DISCOVER THE MAGIC
OF ZEBRA'S REGENCY ROMANCES!

THE DUCHESS AND THE DEVIL   (2264, $2.95)
by Sydney Ann Clary
Though forced to wed Deveril St. John, the notorious "Devil
Duke," lovely Byrony Balmaine swore never to be mastered by the
irrepressible libertine. But she was soon to discover that the human heart—and Satan—move in very mysterious ways!

AN OFFICER'S ALLIANCE   (2239, $3.95)
by Violet Hamilton
Virginal Ariel Frazier's only comfort in marrying Captain Ian
Montague was that it put her in a superb position to spy for the
British. But the rakish officer was a proven master at melting a
woman's reserve and breaking down her every defense!

BLUESTOCKING BRIDE   (2215, $2.95)
by Elizabeth Thornton
In the Marquis of Rutherson's narrow view, a woman's only place
was in a man's bed. Well, beautiful Catherine Harland may have
been just a sheltered country girl, but the astonished Marquis was
about to discover that she was the equal of any man—and could
give as good as she got!

A NOBLE MISTRESS   (2169, $3.95)
by Janis Laden
When her father lost the family estate in a game of piquet, practical Moriah Lanson did not hesitate to pay a visit to the winner,
the notorious Viscount Roane. Struck by her beauty, Roane suggested a scandalous way for Moriah to pay off her father's debt—
by becoming the Viscount's mistress!

*Available wherever paperbacks are sold, or order direct from the
Publisher. Send cover price plus 50¢ per copy for mailing and
handling to Zebra Books, Dept. 2381, 475 Park Avenue South,
New York, N.Y. 10016. Residents of New York, New Jersey and
Pennsylvania must include sales tax. DO NOT SEND CASH.*

The Scarlet Spinster

CLEO CHADWICK

17074

ZEBRA BOOKS
KENSINGTON PUBLISHING CORP.

ZEBRA BOOKS

are published by

Kensington Publishing Corp.
475 Park Avenue South
New York, NY 10016

First printing: June, 1988

Printed in the United States of America

AUTHOR'S NOTE

I have borrowed for Polly's uncle a period from the life of Anthony St. John Baker. Mr. Baker was in real life the secretary to the British Peace Commission which negotiated with the American commissioners at Ghent the terms of peace that brought to a close the War of 1812. He then carried the treaties (three to be signed by the Americans and three by the British) to London for ratification, and thence to Washington.

The portrait of the American Indian which Polly exhibited in her neighborhood circle was inspired by the paintings of Charles Bird King, one of our early American painters. The hair style, ear decoration, and facial markings in Polly's painting are taken from the group entitled *Young Omaha, War Eagle, Little Missouri, and Pawnees,* in the National Collection of Fine Arts, Smithsonian Institution, Washington, D.C. It may be viewed in the Gallery of American Art in Washington.

Chapter One

"Midnight shadowed the dell, the forest and the plain. A cold and boisterous spring day had passed away, and in a deep wood which skirted the shore, a lonely traveler made his way."

Polly Rice picked up the petticoat she was hemming as her father began reading the latest novel to his wife and family. If she sighed as she set herself to the task, no one in the family knew. She *was* content, truly. It was a pleasure to settle once again into the quiet English countryside and direct her attention to rustic interests — the poultry and the dairy, puddings and joints of mutton. She visited the sick, stitched petticoats for her mama's charities, helped her papa with the younger children's lessons. She accompanied her family to church, attended the assemblies in the town, and chaperoned her sister Nettie. The faintest smile flitted across her face as she recalled the last assembly. She'd been seated by a large potted plant, which prevented two gossiping ladies from seeing her.

"Such a help to her mother and father to have Miss

7

Rice home again. Such a pleasant young woman, and not a bit above herself, considering the life she's led these past few years!"

What interested the gossips most, of course, was that at twenty-four she was yet unmarried.

"I wonder why she never married?" the second speaker asked.

At that moment the band struck up a country dance tune, and Polly was never to learn what cause the neighborhood assigned to her spinster state.

But indeed, why should she marry? Her talent with the brush was already bringing her occasional small sums. Surely she could aspire to more. Hadn't the great Turner once remarked that "the child has a way with color"? Moreover, she enjoyed an independent income from a modest inheritance left her by an elderly relative who had taken a fancy to her when she was a child. Her father was in many ways a liberal man and, observing his daughter's always prudent management of her pocket money, had long ago given her complete control of the income from that small fortune. She would have yet a more adequate income on her father's death, and until that unhappy time she could be certain of her welcome beneath his roof.

No, she mused, she certainly had no need to marry to assure her bread and butter. Someday she would set up an independent establishment, but until then she would gracefully conform to country life—she had too much respect for her parents and too much concern for her sisters' consequence to do otherwise—but within herself she guarded and communed with another Polly.

A log burned through and the pieces fell with a crash, requiring that her father halt his reading to re-

8

construct the fire. The day had been unseasonably warm for the first of April, and even with nightfall the air remained almost warm—heavy with imminent rain and the tang of spring. The evening was so balmy that the fireplace sufficed to dispel the chill from the room.

It was a treat for the Rice family to sit before an open fire, for through the winters they warmed themselves before one or another of the stoves ("those iron contraptions," Mr. Rice called them) that her mother had installed for heating. Mrs. Rice, unlike her countrymen and women, liked warmth. She often remarked that it was a wonder that the Romans in the second century could build centrally heated houses in England, while Englishmen in the nineteenth century still shivered and suffered chilblains and runny noses owing to poorly heated rooms. She devoutly hoped, she often said, that when enough Roman ruins were excavated, it would shame inventors into devising better heating systems.

Meanwhile, she made do with cast-iron heating stoves, of both the Franklin fireplace and the German box types, which she had installed in the principal rooms. The effect was not entirely aesthetic, and some of her neighbors complained that her rooms were too hot, but to such criticism Mrs. Rice was indifferent. She had, however, initiated inquiries concerning porcelain heating stoves, said to be in use in the northern European countries and even in benighted Russia, which were supposed to be not only more efficient, but more attractive as well.

Mr. Rice settled himself once again in his chair. With a preliminary "ahem," he reopened the book. "Afar off the traveler espied a glimmering light casting its wavering beam through the gloom . . ."

9

Polly watched the fire with unseeing eyes as it flamed with new vigor. From the review of her present circumstances she was slipping unaware into one of those abstractions that are sometimes called daydreaming, and which for their duration so completely enfold the dreamers that they enter another world. She was, for the moment, enfolded in a quilted robe, riding in a sleigh through the brilliant moonlight of a winter night. The sleighbells were chiming crisply in the sharp, cold, American air. The snow sparkled under the moon, the other young people were laughing and singing, and Alex was holding her hand and promising many birthday kisses. She had just turned twenty-one.

She was nineteen when they received the letter that eventually sent her to America: the letter from her Uncle Peyton telling them of his wife's death. As soon as he could, he came to them, a brokenhearted widower at thirty, who hoped to recover from his grief in the quiet countryside and amid the bustle of his sister's numerous family.

Mrs. Rice let her brother unburden his extravagant sorrow, giving him comfort and reassurances just as in their youth when he was her petted little brother. When she judged he had repeated all the bitter ravings a sufficient number of times and with a sufficient number of variations that his bitterness was purged, she withdrew her sympathy, told him briskly to pull himself together, thrust her youngest child into his arms, and told them both to go look at the new kittens.

Then in the summer of 1814, the Americans, who had been fighting their so-called Second War of Independence, began to make serious overtures for peace. The Tory government, flush with victory over Napoleon and now free to turn all the nation's resources against their former subjects, was nonetheless facing growing discontent from merchants who were tired of losing ships and cargoes to American privateers. The two governments began the studied diplomatic dance leading to a peace conference, and in the autumn of that year the foreign office ordered Polly's uncle to Flanders as secretary to the peace commissioners. Having observed during his visit in the country that Polly was an independent young lady, and also well trained in domestic management by his very capable sister, he requested that she be allowed to accompany him. Reluctantly, Mr. and Mrs. Rice consented.

Ghent had not been as exciting as Vienna, where other diplomatists were settling the affairs of Europe in the wake of Bonaparte's first defeat and exile, but to the country-bred Polly it was an exciting few months, and when her uncle asked her to accompany him to his new post in America, she fervently begged her parents' permission. With even greater reluctance, they agreed.

For the next four years she made a home for her uncle, first in the raw new American capital, Washington City (which had so recently and embarrassingly been set afire by British soldiers), and then again in Rio de Janeiro. It was there that her widower uncle met the wealthy Brazilian beauty who captured his heart and soon became his bride. She was a kind lady, and well aware of the uncle's fondness for his niece, she urged Polly to continue to make her home with them. The proposal was seconded with equal enthusiasm and rather greater sincerity by her uncle, but Polly, wisely

11

recognizing that she would not like being replaced as her uncle's hostess, and furthermore that a new marriage needed privacy to establish itself firmly, thanked them both and refused the offer. So three months past she had bid them farewell and returned to the home and family she had seen but once in the four years of adventure. Now she was just Polly Rice again, daughter of a well-to-do country gentleman.

The truth was — and Polly smiled to herself again — that she had left behind a Past, for in her life as Paula, the English consul's hostess and niece, she had been just a little fast. It wasn't so much a scarlet past as a lovely shade of pink. There were diplomatic dinners, receptions, and teas for the wives of young officers — of course — but there were also dances until dawn, horseback rides in the tropical beauty of Dom Filipe's Brazilian estate, impromptu frolics in America, and sleigh rides in the snow. And ah, the kisses! The dark Filipe, heir to a fortune in land and slaves, and her handsome young American friend, Alex . . . Well, if there were any in England who knew that Polly Rice was once a dashing young lady known as Paula Rice, and much too fast for a proper English country lady, they were few — and even they had no doubt forgotten such gossip as there might have been, now that she had disappeared into the country. Her uncle had never reprimanded her for the youthful flirtations and discreet romances. And after all, good Queen Bess had died a virgin, and she had allowed many more liberties with her person than Polly ever had.

Polly again picked up the petticoat lying neglected in her lap while she dreamed of past pleasures — pleasures that were best forgotten. It was a silly story Papa was

12

reading, to be sure, and had little relation to any events she had ever witnessed or feelings experienced, but they were not a critical family about their entertainments.

That same evening, not far away, in an elegantly comfortable sitting room, another family also sat before a fire — a father, a mother, and their only son just come from London.

Sir Harry Moresby, breaking a cozy silence, commenced upon a subject that occupied his mind more and more frequently of late. "You know, Frederick, you must marry sometime. You are thirty-three years old . . ."

"Thirty-two," Frederick's mother interrupted. "One would think, Harry, that with but one son you might remember his age!"

"Thirty-two, thirty-three — it doesn't matter. What matters is that we do have but one son and that he is far past his first youth."

Lady Moresby turned to her son. "Really, Frederick, your father is right, you know. I shouldn't mind, actually, if the estate passed eventually to your uncle's heirs if that whole branch of your father's family weren't such frightful fools! I couldn't bear looking down from heaven or wherever and watching them gambling Moregreen away, or letting the farms all run to weeds and the tenants' cottages tumble down. . . . I am quite certain that is just what would happen. Any family with that silly woman Letitia Reason at its head just naturally has to have loose screws. If ever there was a misnamed person!"

Sir Harry smiled fondly at his wife. "Although your mother's prejudices are not always mine, Frederick, in this case we are in perfect harmony. I'd even be willing for you to adopt an heir from among the family once I'm gone, but with one of my brothers married to a foolish woman who has given birth to a brace of even more foolish children, and my second brother a bachelor, I haven't that choice. Have you any acceptable bastards, by any chance?"

"I take care not to have," Frederick answered—a bit priggishly, his mother thought. Really, Frederick was getting so stuffy!

"Now for instance," Sir Harry continued, "if Mr. Rice was my brother, I'd have no end of choices. How many boys has Giles now, Eleanor? Four, is it? Five?"

Lady Eleanor Moresby looked thoughtful. "So many families seem to run to all girls or all boys, but the Rices are such a nicely balanced family. Now let me see. There are seven children. There's one boy, Peter, who I believe is in law, and there are two young ones yet at home. That's the three boys. Then there's Gussie, who's married and lives in London, the baby that died—and of course doesn't count—then Nettie, who's been permitted only recently to attend the assemblies, Francie, the youngest girl, and Polly, who's back home again. . . ."

Lady Moresby's countenance shifted subtly from thoughtful to speculative. "Polly hasn't married," she remarked, with a glance at her husband.

Frederick, slouched in his chair, his long legs stretched out before him, his eyes on the fire, lazily observed, "How fortuitous. An unmarried lady just a mile distant, and the daughter of our own dear

14

neighbor at that!"

"Well, Frederick, it is rather obvious. And I'm sure I would never have thought of it if she weren't so eminently suitable. Polly is virtuous, dutiful, kind . . ."

"Yes, and she is probably also plain, prim, and given to sermonizing."

"I doubt that latter very much, Frederick," his father said. "I don't know the girl as your mother seems to, but any child who grew up in that family is unlikely to sermonize. They all read novels, you know."

"I know Peter Rice very slightly. He's certainly a serious chap."

"Well, Polly is neither plain nor prim. She has her mother's coloring and her father's good looks. I wouldn't say she's beautiful, certainly, but she looks very well, and her expression is so lively that one soon forgets whether she's pretty or plain. But I appeal to you, Harry. What think you of her looks? I know men sometimes have different tastes than ours."

"She has a nice enough figure and face. You might remember her, Frederick. Polly's the second eldest — am I right, Eleanor?"

"Yes. Peter — the one in law — is the oldest. Polly would be, oh, about twenty-four or twenty-five now."

"And still unmarried?" Frederick asked, with a lift of one eyebrow.

"How can you be so uncharitable? She's eight years younger than you are, Frederick."

Sir Harry took a thoughtful sip of port. "I do think you might remember her. Those children always have been all over the place." He paused to consider the arithmetic. "But then I doubt a young buck of twenty would notice a girl of twelve or thirteen."

15

"Or a boy of fifteen a girl of seven, I should hope."

"No, of course not," his mother agreed. "And anyway, she had just grown up when her aunt died and her uncle asked for her to come with him to Ghent and then to America. Just the age when you might have noticed her! Such a tragedy it was for him — Polly's uncle — but such an opportunity for Polly! I confess, I do wonder how she manages to settle so comfortably into the dull life we all lead here in the country! But she seems perfectly content."

Frederick yawned and stood up. "I'm sure, my dear father and mother, that she will make someone a superb wife. Now if you will excuse me, I believe I'll go to bed."

A silence endured his exit for all of three minutes, until Sir Harry and Lady Moresby were certain that their only offspring had indeed gone off to bed.

"You know, Eleanor, you've had an excellent idea. I suppose you can find it within your talents to get the courtship under way within the week?"

Frederick rose for an early breakfast but, on entering the breakfast parlor, found his mother there before him, artistically arranging several sprays of pussy willow in a tall vase. The family sitting room and the breakfast parlor, although smaller than the long drawing room and the dining room at the front, were nonetheless of generous proportions. It was in these rooms or in the library in the west wing where the family gathered when alone, where Sir Harry or Frederick sat with neighboring landowners, or Lady Moresby with a guest. Like the bedrooms and dressing rooms on the

16

floor above, they were paneled in pine and painted white, furnished more simply and with a greater eye to comfort than the more stately drawing and dining rooms with their Chippendale-designed Chinoiserie furniture and Chinese-patterned wallpapers, but the same quiet luxury prevailed. Frederick, on each return to Moregreen, his family's seat, was always struck by the restful tranquility of the house, and of his parent's lives.

His parents were all that a landholding family, further graced by a baronetcy, should be. Lady Moresby was kind to her servants and to the poor; she managed her household with leisurely ease; she was equally gracious to those of high and low estate. She liked London, and she liked fashion, but she was also content in the country, and never extravagant. This excellent lady, with a maturity beyond her years, had chosen from among a respectable, although not spectacular, circle of suitors to fall in love with a man of equal virtue. As she was pretty, but not beautiful, he was attractive, but not handsome. He liked fashion, but was not a fop. He enjoyed the entertainments of the town, but was a careful agriculturalist and devoted to his estate. In the midst of so much virtue, they might have been dull, but Lady Moresby read novels and kept abreast of politics; while Sir Harry was dedicated to agricultural journals, the newspapers, and political economy.

Frederick bent to kiss his estimable mother's cheek before walking to the window to look out at the garden and the tall yews beyond. Eleanor, the present Lady Moresby and third lady to preside over Moregreen, meanwhile abandoned the pussy willow to rummage about in one of the many drawers and pidgeon holes of

17

a tall William and Mary secretary-cabinet, lavishly embellished with ivory inlay, that stood between the two large windows overlooking the garden. It was the one piece of furniture saved from the fire that had destroyed the original family residence in the time of Frederick's great grandfather.

Lady Moresby took a magazine from the drawer she had been searching. "A new article on roses that I wanted to take to Amelia—Mrs. Rice," she explained. "Well." She poured herself a cup of coffee and sat down.

Frederick served himself an egg with generous helpings of ham and toast, and then joined his mother at the table. She smiled at him as she poured milk into her cup. "Polly says that in Brazil the people breakfast on very strong and very heavily sugared coffee and a plain roll. I must say, I shouldn't care at all for the plain roll or all that sugar, but I am fond of strong coffee and milk in the morning." Lady Moresby, perfectly well prepared to foster an acquaintance between her son and Miss Polly Rice, if not an immediate courtship, sipped her coffee demurely.

"Miss Rice must have many interesting stories to tell after—how many years was it that she was abroad?"

"Oh, four or five." Lady Moresby, aware of the ironic twist of her son's mouth, composed her countenance. "I really don't mean to fuss at you, dear. It's just that we are concerned that you marry soon. It's not only that you're getting older, but you seem so dull."

As Frederick showed signs of real disfavor, his mother hurried on. "Oh, I don't mean that we aren't happy that you're taking on so much of the burden of managing the estate and our investments; we love having you here so often, and it means of course that your

18

father and I can take our little jaunts now, and still feel easy that all will go along well with the animals and the crops. You know your father has never really liked to leave affairs in the hands of a bailiff—however competent. Property will only pay well if managed well, as your father has said many times. But it's just that, well, you know, dear, I never thought I would say so, but I'd very much like to be a grandmother."

Frederick rose from the table to serve himself a second egg. "I will bear that in mind when next I am in London."

Lady Moresby also rose. She lay a hand on his arm. "I have no wish to push you into an acquaintance distasteful to you, Frederick. But it is only common courtesy to acknowledge neighbors. I'll be calling at Tanwell tomorrow. Why don't you join me and renew acquaintance with Polly? If you think her unattractive in face or in manner, I assure you I shall never say another word. But do think, love, what an asset as a hostess and wife a woman would be who has had so much experience in the world. Not just with giving balls and grand dinners, but in diplomacy as well—for example, if you should ever go into politics. And if she is as efficient and levelheaded as her mother—well . . . and think how brave she must be to get along so well in the wildernesses of America!"

"Come now, Mother. The capital cities of the New World are not yet great cosmopolitan centers, but they are surely not located in the wilderness."

His mother sighed as she returned to the arrangement of pussy willow. Such a fine figure of a man, just as his father had been—and still was, she thought, except for just that little roundness to his belly.

19

As Frederick rode out to join his father in a distant corner of the estate which they were considering for drainage, he reviewed his state of mind and found it not entirely to his liking. Truth to tell, he was not as stuffy as he would have his parents—and himself—believe. He had reached a time in life when it seemed he was not sure what it was he wanted. He liked the country, and he sincerely enjoyed attending the affairs of the estate, but a restlessness sometimes overtook him that could not be relieved by indulgence in his former sports and diversions. Neither his former mistress, nor lately the well-chosen damsels of Mrs. Crawford's discreet establishment, gave him satisfaction. Social affairs and flirtations bored him. He was equally bored by mills and cockfights and the male camaraderie of his club. His friends and acquaintances thought his politics mildly radical, but it was a lazy, armchair radicalism. He had no intention of taking any action toward parliamentary or any other reform. The fact of the matter was that his life had gone stale. He supposed it meant that in the natural course of things it had come time to build his nest and find a mate to share it—something akin to his mother's sudden and unexpected grandmotherly yearnings. So it could do no harm to meet the virtuous Miss Polly Rice with an open mind.

Later, Frederick and Sir Harry rode in silence along the lane leading to the stables. Father and son were feeling charitable with one another, each privately considering how remarkable it was that they could agree so well on the best interests of the estate—that Sir Harry should not be resisting change or Frederick over-enthusiastically recommending all kinds of wild and untested schemes.

Sir Harry's grandfather, the builder and furnisher of Moregreen, had mortgaged the land to pay for it. Through the years the estate had provided just sufficient income to pay the interest. Sir Harry had at last paid off the mortgage and reestablished the security of the Moresby properties, thanks to the high grain prices during the Napoleonic Wars and to his own inspired management. Unlike many other land owners, he had refrained during those halcyon years from expanding the acreage of the estate and incurring new debt; he had instead put what excess capital he had into estate improvements and investments in industrial ventures. Had his son been too enthusiastic about spending good money on experimental agricultural techniques, he would have found it difficult to share the estate and its management, however much affection there was between them.

Sir Harry's thoughts began to wander naturally from the affairs of the estate to succession of property, and so, taking advantage of the understanding between himself and Frederick on the former, he ventured to speak again on the latter.

"You know, Frederick, we have no ambitions for a titled or wealthy wife for you. Only that her family be of good standing. Wealth does not necessarily mean good humor or good sense, nor does it promise a woman who can give you companionship such as I found in your mother. And that I would have for you before wealth, or even before passion. I should suppose in any event that you have had your share of passion by now. By the way, do you still keep that young woman you had tucked away in Bay Street?"

"No. She decided nearly a year ago to emigrate to America. She had some money put by, and I settled a small sum on her. She aspires to establish a public house or inn, or perhaps purchase a farm—whatever appears most profitable in such a new country."

"Living like a monk, are you?"

"No. I visit Mrs. Crawford from time to time. But I'm a prudent man, as you know, Father, and I become more so with the years."

"Yes, even in your most rakehell days when we often feared for your life and limb, we were never concerned for either your health or fortune. It was never my way, and thank God it has not been yours, to gamble with either."

"It's you, sir, who I have to thank that I still have both. Too many young men are given the freedom of the town without adequate instruction. How old was I when you showed me the use of the French letter?"

"I suppose the first time I caught you ogling a village girl."

Frederick had in fact been fourteen when his father caught him kissing the notoriously loose daughter of one of the cottagers. They were in a little grove just behind the big barn. The girl's back was against a tree, and Frederick was attempting to embrace her, while she pushed him away. He knew, though, that her intention was not to end his attempts but to make him want more desperately to press himself against her. She had already allowed him more than one kiss that day, and on many other occasions as well. The first time, he'd

22

taken her by surprise. He'd pressed his lips against hers in what he supposed was a kiss. To his chagrin, she burst out laughing. "Oh, you ninny! You've never kissed a girl before, have you? Like this, you baby!" Now, with her back against the tree, they were going through a familiar ritual, leading rapidly in the direction toward which Frederick had aimed ever since the Facts of Life had been described to him and other gaping youngsters, in quite amazing detail, by a sophisticated upperclassman. He knew, as he kissed her eager mouth that a few more rendezvous such as this and he would attain his goal.

The love scene was rudely interrupted by a very determined shove that had nothing to do with the ritual. The girl picked up her basket and, with a defiant glance at someone behind him, turned and strolled away—combining in her walk both an audacious swing of her hips and haughty deliberation. Frederick was suddenly spun about to face his father, who held him firmly by the shoulder.

Frederick, the man, recalling Frederick, the green boy, chuckled.

His father joined his mirth. "Are you recalling the incident with Nellie Pierson?"

"Yes. After all these years, I can at last laugh about it."

"And Nellie, after two babies conceived on the wrong side of the blanket, settled down with a good man. As is often the case, she's trying to make sure that her pretty daughters stay respectable."

Nellie had sauntered away while he stood staring at his father, expecting a hiding at the very least.

Instead, his father had said kindly, "I think you need

a lesson in how to go on in life, young man, and in how a gentleman should behave. Stop looking so frightened. I am not going to punish you."

Frederick took a gulp of air. "Yes, sir." He essayed a brief glance at his father.

"Let's walk over the field," Sir Harry suggested. "I want to check the new fencing."

They walked across a field newly prepared for planting, slipping occasionally on large clods. They inspected the fence, and finally sat down under a tree. Sir Harry lit his pipe. After a few thoughtful puffs, he said, "It's natural, Frederick, that you should be trying out what a man's body can do. What I do not want is that you molest—even at their invitation—girls from a lower station in life. I do not want your mother to have to dismiss all the young maids and hire only crones. And I do not want any of your bastards floating around the countryside, any more than to have my only son fall victim to the French pox."

Sir Harry had gone on to explain some facts of life that the sophisticated upperclassman had omitted—the advantages of respectable houses run by honest madams as opposed to women of the streets, and the possibility of a mistress when a young man attained his majority. The latter, although from the lower orders, had chosen, or had fallen into, a way of life that amounted to a profession, which was different from the easy ways of girls such as Nellie Pierson. Furthermore, there were problems of disease, but which, with care, could be avoided.

"It's called a cundum. They are sold in London, in Orange Street, I believe, or you can often acquire them at a chemist's or at shops catering to gentlemen's needs."

24

While Frederick was recalling the past, Sir Harry had been pursuing a different but similar thought. Breaking into Frederick's reverie, he said, "I suppose it was around that time I began teaching you a few things about gambling, too."

Father and son let the ambling horses halt to munch at a patch of grass while they looked back over the Moregreen fields. In the stillness of late afternoon the only sound was the light brush of wind across succulent grasses and young leaves not yet deepened into summer green. They chatted for a moment about the improvement of pasturage, and then moved on.

Sir Harry brought the conversation back to the discussion of the previous evening. "Surely, Frederick, if you set yourself to the task, you could discover amongst the season's offerings a girl who would suit."

"That I doubt. I know that my old friend Hastings has dealt very well with his little Julie—and she was only sixteen when he married her—but I find the chits too silly and featherheaded. Gallantry and flirtation palled long ago, and all the posturings of courtship would surely bore me to distraction. I need more substance and more steadiness, I think, and am afraid I have not the patience to endure waiting for a young wife to grow up."

"Well, then, a widow?"

"Or a spinster lady?" Frederick asked, with a smile.

"It was only a suggestion, Frederick, and as your mother remarked, an obvious one."

"Well, I am not averse to viewing this paragon. I'll let Mother take me calling at Tanwell. It seems she has a great fancy for the grandmotherly state, and I would be an unnatural son to deny her such pleasure."

25

They dismounted, handed their mounts over to a groom, and strode together toward the house, satisfied that two issues had for the moment been settled: draining of the marsh in the north meadow and an implied acquiescence to marriage.

Chapter Two

Mrs. Rice no sooner saw Lady Moresby and Frederick driving up the lane to Tanwell than a thought struck her. There was a young man very much in need of a wife (already in his early thirties by her calculation), while under her own roof was a daughter who, loved though she was, should be married to some respectable man. Mrs. Rice, who did not circulate in London society, was not certain how respectable Frederick was, but his parents were respectable, and she assumed — quite correctly — that she would soon be able to ascertain whether the son was eligible as a suitor for her daughter.

Tucking stray locks of hair up under her cap, she whisked herself away to the morning room, calling to a housemaid to run quickly and ask Miss Rice to present herself there immediately in order to receive guests, and to send Miss Nettie to the schoolroom to assume command in place of her sister. Picking up a stocking that had met with an accident when its occupant took a tumble, she slipped a darning egg into it and set to work on another of the many chores of keeping her family in good repair. There was a silly notion that such needlework was not genteel, but Mrs. Rice, in the exercise of careful household economy, paid no attention to silly notions.

Servants liked Moregreen for the attention the builder and first proprietor had given to comfortable servant quarters, but they liked Tanwell because Mrs. Rice expected efficient service to be aided by efficient equipment. The pottery, glassware, and cutlery were plain and serviceable so that the maids and the footman need not be in constant fear when handling them, and there were no unnecessary knickknacks or bric-a-brac requiring careful and constant dusting. Supper tables and tea and serving carts were on wheels to relieve maids of carrying trays and making numerous trips between the kitchens and other rooms — particularly appreciated because Mr. Rice so frequently took his tea in his study, located in the far reaches.

They also liked Tanwell because of Mrs. Rice's radical notion that neither she nor her family was either helpless or above menial chores. The Rice children had all been taught to empty their own chamberpots. Only Mr. Rice was excused, this service being performed under command of his valet by the footman. At the moment, as Mrs. Rice plied her needle and waited for Lady Moresby and her son to be shown into the morning room, she was considering the possibility of installing one of those French style shower-baths and a toilet that could be flushed out mechanically.

Polly received the summons from her mother just as the youngest in the schoolroom was finishing his geography recitation. Instructing the three scholars to at-

28

tend to their sums until Nettie could come to them to continue the morning's lessons, she smoothed her skirt, and ran quickly down the stairs. She glanced in the mirror that hung in the entrance hall, just to assure herself that nothing was out of place (for Polly often had trouble keeping quite all together), then passed through the dining room to the cheerful morning room beyond.

It was a day of effervescent sunshine. The breezes that gently moved the curtains at the open windows seemed to beckon her, luring her to the out-of-doors. It was a day that had aroused in Polly's breast a desire to frolic, as in her youth, and she, as much as the youngsters, had longed to escape the schoolroom. Later she would take them with her for a ramble over the fields to explore some of the old haunts of her childhood. She might even turn a somersault. With this thought she tripped into the morning room, mentally turning somersaults, and there her eye alighted instantly on a well-set-up man, with dark good looks.

It was so unexpected — discovering a gentleman in the morning room — that she was a little breathless and came near to trodding on one of the ginger cats that also favored the morning room. Recovering, she laughed and called, "Naughty puss," after the retreating animal before she turned, unembarrassed but still breathless, to cheerfully greet Lady Moresby.

"Polly, my dear, what a delight to have you home!" Lady Moresby took Polly's two hands in her own. "I still cannot believe you are really here after so many adventures abroad! Did you know, Frederick, that . . . but how foolish of me! I haven't introduced you two children."

Frederick had dutifully risen to his feet on Polly's

29

entrance. "Oh, I remember Miss Rice very well—of a number of barefoot, and very harum-scarum children—at least so they appeared to my eye then—I was about twenty at the time and thought myself very much the man about town—Miss Rice was, I believe, the sauciest."

Frederick, after delivering this wheezer, ostensibly to his mother, stepped forward to bow over Polly's hand. "And you, Miss Rice, were perhaps ten years old?"

"You sly fellow!" exclaimed Lady Moresby. "You gave me no hint that you remembered Polly so clearly."

"How do you do, Mr. Moresby," Polly murmured politely. "I'm sure I don't remember the encounter you refer to, but of course I remember you, for you were only one, and so much older and always so elegant besides. But indeed, I'm amazed that you can recall which child was I among such a numerous brood as we were, especially with a sister so like we were often taken for twins."

"Well," said Frederick, "when my mother mentioned that you were home again I cast about among my memories and fished up that particular day, and the moment you walked in, I thought to myself, Yes, she's the one! You gave me quite a comeuppance that day."

Lady Moresby felt at this juncture that it was time to change the subject before her son got himself in any deeper water. Turning to Mrs. Rice, she inquired politely on the state of her tender young plants following the early spring deluge of two days past.

Mrs. Rice, after assuring herself that refreshments were neither needed nor wanted, replied that although some young plants had been washed out, and others beaten flat by the violence of the storm, the majority

30

were recovering nicely. This led to a discussion of flower borders, a conversation between the two matrons that left Polly and Frederick to manage on their own.

Miss Rice, the diplomat's niece, opened the conversation. "Are you at Moregreen for a lengthy stay, Mr. Moresby?"

"Yes, I believe so. I've quite wearied of London, and I've a notion to spend more time on the estate. I've always enjoyed working with dairy cattle, which, as I've undertaken some breeding and upgrading of our herd, balances off my father's greater interest in the crops."

Polly, who had quite wearied of farm talk since her own return to the country, countered gamely, "My mother has mentioned that there is much of interest in breeding . . ."

Before she could complete the sentence a thought struck her which threatened to end in blushes, since her new propriety forbade laughter, but Frederick interrupted with an open laugh that seemed unconscious of the double entendre. "Forgive me, I'm sure you have enough of such mundane talk. I'm told that your interests in the natural world have more to do with wild things than the domesticated creatures. I have perused your book of native American flower engravings with interest."

A bald lie, thought Polly, as she smoothly responded, "It's a matter of opportunity only. One's interest must necessarily derive from the world one lives in. Another month or two at Tanwell and I hope I shall be as capable of discussing the characteristics, habits, and wants of cows and chickens as others hereabout."

"And I hope not — such talk I can hear any day. I'd

much prefer to hear of those things connected with your adventures. I've traveled only in France and Italy, which is nothing very wonderful — while you have seen the Americas! Are those two distant continents as wild and primitive as we are told?"

"Certainly such recently discovered and newly settled continents, where only the few have penetrated to the interior, cannot boast the art, the great buildings, or the settled ways of life that we have always known . . ."

"Miss Rice, I believe I detect a touch of scolding in your tone. I had no intention of suggesting an inferiority — only a difference. I am eager to learn, and would be pleased if you could instruct me."

Polly dropped her eyes and murmured an apology for her overhasty judgment, at which Lady Moresby, having exhausted borders, rose to go. She kissed Polly's cheek, and then, once again taking her hands, said, "My dear, I am longing to see your sketches and watercolors of America and Brazil. Could we not agree on a time and a day?"

"Of course, with the greatest pleasure. But the best of my work is still in London. Perhaps my mother did not mention that the owner of a gallery in London is arranging a small exhibition . . ."

"Why how delightful! When will it be?"

"Not until the fall. I expect, however, that within a month the paintings he has chosen not to include will be returned. And I have many sketches."

"Then we will expect our own small exhibition when they are returned to you. And I shall look forward to your London show in the autumn."

Polly's promise of a private showing secured, Lady Moresby turned to Mrs. Rice. With promises of return visits, to include an exchange of plant cuttings, the two ladies parted.

Frederick took leave of Mrs. Rice and then of Polly. "Perhaps," he said to her, "you would enjoy a drive about the countryside one of these fine days. I haven't visited the ruins of the old abbey since I was a boy and it would be pleasant to do so with somone who may also remember it from childhood." Polly assented to the possibilities for enjoyment in such a trip, and the intended lovers parted.

The moment they were safely under way, Lady Moresby began, "Frederick, you astonish me! *What* was that foolishness? Miss Rice a *saucy* child! I declare! That was a shameless lie — and she caught you out too, for Polly and Gussie do look amazingly like. And *saucy* — I simply can't *imagine* what you were thinking of! I'm surprised she wasn't offended!"

"Stop talking in exclamation points, there's a dear old grandmama. Of course I didn't remember her, but I thought it would make my introduction more pleasing. After all, if I am to woo her . . ."

"Oh, enough, you bad boy." Lady Moresby allowed a few moment's silence before putting the important questions. "But tell me," she finally ventured, "what did you think? Did she sermonize?"

"No, not exactly sermons. There was, after all, very little time."

"Pretty? Did you not think her rather pretty?"

"Pretty enough," Frederick answered.

For all his feigned indifference, Frederick had in fact looked upon Miss Polly Rice with considerable interest

33

and thought himself pleased that he did not find her displeasing. Just the sort to nest with, he thought. A cheerful, bustling little woman, who still seemed to have a level head and serious mind, and who would keep everything in good order, with no rumpled feathers or loose sticks. "She seems indeed most eligible," he told his mother, "quite a bustle, of course, but another visit might reveal the paragon." Privately, his mother thought Polly more precipitate than bustling—she suspected more dash there than Frederick had perceived—but having learned from Sir Harry that Frederick had voiced a preference for steadiness and substance, she refrained from airing this view of the young woman.

If Polly had known that Frederick Moresby thought her a "bustling little woman," she would have been shocked right down to her tripping toes. She might accept "unexceptionable" from old gossips, but "bustling little woman"?—not from a handsome young man—never! It was not a reasonable description at all of a young lady who was once considered fast! Nor would the description have sounded at all right to her old friends, who—conceding that she was often just a bit disarranged and somewhat breathless in action—nonetheless thought her slim form elegant, her manner entirely pleasing, and her diplomatic tact superb. A young English lieutenant in Brazil, with a taste for seventeenth century poetry—and an unfortunate taste for memorizing it—had found it appropriate to recite, as he held her hand and gazed with soulful ardor into her eyes, those lines from Herrick:

A sweet disorder in the dress
Kindles in clothes a wantonness:

34

A cuff neglectful, and thereby
Ribbons to flow confusedly;
A winning wave, deserving note,
In the tempestuous petticoat;
Do more bewitch me, than when art
Is too precise in every part.

And a gruff Yankee ship captain who had put in to Rio de Janeiro for repairs and provisioning had once remarked as he tied up a dangling ribbon — one of those ribbons flowing confusedly, "Damme, Miss Rice, but you're a fine-lookin' woman. If I were a younger man, and not a rovin' sailor at that, you'd have to look out. I'd be after you to marry me, I would."

However, since Polly did not know she had been so disgracefully thought of by Mr. Frederick Moresby, she merely remarked to her mother that he was indeed a good-looking man, if somewhat dull. To herself she remarked, "If only he had more dash!" Dom Felipe had definitely had dash.

Mrs. Rice, in her usual spare manner, said only that Frederick certainly seemed pleasant enough. Not so young Miss Frances. Nettie had released Francie from the schoolroom once her history was read in order to turn her full attention to the two boys — who were much more likely to make mischief than Francie. Thus it was that, on learning from the housemaid just who had come to call, she was lingering in the upstairs hall to catch a glimpse of Mr. Frederick Moresby, whom she had noticed two months past at church with his mama, and thought simply divine. The door had no sooner closed on them than she was down the stairs, and bursting in upon Mrs. Rice and Polly.

"Oh, he's so handsome! Don't you think so, Polly? I'd adore it if you could marry him, Polly. Do you think you might?"

Francie was jumping up and down around Polly like one of those strange seeds called jumping beans, unaware that she was only one of many conspirators bent on bringing two eligible and marriageable people to the altar.

"Frances, mind your manners," said her mother.

"Yes, for heaven's sake. You give me a headache," said Polly. But she gave Francie a little hug, and looked very much as though she might like to jump a bit herself.

"All right, girls," their mother said. "If lessons are finished, I'm sure you can find other useful employment." She quickly straightened such small clutter as the morning visit had occasioned, and quit the room to complete her morning conference with the housekeeper, but before she became absorbed in that daily detail, she had time to reflect that young Mr. Moresby was indeed attractive, and that it would be a most profitable and suitable match should Polly find him pleasing, and he her. Why had she not thought of it the minute Polly returned home?

The friendship between the two families at Moregreen and Tanwell was warm and of long standing despite the greater consequence of the Moresby's, for there was no less regard on their part, and no envy among those at Tanwell. Had there been a half-dozen children of roughly similar ages in each family, an alliance between them would have been thought of, but Frederick had been five years of age when the first little Rice — Master Peter — made his entrance in the world, and with the great weight of his seniority, he had disdained association with the succession of infants across the park.

Although the idea of an alliance between the families was a new idea for both, it hindered neither family from immediate recognition of the advantages once the idea did strike. The Moresbys had only the one offspring, which meant that property would not be divided; furthermore, that one offspring was intelligent, endowed with a strong constitution, and a comely person. Except for the usual escapades of youth, he had always maintained a level head and a clear eye. Indeed, Mr. and Mrs. Rice could not ask for a better match. Nor, for that matter, could Sir and Lady Moresby ask for more in a daughter-in-law than one of the Rice girls—well-bred, well-trained, and good-natured. And not to be discounted, a marriage would seal the long-standing friendship between the two families with the closes ties of shared grandchildren.

Chapter Three

Shortly after noon of that same day, a small dark cloud floated across the sunny sky. Soon other clouds followed, and then more, until the sun was obscured. Within the hour the rain began. Polly's planned excursion to childhood haunts was necessarily postponed.

Francie was the hardest to console, for she greatly admired her newly returned sister, and she loved to hear stories about the familiar lanes and meadows, and what Polly and Peter and Gussie did when they were children: There Gussie put her bare foot smack in the middle of a fresh cow pie, and there Peter caught the tadpole to put in Aunt Cat's tooth glass, and there Polly found the baby squirrel, lost from its nest in a torrential downpour and a high wind. The two little boys, Masters Jonathan and William, of course, knew every corner of both Tanwell and Moregreen, and certainly did not need any big sisters to accompany them on their rambles, but the prospect of confinement was hard to bear. Soon tiring of the amusements still to be found in the old nursery, they descended to the drawing room to entertain themselves by plaguing their sisters.

Polly and Nettie were teaching Francie the elements of whist, an undertaking that required studious attention from the pupil and respectful silence among the bystanders. Jonathan and William were not welcome. They promised silence—they would just look at the big geography book from the library—but soon they were wrestling each other, rolling around and jiggling the folding table—none too steady, in any event—on which the cards were laid out.

Scolded by Polly, they maintained order briefly until an unlucky cat walked by with a tail carried at just the right angle for pulling—an activity that even though only threatened was sure to arouse the indignation of Francie and bring reprimands from both Nettie and Polly. So it went for another ten minutes until Polly lay down her cards and said, "I know, let's play hide and seek—I'll bet I know places to hide that none of you have ever discovered."

It was a statement unlikely to be disproved, for—in lavish contrast to the classic simplicity of Moregreen—Tanwell was a hodgepodge of graftings on a sixteenth century core. The arrangement of the rooms was capricious, and the successive graftings had left many nooks and odd corners. There were, besides the back stairs and the front stairs, a secret stairway to the labyrinthine attics, and—the many children's particular favorite—a caracole stairs fitted into a little circular tower built onto the outside of the house and which debouched into a hidden hallway between two small bedrooms.

Mrs. Rice through the years had replaced and rebuilt and added according to her two principles of util-

40

ity—efficiency and comfort. Tanwell, despite its eccentricities, was not drafty. She had at shocking expense replaced mullioned windows with sash windows, and the shutters with removable glass windows that were used only in winter (and which were the occasion of much grumbling on the part of the gardener, who with his two young helpers put them up each fall and took them down each spring).

She had furnished the house with a similar eye to comfort, as long as comfort did not interfere with efficiency. Wing chairs stood before fireplaces and around stoves, where children could curl up with books in a warm private world on long winter afternoons, and in the corners early eighteenth century commodes held packets of cards, children's picture books, and games collected over the years. Generally, the furnishings and the rooms were like the house—a hodgepodge on which comfort and efficiency were imposed but failed to dominate. It was a house made to order—as Polly suggested—for indoor games of hide and seek.

Francie objected to leaving the whist lessons for such childish entertainment, but her objections lacked conviction, for although she would never have confessed it, she was finding whist boring. Jonathan and William were willing, if not enthusiastic, and the afternoon was retrieved. Polly soon proved that she did know hiding places the others had not discovered, but she kept her secrets, and it was only carelessness that allowed Nettie to spy her as she crept silently through the dining room on her way to home base.

Polly, now "it," hid her eyes, counting slowly to one hundred. Soon all but William were either caught or home free. Polly, softly prowling the library, heard a

41

muffled sneeze, and then spotted a leg disappearing behind a settee. William, caught in the act of emerging, like the fox was going to ground again. She pounced on the leg, pulling him from his hiding place. He wriggled so vigorously in her grasp that she was near to losing him, but she held him fast with one hand, and with the other attempted to tickle him into submission. Stout young man that he was—for all he was only eight and overcome by giggles—he was soon very close to getting the upper hand and tickling her instead. They were on the floor, wrestling and laughing, when Mrs. Rice appeared in the doorway to call a halt to the game.

William was sent after his brother and sisters to tidy himself, but Mrs. Rice detained Polly. "My dear," she said, "I do think it unwise of you to act the hoyden. Both Nettie and Francie look up to you and will try to model their behavior on yours. And the boys need no encouragement to go out of bounds." Then, seeing the hurt surprise in her daughter's eyes, Mrs. Rice was instantly sorry she had spoken. "Dear child, you have been nothing but joy to us since your return. I am, I'm afraid, perhaps too concerned for order and propriety. Do forgive me."

Polly kissed her mother's cheek. "And I, Mama, have perhaps too little concern for order and propriety. You were right, of course. I must stop playing the hoyden."

Her mother's quick apology and admission of fault were, as is so often the case, more effective than any scolding. In deference to her mother, Polly determined henceforward to try for greater dignity.

* * *

42

As soon as the fields were dry again, Polly found opportunity for a ramble, but this time alone as suited a mood—a restlessness brought on, she suspected, by too much propriety. She clapped an old straw bonnet on her head, took up a sketch pad and pencil, and set out across the park with a vague thought of sketching spring wood and field flowers; or perhaps she would make a drawing of Tanwell from the hill across the valley.

She set herself such a pace that she arrived almost too soon at her destination, a meadow above the woods that bordered the meandering stream which ran through the Moregreen and Tanwell parks. She settled herself just below the crest of the north-facing slope, from which she could see, below and to her right, Tanwell, which lay at the end of the little valley formed by the stream, just at the point where it widened. With the peaks and gables of the roof, the combination of stone and brick exterior, the unmatched chimneys, the little tower and the tenacious ivy, Tanwell was nothing less than a gothic delight.

Moregreen, directly across the valley, with its classic Georgian lines, reminded Polly of pleasant visits in stately Virginia homes, which it so much resembled. She drew up her legs, and rested her chin on her knees. From the ha-ha that broke the slope between stream and house, a fine lawn, carefully sylvan and pastoral, rose in three broad, shallow terraces. The drive, emerging from the woods below, gracefully circled the hill and swept past the front of the house.

The consciously simple setting for the gleaming white house that crowned the rise, a jewel against the yews and the short reach of steeper hill behind, pleased

43

her artist's eye. She took up her sketch pad with an idea of a drawing of Moregreen, but the sun was warm, and soon lulled her into a languorous state. She cast off her shawl, loosened her dress at the throat, then slipped off her shoes. Stockings she had wisely left off altogether. She wiggled her toes and then lay back among the springing grasses and early meadow flowers, her shawl for a pillow, her bonnet and sketch pad laid aside and one arm thrown across her eyes as protection against the sun. That she was in one of the Moregreen fields did not enter her mind; she had often come here with Peter and Gussie when they were children, and no one had ever suggested that they not.

She dreamed lazily of new watercolor drawings, and perhaps, with the aid of magnification, studies of the smallest and most insignificant meadow flowers, which passed unnoticed among larger and showier blooms, but that nonetheless had beauty and intricacy. Or an attempt to catch, within the familiar landscapes, the gentler light of England, so new to her eye after the brilliant—even harsh—light of America and the limpid light of Brazil.

It was thus that Frederick came upon her, and before he could turn to hasten away, she had heard him. She sat up quickly, her expression startled, and then on recognizing him, she smiled. "Good day, Mr. Moresby. I hardly expected to meet you here. One of your Ayrshires perhaps, but not you." Then noting the direction of his glance, she hastily pulled her skirt down over the bare legs and feet that had been so carelessly revealed; then with a start her hand went to her collar—although why an open collar, or for that matter a bare ankle, should embarrass her when so many of her gowns were

44

cut so low at the bosom and so high at the hem, she was unprepared to think.

Frederick, who had just come from assisting with the setting of some posts, was himself embarrassed to be confronting a lady in only his shirtsleeves, his collar open, and wearing farm boots besides, although neither his face nor voice betrayed him. "Good day, Miss Rice," he replied, focusing his gaze on her really very nice eyes. He had not, however, failed to note the well-turned ankle and hint of shapely leg. *She might be a village maid out gathering wild herbs, and I a sturdy farmer,* he thought, *in which case he would have dallied a bit, and perhaps have stolen a kiss.* He carefully gave no hint of such thoughts and remarked instead on the pleasant day and favorable weather, to which Polly replied in kind. He then courteously excused himself and set off down the hill, while Polly, watching the broad shoulders and long strides, was cast willy-nilly into those disturbing memories of dalliance in the Americas, all thoughts of painting driven from her mind. . . .

Dom Filipe Ramos Arizaga had been all that was proper, and as their acquaintance deepened, he became an acknowledged suitor. Then came a night on the long veranda of the hacienda house. The breeze was gentle, but sufficient to discourage the mosquitoes that plagued the tropical Brazilian nights. The other houseguests and her host and hostess, Filipe's father and mother, had retired. She knew that she should not have come down to meet Filipe after their elders were abed, but the night was warm and lovely, Filipe handsome and charming, and he had been making love to her all

45

evening with his eyes, and with the seemingly casual touches of his hand on her arm that were in reality caresses. They talked, alone on the far end of the dark veranda, and even his voice seduced her. He kissed her lightly. The intervals of conversation became shorter, the kisses more frequent, and although still gentle, they were more insistent, until at last there were only the murmurs of lovers. In the back of her mind Propriety's voice told her she should not be there alone with him, but she continued to lie in his arms and return his kisses. His hand strayed to her breast, ever so lightly caressed the nipple, and she gasped with pleasure. The voice at the back of her mind became a shout, and she sat up abruptly, pushing Filipe away from her. "No," she said. Then again, more emphatically, "No!"

"Please," he begged.

"No. It is not proper. I can't. My uncle . . ." She began to cry, so great was her physical longing.

Her tears, and the mention of her uncle, brought Filipe to his senses, no doubt thinking of a possible duel or at least an uncomfortable scene. "I have asked you to marry me, my own love. I would not harm you." He thought her tears the tears of a maiden who had narrowly escaped violation, who was innocent of the meaning of her physical signs of arousal. "My pet, my so innocent love, I would not harm you," he repeated. "I forgot myself."

He tried to dry her tears, but she drew back, unable to bear his touch. He was stimulated to even greater efforts to apologize and to comfort and reassure his sweet, his delicate, his lovely, his innocent flower, until Polly, slowly regaining her own control, began to find the scene both incongruous and amusing. What would happen if she suddenly threw herself back into his arms, and confessed the true origin of her tears, she wondered. What would he think of his delicate, his innocent flower then? With the return of her sense of humor, and her sense, she found the right words to release them both. He escorted her to the foot of the stairway leading to the bedrooms above, and bowed over her hand but did not kiss it. He watched her ascend, and then turned—no doubt, she was sure, to find some relief in hard spirits. She was in complete sympathy with him, and only wished she could do the same.

Before they returned to the city, he asked her again to marry him, and again in a more formal petition in her uncle's drawing room. He was a gentleman, and she believed that his ardor was enhanced by his conviction that he had taken advantage of her innocence. He was also a proud man, and on her third refusal, he withdrew to his estates in the country. She saw him only once before she left Brazil, at a formal dinner where they exchanged a few pleasant words, and wished each other well.

But Polly, from that night on the veranda, knew that for all her brave notions of independence, she must find a husband if she were to avoid the scandal of taking a lover. . . .

With an exasperated exclamation she gathered her skirts, picked up her basket and shawl, and descended the long slope toward the stream and footbridge.

A week passed, and another began, and the two families, unaware of the meeting in the meadow, put

47

hopes aside. Then one morning Frederick could no longer tell himself that pressing chores kept him from Tanwell. He finished his coffee, thinking that the Brazilians were right about coffee; it should be good and strong, rather than weak liquid favored by his countrymen. However, he preferred it not with sugar and milk, but a spot of good warm cream from the Moregreen dairy.

Satisfied, he strolled out to the stables and called for his horse. He set off toward Tanwell, where he arrived rather more quickly than intended, since he had only to ride across the two parks—a distance of no more than an easy walk. There was consequently some flutter behind the scenes at Tanwell when Miss Rice was told that Mr. Moresby waited on her in the drawing room, but when she did appear, she was as perfectly composed as if she had not been fussed at by both Nettie and Francie until nearly at the door.

"Good morning, Mr. Moresby. I hope you are well at Moregreen."

"Yes, quite well, thank you, Miss Rice."

Indicating two chairs near the long windows overlooking the garden, Polly said, "Shall we sit over here? My mother will be in directly."

"Thank you, no. I was riding past and it struck me what a marvelous day it is—just the kind of day for visiting the ruins of the old abbey. Perhaps you would enjoy the drive I mentioned when I called with my mother?"

"Right this very minute, Mr. Moresby?" asked Polly, restraining a hope that Mr. Moresby might have a little dash after all.

"I wouldn't think of giving you such short notice.

Perhaps this afternoon?"

"Why, yes. I'm sure Mama has nothing that needs doing. I'd be happy to accompany you." Well, dull dog or no, he was almost as good looking as Francie thought him, Polly reminded herself.

Frederick chose a pace that would afford peace of mind should Polly prove a nervous passenger, and which also permitted ample leisure to view and exclaim on the beauties of the countryside. April was now nearly spent. Pear and apple blossomed pearly white and pale pink against the new green of field and hill and hedge. The elms were just bursting into leaf, the grain was well up, and the calves and colts, now past their tottering infancy, frolicked about their mothers.

Frederick pointed out a decaying manor house, inhabited by an aged farmer, a cantankerous and misanthropic bachelor. "Do you remember old Amos?" he asked. "He's nearly ninety now."

Polly did remember old Amos, and she remembered his peach orchard also.

"Yes, and he guarded it well," Frederick said. "He had the reputation for being so mean he would whip anyone caught in it. But such a temptation those peaches were! We made careful plans, my friends and I—you remember the Somersall twins?" Polly nodded. "Well, the twins and I made careful plans for raid on that orchard, and it was so well executed that he never caught us. We thought ourselves very clever, but I daresay it was old Amos who was the clever one. He would never have whipped us had he caught us, so he let his reputation stand, and achieved his purpose. It was

49

much easier to raid other orchards."

Polly smiled. "His reputation had certainly grown by the time my brother and sister and I were of an age to steal peaches. By that time it was well known that he could turn children into salt with no more than a glance. Oh, but we told each other such delicious tales of Old Amos and his frightening ways. I wonder if he knows that he was responsible for so many excruciating thrills?"

"I wouldn't wonder but he did. My father drives over to call on him now and then, and finds him only mildly disagreeable. The old fellow speaks well of your mother, by the way."

A silence fell as Frederick negotiated a short steep hill and a dangerous curve at the foot. He was gratified that Polly refrained from screaming, or squealing, or otherwise exhibiting any nervous mannerism, although the curricle tilted alarmingly on the steep grade. Polly merely braced herself in order not to slide onto the floor.

Once past the difficult spot, Frederick thankfully increased their pace before continuing. "Old Amos's peaches were the best in the country, though. Well worth a whipping, even if not worth being turned to salt. I wonder what kind they were."

"My mother has two young trees—cuttings that she grafted on common root stock. Old Amos brought her the cuttings one day, but refused to tell her the name of the variety. Last year, she says, they bore a few fruits that were excellent, and she looks forward to a larger crop this year."

"Your mother is one of the best farmers in the neighborhood," said Frederick, "and a genius with fruits and flowers. Perhaps that's why Amos speaks so well of her."

Frederick halted the horses near a small shady copse. "After we tour the ruins we can rest here. It seems a comfortable place to spread the picnic your mother sent with us."

As they left the shelter of the copse and saw the ruins before them, Polly exclaimed, "Someone has cut the trees!"

"Yes, I heard they had been cut. The price for good oak was high a few years back. And visitors are evidently expected to follow the path the landlord has marked out and not go wandering around his meadow," Frederick observed as he guided her toward a rickety stile that gave access to the meadow.

"I don't recall that there was a fence," Polly said as Frederick handed her down the other side. "Is the landlord another cantankerous old fellow?"

"No, only greedy."

The ruins were less than either Polly or Frederick had remembered. There were crumbling walls, one fragment rising to a height of ten feet, an arched doorway, a few paving stones still intact, and piles of stone enclosed in tangles of woodbine and briar. They traced the outlines of the building, told each other what little—and uncertain—history they knew of the place, and then, warm from unrelieved sun, returned to the copse and gratefully settled themselves on a rug to rest and take their picnic tea.

"Tell me," said Frederick. "When were you in America? My mother says it was soon after our second American war."

"Yes, my uncle was sent to Flanders when the peace negotiations were opened with the Americans at Ghent in 1814, as secretary to our peace mission. He delivered the ratified treaty to Washington City and remained as chargé d'affaires until Sir Charles — our minister — arrived. Then he was engaged in negotiations over boundary settlements with Canada, and an agreement for permanent naval disarmament on the Great Lakes that lie between Canada and the United States. He's an excellent negotiator, the soul of tact and patience, and with the future relations between Brazil and Portugal so uncertain, was considered the perfect choice for our legation in Brazil. But I admit that during the first year in America I was more involved in the problems of housekeeping than diplomatic affairs. Which also required a certain skill in the arts of negotiation, I might add."

Polly had been fumbling ineffectively with the cap of the flask her mother had provided containing a refreshing and fruity punch. Frederick took it from her and with a deft twist opened it. Polly took two cups from the picnic basket and unfolded the napkin that held the little buns, which were another specialty of her mother's kitchen. When their simple tea was laid out, Frederick asked, "You know, I've always wondered; did Mr. Madison really run away when our soldiers entered the capital city? Did he really abandon the presidential palace, as our papers reported here?"

"Oh, no. He'd been to inspect the troops. It was Dolley — Mrs. Madison — who had to flee. She saw to the removal of Mr. Washington's portrait, then took the silver and some state papers and fled to the country. She makes the description of her flight seem quite dramatic now, and even amusing, but I'm sure she was terribly worried about Mr. Madison — 'Jemmy' as she calls him. She really is the most amazing woman. She dips snuff, she gambles, gives balls and levees with not the slightest sign of effort. And she engages in a constant round of calls—she is just irrepressible! Even in the abominable Washington climate she retains her energy."

"Washington has an abominable climate? I would have thought it rather mild and agreeable."

"No, indeed. In summer the whole diplomatic corps—and most of the American officials too—move to the country. Ordinarily it's hot, and muggy; one of the French staff said the climate reminded him of African jungle. In the summer when it rains and in winter after the frequent thaws the streets are ankle deep in mud. People were often late to engagements because of the mud in the streets—I could keep two laundresses employed full time. But there . . ." Polly brought herself up short. "You can't have any interest in such details of life in the New World as how many laundresses my uncle's establishment needed. Tell me what interests you, and I'll try to answer like the wise and observant traveler my uncle tried to teach me to be."

Frederick had always had an interest in Thomas Jefferson, for all that the noted American was a Francophile. Although Polly had met the great man only once, on a tour into Virginia to visit Mr. Madison at his plantation, she had heard many stories of Jefferson's years in Washington with which to amuse her listener. "My uncle says he is an enigma. He told the French minister once that if he insisted on wearing gold lace that boys would follow him in the streets."

Frederick failed to smile; he looked merely puzzled.

"It was thought very funny at the British legation,"

53

Polly concluded lamely.

"So you met Mr. Jefferson when you were visiting Mr. Madison? You know," he said thoughtfully, "I have never quite believed the picture of Mr. Madison that was painted by our newspapers since I read a pamphlet of which he was author, concerning agriculture and the preservation of nature's balance, which struck me as exceedingly well thought out."

"Oh, he is held in very high regard in America—at least by most—and our minister, Sir Charles, always regarded him highly. He's called the father of their constitution, and is believed to be brilliant. So is Mr. Jefferson, who was visiting when Uncle and I were at Montpelier, but neither he nor Mr. Madison seemed inclined to show their brilliance on any other subject than agriculture—chinch bugs in the wheat, grafting fruit trees, and how to keep the squirrels out of the corn—what we call maize, you know—Indian corn. My uncle, who much prefers politics, was quite put out with them. I, of course, spent my time with Dolley or the other ladies, and such young gallants as cared to escort us when we went walking or riding. Except in the evenings, when Mr. Jefferson sometimes played his violin for us, and the talk was of literature and art, and a little of world affairs."

Frederick also admired and was curious about Benjamin Franklin. He had read several of his writings, particularly those devoted to science. Here Polly had to plead ignorance. She had read none of his works, nor heard any tales, except that he had been a most wily ambassador to the French during the American rebellion—now nearly fifty years past. So Polly became the listener, learning about electricity, balloon ascensions,

54

and the future of boats powered by steam.

The shadows were growing long when they quit the copse.

As Polly reviewed the day, sitting in the chair by the window where each night she brushed her hair, she came to a decision, confirming her earlier half-formed impulse. Surely at twenty-four — nearly twenty-five — she could demand independent control of her small fortune and — equally important — independent control of mind, spirit, and body — the independence she had so feared to lose when she was younger and less assured. If Frederick Moresby should appear interested, she would encourage him. He had so much to recommend him: good looks and fortune . . . excellent parents who would make her welcome as a daughter, and he had given her a pleasant, if serious, afternoon. A small matter; she was a diplomatist's niece and accustomed to serious-minded discussions.

However, Polly's thoughts did not linger long on the afternoon's conversation, but returned to Frederick's good looks.

He reminded her of Dom Filipe, with his dark hair curling on his forehead, but it was not really a physical resemblance. It was more . . . what? More a feeling of attraction to the man. Polly's traitorous thoughts returned, against her will, to memories of kisses and caresses, thoughts that had of late been too persistently popping into her head for peace of mind.

Why had she refused Filipe's offers of marriage? She hadn't loved him, she was certain; a turbulence of the senses at a man's touch, and a weakening of maidenly

55

restraint is not love, but something else. And without love it had not been possible to cast her lot forever with a foreign husband in a foreign country — and a country, moreover, where women had even fewer rights than in England. Not to mention Filipe's slaveholdings. She could never have adjusted to that.

And Alex. Never a suitor, really, and certainly too young for marriage when she had known him in Washington. But ah, such sweet kissing! How nice it would be for once to proceed to the end of that road! What was it like to lie all night in a man's arms? Polly skittered away from the thought, for it would lead only to discontent, and she had a vague feeling that it might be unhealthy. The healthy — and the sensible thing — was to marry. Men and women who had no great love for each other, at least as far as she had observed, often had dozens — well, maybe half dozens — of children, so love was obviously not an essential. Mutual respect and a personable face and figure would certainly do. And she had not long since left just such a man — a man she believed she could respect.

Frederick called often at Tanwell after that day, and it was understood by all that he was courting. Polly rode with him, went driving with him. They met at assemblies in the town. They went on outings together, Polly sketching while Frederick fished. The Moresbys dined with the Rices and the Rices (those above the age of fifteen) dined at the Moresbys. Frederick and Polly discovered that they both liked to dance; that they played whist by the same theories; that they shared a disinterest in ruins; and that neither very much liked

56

mutton. All this was encouraging for a marriage without conflict. Further, they discovered in each other a directness and independence of mind that each could respect in the other. Polly restrained her more lively and flirtatious impulses, convinced by her mother that somehow such behavior was unsuited to one of mature years and advancing age—one who, moreover, was admired and looked up to by younger sisters. And Polly, despite her dishabille and her playful impulses, did have a strong sense of personal dignity. It was that dignity which had made her so long reluctant to surrender herself in marriage, and which was forever in a state of tension with her romantic streak, her playfulness and her passions. She responded, unconsciously, to Frederick's seriousness, as he responded to her dignity, and both repressed the self-knowledge that whispered of deceit, and of the repression of essential elements in themselves. They had made their decisions, he for his reasons, she for hers, and once set on their courses were determined not to deviate from them. Arranged marriages were so commonplace that they saw nothing remarkable in arranging their own. Each set out to accommodate the other, and to make the best of what would be a contractual relationship.

All in all, Polly demonstrated herself to be virtuous, sensible, and unexceptionable. Frederick, convinced that his restlessness merely required a mate to put in a nest, and once determined that Miss Rice would be a compatible nest mate (and, he secretly thought, her independence of mind would no doubt free them both from unnecessary intimacy) was careful to betray no hint of that restlessness which often urged him to put spur to his horse, or to be in any way other than dull

Mr. Moresby. But Frederick also remembered those well-turned ankles and the glimpse of shapely legs, which suggested perhaps better than he had any right to hope on the subject of his mother's prospective grandchildren.

Chapter Four

Polly's water colors and sketches arrived from London, carefully crated and in the care of a young art student named Higgins, who managed to parlay an invitation to rest a day into nearly a week before undertaking his return journey. Mr. Higgins mooned about at Polly's side, plying her with compliments and suggestions for new paintings while bemoaning the absence of the sublime in the pastoral vistas of the neighborhood, until Frederick began to feel his fingers itching to strangle, and Polly could hardly maintain a well-bred sobriety of countenance.

Mr. Higgins was finally dispatched by Mr. Rice, who took to demanding his company for morning strolls, afternoon chats, and evenings in his library, during which he talked steadily and in exhausting detail of art and artists through the ages. His brain awash in facts, the young artist retired to the safety of his London peers, who were willing to deviate occasionally from the subject of art to discuss women and politics.

Mr. Rice could not help puffing himself up before

the assembled females as they sat at their first family dinner in nearly a week.

"I should have thought," he began, as he contemplated a gooseberry tart, "that someone might have congratulated me."

"For what, Papa?"

"Why, my dear, for ridding our household of a pest."

"A pest, Papa?" asked Francie, puzzled, thinking of the bat that had found its way into her bedroom, and the skunk with which one of the housecats had insisted on doing battle.

"He means Mr. Higgins, Francie," said Polly. "And we do congratulate you, sir. Your performance was inspired."

"Yes, indeed, and we will be able to thank you that we will never again have to put up with any of Polly's artist friends," observed Mrs. Rice dryly. "No doubt Mr. Higgins has reported to all his friends and acquaintances that Tanwell and its proprietor are to be avoided at all costs."

"Perhaps," responded Mr. Rice, "but I suspect that Mr. Higgins's friends (if he has any) are aware that he is a prosey bore and are amused that he has met his match. Polly's friends will be willing to chance an encounter with an ogre in order to see her."

"An ogre is hardly the descriptive word," said Mrs. Rice, exercising a privilege of long standing for the last word.

"Well, well," Mr. Rice murmured, preliminary to a change of subject. "I have been waiting for the announcement of your exhibition day, Polly, the one for your family. The little sketches that accompanied your letters were like the fragrances that drift from the stew-

60

pot: they whet the appetite for more."

"A stewpot is not the most elegant simile, sir, but indeed apt. I discover I have everything from a quick sketch of my two laundresses in Washington City hard at work over their tubs to some watercolors that Mr. Higgins insists are 'utterly sublime.' And I am puzzled that some paintings and drawings that I have considered my best were rejected for exhibition in London, while others with which I was never satisfied were chosen."

"Are you certain the man who made the selection is competent?" asked Mrs. Rice.

"Oh, yes. He did excellently in choosing among my botanical drawings and supervising production of the engravings. He was recommended not just by a friend, but by Mr. Benjamin West at the Academy. And my brother Peter testifies to his honesty and reputation."

"It's well known," observed Mr. Rice, "that artists and writers are not the best judges of their own work. The artist, for example, may be attempting to record a landscape in exact detail, and exactly how it looks in the glow of a sultry sunset. But suppose that at just such a moment in a similar spot he was moved to make an offer to a young lady. Now, if the marriage turned out well, he will have a fondness for his painting, quite aside from its value as a work of art. On the other hand, if he has wedded a shrew, although he catch the flaming red and the burnt gold to produce his greatest work, there will always be a ghost hovering over the painting to diminish its value in his eyes."

"A ghost, Papa?" asked Francie. "Why should he see a ghost?"

"Why, my dear, it will be the spirit of his wife, who is

a very nasty woman, railing at him constantly for wandering off into the country with a paint box when he should be helping her in the shop."

"But if she's not dead, how can she be a spirit?"

"I know how to explain it to her, sir," Nettie volunteered.

Mr. Rice peered down the table at his third daughter. One almost forgot she was present, sometimes; she was so still and with an expression on her pretty young face that even her family often mistook for abstraction. But it was just her way of listening, for all at once her face would light up with the intelligence that so delighted him. "Very well, Nettie. I'm sure we all will be interested to hear your explanation."

"Do you remember, Francie, last summer when Mama set us to sorting over the bed linens for stains and worn places?"

Francie was not much given to remembering the routine details of her life. "I guess so," she said uncertainly.

"Don't you remember how we decided that some of the worn spots didn't really need darning yet, because we knew that we would have to do the repairs and we both hate darning?"

Carefully not looking at her mother, Francie murmured again, "I guess so." She would have liked to help herself to another gooseberry tart, but thought it would be impolite to interrupt Nettie.

"Oh, of course you remember, silly. And then we began feeling naughty. It was just like Mama was standing there looking over our shoulders and telling us that the sooner a worn spot is mended the less work in the end—that problems are best attended when they're

62

small because if not, they just get bigger and harder to solve."

"Yes! I do remember. And I was glad, after all, that we thought of what Mama says, because I won't have to do so much darning."

"A lesson well learned, Francie," her father remarked approvingly.

"Oh, I didn't mean that, although it's true, but if we'd left those spots 'til next winter, maybe Nettie will be married by then and I'd have to do them all by myself."

Nettie cast an exasperated look across the table. "Really, Francie, you can be the most amazing slowtop! I'm not talking about learning a lesson in housekeeping, but that Mama's spirit was sort of there reminding us of what we already knew."

"Oh!" Francie at last saw the object of the lesson. "Oh, just like the painter's wife!"

Amid general kind laughter, Mr. Rice said, "Except that your mother is not a shrew, but a wise woman. If I painted the landscape where I proposed to your mother, I'd like it excessively."

Mrs. Rice rose from the table, ruining all Francie's chances for another gooseberry tart. "How odd, Mr. Rice, for if I remember, you made your offer in my father's drawing room on a gloomy winter morning."

"Ah, perhaps, my dear, but I remember it with sunshine and the scent of roses."

Mrs. Rice chose not to respond to this sally, saying only, "Shall we go, girls, and leave your father to his port?" But as she passed his chair, she lightly touched his shoulder. They had dealt well together through the years. Odd, she thought, as she led the way down the hall. Two people could hardly have seemed less

63

suited—the son of a rake and the daughter of a parson. But she had had the energy he lacked, and it was that very lack that had left her free to make decisions without his interference. And it was her love of farming and efficient management of affairs that left him free to indulge his scholarly interests. Had the two of them tried to tred the paths society ordinarily marked out for man and woman, what a botch they would have made of it! She a criticizing shrew, and he unable to keep their comfortable fortune in land and investments intact, let alone increase it as she had.

Her husband was a student of art, an expert in architectural styles, widely read in literature, history, philosophy, and geography. He took great pleasure in teaching his children (once they reached the age of reason) and in tutoring an occasional neighbor youngster for his examinations, but he had no interest in the management of either capital or land, and a perfect horror of managing labor. He had a great interest in the new science of political economy, for although he would have been incapable of figuring simple interest, he had a perfect comprehension of economic theory, and could number among his many scholarly correspondents the outstanding economic philosophers of his day.

When their neighbor, Sir Harry, wished to talk economics, he sought out Mr. Rice, but when he wanted to talk farming, he sought out Mrs. Rice. It was she who supervised servants and laborers and dealt with the farmer who oversaw the management of the fields and plantations, to whom the neat farm house was due, who supervised the construction of the small orangery, and to whom the fame of Tanwell's nursery beds and the growing fame of its orchards could be credited.

Efficient and practical, Mrs. Rice was the very opposite of her husband, and she had borne it all (including eight children, only one of whom had been lost in infancy) with nearly perfect equanimity. Although she had no objection to listening to Mr. Rice reading from a good novel, she had no interest in books other than the practical. She subscribed to botanical journals, and read perfect tomes on farming and husbandry. She was among the first to purchase Dr. Hunter's cookbook, and the very first in the neighborhood to serve one of the daring curry dishes that he offered along with much useful and useless advice. It was in just such actions that Mrs. Rice revealed the fire in her own soul—a fire long since banked, and now nearly extinguished by the demands of ordering a large household, a farm, and a husband who would have let it all—fortune, estate, wife, children—fall into ruin and want from sheer inattention.

A memory she could not quite formulate bothered Mrs. Rice as she picked up her mending and observed her daughters. Francie went to the pianoforte to tinkle out some light country airs; Nettie picked up a book. Polly took out her sketch pad. "May I make a sketch of you, Mama?" she asked. "That cap is so enchanting." The memory she searched for was forgotten, as Polly fussed with the direction of the light and the angle of her chair.

It was not long before Mr. Rice joined them, for he took little enjoyment from sitting alone drinking port, and preferred the comfortable evenings in the drawing room with his family. Jonathan and William were called from the old nursery, where they were still re-

65

quired to take their meals, and Mr. Rice picked up the current novel for an hour's reading. The Lonely Traveler had long since found his home and his lost love; the Rice family were now embarked with a Spanish count and his daughter on a voyage to Italy, and about to be taken by Barbary pirates.

As Mrs. Rice's mind wandered from the novel—the author was taking an unconscionably long time to effect the capture—she recovered the memory: she had chided her graceful daughter for acting the hoyden, when she had merely been entertaining the youngsters. It had hurt Polly's feelings, and she was sorry for that. Well, there was no taking it back, and she had apologized. No use crying over spilt milk. The thing to do is to promptly wipe up the spill and then put it out of one's mind.

Good lady through she was, she was not given to introspection, and so did not pursue to its genesis the fleeting discomfort of the memory. If she had done so, she might have recognized that it was her consideration of the unconventional arrangement into which her marriage had naturally fallen that had led her to remember that she had scolded Polly for a lack of propriety. If she had then thought about it more carefully, she might have recognized that her successful marriage contained a lesson at least as important as that worn spots in bed linens should be promptly darned: convention could sometimes give way to personal inclinations without harm, and sometimes even for the better.

Polly's exhibition was planned to include only the Moresby's, but word got out, as word will in small communities. The rector expressed interest; and Squire Ruggles, whose nephew had emigrated to the United States, had several times mentioned his desire to see scenes from America, "although Brazil could go hang" for all he cared. A Mrs. Montout, who visited in the neighborhood, had a distant connection in America, and on the basis of this connection secured an invitation by hints so broad that they more nearly constituted demands. The exhibition soon became an exhibition to be followed by a luncheon on the lawn.

Rather than show only her best work, Polly chose drawings, watercolors, and sketches that most clearly depicted people and places in the New World, including some of the preliminary drawings for the botanical paintings that had been the basis for her book of engravings. She chose the morning room for her exhibition. The light was favorable in both the morning and early afternoon, and tall French doors opened onto a narrow terrace and stretch of lawn where the luncheon tables could be arranged. An ancient sycamore tree spread its thick shade over one corner of the lawn and supported two swings on one mighty limb, and a third swing on another limb of only slightly less impressive dimension. In another corner of the lawn three willows provided canopies of slender drooping branches. And should there be rain, the dining room was just down the hall.

Exhibition day dawned fair, as the footman's grandfather, who was known in the neighborhood for accurate weather forecasting, had predicted it would. After some discussion, the tables were set up under the willows. Cushions and small rugs were scattered around the lawn, and benches were brought from the garden.

67

Neither Polly nor her mother had been certain of the procedure for an exhibition and luncheon, and had at last decided that Polly should remain in the morning room during the first hour in order to answer any questions the scenes might stimulate, after which she could mingle freely with the guests on the lawn, while the guests would be free to wander in and out of the exhibition room as they pleased.

She stood now by the door, making one last assessment. She had included drawings of the American president's residence as it looked under repair after the fire set by British soldiers in the late war, other public buildings in Washington City, and the British minister's residence. There was a watercolor of the Great Falls of the Potomac several miles above the city, and another of dark, brooding Pennsylvania forest, both to satisfy interest in the sublime. There was a portrait in bodycolor of an Indian chieftain in full regalia, and several watercolor and pencil sketches of American scenes: the horse races, a slave market, and the New York-Washington steamer. She had also drawn Mr. Madison's country residence, Montpelier, where she had met Mr. Jefferson, and some scenes from New York City and the mountain settlements of western Virginia.

The Brazilian scenes were similarly varied. There was a painting of Dom Joao in a royal procession; a whimsical drawing of European botanists conferring about a strange plant in the botanical garden Dom Joao had established for the study of New World flora. She had included a painting of the Sugar Loaf—the amazing hill that guarded the magnificent harbor of Rio de Janeiro, and another of the harbor with ships from many countries at anchor. There was a convent, a

68

slave pen, and a group of nuns doing their marketing, as well as scenes from the countryside. A stewpot, indeed, she thought to herself.

"Good morning," Frederick said behind her.

Polly jumped. "Oh! I didn't hear you."

"I'm sorry. You must have been deep in thought, for I certainly made no effort to be silent."

"I was wondering if I should move that gouache of the New York harbor farther away from the Pennsylvania forest. Even though I've tried to present a sequence based on geography, I'm afraid the colors in the forest painting are dulled by those in the gouache."

"That's much too technical for me, I'm afraid."

"It has to do with color theory. You see—"

"No, no. No theory please. I want to enjoy the exhibition as sensibility, not sense. And I've come early for my promised exclusive showing." He drew her arm through his and led her into the room. "Now, what is this charming landscape? You see, I refuse to follow your chronological thinking. . . . Is that not sensibility?"

As they slowly toured the room, Frederick's admiration of Polly's work grew. He had considered her engravings of American native plants competent, and the accuracy of the representation of botanical parts excellent, but he had not thought them anything extraordinary. This work, liberated from the demands of scientific accuracy, was freer and lovelier.

"You know, I've seen the sketches you've made on our walks, and the amusing drawings—the fish I caught that day by the stream flipping around in the grass and I trying to catch it, for example—but never a finished painting. I had no idea you were so good."

69

Twenty minutes later, reassured by Frederick's appreciation and by his calm presence, Polly thought she might almost enjoy herself in the hours ahead. She would have liked to put her arms around his neck and thank him with a kiss, but she merely said, "I don't believe any but the most egotistical of artists could look forward to even the smallest exhibition of their work without nervousness, but you have made it seem much less frightening. Thank you, Frederick."

He wanted to say that she was beautiful, glowing with the realization that her work was good, with anticipation and excitement, but he confined himself to patting her hand.

Just then Francie stuck her head in the door, so excited that she did not notice the intimate mood into which the two occupants of the room had fallen. "Polly! Polly! Someone is coming! Oh, isn't it exciting?" And Francie, as was her wont when excited, began jumping up and down.

Frederick put his hand on Francie's shoulder. "You are a regular jumping jack, Francie. I believe you have springs in your knees."

Francie giggled, but could think of nothing to say to this elegant gentleman who was courting her sister. Frederick bowed to Francie, then took Polly's hand again and lifted it to his lips. "I will leave you now to receive your guests. I will return with my parents, but I'm glad I had an opportunity to see your work with you alone. It is very good." Less seriously, he added, "When this afternoon is over, you will be hailed as an important personage by all who see it. When travelers pass through the neighborhood, and inquire who of importance lives hereabouts, people will say, 'Why Miss

Polly Rice, the artist, you know.' "

Polly laughed, as he had hoped. As voices reached them from the terrace, he bowed again, and departed to await the arrival of Sir and Lady Moresby.

Other guests came quickly on the heels of the first, and soon Polly was so beset with questions that she had no time to consider her own fears of artistic failings. Certainly these viewers were not inclined to be critical, although several remarked on the daring color in the paintings. They accepted the exhibition as Polly intended it: as a "journey to the Americas."

Mrs. Montout, who had claimed her invitation on the basis of a relative in America, remarked, "Oh, yes, Basil mentioned the magnificence of the Falls of the Potomac," a refrain repeated with each of the paintings, and that led Mrs. Rice to observe later than one would have thought Basil had followed Polly around carrying her paintbox.

The rector tsk-tsked over the scene of the Washington slave market. A disgrace, he declared, in the capital city of a Republic based on the principles of philosophers such as Locke, Rousseau, Montesquieu, and Paine. The Brazilian slave markets he thought not surprising. What could one expect of an appendage of an autocratic Catholic kingdom such as Portugal?

Frederick returned, accompanied by Sir and Lady Moresby. Catching Polly's eye to give her an encouraging smile, he led his parents to the landscape that had first attracted his attention and then left them to their own impulses. Spying Mr. Rice on the terrace in conversation with a neighbor he had not seen for several months, he left the morning room to join the gentlemen.

71

"What a magnificent fellow!" Lady Moresby exclaimed to Polly, as she studied the portrait of the Indian.

"Where did you meet Red Indians, Polly?" asked Sir Harry.

"They came to Washington to make treaties with the government over land and rights," Polly explained. "I saw the Indian in the portrait passing in the street in front of our house in Washington, and later at a diplomatic reception. I drew his costume and—decoration, I guess one would say—from memory."

"Imagine, the noble savage traversing the streets of a civilized capital!" a lady viewer whispered. Then remembering that civilized people had not been established long on the North American continent, and that even representatives of civilization were reported to become somewhat barbaric in the new environment, she asked uncertainly, "Washington City is civilized, isn't it?"

"Why do they paint themselves that way?" Lady Moresby asked, to draw attention once more to the portrait.

The portrait showed the Indian's head and shoulders. A string of glittering beads about his neck was barely visible above the closely wrapped robe. Except for a crest of hair that ended high on the crown, his head was bald as an egg. More startling yet, the shaved portions were painted bright red. Jagged green and red streaks decorated his cheeks. Finely braided black and white cords were looped around his ears and through a ring of skin formed by the earlobe. "The Indians sometimes slit the earlobes and stretch it, so that it almost looks like the ring in a gypsy's ear," Polly explained.

72

"How odd," Lady Moresby remarked. "The South Sea explorers report the practice among some islanders. According to their accounts, some of the ear loops are stretched almost to a level with the chin."

"Barbaric!" exclaimed one of the ladies.

"I think he's beautiful," Nettie said. She turned to their neighbor, Squire Ruggles, who had just come up beside them. "Think how much more interesting you would look, sir, if you painted your face all red and green stripes like this Indian."

"Why you saucy puss. I'd look like a silly macaroni."

"It's a wonder the macaronis never took it up. It would have looked fine with their crazy pants and lurid waistcoats," Sir Harry observed.

The squire was soon transfixed before a drawing of an ox and cart among the Brazilian scenes. Polly, noticing his interest, paused beside him. "Do you like my ox, sir? I'm sorry that I didn't do more agricultural scenes for you country gentlemen, but—"

"No, no," interrupted Squire Ruggles. "Can't expect a lady to be interested in such stuff—unless she's your mother, of course. But I can't help noticing what a poor beast the creature is. Never gets enough to eat, or I miss my guess."

"That's true. The animals are very poorly cared for in Brazil—with the exception of the blooded stock, of course."

"Well, the picture is uncommonly good, if I do say so. What a comparison with my Caesar—my prize ox, you know. Stands fourteen hands, and weighs near a hundred and sixty stone." The squire paused. "Don't suppose you'd agree to paint him for me? I'd be happy to pay, of course. Don't know why painters shouldn't

73

get good money for their work, any less than masons or harness makers."

Polly laughed. "I'd be delighted to paint your ox — or make a drawing like this one, if you prefer. But I wouldn't want money for doing it."

"Well, well, we'll see about that, missy. Never sell your work for nothing. You promise to make me the picture and we'll dicker over price later. Is it a bargain?"

When Polly agreed, he said, "All right, that's the way we leave it. Now here's somebody else wanting to talk to you, so you just run on. But first your hand on it."

Polly gave him her hand. "It's a bargain, sir. Please send me a note when you're free to plan the drawing — or the painting — and I'll ride over to discuss it with you and to make some preliminary sketches of — Caesar was it?"

After the last guests departed, the Moresby and Rice families gathered on the north lawn. Polly collapsed on a bright-colored rug, where Frederick joined her. Jonathan and William were in the swings, and Francie, tired of being grown up, joined them. Nettie collected cushions from other rugs scattered around the lawn and made herself a comfortable nest at her father's feet. Servants moved quietly about, removing the party paraphernalia. The midsummer scents of new-cut hay and sweet clover drifted across the lawn on the gentle and vagabond currents of a still afternoon.

"This has been a perfect year for clover," Mrs. Rice remarked. "I've never seen it bloom so luxuriantly."

"It smells heavenly," Nettie sighed.

"It was a wonderful afternoon, Amelia," Lady

74

Moresby said to Mrs. Rice. "Only you could find a cook in the village who could prepare such repasts. With Polly's paintings and this lovely afternoon, I feel a surfeit. So much beauty at once . . ."

"A perfect afternoon should be capped with a perfect wine, and I just happen to have a bottle of Moselle that, if it's as good as the others of the same year, should be superb." Mr. Rice called to one of the servants hired for the day. "Send a footman to me," he ordered.

When Robert appeared, Mr. Rice gave instructions for glasses to be brought and the wine to be selected. "Glasses for everybody — the youngsters too!" As Robert started toward the house, Mr. Rice called, "And ale for everybody in the kitchen when you've finished the work of cleaning up."

They chatted languidly as they waited for the wine. The day was so still that it seemed to slow the senses — so still they could hear the cattle lowing as they were brought up to the farm barns for milking. Nettie, leaning on her father's knee with his hand resting lightly on her head, fell into a somnambulant state. Jonathan and William no longer pumped the swings to dangerous heights as they shouted challenges to each other, but were unenthusiastically wrestling each other in the grass. Francie remained in the swings, where she was swinging leisurely back and forth, dreaming some vague young girl's dream.

"We'll all be asleep in a minute," Polly said. "When Robert comes with the wine, he'll find us like people in the old fairy tales, or the characters in *A Midsummer Night's Dream* — enchanted — under a spell — sound asleep."

"It's just the kind of afternoon for falling under an

enchantment," Frederick said, his eyes on Polly.

Lady Moresby restrained herself from glancing at her husband. Polly was looking almost beautiful today.

"Except," Polly was saying, "for this ant crawling across my hand." She gently brushed the ant away, but she had broken the spell, and Lady Moresby could have shaken her. Oh, well, she thought, as Robert appeared, reverently transporting the wine, and followed by a maid carrying a tray with glasses. The youngsters were called, and the glasses filled.

"Shall we drink a toast to the success of Polly's first exhibition?" proposed Sir Harry.

"And another to Amelia and her luncheon," suggested Lady Moresby.

"To Mr. Rice for this excellent wine," said Frederick. "And to Polly," he added, lifting his glass.

Chapter Five

Frederick had nearly blurted out a proposal in the aftermath of Polly's exhibition — when he was full of admiration for her talent, dazzled by the glow of her excitement and happiness, and not a little affected by wine. But he waited, restrained by habitual caution. A hasty proposal, brought on by a momentary enchantment, had doomed more than one man to a life of misery. He did not, of course, believe that life with Polly would be misery, but nonetheless, a step like marriage required sober thought.

She remained much in his mind in the days that followed. He remembered how she had laughed when he joked her nervousness away, and how her eyes had lit up when he praised her work. He put himself to serious consideration of that subject. If he offered for her, he would be marrying a woman endowed with a talent that should not be subdued or ignored. He felt just a little in awe of it. But then, a woman with a strong interest of her own was less likely to be demanding of her husband's time and attention, and much less likely to re-proach him for the pursuit of interests more appropri-ate to a bachelor than a married man—even though just then Frederick could not think of any bachelor pursuits that still interested him. He recognized that that very lack of interest was what was leading him to marriage, indicating as it did that he was ready to settle down. So his thoughts ran on, fitting Polly into the marriage of convenience he had determined to make.

After a week of careful consideration, Frederick judged that he was no longer under any lingering influ-ences. He was, so to speak, sober. His acquaintance with Polly was now of sufficient duration that a pro-posal would not be considered improper. It was made, and accepted, with an admirable frankness on both sides.

Frederick began, as they walked along the stream bordering the parks: "You are no doubt aware, Polly, that I have come to have a high regard for you, and that I have in fact these last weeks been courting you with the hope that when this moment came, you would honor me by promising to become my wife."

Polly replied with equally succinct formality, and with just a flash of that sparkle that had enchanted grave ambassadors, handsome officers, and dashing Americans, South and North. "I had, yes, come to suppose that your attentions might lead to this end, and you in your turn must realize that I have given you every encouragement. My answer, of course, is yes."

Frederick bestowed a kiss on Polly's brow, and an-other, carefully formal buss, upon her lips. She con-trolled the impulse to put her arms around his neck and kiss him properly. She merely took his arm and said,

"Can we walk a bit, and talk?"

He acquiesced, and Polly began to state her terms. "I fear you may wish to retract your offer"—she smiled to lighten the words—"when I say that I do reserve a few conditions."

Frederick assured her he would not, and she continued. "As you know, I have had complete control of a small inheritance since I was eighteen, and as you also may know, I will come into something like two thousand pounds on my father's death, the earnings from which I would also expect to control. And, of course, any earnings from my paintings or engravings."

"I have told you, Polly, that I admire your independence. I should not object. We are too old, the two of us, for youthful romantic excesses and other foolishness . . ." (Frederick believed that by this clever circumlocution he was reinforcing the idea that theirs was a marriage of convenience) ". . . but we have respect for each other, and admiration, and I believe we shall make a most successful marriage."

Polly would have preferred an argument rather than such ready agreement. Points too easily won, she had learned from her diplomat uncle, were always subject to suspicion. But she only answered, "Thank you, Frederick."

So they strolled on, settling such affairs as when to announce the engagement, when and how Frederick would approach her father, whether she should tell her family first, and even the wedding date (Polly thought the Christmas season would be nice), and where they might honeymoon (Frederick thought France, perhaps Italy—even, daringly, North America)—all those details that must be settled before a marriage, and that

79

could be settled without delay since there was no pressing need, as there must be between true lovers, for clarifying all the little misunderstandings that preceded the discovery that they loved.

That evening each announced the decision to a delighted family. The following morning Frederick waited upon Mr. Rice; Lady Moresby and Mrs. Rice met later the same morning; in the evening the families met for a late supper; and it was done. The friendship between Moregreen and Tanwell was reinforced; Lady Moresby and Mrs. Rice could think about grandchildren; Sir Harry could think about succession of property; Mr. and Mrs. Rice about a well-settled daughter. Nettie and Francie engaged in lively thoughts of romance and bridesmaids' gowns; the two young brothers wondered why a silly old engagement should so excite their elders. Even the servants were pleased, for Polly's courtesy and friendly manner had won her the approval of the household and farm staff. It was a perfect day for everyone, except possibly the two principals.

Polly, in her bedroom tucked under the eaves at the end of the second floor hall, suffered a crisis of nerves such as she had not experienced since she hostessed her first formal diplomatic dinner. What had she done? She sat for a long time in the chair by the window, looking across the park toward Moregreen. The scent of nicotiana hung in the air. In the garden below her window, a clump of tall foxgloves, their bells satin white, gleamed in the shimmering light of the waxing moon. Didn't the country people associate foxglove with some kind of midsummer sacrifice? Was she sacrificing herself on an altar of frustrated passion and morbid curiosity? Was it a midsummer madness? Her eyes grew

80

heavy and she went to bed, only to wake again, and to toss and turn until near morning, when she finally slept.

Although she had slept so poorly, she rose at her usual hour, added a dash of artificial color to her cheeks, chose her most cheerful, bright-hued morning gown, and went below for breakfast. The first crisis had passed. But as she picked up the newspaper, she noted the date. In less than two weeks, the Americans would celebrate their independence, and only yesterday she had given up hers. The omens did not seem auspicious. She shook off the thought, and served herself an egg.

Frederick had spent an equally uneasy night, and although he, too, presented himself for breakfast as usual, and with the outward calm that had become his habitual mask, he wondered at his agitation. Perhaps all men suffered such second thoughts at the prospect of losing their freedom, even those marrying women they passionately loved. Later in the morning he found an opportunity to confess his doubts to his father, phrasing the question lightly and putting it almost negligently.

"Of course, very natural," said Sir Harry, anxious to reassure his son, and too pleased with the match to probe Frederick's fears. "I was in the same state after I offered for your mother. I've known men who actually developed symptoms of panic—but who settled in very nicely—snug as could be—once the vows were taken. No, no need to worry."

So Frederick's father reassured him, and Frederick reassured himself, and with a little effort came to believe that he had done exactly the right thing. He was fond of Polly and she of him. And he *had* been dazzled the day of her exhibition; that he couldn't deny. But he

81

found it necessary to run down to London for a week or two to attend to some business.

Mrs. Rice, meantime, was considering that she must now undertake the duty of instructing her daughter in the facts of marital life. Accordingly, when the following afternoon she was returning from the orangerie and found Polly sitting alone on a garden bench, she took a seat beside her. Sighing, she remarked on the unusual warmth of the day, to which Polly readily agreed. Mrs. Rice admired the drawing Polly was completing of a single, drooping branch of roses and, these formalities taken care of, plunged in. The sooner started, the sooner finished. "I have been hoping for an opportunity to speak to you alone," she said.

"Yes, Mama?" Polly replied, somewhat absently, her thoughts still on her drawing.

"If this is an inopportune time . . ."

"No, no, not at all. Forgive me for my distraction. I was just coming to the conclusion that I had exhausted my creativity for the day."

"I shan't be long with what I have to say. It is just that now you are affianced, I think it right that you should be made aware of the rights and duties of marriage."

"Oh, Mama." Polly laughed. "I believe I know what the 'duties,' as you call them, are. I must honor and I must obey my husband, and in return he is required to see that I am fed and clothed. It is also my duty to produce a sufficient number of children that Moregreen and any other Moresby property pass on in a direct line of inheritance. Am I correct?"

"That is very flippant, Polly. I would have liked to

have heard something about mutual affection and respect."

"We have that, Mama. In fact, more so than I had hoped. I am really very fond of Frederick. And he has assured me that I may retain control of my own small fortune."

"Well, if managing one's own money has anything to do with respect, I suppose you are right, and Frederick does seem to hold you in affection and esteem. But what I wished to speak to you about was the satisfaction of passion. You should know, Polly, that men are not like us. They must, er, satisfy physical passions."

Polly twisted the rose she had been studying. "We do not have physical passions, Mama?"

Polly's mother shot her a shrewd glance—her daughter was, after all, twenty-four, and she had traveled in worldly circles. "It is not thought proper," she answered cryptically.

Polly replied slowly, "Why is it not thought proper?"

"I don't know, my dear. Perhaps it is even unfair. I can, however, tell you this: gentlemen of breeding do not expect their wives to demonstrate passion—that is reserved for their mistresses. Frederick will expect his wife to submit willingly, but he will not expect her to act like a courtesan."

Polly, her eyes on the rose in her hands, asked in a low voice, "How can you know, Mama, what Frederick will or will not want?"

"I cannot, of course, know the mind of another. All I can tell you is what I have learned from my experience and the experience of other women of my acquaintance. I—and I thank God for it—have not had to bear the ignominy of knowing I shared my husband with a

83

mistress, nor has Frederick's mother, but innumerable women of our acquaintance—as I am sure Lady Moresby would confirm—have been required to resign themselves to the fact."

"Some, I would guess, with relief, if they are denied passion as a reward for duty."

"Yes, some with relief," her mother answered. "You realize, I am sure, that some women prefer that their husbands take mistresses. Childbirth is not easy."

"But you, Mama . . ."

"I was very fortunate in that I had an easy time. It is not always so, as I'm sure you must know."

A silence followed, which Mrs. Rice broke. "My dear, I am only cautioning you—trying to explain to you the facts of marriage and of propriety."

Polly could find nothing to say but to thank her mother for her advice and to assure her that she would try her utmost to be a good and faithful wife. Mrs. Rice chose to be content with this dutiful assurance, and left her daughter to finish her drawing. But Polly's restraint was not acceptance. She did not aspire to be a good, faithful, and passionless wife! Damn, she thought, using her favorite private expletive, what am I marrying Frederick *for*, if not for an acceptable expression of passion? Had her experience in these last years left her unfit for a life in the country and the role of wife to a serious and respectable gentleman?

Polly, unlike many women attached closely to the diplomatic service, had never developed a fondness for serious politics. The intrigues of diplomats and the development and pursuit of national policies had failed to arouse her interest, and she had paid only the attention necessary to fulfill her role as her uncle's hostess.

Unlike yet other women, she had never been interested in the endless rounds of gossip: the intricate personal intrigues and the pecadillos of the diplomatic community. In America she had preferred the company of a set of young people whose interests centered on dancing, parties, horse-racing, and flirtation; such serious interests as she had at the time were limited to observations of the manners and customs of the Americans and the natural wonders of the great continent that was theirs, all of which she tried to capture with her brush and pencil. In Brazil she had preferred the artistic and scientific community which the Portugese king, Dom João, had encouraged during the Brazilian exile forced upon him by Napoleon's invasion of his country. The new botanical garden, the discoveries of the German botanists, the inspiration of the French artists and of Maximillian and Thomas Ender and their Brazilian scenes—these had been Polly's serious interests. And for the lighter side of her life, novels, shared often with Lisette, the daughter of one of the French artists who, like so many Europeans, had thrilled to the promises of a new world, and who had eagerly responded to invitations from the exiled king. Among the novels were many like those her father often read to his family; but there were others that ranged from the racy to the pornographic.

While Polly sketched, Lisette, a superb linguist, read aloud, in a running translation from the French to the English. When she was hard put to find the English word, they puzzled out the meaning together. They felt young, modern, republican, and very daring. Lisette, child of revolution, who had grown up among artists, was more familiar with the risqué than Polly, but Polly

85

was more familiar with the pornographic. Even the most startling of the French novels could not compete with the little booklets that had been surreptitiously vended to the girls at the proper school for females in which she and Gussie had each spent three years. There always seemed to be something deliciously naughty even in the worst of the French novels, compared to the common vulgarity of the little booklets by which Polly, like many other English girls, had been introduced to a side of life about which so much was hidden, and when discussed, so often only in whispers or by innuendo. The naughty French stories had been the antidote to that vulgarity, but vulgar or no, the little booklets had revealed a good deal to their readers that their parents and guardians, and later many of their husbands, never suspected they knew.

Would she, in fact, find herself cast off by Frederick if she should allow any of the emotions aroused by Filipe to burst forth once again? Another moment of fear at the course she had chosen caused her to tremble. She regarded her hand, still holding a rose from whose stem she had been carefully stripping the thorns as her mother spoke. "What is the matter with me?" she asked herself. "I must marry and take my chances; or I must live the life of one of the little Brazilian nuns, not only without the hope of passion, but without children, without the companionship of a man, with only my work and my status as spinster auntie." The latter was a positively chilling thought! Or, she conceded, a scandal . . .

Her drawing no longer beckoned. Despite the unsuitability of her dress for riding, she went directly to the stable and called for her horse, sending a groom to retrieve her drawing materials and to take them to the house. As soon as she was out of sight, she tucked up her skirts more comfortably, and letting the little mare amble along the hillside, directed her to a vale where, in the solitude and beauty of the spot, she could recover her inner calm.

Although Mrs. Rice told herself her duty had been done, she was not able to put out of her mind the business of preparing Polly for her forthcoming marriage. She could not quite convince herself that she had done the chore adequately.

She believed, as she had told Polly, that passion was not expected from wives, and nothing Mr. Rice had ever said or done had made her think differently. She had carefully schooled herself to the most passive expression possible; many times her teeth had nearly pierced her lip as she attempted not to cry out in her transport. It was that very passion that made her so vulnerable, and she had often, even in the pleasureful aftermath of the marriage act, cursed the treachery of her body. But after Francie, fear of another pregnancy had conquered her baser needs. To her husband she excused herself as unwell. It was only after she noticed his eyes hungrily following a young maid that she indicated to him her recovery. There had been no further danger signs from Mr. Rice thereafter, but she had suffered, for she also believed that her regrettable inability to control the spasm of pleasure was responsible for her excessive fertility. She schooled herself to detachment, and Mr. Rice for his part tried to practice Onanism. Mrs. Rice knew nothing of sexual methods other than the single copulatory position deemed "natural," and if she had she would have considered them perverse. Onanism — withdrawal — was an acceptable method of avoiding conception, but left her unsatisfied and restless; that her husband could give her pleasure without penetration was unthinkable; and that she could give herself pleasure would have been morally reprehensible. For his part, Mr. Rice, although certainly aware of many variations in acts of love and sex, would never have expected his wife to engage in them, associated as they were with the libertine ways of his father. Nor, for that matter, could he use a French letter, even in the most respectable coupling, for it was too closely associated in his mind with elegant French whores, the means by which his father had introduced him, at the age of thirteen, to sex.

After two years of restraint, which Mrs. Rice remembered as unhappy years altogether, she began to think that although she had not yet passed the change of life, that her childbearing years were over. For four years harmony was reestablished in the marital bed and her body at peace. Then she became pregnant with Jonathan, followed closely by a second pregnancy with William.

She was thirty-eight when William was born, evidently fertile again, and with several years more before she would be liberated by menopause. It was then that her talent for efficient management was aroused to serve her in this most intimate of causes. An elderly and ailing relative in London provided the excuse to visit that city where, sometimes using a false name she questioned accoucheurs and midwives, matrons of lying-in hospitals, and even visited a famous madam.

She learned a great deal of absolutely startling and admittedly fascinating information, which did not change her beliefs one whit, but she did find the answer to her immediate problem — a means to avoid pregnancy, keep her husband away from young maids and satisfy her own treacherous body. Oddly enough, her first clue had come from Mr. Rice, who in his study of economics had read of a method suitable for women. But she had never told anyone, least of all her husband, what she had done in London, except to mention one discussion with a well-known accoucheur, who had recommended the same method as the economist. (Interestingly enough, so had the madam.)

She would have liked to have given their elder daughter, Gussie, when she married, and now Polly, the benefit of her experience, but she could not. A natural reserve, a reluctance to reveal even a hint of an intimate and private relation, was coupled with delicacy and with the conventions of her society and time. Well, she thought, Frederick had no doubt had experience and will know what to do, just as Giles had. Her marriage night had not been so frightful. And if her daughters became pregnant too frequently, or their health or lives were endangered, she would steel herself to speak. With that thought she contented herself, and turned resolutely to the household accounts, at which Polly found her an hour later.

When she returned from her ride, Polly went to the dairy for a glass of cool milk, and then to the kitchen for two thick slices of bread and butter.

She looked in on her mother, busy at her desk in a

corner of the library. When Mrs. Rice looked up questioningly, Polly said, "Mama, I've decided exactly how I wish to finish my drawing. If you will excuse me, I will make my dinner of bread and milk and continue working until the light is gone."

Later, even as the light faded, she felt the drawing was emerging as she wished, and knew that another crisis had passed. She had achieved once more a measure of serenity and confidence in a future with Frederick.

Chapter Six

Two days after this event, the footman returned from an errand in the village bearing a letter. Mrs. Rice, who was sitting in the morning room with Polly and Nettie, put down the shirt she was sewing, and observed, as she broke the seal, "From your Aunt Grover-Morton."

"Aunt Cat!" exclaimed her two daughters.

"Aunt Cat never writes letters," said Nettie. "What can the matter be?"

Mrs. Rice, with a quick glance over the top of her spectacles, commanded silence while she read.

"Well, it seems your aunt will be visiting us earlier this year than usual."

"And what," asked Polly, "is the reason for such haste? Doesn't she still customarily visit in August?"

"As we know, your cousin Clarissa suffered numerous colds this past winter and also a case of severe putrid throat. Her health has been damaged by the repeated illnesses and her doctor recommends that she spend the summer away from the city, but does not recommend either Bath or the seashore, which are too crowded and noisy. They come to us now, should we concur. Although how Catherine expects us to concur

91

I'm sure I don't know, since they arrive within two days."

"That's the extent of it?" asked Polly. "In two such close written pages, that is all?"

"That is the essence," said her mother, with a small smile, as she handed the letter to Polly and took up her sewing.

"Lord bless us!" exclaimed Nettie, reading over Polly's shoulder. "Aunt is as wordy when she writes as when she talks."

"I'd forgotten Aunt Cat's volubility." Polly refolded the letter. "I suppose Clarissa is a young lady now."

"Oh, yes," Nettie replied. "She's pretty, and clever, and just lots of good fun."

"And not too insensible, either, considering that from the age of eight she's been under your Aunt Catherine's wing," their mother added.

Catherine Grover-Morton was the sister of Mr. Rice, and Clarissa the daughter of their deceased younger sister. The latter had married a man who, although of no particular distinction, had later achieved sufficient prosperity in trade to leave his already motherless little girl well provided for when he, too, was overtaken by untimely death. Aunt Cat, whose own short marriage had not been blessed with issue, had taken her sister's orphaned daughter to her heart, and raised her as her own.

Mr. Rice, when he heard news of the imminent arrival of his sister and niece, although he seldom concerned himself with financial matters, grumbled about the expense of feeding his sister's horses. "You must make certain," he instructed Mrs. Rice, "that she sends them back to London immediately."

"If you're concerned, tell her yourself," said Mrs. Rice, with uncharacteristic snappishness, and an equally uncharacteristic flounce out of the room that left her daughters and husband with mouths agape. She returned in minutes to apologize and, with a sigh, to explain herself. "It's not just that we will have to hire an extra servant, but the housekeeper had just warned me—threatened, actually—that if 'Mrs. Cat is still on the vegetable regimen like that heathen poet she talked about last year,' Cook will surely quit. Bread and raisins for dinner is an insult to a respectable cook, it seems."

The arrival of the two guests was throwing everyone into such a fuss that Polly began to wonder if memory betrayed her. Only that morning the footman, young Robert, had approached her and, with much apologizing and excusing, had asked her to tell Mrs. Rice that he absolutely would not clean Mrs. Cat's canary cage again this year. Polly recalled her Aunt Cat as a pleasant, rather featherbrained woman, and Clarissa as an awkward but well-behaved child, both of whom fit into the household without undue difficulty. When she asked her mother if in her youth she had not realized what Aunt Cat's visits entailed, Mrs. Rice replied yes, Polly had perhaps forgotten.

"Are Aunt Cat and Clarissa so disturbing to our routines? Or unpleasant company?"

"No, nothing of the sort. Aside from the fact that Catherine is a rather silly person, they aren't difficult guests. Perhaps it's because Catherine seems to stimulate confusion, and so we take extra precautions before her visits in order to *prevent* confusion. Heaven knows, though, after all these years their arrival should be as ordinary as a call from the neighbors. I just don't know,

93

child."

Aunt Cat arrived soon after, with all the hurly-burly of a traveling show that her family had come to expect. Her little pug dog was the first to descend from the coach and, in order to establish his presence, immediately watered his favorite bush. This accomplished, he ran around the family party gathered on the steps, barking and backing and growling. Little Pug always arrived like a lion, and as inevitably went out like a lamb—but until one or another of the several cats lost patience and with a few well-directed swats put him in his place, he remained a lion among beasts. Following Little Pug, the bird cage was handed out, with the two canaries, which would later cheer the mornings with sweet song from their cage on a stand in the morning room, brought out each year for one or another of the long line of canaries on which Aunt Cat doted. The next to alight was the ladies' maid, who always accompanied Aunt Cat and Clarissa on their travels to serve both mistress and niece. She turned to assist the next to descend, Aunt Cat herself—plump, smiling, and talking.

"Oh, what a frightful journey. We have been caught in a rainstorm, and severely misused at the White Ox, which as you may know, Amelia, has a new owner . . . lovely to see you, my dears." Here she paused to kiss her sister-in-law and her nieces in turn. "And this is Polly, isn't it? My what a lady you've become! And here is Clarissa . . ." as Clarissa at last emerged from the carriage, ". . . such a terrible winter the poor girl has had. Two months—imagine—two whole months in bed. She missed the entire season. And even yet she has not fully recovered. As I told you in my letter, Amelia . . . Clarissa, dear, do look to Little Pug."

The three young ladies of the house now took charge of Clarissa and Little Pug, leaving their mother to urge Aunt Cat into the house, and the servants to complete the unloading of the baggage, to see the coach and horses to the stables, and the coachman to his quarters.

"I have the most lovely house gift for you, Amelia! But I'm so afraid I may have packed it in the trunk."

"How nice, Catherine," they heard Mrs. Rice say as she urged Aunt Cat toward the stairs. "I can wait until you are settled and your trunk is unpacked, I'm sure."

Polly remembered Clarissa as an ungainly girl, who although small for her age, had all the clumsiness usually associated with children who grow too tall too soon. The willowy and graceful young woman she now confronted bore so little resemblance to that child that Polly involuntarily exclaimed, "My dear, I wouldn't have known you had we met in the street. You have become so lovely!" Clarissa's reply was perfectly correct, with such a proper mixture of modesty and calm acknowledgment of the compliment, that Polly was even more amazed. The young Clarissa, although well behaved, had been as graceless in her manners as in her movements.

Clarissa was equally surprised by Polly, whom she remembered from the vantage point of fourteen years, when a nineteen-year-old seems all that is sophistication and elegance. Clarissa was now just past nineteen herself, and here was that same Polly, looking not at all sophisticated, a little disheveled, and with just the faintest beginnings of lines at the corners of her eyes.

That Polly's wrinkles would follow the lines that laughter traced in her face, rather than the lines that would etch the faces of the scolds and the petulant would never have crossed Clarissa's mind. She was yet so young, and so accustomed from her London upbringing and the influence of society friends to thinking any mark of age the beginning of the end, that Polly seemed nearly as dried up and passé as their Aunt Cat.

Among them all, hostesses and servants, they at last saw Aunt Cat and Clarissa, with Little Pug, settled in the adjoining chambers that were together referred to as the spare room. The maid was shown above to her room in the servants' attic, the canaries' cage was safely placed on the stand in the morning room, and the luggage taken out of the entrance hall and carried upstairs. The Misses Rice then sat down in the drawing room to wait for their guests to refresh themselves after the journey, while their mother hurried off to her husband's study to advise him that his sister and niece had arrived and would be taking tea with them soon. Perhaps, she suggested, since Aunt Cat was his only living sister, and Clarissa the only child of his deceased sister, he would like to greet them?

The scullery maid had been assigned the task of cleaning the bird cage; Aunt Cat, it was soon learned, had given up her vegetable regimen, and the horses were promptly dispatched back to London. The family had no sooner made these and other adjustments to the guests, and the guests accommodated themselves (or resigned themselves, as the case might be) to the rhythms of country life, when a new excitement stirred the neighborhood—the letting of Crossfield Cottage to two young men from London.

Polly was the first to hear the news, for she enjoyed exercise more than the others, and so it was she who walked into the village to buy some flannel and several other items for her mother and to post letters for her father. Mrs. Leach, the postmistress, sat at the center of one of the webs of village gossip (Mr. Ludlow, the proprietor of the public house, sat at the center of the other), and this day the most exciting news was the latest addition to local society.

"Yes, my dear. Crossfield Cottage is rented at last. Such a shame it was that Mr. Tomkins let it stand vacant so long. He can be thankful, I assure you, that he had the good sense to engage my nephew to look after the grounds for him and keep an eye on the house. Why, just the other day the surgeon's house was broken into while he was away in London. I told him at the time he should not give his housekeeper leave to visit her sister at the same time he himself was away, but he wouldn't listen to good advice—oh, well, my dear," Mrs. Leach wound up, "we none of us want advice, do we now?"

"And who has taken the cottage, Mrs. Leach?"

"Two young gentlemen—or perhaps not so young. My nephew says one of them looks not quite in the first flush of youth, but then not at all old either. But dearie me, I can't recall the names for anything. One of them stutters and the other is foreign—American, my nephew says, but whether from Canada or that upstart country where you went with your uncle I can't remember, if he even told me, which I begin to doubt. Whichever, I expect the foreign one will be glad to meet

97

someone who once set foot on his own native continent and who can understand him too. My nephew says that what with one stuttering and the other talking so funny, it's a fair riot to listen to."

"Once you accustom your ear to it, the accent isn't so very different from ours. And, of course, the Americans say we have more different accents in our one island than they have in their whole expanse of seacoast and interior, and that we shouldn't say a word about the way they speak."

"Well, of course, English was our language first, but then, now that you point it out, my dear, I will admit that some of our very own people are not always the easiest to understand. I determine right now that I will keep a straight face and listen very hard when the foreign gentleman comes for his mail. And as for the stutterer, my own dear Mr. Leach once knew a man who stuttered, and he says that for all that, he was as smart as anyone could want to be."

Polly lingered several minutes more to hear about Mr. Leach's acquaintance, and then the roster of births, deaths, and doings—including the break-in at the surgeon's—for to hear the news of interest, one was required to hear everything.

When Mrs. Leach had exhausted fresh gossip and begun on events more distant in time, Polly excused herself and hurried on to make her mother's purchases. She was just emerging from the shop, her head so full of an idea for a drawing of Clarissa posed against a background of hollyhock that she did not see the young man passing by, in an equal hurry, and with his thoughts likewise somewhere other than minding his own progress down the street. They collided with such force that Polly was nearly knocked off her feet, and in catching herself from falling lost her package. Since the first available support at which she clutched to steady herself was the very same young man, the two spent several seconds in inarticulate apologies as he steadied her; then, as he stepped back to hunt for her package, they for the first time looked directly into each other's eyes. Recognition dawned. She gasped in surprise; he exclaimed.

"Alex!"

"Paula!"

She reached out her hands to him with impulsive cordiality and long-standing affection. He clasped them in both his, and then, with an even warmer impulse, he raised them to his lips. "Paula! The most sparkling hostess His Britannic Majesty has ever been so kind to bestow on us benighted colonials! I heard your uncle had remarried and that you'd returned to England, but couldn't remember where your home was for the life of me. I ran into old Perkins in London and asked him, but he uumphed and hummmphed and gargled and finally said he thought, uummmph, gargle, someplace in Cambridgeshire."

"He would!" Polly laughed. "He never could remember anything, even to tie his own cravat. But you, Alex. Just look at you! Still as handsome, and breaking hearts in a dozen countries, I'll vow. Whatever brings you here? And your mother and father . . . how are they? And all our friends in Washington . . . oh, I'm so eager for news!"

"Slowly, slowly, Paula. Too many questions at once."

Another gentleman had observed this enthusiastic and warmhearted greeting, and had now made his way

99

across the street.

"Good morning, Polly."

"Oh!" She slipped her hand from Alex's warm clasp. "Frederick. You . . . surprised me."

"Yes, I didn't think you saw me," he said, as he took her now freed hand in his.

"Oh," she said hastily, "Frederick, may I present Mr. Alex Chapham, from America. Alex, this is Mr. Frederick Moresby, my fiancé."

Alex put his hand out, in the egalitarian French and American manner, as Frederick bowed; then Alex bowed as Frederick extended his hand.

"Stop, for goodness' sake," Polly said, too distracted to laugh. Nor did the gentlemen. Fredrick smiled and offered his hand to Alex, who shook it, and then did laugh. "I'm happy to make your acquaintance, sir," he said.

"I didn't know you had returned from town, Frederick," Polly said (with, as she later reflected, the most awful gaucherie).

"I just returned last night, but too late to call on you. In fact, I called this morning, and have followed you into the village thinking you might like a morning drive." Frederick turned to Alex and asked politely, "Are you with your Foreign Office, sir?"

Alex, who had been taking the opportunity to retrieve Polly's lost package, straightened. "Yes, I am. I met Paula in Ghent. Although"—he came close to winking at her—"I see she has turned back into a Polly."

"You are now stationed in England?" Frederick asked.

"No, I've been assigned to our legation in Germany, but I have several weeks free, so I thought to make it a slow trip, stopping for a time in England to visit old friends."

"You have friends in the neighborhood?"

"Not a soul, until I ran into Paula — most literally ran into her, I'm afraid. But pure luck brings me here. I couldn't find anyone in London who knew where she'd gone — although many remembered her." Alex smiled down at her. "Now that we have met so opportunely, I hope I'll be permitted to call and to pay my respects to your father and mother and to your sisters." Addressing Frederick once again, Alex said, "Paula used to read us letters from her little sister — Nettie, wasn't it? Such funny, sober letters they were. We missed not only Paula — Polly — when her uncle was ordered to Brazil — we missed Nettie and the whole family."

"I'm sure my mother and father will be delighted to receive you," Polly said. She turned to Frederick. "I do believe that Alex must be the foreign gentleman who talks so very funny and who has just rented Crossfield Cottage . . ." She flashed an arch look at Alex from under her lashes.

"And how did you know that?" cried Alex. "Is the news out so soon?"

"Oh, yes indeed. You must remember that we have no great events to occupy us here; all manner of little happenings are our news — and when a cottage is let to two gentlemen, one with a foreign accent, and one with a stutter . . ."

"Here, who's been telling you all this? Clancy does have a stutter, but only when he's pressed to speak quickly, or when he's under some kind of strain, but he's the best fellow in the world. I hope you'll let me bring him to call, Polly. You'll like him, I know. Met

101

him when Father sent me over here to polish me up a bit before I set out on my career. Clancy took me under his wing and kept me from making some foolish mistakes. The poor fellow needs cheering up—he's had a bad time of it recently."

"Are you speaking of Clancy Danver, Earl of Bolling?" interposed Frederick.

"Yes. Are you acquainted?"

"We belong to the same club. I presume you're speaking of Bolling's recent divorce?"

"Terrible thing. Poor chap's thoroughly cut up about it, and when he said he wished he could get away from London and the town gossips for a while, I said to him, 'Well, fine, let's. I'm at your service, old fellow.' And here we are."

At this juncture, Alex, glancing past Frederick, saw the object of discussion making his way toward them. "Here's Clancy now—tired of waiting for me on the High Street corner, I expect. Clancy! Clancy, old fellow! Look who I've met here! Ran into her hurrying to meet you."

The man who approached them, although of medium height, looked smaller, as much from his air of diffidence as from the slightness of his frame. His eyes were brilliant blue and would have been unusually arresting, except that he seemed to have difficulty focusing them upon a single person or object. His gaze met Polly's and quickly slid away, although his greeting was courteous.

"D-delighted. Looked for you in London, Alex d-did. T-told me all about you. You must be d-d-d—" Lord Bolling appeared unlikely to ever get past the next delighted, and Alex relieved him of the necessity to do

102

so by exclaiming, "Here now, we've forgotten Poll—Polly's—package!" and on delivering it into Frederick's care, called his friend's attention to the fourth member of the group.

As Frederick acknowledged Lord Bolling's greeting, he was remembering that he had always thought Bolling something of a fool, not because of the stutter, which under most circumstances impeded him little, but because of the inanity of his remarks. His recent difficulties seemed to have left him in even worse condition; his stutter was worse, his gaze unsteady, his handclasp languid. He seemed to be composed of rags, and his eyes as uncontrolled as loose buckshot rolling around in a dish, except that they rolled in unison. Frederick, in order to spare Lord Bolling from exertion, welcomed the two men to the neighborhood at greater length than was usual for him, offering them the privileges of his estate—although not yet the season for hunting, the fishing was fine—and otherwise offered the hospitality of his house and home. With these and similar pleasantries from the other three (Lord Bolling offering inarticulate sounds), the company parted; Frederick and Polly in one direction and Mr. Chapham and Lord Bolling in the other.

Frederick forbore to question Polly on her previous acquaintance with Mr. Alex Chapham, adhering firmly to the rule of mutual independence he had hinted at in his proposal of marriage, and merely remarked that she had apparently used a more formal name abroad.

"Oh, that's just a name Alex gave me, and that I

103

adopted in a foolish youthful desire to add to my consequence."

Frederick merely replied with a fond smile that she no longer had any need to inflate her consequence, if she ever had.

Polly was eager to tell Frederick all about the fun of those years in Washington, and how kind Alex and his family had been, and was vexed that he gave her no opening. She had been so young, oppressed by her duties, still inexperienced, and she had needed youthful friends and youthful fun. She wondered if this was what Frederick meant by "too old for the romantic excesses of youth"—if it meant that he would never be curious about the other men in her life. Then she scolded herself soundly. This was what she had intended for her marriage, was it not? It wasn't that she wanted him to be jealous, she thought, but just that she wanted to tell him about herself, and Alex Chapham was part of the telling. So—Frederick having little to say about his trip to London, since his activities there would not bear a discussion with his affianced—the ride home was occupied with the affairs of Lord Bolling.

Bolling, it seemed, had had the ill luck to be accepted by a lady of easy virtue and independent fortune, who once wed to a title considered herself settled in all she wanted in life except the pleasure of the bed. She had remained faithful for the year required to give her husband an heir. That chore accomplished, the lady sought more handsome and less staid companionship, but with a lack of discretion that even a sophisticated society found unacceptable. She took up, in rapid succession, one after another of the young, handsome, and

104

ingratiating men who hovered on the fringes of society, and who were always ready to trade their favors to wealthy patronesses for money and gifts. Then the heir she had presented her lord most unhappily fell victim to an infant malady, and although she was willing to pay for her title with another season in her husband's bed, that gentleman had forsworn her favors forever. Her affairs thereafter were conducted with increasing flagrance and decreasing taste; Lord Bolling ceased to go into society and avoided all his acquaintances, although — from what Frederick knew of Bolling's mother, who had a tendency to vapors and lamentations — he had wisely refused to accept the solace of shelter on his country estate. Finally, rumor had it that the wanton wife was pregnant, and since it was common knowledge that she was no longer welcome in the marital bed, divorce was inevitable.

"What a sad story," said Polly. "Has she been confined with the infant yet?"

"The rumor is — and you realize that what I've told you is largely rumor — that she had her confinement while visiting relatives in the north of Scotland, and the child has been left with them. She is now back in London, has set herself up in an independent establishment — on a very generous, and unnecessary, settlement from Bolling, by the way — and means to open a salon for the literary. It remains to be seen whether she can carry it off."

Polly was considering other matters. "How can the gossips know that she actually was expecting a child, or that if she in fact was, that she permitted the pregnancy to come to term?" Polly felt rather than saw Frederick's startled glance, and continued, "Really, Frederick, I wonder at you men! You tell me a story that is repeated in every club and drawing room in London, by male and female alike, and then wonder that I should ask forthrightly if her pregnancy came to term. Every wit in London knows the use to which the tops of sabina are put. And surely you know that there are women in the village—and one among the cottagers on your estate, if I am not mistaken, who give aid to girls who have had the misfortune to find themselves paying for succumbing to the same urges and wants as their sometime lovers. I am sorry Lord Bolling was cuckolded, and I am sorry for his hurt, but the former Lady Bolling seems to have been condemned not for her actions, which are not so very different from those of many men—who seem to think it perfectly proper to keep a string of mistresses whether married or not—but because she is a woman."

Frederick, somewhat taken aback, said, "You have taken up the cause of female rights?"

Female rights was an interesting subject—Polly was quite in sympathy with the women who spoke out on women's rights—like the notorious Miss Mary Wollstonecraft, but she had more recently read a book which (rumor had it) was the work of Miss Wollstonecraft's daughter, named Mary for her mother, and now the wife of Percy Shelley.

"Oh, Frederick! That reminds me! Have you read *Frankenstein* yet? It's a silly book, but a chilling theme."

The remainder of the journey was spent discussing the merits of novels as intellectual fare, Polly arguing in favor, and Frederick, who read novels only in secret, standing out for more sober works, such as Ricardo's *Principles of Political Economy and Taxation.*

As they entered the drive at Tanwell, Polly asked, "Did you meet my aunt and my cousin when you called?"

"No, I spoke only to your mother, and drove immediately on to the village."

"Then you must stop to make their acquaintance."

They found Mrs. Rice, Aunt Cat, Little Pug, and the two canaries in the morning room, where the ladies were engaged in looking through old botanical magazines. After Frederick had been presented to Aunt Cat, and had made all the formal acknowledgments required, Mrs. Rice sent them to the shrubbery, where Nettie and Clarissa were taking their morning exercise.

"Perhaps they're in the summer house at the end of the gardens," said Polly, when they failed to find the girls. "They like to go there to read and sew and gossip."

The garden was crisscrossed and woven with paths laid out for easy access to beds, for although Mrs. Rice was familiar with the schools of landscape gardening, her interest was plants; and design had inevitably given way to the need for space. Thanks to Polly, she possessed some of the earliest specimens of hardy flowers native to the Americas, including a rare plant called a petun, from seeds Polly had sent from Brazil. It was for her mother's pleasure that Polly had first undertaken the sketches of American plants, and which eventually grew into the book of engravings that had already won her some small fame and modest income.

Frederick and Polly walked arm in arm along one of the many grassy paths, enjoying the pristine silence of the garden, which was disturbed only by the heavy thrum of bumblebees among the snapdragons. Polly paused beside a clump of pink and pale yellow spikes. "Look how perfectly the bees fit into the flower," she said. "Have you ever noticed? It's almost as if the flower and the bee were made for each other."

Frederick plucked a flower, and pinched it to make it snap, but restrained the sudden impulse to playfully use it to take a snap at Polly's nose, which was really quite as nice, he was beginning to think, as her pretty eyes and shapely ankles. "Are you interested in horticulture like your mother?" he asked, thinking how charming was the faint sunburn that decorated the very top of her nice little nose. Had he not cherished a profound prejudice against driveling poets he might have considered writing a few lines.

"Oh, no. I'm afraid my interest is not in the growing, but in the enjoyment of flowers, especially the pleasure of painting them."

Frederick dropped the flower in his pocket, fearing Polly might think it sinful to dispose of beauty by such callous means as tossing it into the shrubbery. She took his arm again and they walked on.

The summer house was situated on a pretty little rise, gleaming white among the close-growing greenery that shaded it. As they approached they heard low murmurs and then Nettie's voice rising clear, fluting, strong:

> " . . . long time they lay
> Fondling and kissing every doubt away;
> Long time ere soft caressing sobs began
> To mellow into word, and . . ."

"Merciful heaven," whispered Polly. "That's Keats — his *Endymion.*"

The sound of their footsteps carried well in the stillness, and a sudden silence fell in the summerhouse, followed by a scuffle, which proved only partially successful. A volume of Byron lay still open on a corner of one seat as Polly and Frederick entered, although on the other seat the two girls were virtuously bent over a small volume of essays. Their two elders gave no hint that they had heard Nettie's dramatic reading. Clarissa and Frederick were presented to each other, and the elders invited to be seated. Frederick casually moved the Byron aside, noticing as he did so that the girls had earlier been reading a very improper tale.

Clarissa, more artful than Nettie, observed to Polly that they had spent a delightful morning reading, and casually lay aside the volume of essays. Frederick, however, was not to be so easily gulled, nor so willing to let the girls escape. Picking up the volume of Byron, he said, "Nettie, I didn't know you were a reader of Byron."

Nettie cast a frightened glance at her sister, but Clarissa smoothly intervened. "The book is not Nettie's, but mine. Are you admirer of Lord Byron, Mr. Moresby?"

"I find something to admire in his poetry, yes, but I prefer Shelley for the political content of his work. I can't say that I always approve his political positions, but I believe he is sincere."

It was now Polly's turn for surprise. Frederick reading poetry? But then, of course, he would single out the political rather than the lyrical or romantic.

109

"I am afraid," said Clarissa, "that I find poetry a poor vehicle for political sentiment, which — I have always supposed — should be based on the intellect, not the passions. Don't you agree, Polly?" Without waiting for an answer, Clarissa continued, "I look for romance in poetry, and for sincerity of emotion, and that I find in Byron. But . . ." She lifted a cushion and took up a volume (hidden accidentally, no doubt, in place of Byron): Sir Walter Scott's *Marmion*. ". . . I also find pleasure in a good rhyme and a well-told tale, especially if it's a romantic tale." She opened the book to Canto V, and began to read:

> *"O, young Lochinvar is come out of the west,*
> *Through all the wide Border his steed was the best,*
> *And save his good broadsword, he weapons had none;*
> *He rode all unarmed, and he rode all alone.*
> *So faithful in love, and so dauntless in war,*
> *There never was knight like the young Lochinvar."*

Closing the book, she said, "Now there is a fine romantic poem — the fair Ellen, about to be wed to 'a laggard in love, and a dastard in war,' is saved by the brave Lochinvar. I don't believe that Scott writes with depth of feeling here — he merely tells a tale — but it appeals to us, the fair sex, as you men call us, because we, too, are often wed against our wills to laggards in love and dastards in war, and so we read romances and dream of our brave Lochinvars."

Frederick smiled. "You dream of love and romance as others dream of someday visiting the Sandwich Islands or Tahiti. I suppose that romance has many as-

110

pects, but I for one find poets' overwrought tales of passion a bit too fanciful."

"You have never pined after a fair maiden, then, sir?"

"We men are supposed to pretend to pine, according to the fashion, but I must confess that although I have seen men overwhelmed by a beautiful face and figure, and others charmed by a witty mind, I have seldom seen or heard of anyone swooning for love."

"It is just such prosaic natures as yours that leave us poor females so susceptible to the romancing of poets," replied Clarissa. "But now I have done. I will not even solicit my cousin Polly's opinion, for I suspect that she will come down against romance as well; nor solicit my cousin Nettie, for I know *she* will favor romance. No," she said as Polly appeared prepared to defend herself, "I will argue no more. Tell us, rather, some tale of the village. I know from past years that when one returns from posting a letter, one always has news to tell. And how is Mrs. Leach? Is she still among the living?"

Polly laughed, suddenly remembering that, indeed, she was the bearer of news, and she soon had Nettie in a pleasant thrill of excitement thinking of the foreign gentleman—and an acquaintance of Polly's besides. As for Lord Bolling, Clarissa remarked that although she had never met him, she had always been sorry for him—his lady was so indiscreet, to which Polly replied with some asperity that perhaps the lady had been reading Lord Byron—or perhaps even Keats (at which latter name Nettie blushed guiltily), and that rather than merely reading romances and longing for her brave Lochinvar, she had gone out to look for him— whereat Frederick favored her with another questioning look.

They whiled away a half hour in discussion of Lord Bolling and Mr. Chapham and how Polly came to know the latter, for unlike Frederick, the girls had no reserve about questioning Polly on her former acquaintance with young men. They remarked on how very unusual was the coincidence of meeting him in front of Mrs. Wagner's shop, and at the end, Frederick discovered he had promised Nettie a ball and had sworn that he would be certain to invite the newcomers. Frederick rose to go, and Polly with him, leaving Nettie and Clarissa in the summerhouse—no doubt to sigh over the cruel partings of lovers, and their pantings and repinings.

Polly sat down on a garden seat to watch Frederick's curricle disappear down the drive. Her mind, however, was far from her future husband. She was engaged instead in distracted musings on her own mixed and contrary feelings. Was Clarissa too worldly, and a bad influence on Nettie? She had been cross with Clarissa for mentioning Lord Bolling's divorce, and was certain that at that very moment Clarissa was telling Nettie the whole story. But then, was she too protective of Nettie? The carryings on of the rich and the titled were not too different from those of the poor and untitled, and certainly Nettie knew that their neighbor, Squire Ruggles, and a natural daughter—a bastard, not to mince words—whom he had educated and seen well married. He spoke of her openly, and it was general knowledge that he sent little gifts to his perfectly legitimate grandchildren, and had named her in his will. Among the villagers and laborers also, illegitimacy and infidelity

112

were hardly unknown. Nettie could not have lived so close to the local folk unaware of such things. Furthermore, she could not have grown up in the country, among the breedings and birthings of farm animals, not to mention the numerous cats under her very nose, without knowing something of elementary facts, perhaps even more realistically than Clarissa.

Yet Clarissa's knowledge was different. Polly returned to her previous judgment: worldly. It was to be expected, of course, since Nettie had the innocence of manners that came from country rearing; she had visited London but never had a season, while Clarissa had always moved in sophisticated society. She would not like Nettie to become too hardened, or too accepting of humanity's pecadillos, or to lower her own standards.

Yes, she had been cross with Clarissa for that reason, but she herself had defended the former Lady Bolling, whose indiscretions could hardly be excused, even had her husband been a laggard in love or a dastard in war — which latter at least he surely had not been. Perhaps, however, a laggard in love? Polly's conscience pricked her again — she had sounded very much an advocate of Mary Wollstonecraft's ideas of free women and free love this morning. Next she would be taken up vegetarianism, like Miss Wollstonecraft's son-in-law — or her own Aunt Cat.

And what about the poets? (Excepting Sir Walter Scott, of course, who was her father's favorite.) Whether to speak to Nettie about reading literature her father had forbidden, whether it really ought to be forbidden (Polly did not agree with her father on this point), and if not, how to protect Nettie from possible negative influences while yet leaving her free to enjoy

113

all that was good and beautiful and exciting in the young romantic poets? While puzzling through these dilemmas that have plagued the guardians of the young since time began, Polly failed to remember those little naughty booklets, those racy Frency novels, and she also forgot to wonder if the exposure of Nettie to controversial poets and the doings of the ton were truly sufficient cause for the annoyance she felt with Clarissa.

In the summer house, Clarissa and Nettie had not yet returned to their volumes of erotic poetry, or even to the Bolling scandal, but were once again reviewing in detail Clarissa's problem.

It had been no more than a day or two before everyone in the family and most of the servants knew that Clarissa had received an offer from a titled gentleman; and that Aunt Cat and the men who held her fortune in trust considered it an offer too eligible to refuse. The gentleman was a widower, with children nearly the age of Clarissa, but he seemed not to be seeking a mother for his children so much as an ornament to hang on his arm. After careful investigation of his finances and his character, the trustees had solemnly given their approval. The widower was willing to pay a good deal for his bauble, so much, in fact, that no good banker could refuse. The two other trustees, merchants and former associates of Clarissa's father, were dazzled by the title. Aunt Cat was dazzled by everything. With such unanimity among them, they had concluded to issue an ultimatum. If Clarissa refused, her yearly allowance would be cut to the minimum, and control of her for-

114

tune, which the trust stipulated could be hers at twenty-one, should her trustees agree, would be held until she reached twenty-five, the age at which under her father's will she could take charge of her fortune. A cut in her allowance would not have bothered Clarissa, for she'd always been able to wheedle Aunt Cat for money, but Cat's funds had also been tied up in trust by her very sensible husband and in-laws, and—as she was in the habit of telling Clarissa—her money was tied up *forever*, while Clarissa, no matter what happened, could have her money when she reached twenty-five. As it was, her allowance was shockingly niggardly and her expenses considerable. With this as an excuse, Aunt Cat stood firm against supplementing Clarissa's reduced allowance.

"But Clarissa," Nettie said, "they can't *make* you marry him. All they can do is parcel out your own money in dribs and drabs."

"*All?* Really, Nettie, you just don't know what it's like in London, stuck out here in the country like you've been! I have to have money for clothes . . ."

"Clarissa Knight! I declare! How can you need clothes? You *have* clothes, lots and lots of clothes."

"Well, you will soon understand, now that my uncle has finally given you permission to come to us this winter and to be presented during the season."

The delights of London distracted them for a short time, but Clarissa soon found the subject leading back to money.

"So you see, one must have clothes—and the worst thing is that I'm nineteen."

"Well, so am I, almost. What's so awful about that?"

"You *are* an innocent looby! I've already had one

115

season, then I missed last season, and I'm still not married . . ."

"Who's a looby?" Nettie and Clarissa had known each other a long time. "*You're* the looby. If you want to be married so badly, you can just marry the earl, or the duke, or whatever he is. Really, Clarissa, I think you are lacking in brains."

Clarissa's jaw set in stubborn distaste. "I *won't* marry a man who's forty years old and has false teeth, no matter what his title is. And anyway, he's not a duke or an earl—just a baron, which isn't much. There are bushels of barons. If he *was* a duke I might accept him . . . but even then . . ." Clarissa looked thoughtful. "But I just know if I have the right clothes, and can go to Almack's and to balls and suppers and drive in the park . . . I just *know* I can meet someone young and handsome and rich. And maybe with a title too. I was too green my first season. But I have address and consequence now, if I do say so, that I couldn't have at seventeen. But if Aunt and my odious trustees won't even allow me enough to buy one or two ball dresses, I won't be able to go anywhere, and if I'm not seen, I won't meet the right men."

"Oh, Clarissa, you are so funny. You mean if you are not seen you will meet the *wrong* men?"

Clarissa was not unable to laugh at herself, and with her good humor restored, she replied, "Just let me say this, Nettie, that you've not yet realized how important these years are. The happiness of the greater portion of our lives depends on the men we marry. What happens to us now determines the whole course of our future. I, at least, intend to secure my future well. Just listen to what Lord Byron says. His *Don Juan* may be scandalous

116

and not fit for our eyes, Nettie, but he understands what I've just said." She picked up Byron's latest book of verse. "Aunt Cat doesn't know I have this, and don't you tell. Do you think Polly will tattle?"

"Of course not."

Clarissa thumbed through the pages, "Here it is. He says women revenge themselves on men, and then in this verse he goes on:

"They are right; for man, to man so oft unjust
    Is always so to women; one sole bond
Awaits them, treachery is all their trust;
    Taught to conceal, their bursting hearts despond
Over their idol, till some wealthier lust
    Buys them in marriage—and what rests beyond?
A thankless husband, next a faithless lover,
    Then dressing, nursing, praying, and all's over."

Clarissa looked up at Nettie. "In the next verse he says that some wives run away, others take to drink, or pray . . . oh, all kinds of things—even write novels, whatever that means."

Nettie looked thoughtful. "What would you do, Clarissa?"

"Well, I certainly wouldn't drink. I abhor the stuff. I should take a lover."

"But lovers are faithless too, he says."

"Then I should take another. But enough of that. I want to read you the rest of *Endymion*. Keats is not well thought of, but I just adore him." As Clarissa searched through the volume to find the page, she added one last observation. "Another thing that makes my life a pur-

117

gatory is that Aunt Cat fusses all the time. You know how she went on at me the other night, until my Uncle Rice made her stop."

"Yes, you poor love, I know. But remember, they can't make you marry him, and I'll bet Aunt Cat wouldn't hold out long if she saw that any shortage of funds meant you couldn't go to balls, because then she would have less excuse to go.

"There are still the trustees. What will influence them — and Aunt Cat — is that I attract another man of at least respectable fortune and consequence . . . or I could elope with a rich man — then control of my fortune wouldn't matter. . . . Ah, here's the page. Just listen to *this*, Nettie."

On the drive back to Moregreen, Frederick was also pondering love and marriage. His London visit had been neither soothing to his spirit nor calming to his unease. He had spent half his time wishing he was back in the country, even as he pursued his business with all outward signs of attention, and his pleasure with all outward signs of enjoyment. In fact, the business matters were twice as irksome as he had expected — possibly because they were mostly invented — and the pleasures were dull. At Mrs. Crawford's superior establishment he suffered one of those embarrassing male failures, and although he blamed an excess of port and the inferior quality of his prophylactic, and although he subsequently redeemed himself satisfactorily, he could not quite accept his own excuses. Either he was too old for such ventures, or his engagement had somehow shackled that element of his psyche which an Austrian physi-

118

cian would later in the century label *libido*. He was aware that he missed Polly, which suggested he had made the right decision, and that he would (and could) be a model husband. He had needed this London interlude to prove it to himself.

Consequently, on his first morning back in the country, he dutifully set out to call on his betrothed, only to find her not at home. Then, after following her to the village, his first sight of her was the radiant vision in front of Mrs. Wagner's notions shop, smiling at the careless golden curls of a damnably good-looking fellow, who was kissing her hands with unwonted fervor. Frederick hadn't liked it at all. But since he himself had suggested that the two of them were too old for romantic foolishness, he could not (*would* not) be jealous, nor question Polly about friends from her past. Nonetheless, on the drive to Moregreen, and off and on for the remainder of the day, the memory of Polly and that Yankee Doodle disturbed his recently acquired complancency.

Chapter Seven

Alex and Lord Bolling called at Tanwell the following morning, greeted at the gates by a very dirty pair of boys who had been making use of their summer freedom from books and lessons to put as much distance between themselves and the house and propriety as their mother would tolerate. The summer world of young Jonathan and William Rice was in the stables, the barns, and the outlying acres, which latter provided opportunity for illicit swims, interesting explorations, and feathered targets for slingshots.

Yes, they told the visitors, this was Tanwell, and yes, their parents and sisters were at home — at least they guessed so, but they hadn't been in the house since shortly after sunrise. Jonathan and William having diverted discussion to their own affairs, seemed about to launch into a detailed description of their activities since the sun rose, so Alex called a hasty thank-you and, with a flick of the reins, proceeded up the drive.

After waiting on Mr. Rice, a ceremony as short as he and they could contrive to make it, they found the ladies in the morning room. It was a daunting experience for Lord Bolling, who was rendered incapacitated by so much assembled femininity and, after stammered responses to introductions, lapsed into silence. Alex, to whom feminine company was more stimulating than otherwise, was left to remark on the pleasant prospect of the north terrace and lawn, and to comment on Aunt Cat's canaries and, in short, to make himself and his companion known to Mrs. Rice and Aunt Cat as respectable and proper company for the younger ladies. Having satisfied all the requirements of polite intercourse, Alex rose, imitated by Lord Bolling, with promises to call again the following day.

Intimacy between Tanwell and Crossfield cottage went forward so rapidly thereafter that within a week the visits had become nearly daily affairs. Frederick found himself soon drawn into the intimacy. Both Alex and Lord Bolling were enthusiastic fishermen, and when Frederick joined them in this pursuit, he found Alex to be as easy with men as with women. Even Bolling showed some spirit and intelligence when free of club and drawing room, of women, and of the suspicion that every raised and unfurled fan hid whisperings of his cuckoldry. Alex showed a flattering interest in Frederick's proposals for upgrading his dairy herd by selective breeding; he was an enthusiastic pupil of English politics, and equally enthusiastic about the gentle beauty of rural England (as orderly as a formal garden, he said). Indeed, thought Frederick, there was no end to his enthusiasms.

Frederick soon heard that the young men were making inquiries after mounts in the village, and immediately offered the pick of the Moregreen stable for their

122

use during the remainder of their stay.

"Too generous. G-g-grateful, I'm sure, b-b-b- . . ."

"What Clancy wants to say," intervened Alex, "is that he has decided to send for some hacks from his own stable. We decided to come into the country on the spur of the moment. Took the first reasonable rental that offered. We thought we might drive on to the lakes and do some walking tours. You should see the guidebooks we carried!"

"Still m-may," Clancy added.

"Hugger-mugger, old fellow. Once get you settled someplace and you're the devil to move."

"All the more reason you should accept the loan of two horses from the Moregreen stable. I can, incidentally, also recommend a groom to you. The younger brother of our own head groom is currently looking for a situation. His employer in London sold his stable. He would be grateful, I think, to have temporary employment in the neighborhood. Once he demonstrates his worth to you, you may be able, Bolling, to recommend him to an acquaintance. He's certainly deserving. I'd like to take him on myself, but we have no positions open at Moregreen."

Put in such light, Frederick's generous offer seemed almost like charity to the unemployed. They walked to the stable for an inspection of horseflesh, and immediately approved Frederick's suggested choices. As they acquainted themselves with their new mounts, Frederick spoke to the head groom, who confirmed that his brother was available, and could find quarters for the animals in the village. The three men then strolled along to the exercise yard.

"What a fine horse!" exclaimed Alex, as he caught

sight of a tall gray stallion. "Do you race him?"

"I'm thinking about it. Although we've never aspired to a racing stable at Moregreen, we do race our best horses from time to time."

"Win now and again, too, if I recall," said Bolling. "Wasn't that chest-chest-n-nut gelding in the Newmarket in '16 an entry of yours? What was his name? Top Gallant . . . something like that, wasn't it?"

"My Gallant. Named after an old admirer of my mother's, who my father always referred to as a gelding." Suddenly bethinking himself, and that Bolling might be sensitive on the subject of virility, Frederick hurried on. "A fine horse — had we known he would develop into such a fine animal, we'd never have had him gelded. Unfortunately, it's not always clear what a horse will become in maturity. We lost an excellent stud."

Lord Bolling seemed unaware that he might be thought sensitive about references to diminished masculinity. "Hear that racing's quite a p-passion in America. Ain't that so, Alex?"

"That's right — the October races in Washington bring out everybody right up to the President. Heavy betting, too. It's the only sport I'd be willing to lay a bet on. I'm afraid I'm just not a gambling man."

"Nor I," said Frederick.

"Well, in m'younger days," said Bolling with a reminiscent smile, "I liked to lay a spot or two on the mills. The fights, y'know," he explained to Alex, in case the American did not understand the argot. "And admit, dropped quite a lot in g-gaming. Lost a pretty little p-property down in Kent, but it brought me to my senses. Haven't gambled since. Still regret losing that

124

p-property."

So it was that Alex and Lord Bolling were introduced into the Moresby household, where they quickly found favor with Lady Moresby for their good manners, and in the case of Alex, for his ready conversation. Even Sir Harry found something to admire in the visitors, for Alex showed a good deal of interest in the latest theories of scientific agriculture, in which England was a leader, and Lord Bolling had recently taken the notion that attention to his agricultural properties might provide him an escape from the London gossips.

The intimacy between Tanwell and Crossfield Cottage soon led to frequent invitations to family dinners. It was not long before Mrs. Rice dispensed with formal service, and the young men, including Frederick, were soon serving themselves from the dumb waiter, a many-tiered stand on which the various dishes were placed, and that occupied one corner of Tanwell's Elizabethan dining room.

The dining room, with its quantities of rich Elizabethan moldings, was the only visible remaining evidence in the Tanwell interiors of its sixteenth century core. Generations of children had climbed on chairs and stools to exclaim over the carved boars, dolphins, and grotesque faces that decorated the wood-paneled walls of this room. A particular favorite was a horrifying serpent tempting an interestingly unclad Eve; and an equally interestingly unclad Adam gazing up into an apple tree — unaware of the conspiracy that, to his future detriment, was going on in the panel behind him. The following panel, showing the bare backsides of Adam and Eve departing the Garden of Eden, was somewhat less interesting, and their subsequent fully

125

clothed biography of little interest at all.

Alex took delight in the generously overblown decor, so evocative of England's long history, and especially its contrast with the Sheraton sideboard, boasting the latest in efficient gimcrackery, and with the streamlined efficiency of the wheeled serving carts that eased the labors of maids and footman. He accused Mrs. Rice of being an American at heart—intrigued by labor-saving equipment, and given to an almost American informality, as witness the self-service comings and goings to the dumb waiter. Mrs. Rice, whom no one but Mr. Rice had ever teased, only smiled and murmured, "Perhaps so."

Across the park at Moregreen a more formal spirit presided. Lady Moresby, as intimacy increased between Moregreen and the Cottage, determined on a neighborhood dinner party. After consulting her husband and son and studying the calendar, a date was set.

"I don't see how I can accomplish it any sooner than two weeks," she told Sir Harry. "You must be in London for two days next week, but can't tell me yet on what days; Amelia and I must attend a meeting of the garden committee in town on Thursday. Then on Monday of the following week you and Frederick are expected to attend the county Agricultural Society meeting. Does two weeks from today seem acceptable to you? Let's see, that would be the thirtieth. I was thinking it might be an informal engagement party, just among our neighbors, and the thirtieth would coincide nicely with the announcement in the papers."

Sir Harry, who would have agreed to any available date, gave his assent and returned to his paper. Shortly, however, his wife was making small exasperated sounds

126

that he knew were intended to elicit a sympathetic query from her mate. On making the required query, he learned that she was having no little trouble composing a guest list. Of those in the county among whom they visited, many were at the seashore or enjoying travels on the continent. And there was the problem of Alex.

"Alex Chapham is delightful," Lady Moresby observed to her husband, "a diplomatist through and through, but so soon after another war with America it is just a little difficult socially. I can't ask the Paunceforts—you recall that Mrs. Pauncefort's family were colonials; but they opposed the rebellion and lost everything when they fled the colonies. Even though she was only a child at the time she's kept her resentment at high boil . . . one does tire of hearing about it whenever America is mentioned. Just imagine how she would take on when she discovered Mr. Chapham's origins! And the Darrows—it was only a few years ago—was it five? Six? Anyway, only a short time ago that old Admiral Darrow was shipped home from America in that rum barrel."

"It was 1814, the year we took their capital. And he was sent home preserved in good Jamaica rum, not in a rum barrel."

"I fail to see the distinction. Were he and the rum not both in the barrel?"

"You make it sound like a barrel of sea biscuit."

"Well, the barrel is the important thing to them. They keep it in their small gallery below his portrait. Did you know that?"

"No, I can't say I did."

"Mrs. Darrow goes on all the time about what good

127

friends he was with Admiral Hornblower, and their connection with the Wellesleys through him, although I'm quite certain that all intercourse between the Admiral and . . . what is Admiral Hornblower's wife's name? A Wellesley, of course, but what was her Christian name? Oh, well, I'm certain that between the two families intercourse was limited even in old Darrow's time, and is nonexistent now."

"Barbara, isn't it?" Sir Harry suggested.

Lady Moresby looked at him blankly. "What?"

"Barbara—Lady Barbara Wellesley—Hornblower's wife."

"I believe you're right. Well"—Lady Moresby turned to the next name on her list—"I have a dinner party to arrange and shouldn't be gossiping."

A short silence followed.

"The trouble with the Herberts is that they have only girls left unmarried."

"And what makes that so terrible?"

"Well, one does like to balance the sexes, and we are long on females already. I need men."

Sir Harry tapped the tobacco from his pipe. He stood up, stretched, and then lay his hand affectionately on his wife's shoulder. He bent to kiss her. "Well, my dear, I will leave you to your chore. I'm sure you will manage."

"Reverend Littleton and his aunt and Squire Ruggles and his family seem the only possibilities," Lady Moresby said. "Perhaps it's best after all. That makes eighteen, with just enough people for two whist tables—Catherine seldom plays whist; she simply hasn't the necessary concentration. She does play the pianoforte beautifully, though. It's one extra girl for

128

dancing, that is, if Francie is permitted, but that can't be helped, and it's not so many dancing that we will need to clear the dining room and hall. That can wait for the ball that Frederick says he has promised Polly's sisters. I wonder why your ancestor neglected to include a ballroom in this otherwise fine house? Although where Frederick thinks he will find enough people for a ball, even if I invite families from five counties . . ."

Sir Harry retreated.

Mrs. Rice looked into the library, where she at last discovered Polly. "Am I interrupting, dear?"

"Yes, ma'am, you are—but very fortunately. I promised myself an hour of leisurely reading, and it is now three hours, I'm afraid."

"What are you reading, love?"

"*Emma,* by Miss Austen," Polly said as she looked around for something to use as a bookmarker.

"Oh, yes. Your father read it to us when it came out two or three years ago. I was diverted, but Nettie and Francie didn't like it. I believe neither the heroine, the hero, nor the story was romantic enough for them."

Polly tore a corner from a newspaper she found lying on a chair and, after placing it between the pages, closed the book. "I'm diverted also. Emma isn't a very nice heroine—although she certainly is patient with her fussy father—but she pleases me. Although I suspect she will learn the error of her ways in the end and be happily wed, she is nonetheless a relief from the virtuous heroines usually encountered in novels. I can sympathize with her, for I often feel less than unselfish and not very good or charitable."

Mrs. Rice demurred at Polly's self-criticism. "None of us is perfect, of course, but then, I've always thought it sensible that our maker—be it God or nature—allowed us a few faults."

"Why, ma'am, you are a philosopher."

Mrs. Rice sniffed. "Never."

Polly laughed and gave her mother a hug. "Well, that's all neither here nor there. Did you want me for something?"

"Yes, I did. I wonder if you could accompany me to visit Martha Riggs? The baby has a fever, Mary tells me." Mary Riggs was the eldest of a family of numerous children. Mrs. Rice employed the eleven-year-old girl as a scullery maid, more as an act of charity than for her own needs. That did not mean, of course, that Mary was not expected to work diligently for her pay. "I'm going to take Martha an infusion for the child. I wouldn't bother you, but Nettie has gone on an errand with Francie, Clarissa is resting, and the maids and the footman are busy—summer is always such a busy season—and there is no one to accompany me."

"I'll just run up and change my shoes and get my parasol."

"A hat would be better. We have several things to carry. Come to the kitchen when you are ready. We'll take the path across the fields."

Polly found her mother in the kitchen just finishing the packing of a basket. "That looks like more than an herbal infusion, ma'am. I see cakes, and a jar of broth, and eggs, and a cheese . . ."

"Yes, the poor children need strengthening food."

Mrs. Rice tucked a clean white cloth over the top of the basket, and Polly picked it up. "I'll carry it, Mama."

130

They passed through the kitchen garden, where the gardener was picking beetles from the potato vines and dropping them in a can. "I'll just stop by the garden house for a moment. I have a geranium for Martha, and a potted mint."

The garden house was a jumble of discarded flats, stacked cold frames, neatly arranged tools and implements, and in an extension under a slanting glass roof, plants in pots in various stages of growth. Mrs. Rice selected a vigorously flowering plant. The bright red blossoms glowed among the green leaves.

"Here." Polly held the basket out to her mother. "You take the basket and let me carry the geranium. The basket is less awkward. How gorgeous it is," she exclaimed as they made the exchange.

"Yes," said Mrs. Rice, as she tucked the mint in the basket. "I always try to include a pansy set, or a potted plant when I take a basket to one of the poor. They need beauty more than the rich or well-to-do."

"What a lovely thought."

Mrs. Rice sniffed deprecatingly in reply.

They let themselves out of the gate and took the path that skirted a turnip field. "I try to encourage gardening—potatoes and vegetables—such truck, and a few herbs like mint and chamomile, but I also try to encourage a few flowers. A bit of beauty in the dooryard might soften some of the hard heads that too often afflict the poor."

"Hard heads?"

"Too many of these people are unwilling to make the changes that would render their lives a little less drab. Mary's mother—Martha Riggs—tries, poor soul, but with so many babies, and taking in washing, she's too worn out to do much more. The geranium will be easy to care for. It needs only watering and dry leaves picked off. Furthermore," continued Mrs. Rice after a short pause, "Martha has a less than worthless husband. I suspect that he is lacking intelligence as well as diligence and most of the other virtues. Each time Martha confesses to another future arrival—that 'it's happened again,' as she says—he beats her. She was only recently brought to bed for the seventh time."

Further discussion was prevented by their close approach to the Riggs's cottage. The family lived in a little hamlet of four shabby cottages. The inhabitants cultivated small patches of ground that their ancestors had salvaged from one of the early enclosures of common land, supplementing this meager subsistence by taking in washing, odd jobs of all sorts, and day labor on the surrounding farms and estates. Success in placing a child in service somewhere was regarded as the greatest good fortune that could fall to a family.

The Riggs cottage was as shabby as the others, but the interior was neat and clean. A little girl whom Polly thought to be no more than six or seven years old was scrubbing the stone floor, and a boy equally young or younger sat in a corner shelling peas. A toddler, and another child a little more than a year old, sat wide-eyed in a corner. The latter, only recently weaned in favor of the new baby, sucked a sweetened rag, commonly referred to as a sugar tit.

Mrs. Riggs knelt by the hearth holding the whimpering baby in one arm, while stirring a pot with her free hand. One enormous drooping breast was exposed, the aureole around the protruding nipple dark brown against the white skin. As she rose to greet Mrs. Rice

132

and Polly, she absentmindedly stuffed the nipple into the whimpering mouth. The baby sucked for a few seconds, then released the nipple and resumed its frail keening. As Mrs. Riggs gestured, or as she moved about the room, her breast jiggled against the baby's mouth and cheek, which set it to rooting over the great expanse, at which Mrs. Riggs absently stuffed the nipple into its mouth, and the entire drama began again.

Mrs. Rice, after interrupting the mother and infant long enough to lay a hand on the baby's forehead, unpacked the basket, telling the little boy to put the cheese away in the makeshift cupboard. She set the geranium and the broth on the table, issued instructions on the care of the flower and the administration of the broth. She then sent the little girl, who had finished her scrubbing, for water and, when she returned, put it to boil.

"You know how to make a tea from mint, Mrs. Riggs, so I will leave that task to you. I've brought you several stalks and one plant, which you should set out soon. It should do well anywhere in your garden. Give the baby my infusion with a little mint tea."

She then surveyed the room and asked where the peas came from.

"The squire's wife sent a whole sack over. They'll be a godsend this winter." Mrs. Riggs's face suddenly crumpled. She used her free hand to wipe her eyes and nose, setting the breast to jiggling and the baby to rooting again. "I don't know what I'd do without you and Miz Ruggles, ma'am. I try, but I just can't get anywhere." She gestured around the room. "There's always another one, and Mr. Riggs . . ."

"There, there," Mrs. Rice intervened, patting her on

the shoulder. "You do the best you can, and better than could be expected."

The baby had released the breast again, and the irritable keening increased in volume. Mrs. Riggs with a gesture of impatience thrust the nipple at the baby's mouth, only to have it loose its hold once again. She was now crying in earnest. "Oh, ma'am. I'm afraid I just don't have any milk this time. You know, ma'am, I always had plenty afore. Why, just let a little one cry and the milk would run out. Wet my dress, it would. But I'm too worn out this time, ma'am."

Mrs. Rice took a handkerchief from her pocket and gave it to Mrs. Riggs. "Dry your eyes and blow your nose. Take it," she urged as Mrs. Riggs hesitated to use a lady's handkerchief. "Send it back with Mary when you've had time to wash it."

"Oh, ma'am," Mrs. Riggs began again.

"No more, now. Your Mary's a good girl, and so are these little ones, and I hear your Robbie has found a place in town with the surgeon."

"Yes," Mrs. Riggs said, wiping her eyes. "I've been blessed with good children. That's why I feel so bad when I think I just can't bear another . . ."

Mrs. Rice was rapidly approaching exasperation, a state she tried to avoid when calling on the poor. "You're tired now, with care of the baby. I'll tell Mary to stay home tomorrow to help you out." Then, as she caught the fear in Mrs. Riggs's eyes, she added, "Don't worry about her wages. Mary can make it up sometime when I need extra help. And I'll send some good boiled milk tomorrow when you've got the baby's fever down." Mrs. Rice turned to her daughter. "Come Polly, we must be getting back. Good day, Martha."

Polly, who had spoken no word other than a greeting to Mrs. Riggs, gently set the toddler on its unsteady feet. The little mite had laid hands on her skirt and pulled her toward a stool and, as soon as she sat down on it, had crept into her lap. The child had hardly moved, except to press itself against her, and she found herself cuddling it, her heart filled with pity as she realized that the little thing was starved for such cuddling. The one-year-old, deserted by its older sibling, had simply curled up and gone to sleep, still sucking the rag.

As they left the house, a scowling man stopped them. He was neatly and cleanly dressed. His worn flannel shirt had been darned in several places and his pantaloons were neatly patched, all of which was testimony to his wife's fastidious care rather than to his own personal inclination. He touched his hand to the brim of his hat, but continued to scowl. "Good morning, ma'am. Good morning, Miss Rice."

"Good morning, Mr. Riggs."

"I hopes ye're well, ma'am." The polite greeting did not erase the scowl.

What an ill-natured man! Polly thought. He looks as though he'd like to do violence. Of course, a man who beat his wife for getting in the family way, when it was he who got her that way, must have some propensity for violence.

Mrs. Rice, her voice markedly severe in tone, replied to the man's greeting. "I'm very well, thank you. Your wife, however, needs a rest. I'm sure you understand me."

"I understand ye vury well, ma'am, and with all respect I'm tellin' ye to mind y'r own business. You got

135

no right to meddle or to preach sinful ways to my woman."

Polly looked at the man in astonishment. That one of his class should speak to her mother in this way was shocking. She had become reaccustomed in Brazil to servility among the lower orders, so strikingly absent in the United States, but here in her old home her mother was respected not just for her superior birth, but for her good sense and good deeds. And that anyone should suggest that her mother preached sinful ways was astonishing; Mrs. Rice was a model of matronly propriety.

"She is not your woman, Mr. Riggs. She is your wife. And I am not preaching sinful ways. I am giving sound medical advice."

"I'm warnin' ye, ma'am. There's others that thinks like me. I wouldn't want ye to come to any harm, ma'am."

"And I'm warning *you,* Mr. Riggs. Another child and you may lose Mrs. Riggs. Your wife is too worn out to sustain another lying-in. Especially when she receives a beating for it."

"Watch your tongue, ma'am. You got no right to speak to me such like."

"And you have no right to treat your wife like an animal, Mr. Riggs—in fact, I wager you treat your hound better."

At this point Polly felt that intercession was essential. "Come, Mama. We must be getting back. Papa will be wondering where we are. Good day, Mr. Riggs."

As they walked away, Polly held her tongue. Surprisingly, so did her mother. However, when they were out of sight of the man, and after several furtive glances behind to make certain that he was not following them, Polly asked curiously, "What on earth was that about? That man threatened you."

"Yes." Mrs. Rice sighed. "I have been telling Mrs. Riggs about birth limitation."

"Birth limitation?" Polly could not have been more unbelieving if her mother had been telling Mrs. Riggs she should fly to the moon.

"A brute of a man," Mrs. Rice said. "He refuses to acknowledge that he has any responsibility in the matter."

Polly preferred to pursue the more interesting subject of her mother's radical actions than Mr. Riggs's bad temper. "It's unfortunate that there is not available to the poor some means other than Mr. Malthus's recommendation of 'moral restraint.' It's difficult to imagine Riggs in possession of any moral feeling, let alone moral restraint."

Mrs. Rice chose to ignore the reference to Malthus, a gentleman of whom her husband often spoke when discussing economics. "The sad thing is, it is unnecessary." She gestured toward a boulder by the side of the path that had been placed to mark a property line. "Let's sit here for a moment in the shade."

Mrs. Rice removed her hat and fanned herself. "I have spoken to Mrs. Riggs twice about her excessive fertility and meager resources, and explained to her that she need not be constantly increasing." She fell silent, organizing in her mind exactly how to continue with this delicate subject, which had been forced upon her by Riggs.

Polly, who recognized her mother's embarrassment, said, "If you are referring to . . . mmm . . . 'cundums,'

137

I believe they're called. I know in French it's *la capote anglais*. Aren't they too expensive for the poor to afford?

Mrs. Rice smiled sardonically. "I believe we refer to them as French letters."

"Oh, really, Mama? How interesting." She did not mention that in the naughty little books of her youth they had been called "scabbards," "instruments of safety," "machines," and innumerable other circumlocutions.

"Yes, very. But I refer not to the French letter, but to a simple device that any woman can make, and which happens to be recommended by an economist quite as well known as Mr. Malthus."

Polly looked at her mother in surprise. "I didn't know you read the economists, ma'am."

"Well, I don't. But then, one can't live with your father without beginning to think that one has. In any event, I refer to Mr. Bentham, and a method he recommended for reducing the poor rates—the use of a small round piece of sponge, with a thread or penny ribbon attached, that a woman can use to protect herself. Naturally the man had no concern for the health or welfare of women—just reducing taxes—but that's an economist for you."

"I see." Polly thought a moment. "You mean that she inserts the sponge in, uh . . ."

"Yes." Mrs. Rice had no doubt they both knew where, without further discussion, and if Polly didn't know now, she soon would. "The sponge provides a barrier against the man's seed. It is not certain, of course, but it is nonetheless surprisingly effective."

"But doesn't it impede the, uh, intimate relation?"

138

This isn't the easiest subject to discuss with Mama, Polly thought, keeping her eyes carefully fixed on the landscape.

Mrs. Rice, however, was finding it easier to speak to her daughter than she had expected—almost as easy as when she lectured poor drudges like Mrs. Riggs.

"No, not if properly prepared and placed. I myself used it after the birth of William, until I was certain I had passed the change of life. It was recommended to me by a London accoucheur, a man of the highest eminence. Otherwise"—again the fleeting sardonic smile—"I suppose you would have two or three more little brothers or sisters."

Polly was trying to absorb this stunning glimpse of her parents' private life and the possibility that passion might survive the years.

"I will show you how to make and use one of the devices at the first opportunity," Mrs. Rice said as she rose. "Some recommend that it be removed immediately after," she continued, as they set forth once more, "but I believe it more effective if left in place for several hours. One must, of course, wash it very thoroughly after each use . . ." She chatted on, describing the method, the women to whom she had recommended it, the inability of some to use it, the objection of husbands who believed any attempt to prevent babies to be a sign of loose morals. "But in my opinion," concluded Mrs. Rice, "that usually means that they refuse to wait a few minutes, or that they believe that without the fear of a baby their wives will sneak out with some other man. Or both."

Really, Mrs. Rice thought when they parted—she to attend a household chore and Polly to return to her book, having lost so much of the afternoon anyway—it was quite easy to discuss these matters with her daughter. She should have taken the plunge long ago when Gussie was married. Well, she hadn't, and Gussie was only in her second pregnancy. Nonetheless, she must make the effort when next Gussie visited. Or better, Polly could do it. At which it occurred to her to wonder how Polly knew about cundums, and to reflect that it was just as well that she would soon be marrying. The human body, as Mrs. Rice knew, imposed its demands.

As Polly and Mrs. Rice were walking across the fields to visit Martha Riggs, Frederick was riding home from the village. On an impulse, he turned up the drive at Tanwell. Since he had just left Alex and Bolling, this would be an opportunity to see Polly alone. Perhaps she would like to take a late afternoon ride with him.

He was shown by the footman into the drawing room. "I will inform Miss Rice of your presence immediately, sir," said Robert, with what he thought was proper pomposity. Robert was having a difficult time keeping fixed the rigid expression that was supposed to mark the superior footman who hoped to become a butler. Mr. Moresby had known him ever since he was born, and he found it hard to change their relationship. He made therefore a too hasty exit, while Frederick, amused, sat down to wait for Polly and to contemplate Elizabethan candlestands on spiral twist-turned posts, side by side with modern four-candle torcheres and mirror-backed wall sconces to concentrate the light. A strange and somewhat dangerous-appearing contraption stood on an oak table, though it proved, after a

140

somewhat furtive examination, to be a lamp. Mrs. Rice, as she had recently remarked to Frederick, believed good light saved eyesight and prevented excessive weariness, thus improving the efficiency with which tasks requiring the eyes were performed.

When the door opened, he turned expectantly to greet Polly, and then hid his disappointment when Clarissa came into the room.

"Good afternoon, Mr. Moreseby," she said, holding out her hand. "I have come to tell you that Polly has gone out — an errand in that little hamlet across the fields, the housekeeper says."

"I'm sorry I've missed her. Will you tell her for me?"

"Of course," Clarissa said as she seated herself. "I was just about to take tea. Will you join me?"

"Thank you, Miss Knight. It's kind of you, but I must be getting home."

Clarissa pouted prettily. "Then I shall have to take my tea all alone."

There was something in her voice that invited — almost demanded — a response, and Frederick, with a sigh, made the effort. "In all this vast household, surely there is someone at home to keep you company."

"I am afraid not. Polly and Aunt Rice have gone on their errand of mercy — a sick infant, I believe. Nettie has driven Francie to the village for her music lesson. Aunt Cat is not feeling well and absolutely refuses to take tea with me. No one ever takes tea with Jonathan and William, and Uncle Rice always takes his alone. I just would never dare to ask him to join me." Clarissa lowered her eyes with a pretty flutter. "I wonder at myself that I dared ask you." She clasped her hands gracefully together in her lap and, looking up at him

141

shyly, said, "Even in a big household it can be lonesome for a visitor, however fond she may be of the members of that household."

Frederick's sympathy was aroused, despite his anxiety to be gone. Instinct was warning him that tea alone with Clarissa was not the safest undertaking. This gentle flower was not the young woman he had met in the summer house or become acquainted with in subsequent visits to Tanwell and in excursions about the countryside. On the other hand, there was nothing unusual in a young woman becoming homesick. Nonetheless, instinct still told him to escape, so he took the opportunity of her earlier, unfinished remark to at least make the attempt.

"I apologize for my dress. I have been to town on estate business, and on impulse thought Polly might like to take a late afternoon ride with me."

"Oh, what a delightful idea! The cool of the late afternoon, and to revel in the breeze on Crown Hill! She will be so disappointed! But then, of course, you are disappointed too. Do take tea. Perhaps Polly will return before we finish and in time for the outing."

Clarissa had hit exactly the right argument. Frederick capitulated. Tea was rung for, and somehow Frederick found himself settled by the long windows with Clarissa, discussing plays they had both seen performed. *Romeo and Juliet* provided Clarissa the opening for a discussion of romance and inevitably led to a discussion of the interference of elders in the lives of the young—most particularly in whom they should marry.

"I believe we owe something to our parents' generation and to our forebears," Frederick said. "And most particularly when their lives have been upright, and when our present leisure is the result of their prudence and good management. Of course, in the case of depraved parents, or ancestors who have squandered wealth and substance, the matter is different."

"It is also different, is it not, in the choice of a life's companion? Surely the young should have the right to choose the person they will go through life with." Clarissa looked away, toward the lawn beyond. "What could be more unendurable than to share the years, to live in intimacy, with someone one dislikes?" She lowered her eyes, and then quickly looked up again. He saw two large brown eyes, heavily lashed, swimming in tears. A tear fell, but nonetheless, Clarissa sat straight and proud, her chin up. She dashed away another tear with a gesture of defiance. As Frederick leaned forward, ready to speak a word of comfort, she said, "I am sorry. It is a subject I should not discuss, for it touches me too closely. I am to be wed to a man whom I hold in great dislike. But it is my problem, and I am sorry to have subjected you to this scene. I shall just dry my eyes, if you will excuse me, and then I shall offer you a second cup of tea. We will talk on happy subjects, Mr. Moresby, and I shall soon forget my distress, for I am determined to put it aside during this interlude among so many rural beauties."

Frederick felt some straightforward practical advice was called for, and said, "You cannot be made to marry, you know."

"Legally, perhaps not. But guardians and trustees have means to be persuasive, especially with one like myself who has been so long dependent on the kindness of others. I cannot discuss the subject further. It was wrong of me to tell you. Would you mind, Mr.

Moresby, if we did not take a second cup of tea? I believe I shall go out for a walk. Perhaps I can reach Crown Hill in time for the sunset. As music soothes the savage breast, beauty soothes the anguished heart."

There was nothing for Frederick to do but invite Clarissa to ride with him.

After parting with her mother, Polly returned to her book, but was unable to concentrate on the words. She could not get out of her mind the confrontation with Riggs. As she reviewed the conversation she was struck with special force by Riggs's statement that he was not the only man who disapproved of her mother's activities and who thought she "had no right." With an exclamation of annoyance she put down her book. She must speak immediately to her father, difficult as it would be to broach such subjects.

"Come in," Mr. Rice called as she knocked on the door of his sanctuary. "Polly. To what do I owe this pleasure, child?" He arose and placed a chair for her. "Sit down, my dear."

Polly seated herself but discovered that she was at a loss how to begin, how to proceed, and how to phrase her statements with the necessary delicacy. "If you will give me a moment, Papa, to collect myself."

"Of course." A small tremor of foreboding passed through Mr. Rice's mind as he once again took up his pen and pretended to return to his work. When Polly stirred, he looked up. "Are you now prepared?" he asked, with a kind and encouraging smile.

"I'd like to speak to you, sir, about something that happened this afternoon, but I must first ask you if you are aware that my mother, when visiting the poor, also gives advice on the use of a device that helps the women to guard against more babies."

"Yes, I am aware of it."

Relieved, Polly then recounted the scene with Riggs. "I am convinced, sir, that he was threatening my mother."

"I fear you are right. I've known for some time that there are mutterings. Her farmer came to me with some very unpalatable gossip. I've forbidden her to go out alone—even to ride around the farm. But she's a strong-minded woman, and unless it affects her children, she will continue."

"It would certainly affect us if she were harmed."

"Your mother, however, is thinking of some social consequence; that you should be cut by neighbors, or by friends."

"I hardly feel that is sufficient reason for her to give it up. It's good work, sir. It must not be good for a woman's health to bear one child after another. And with fewer mouths to feed, a small income can be made to provide better for each one of the children."

"There is some argument that it would mean fewer workers and therefore higher wages. Good or bad, depending on whether one is an employer or one who is employed."

"I don't think Mama would find that the best argument, sir."

He smiled. "No, she wouldn't." Sobering, he said, "You suggest, then, that she continue?"

"Yes, if her safety is not endangered. I'm relieved to learn that you have suggested some caution to her. I'm not concerned for any consequences other than her safety. Our social standing in the community is of little consequence."

Mr. Rice gave her a long look. "Be careful what you are saying, Polly. Ostracism is a terrible punishment, as even the savages are aware."

Chastened, but unconvinced—how, after all, could a family such as hers suffer ostracism?—Polly returned to the library and to her book. She was interrupted first by the footman inquiring if she wanted tea, by which means he managed to inform her that Miss Clarissa had taken tea with Mr. Moresby and then gone riding (of which he strongly disapproved, as an admirer of Polly). Then she was interrupted by Francie and Nettie also inquiring if she had had tea, then by Jonathan and William, to inform her that one of the cats had chosen to have her kittens in the barn—eight of them, and would that excessive number require that some be knocked in the head?

They wanted her to come with them immediately to help decide which ones to save, and spoke loudly and with great relish of the possible killings, a relish that Polly detected to be no more than a brave front—little boys in a mistaken attempt at manliness, for they, like the whole family, had a weakness for cats. Mrs. Rice, of course, claimed that she kept cats to keep the mice down, a necessity in such an old house as Tanwell, but her family were no more taken in by that than Polly was taken in by the bloodthirsty remarks of her young brothers.

She promised to visit the kittens later, but then, aware of their disappointment, felt guiltily neglectful of

146

the duties of a big sister. She should have gone with them, for they quite obviously very much wanted to show her the kittens themselves. She went to the door and called to them that if they were in the barns at milking, she would come to see the kittens then.

As soon as they were gone, she slipped out of the house. She hoped that she would meet no other members of her family or the serving staff before she reached a bench in the far corner of the garden where she could not be seen from the house, so she could finish the story of Emma. She read until a passage in her book reminded her with a guilty start that she had promised to meet Jonathan and William in the barn.

She was just passing the stable when Frederick and Clarissa returned from their ride.

"Hello, Polly," Clarissa called gaily. "Mr. Moresby has been *so* kind. When he didn't find you at home, I offered myself as substitute."

Frederick dutifully helped Clarissa dismount, but could find nothing to say to Polly except to greet her, and to give her a one-adult-to-another smile. Rotten luck, he thought, but of course neither he nor Clarissa had had any intent of hiding the fact that they had ridden together.

The groom who had accompanied them led Clarissa's horse away, as Clarissa, smiling happily up into Frederick's face, said, "Now you *know* I did."

"Did what?" Frederick asked, wondering if he had spoken unaware and, if so, what he had said. "Pardon me, Miss Knight, I wasn't attending."

"Offered myself as substitute." She turned to Polly. "I was very naughty, Polly. I hinted so openly that I should like to ride, that Mr. Moresby simply couldn't

147

avoid inviting me."

Frederick found himself protesting that indeed, he had been delighted, and then wishing he'd not been so generous with his gentlemanly assurances. The chit had forced him to issue the invitation, and now she had forced him to deny he had been forced. Frederick was feeling manipulated and vaguely guilty, even though Polly seemed not at all concerned.

"I was just on my way to see the new kittens in the barn," Polly said. "I promised Jonathan and William, so I must hurry on. Will we be seeing you for dinner tomorrow, Frederick? My mother is expecting you."

"Yes, I shall be there. Tomorrow morning perhaps you and I can have our ride." Frederick emphasized, ever so lightly, the "you and I."

Polly understood, and smiled into his eyes. "That would be very nice. I don't suppose you have any interest in the new kittens?"

"Thank you, no. I must be getting home." He bade the woman and the girl goodnight, relieved that Polly showed no sign of annoyance.

Polly and Clarissa turned toward the barn. They had gone only a few steps when Polly suddenly remembered that she had made another promise for the morrow. "Do wait for me a moment, Clarissa. I must tell Frederick something."

She lifted her skirts to facilitate hasty progress, calling after him.

He reined in his horse and turned. "Is something wrong?" He was amused by her haste and admiring of her light-footed progress.

"No, it's only that I'd forgotten that I've arranged to go to the squire's tomorrow morning. Do you remember my promise to him to paint his ox?"

"Perhaps we can ride over together," Frederick suggested. "There's a horse he wants me to look at."

"I'd be grateful. You can keep the squire from standing over me."

Clarissa was waiting for Polly by the gate into the barnyards. "Goodness," she said. "Such amazing energy you have, Polly. I wish I had such energy, but since my illness, I find I tire too easily. Riding, however, strengthens me. Did you know, Polly, you have ripped your skirt? It was so nice of Mr. Moresby to ask me to ride with him. I have been feeling such a return of health this afternoon!" Clarissa chatted on about kind Mr. Moresby and what excellent and pleasant company he was, to which Polly readily agreed. She was perfectly aware, however, that Clarissa thought her a hoyden, and wondered if Frederick had thought so too. She resolved once again to cultivate greater sobriety of manner.

Clarissa, an expression of distaste on her face, was picking her way toward the barn, where Jonathan and William eagerly awaited them. "Really, I can't imagine what possessed me to come with you, except that little kitties are so adorable."

"I'm afraid these won't be so adorable, since they are newborn, and probably look more like mice than kittens. And I should warn you," Polly added on a mischievous impulse, "that Jonathan and William expect us to choose which ones to save from being knocked in the head."

"Oh, how *disgusting!* How can you be so cruel? But I suppose it's the way with country people."

Polly laughed. "Now Clarissa. You've been coming

149

to the country for long visits ever since you were eight years old, and are as familiar with barnyards and barns as I am, and no one, I should think, could be blind to the cruelties of London life. Hasn't your heart ever bled for an old, decrepit hack horse, which should long ago have been turned out to pasture?"

"I was only a child when I climbed around barns," Clarissa said defensively.

Polly was spared an answer by Jonathan and William, who led them up into the loft (Clarissa proceeding with as much agility as any of them, Polly noticed). The mother cat rolled away slightly to make proud display of her babies, with a low, sweet trill that they interpreted as "Aren't they all beautiful?"

"And they are too beautiful to knock in the head, don't you think so, Polly? Don't you, Clarissa?" William asked belligerently.

"Of course," they both agreed.

Chapter Eight

Alex and Lord Bolling arrived the next morning, only to be told that Miss Nettie and Miss Clarissa, with Miss Francie, were in the summer house, and that Miss Rice had just been observed going that way too. They found the three girls charmingly arrayed for an indolent summer morn, but Polly was afoot and dressed for riding.

After the general greetings, Polly said, "You all must excuse me. I've put off too long my promise to paint the squire's prize ox." Deepening her voice and shifting her stance, "Stands fourteen hands and weighs a hundred and sixty stone. Fine animal, missy."

"Oh Polly, are you *really* going to paint an ox?" Clarissa asked. "The squire never did have any sense of propriety."

"I don't think there was any lack of propriety in Squire Ruggles's desire to have a painting of a magnificent animal," Polly replied. "And I'm sorry if I seemed to be making fun of him. We've always enjoyed his bluff and hearty ways, and appreciated his good heart too.

151

I'm happy to paint his ox."

"Come, come, Poll, you're too harsh on the missy," Alex intervened with mock severity. "You must remember that those of us who are not country bred do not always appreciate such wonders as a prize ox. But I, for one, am willing to gaze with admiration on the beast. I will accompany you if I may."

Francie at that moment saw Frederick approaching the summer house. "Here comes Frederick," she announced, and as he entered, also dressed for riding, she said, "Oh, Frederick! Guess what? Polly is just going off to paint the squire's ox!"

"Is she now?" Frederick tweaked Francie's ear, and she in turn grinned up at him. She was going to enjoy having him for a brother.

Frederick greeted the others and then turned to Polly. "I'm sorry if I've made you wait."

"I am just ready now."

"I, too, have offered myself as escort, sir," said Alex. "Let's leave Clancy here with this bevy of beauties and be on our way."

"I see no need for both of us to go," Frederick replied, and immediately reproached himself for the stuffiness of his tone. "But if you would like to see the ox and something of the countryside, Polly and I will be happy to have you accompany us."

Well, thought Polly. Just who does he think he is? Surely it was my right to invite others to join us, not his.

But Alex was not to be dismayed. He preferred Polly's company and Frederick's to the young missies, and if he wasn't mistaken, Bolling was somewhat taken with Nettie. It would do the fellow good to be left alone with

152

the bevy for a time. "I appreciate your offer, sir," he said to Frederick.

"P-p-perhaps we all should go." Lord Bolling had at last found voice. The prospect of being left alone in the company of so many females was as always daunting.

"No, no, Clancy old fellow. You stay here with Nettie and Francie and Miss Knight. They will read you shocking poetry and feed you grapes and comfits, and take you strolling down garden paths. I've spent many hours sitting by Polly's side as she sketched, and I know from experience that she demands perfect quiet from her companions. Frederick and I can hold our tongues as we are required, but I fear should we take these lovely ladies along. No, Clancy. We leave you to entertain and to be entertained."

Frederick, ashamed of his previous pomposity, and aware that Polly had shot a resentful glance his way, was careful to include Alex in such conversation as the ride to the squire's permitted, and resolved to apologize to Polly at the first opportunity. But when that opportunity came, as Alex bantered with the squire, who had been awaiting them at his doorstep, she seemed to have forgotten her momentary irritation. Better, he thought, to let it pass.

"Got your note, missy," the squire told Polly, "And I've got Caesar penned up where you can get a good look at him. I'll leave one of the younguns with you, and meanwhile take these gentlemen around to have a look at the crops. And the missus is expecting you all for a dish of tea when you finish. How long do you reckon it'll take to paint old Caesar? Just so I can have these gentlemen back in time, you understand. And missy, Mrs. Ruggles says you're to come right up to the house when you finish, or if you need a rest or anything."

"I'll make several sketches of Caesar first, and from those I'll make a preliminary drawing for you. The sketches will take perhaps two hours. The drawing I'll do at home, and send back later for your approval before I start the actual painting. So we should tell Mrs. Ruggles two hours. I'll run in now to say hello, and tell her how many of us to expect."

When she returned, the squire said, "Now here's young Tom, ready to sit with you, and try to give you lots of advice, I don't doubt." He turned to the youngest of his several offspring, and admonished him, "Now you keep quiet while Miss Polly is working, you hear? You've got a rousing good story there, I see, so you can just read and keep quiet and see that nobody bothers her. Understand?"

"Yes, sir," replied the young man. He smiled tentatively at Polly. He was looking forward to a few quiet hours to read without interruption, a rare pleasure in the household of which he was a member, and one, moreover, where too much reading, especially reading for amusement, was considered a sign of sloth at the very least, and possibly of some mental imbalance. His father did approve "a rousing good story" now and then, though, and that was what he presently had in hand.

They were just ready to start when Mrs. Ruggles appeared at the door, calling Tom. While he ran back to the house, Polly seated herself on a bench under a tree, and the men prepared to remount.

"Want you to look at a horse of mine, Moresby," the squire said. "You're a great judge of horseflesh. I'm

154

thinking of keeping him for a stud."

"I'd be glad to look at him, sir. You should know that Mr. Chapham here has as good an eye as mine, perhaps better."

"I doubt that," Alex protested, "but I shall be equally happy to see the animal. Where I do shine is pronouncing judgments, however poorly I make them."

"The animal has the endurance and strength, and by God, I never saw a horse so warm after the mares, but the conformation . . ."

The problem of conformation was lost to Polly as the men rode off in great good humor. Well, so much for sitting quietly by my side as I paint, she thought with amusement.

Tom was not long delayed, but when he joined her, his face was scornful. "Ma's so silly," he said as they walked toward the pen where Caesar awaited immortalization. "I had to go back just to get this old cap."

"Well, the sun can be hot, you know. You wouldn't want your brains baked."

"Oh, brains can't bake. Mine'd been baked before this if they could."

Polly changed the subject. "What are you reading, Tom?" she asked him kindly.

"A smashing story, ma'am. It's Captain Bligh telling about the mutiny on his ship and how he, and the men Mr. Christian put off the ship, sailed thousands of miles in one little boat to get home again. I haven't finished it yet, but I know he got home because he wrote this book, don't you see?"

"Yes, I've heard of Captain Bligh's great feat, but I've never read his account of it. Is it very exciting?"

"Oh, I think so, ma'am! I'd like to go to sea, but Pa

155

says I should have thought of it when I was twelve—he says fourteen's too old, and anyway, there's no fortune in it now Boney's gone. Would you like to borrow the book, ma'am? I'll bring it over to you when I finish." It occurred to young Tom that in pursuit of such an errand he might see Francie, an older woman who at the moment he was worshiping from afar. "I'd be real pleased to lend it to you, ma'am," he repeated, with even more eagerness.

"Why, Tom, that's very generous of you. I'd like to read it. But you needn't ride all the way over to Tanwell. I'll be sending over a servant with the preliminary drawings of your father's ox, and you can send the book to Tanwell with him."

Seeing the opportunity of a possible sighting of Francie fleeing from his grasp, Tom said hastily, "Oh, I'm near finished. I expect I'll have it done long before your drawing—drawing's so hard and all. I wouldn't mind at all riding over to Tanwell. Why, I ride twice that far some days when Pa's in a whirlwind."

"In a whirlwind?"

"That's what Ma calls it when Pa really gets going on something. You know, like when it looks like rain and the hay ain't in yet."

"Well, all right, if you're sure it's no trouble."

"Oh, no, no trouble at all. I assure you, ma'am."

By this time they had reached the pen. "See—" Tom pointed proudly. "Pa fixed up this kind of high chair for you so you could get a real good view of Caesar, and then from the high ground up there under the tree you can get another good look at him."

"Caesar isn't vicious, is he?" Polly asked. The "high" chair looked rickety. "I wouldn't be afraid to sit in the pen with him. It's a very ample pen, and if I sit right over there near the gate, I can get out quickly should he take exception to my presence. Or if there's no time for the gate, I can climb the fence."

Tom eyed her skeptically. "Climb the fence?"

"Yes, climb the fence. Do you forget that I grew up in the country too? I climbed lots of fences when I was younger, and I assure you I've not become so old that I've forgotten how."

"Well—" Tom was dubious. "Old Caesar's never been known to get mad at anybody, but I don't know what Pa would say."

"Then we won't tell him. I promise, if Caesar gives me one cross look, I'll jump right over the fence."

"Oh, pooh," Tom was emboldened to say. "You couldn't jump over that fence."

"Just a manner of speaking, Tom, meaning that I would climb over quickly."

"Oh. I thought you was bamming me. I can vault the fence but not quite jump it."

"No, it's much too high for jumping."

Tom helped Polly set up the stool she carried with her, during which old Caesar continued to phlegmatically chew his cud, not bothering with even a curious glance, let alone a cross one. Tom settled down on the grass by Polly and opened his book as Polly opened her sketch pad. Both were soon deeply engrossed.

Polly showed her sketches of Caesar to the squire and discussed the pose he preferred for the painting, and she was then free to drink tea and make polite conversation with the squire's "missus," who had been more

157

than adequately entertained by Alex and Frederick meanwhile. After a good neighborly gossip, as Mrs. Ruggles put it, and a lot of hen talk, as the squire put it (winking broadly at Alex and Frederick), Polly rose to leave. As Mrs. Ruggles saw her out — waving a maid-servant aside — Polly took the opportunity to say a word about her kindness in sending dried peas to the over-burdened Martha Riggs.

"Yes, the poor dear," Mrs. Ruggles replied. "Some women pray for children and are never blessed, or are blessed only once, like Lady Moresby. Or like my poor sister — all her confinements end with stillbirths. And then there are others of us who can't stop. I remember when my own young ones were coming too fast for comfort, even though I had the help of two or three servants, a nursemaid, and a cook. Not to mention a good husband who doted on the little ones." Observing that the men were standing out of earshot in the sweep waiting for the horses to be brought round, she added, "Childbirth is a burden laid on us, my dear, much as we love our children, and however much we enjoy them when they grow up and begin to bring us grandchil-dren. I can guess how Martha Riggs feels."

At Polly's look of surprise, Mrs. Ruggles gave her a motherly hug. "I shouldn't be saying such things to a young lady who's just gotten herself engaged. Oh," she said laughing, "I know you haven't officially announced it yet, but we all know. Why—"

Just then the squire called, "Now, Mother, let the missy go. These horses are wantin' to get home to their dinner."

Polly never heard what Mrs. Ruggles intended to say, but not to be denied, the good woman said it to her husband instead. "Anyone can tell by looking at that young man that he's head over heels," she said, as they watched Polly and her two escorts depart down the drive.

"Maybe so," replied the squire. "Those were sure some fine pictures of old Caesar. Miss Polly says I can have 'em all when she finishes the painting."

"Oh, go on," replied Mrs. Ruggles, laughing.

When the invitations were received at Tanwell for the Moregreen dinner party on the thirtieth of July, Polly and Mrs. Rice looked forward to no more than a pleasant evening and an excellent dinner, but elsewhere the invitation stirred a variety of expectations in a variety of female breasts. Francie, because she was to be allowed to join the company, nursed a thrilling anticipation of adulthood, which she translated as grown-up parties and people listening to what she had to say. Clarissa thought of Frederick, whose interest, she felt, had been stimulated. Nettie was thinking of dancing and, moreover, of waltzing.

The difficulty was that Nettie did not know how to waltz, nor was she sure her father would approve. She therefore applied to Polly (who had been taught the waltz by *none other* than Dolley Madison, the wife of a former *president* of the United States) to convince her father that dancing within an encircling male arm was harmless and not an invitation to degeneracy.

It was not an undertaking of which Polly had much hope, although her father was such an odd combination of liberality, moral rectitude, and prudery that one could never anticipate him. She supposed, however,

159

that his unpredictable character was not surprising, all things considered.

Mr. Rice's father, Polly's grandfather, had been the third son of a Ducal family allied with one of the great houses of France. His connections were, of course, excellent, but he had chosen the more rakish offspring of the aristocracy as his set, spent his time between Paris and London, and eventually achieved a reputation as a rake in his own right. Polly's father had seen men who could claim the best in breeding rotting with venereal diseases, and scions of the noblest and wealthiest families who took exquisite pleasure in delivering crushing set-downs to their social inferiors. He had fled from this milieu, cut all connection with his father's titled family, and married the daughter of a country gentleman whose Methodist leanings had eventually led him to preaching.

Fortunately for the future well-being of his family, Mrs. Rice brought him a generous dowry, now invested in the Funds and providing a modest but steady income from interest. Then shortly after his marriage, owing to untimely deaths and poorly drawn wills in the male line, he succeeded to the ownership of Tanwell, a 310-acre estate. Equally fortunate, such money as his rakish father had failed to squander on liquor, gambling, horses, trips to Paris, and expensive wenching went into properties a short distance outside London, which were making the Rice family very wealthy indeed. Mr. Rice could well afford the complete break he had made with his aristocratic connections.

When he was recalled to mind by any of his relatives, it was in such passing ruminations as, "I say, whatever happened to young Giles?"

"Cousin Giles?"

"That young sprig of Laurie's."

"Laurie?"

"You know—third son of the old Duke. Used to spend a lot of time in France till the trouble over there."

"Oh, yes, terrible cutup if I recall."

"My yes, never saw his wife again after Cousin Giles was born."

"Small wonder. She died in childbed if I remember."

"Believe you're right. Not long after the Treaty of Paris—'63 was it? '64?"

"Although now I think of it, there were two girls. One of them married Grover-Morton's boy—got himself killed in the war with the Americans."

"Catherine Morton! Is that right? I'd forgotten she had a connection with the family."

"Not surprised. You've been buried out here in the country so long."

"What did happen to young Giles, by the way?"

"Believe the young fellow married into the bourgeoisie, or maybe she was just a Methodist, and buried himself somewhere in the country. Inherited an estate from his mother's family."

"A Dunnington, wasn't she?"

"Believe so."

A ruminative silence.

"Are you sure Catherine Grover-Morton is young Giles's sister? I've got it in my mind she was the daughter of the second brother, George, you know. Got his head knocked in when his carriage overturned."

"Maybe so, but I thought George had only boys."

And so the conversation would meander on, tracing remote relatives, and "young Giles" would not be re-

161

membered for another several years. Mr. Rice, knowing how easily distant connections are forgotten, was confident that his own children would take their places in what he foresaw as a rising middle class, free of the fetters of aristocratic prejudice. Mrs. Rice, although she accepted the High Church to which Mr. Rice paid allegiance, had no ambitions to be other than bourgeois, or for that matter, other than a Methodist. In fact, she intended to insist that Jonathan and William attend a dissenter school, where they could learn science and other practical subjects, instead of a lot of dead languages.

Catherine—Aunt Cat—was in fact "young Giles's" sister, and not the daughter of his father's brother, George (second son of the old Duke). She and her sister, Clarissa's mother, had been packed off to a country town after their mother's death, where they grew up under the care of a lady who gave them to know that their father's life was disgraceful, but their aristocratic connections a matter of pride. Each sister learned half the lesson.

Catherine was too giddy for an excess of rectitude, and too like her father to disapprove Society. She married a gentle young man with a pretty inheritance (Grover-Morton's boy), and after his death (he got himself killed in the American rebellion) lived in London, where she maintained a foothold in the upper classes. But for all the feebleness of her mental powers—more a matter of lack of exercise than lack of wit—she had a kind heart and a generous soul.

Her sister, Clarissa's mother, ran away with an unpretentious young man of common birth but of exemplary moral quality who later became rich in honest

162

trade. He proved to be also an exemplary husband and father, and they lived comfortably together until she died. After a brief period of distracted grief, he realized that he must make careful provision for his little Clarissa, his wife's death having proven how uncertain is one's tenure on earth. He had no intention of leaving his daughter to the care of such a featherbrain as her Aunt Catherine, and had not named her a guardian in his will. Rather, he gave Clarissa into the care of his brother-in-law, Giles Rice, who was named her guardian. He did not, however, name his brother-in-law a trustee of whatever fortune he might leave the little girl, being cognizant of Mr. Rice's lack of financial acumen. The money was left in the care of two business associates and his banker, with the provision that a generous allowance be provided for Clarissa's expenses.

That Clarissa was eventually given into the care of her Aunt Cat was due to an excess of youngsters at Tanwell. Consequently, when Catherine begged her brother to let her have the little girl, he consented, and Mrs. Rice, whose own children took as much of her affection as she could spare, made no objection. Moreover, she had just begun to suspect another pregnancy, which had occasioned a temporary and unfamiliar feeling that she could not quite manage it all. Clarissa had received an abundance of love from her aunt, and so over the years Mr. and Mrs. Rice closed their eyes to any deficiencies in Clarissa's upbringing.

Both had soon discovered as well that any attempt to interfere with the aunt's decisions was likely to bring on tears, accusations, and florid lamentations. Cat would cry that they did not trust her, that she was sure she did the best she knew how, that she herself had been a

163

motherless child, left to rusticate in a country town with no pretty dresses or other joys, and she could not bear that her poor Clarissa should suffer a like fate. And so, over time, they gave up even a vestigial responsibility, and Mr. Rice abdicated the role of guardian.

While his sisters were rusticating in the country town, Mr. Rice—the young Giles—had remained under his father's care, but far from following in his father's footsteps, the lascivious household in which he was reared had nurtured a repulsion for his father's way of life and a longing for retirement and rectitude. The bawdy close of the eighteenth century, and the fast regency society of the early nineteenth century repelled him, and from his sons as well as his daughters he demanded a strict code of conduct that bordered on Methodism.

He had not, however, become conservative as the French revolution and then the Napoleonic conquests challenged the old ways and threatened insular security. He had been known to champion greater freedom for women to manage their own affairs, and he had encouraged his daughters to study mathematics, geography, and the great classics of English literature. When Polly showed talent with the brush, he hired excellent teachers and encouraged her to strive for more than the pretty pictures young girls were expected to paint. He enjoyed, and moreover read aloud to his family, novels of neither literary nor moral worth; he countenanced participation in rural merrymaking that was often as bawdy as it was rowdy. He had never protected his daughters from the facts of the stable, chicken run, or barnyard. Still, Restoration poetry and the plays of Congreve were kept behind locked doors; he had not taught his daughters French, which was the language of innuendo and naughty books. He allowed his daughters the satirical realism of Fielding, encouraged them to read Scott, Burns, Wordsworth, and Coleridge, despite the "inflammatory minds" of the latter two (at least in youth), but the younger romantic poets, whose scandalous lives emphasized the lush eroticism of their poetry, were forbidden.

How could Polly best convince such a thoroughly capricious and unpredictable man that the waltz was neither lascivious nor an indication of moral laxity?

She chose her moment carefully, conspiring to meet Mr. Rice as he returned from a late afternoon stroll through the orchard. Hooking her arm through his, she said, "Papa, I have a petition to present."

"So, my dear, what is it?"

"Remember, when you were speaking with Frederick the other night of the changes we can expect in future from the application of steam power to machinery?"

"Indeed I do, but I find it hard to connect such a discussion to any petition I might receive from my daughter. You are not wanting to study engineering, are you?"

"Of course not. I am merely introducing the idea of change—of new ways and new habits."

"Ah. An escapade is contemplated."

"No, Papa. Only that you give permission for me to teach Nettie some of the dances I learned in America. I merely seek the assurance that you approve before I undertake to do so. Or rather," she hastily amended, "your permission that I may do so."

"Well," said Mr. Rice. "Come and sit down and tell me about these dances you learned in America. Wild

Indian dances, were they?"

"No, Papa. Don't laugh at me," Polly replied. "I was thinking of some of the country dances I learned one summer when we spent some time among the Germans in Pennsylvania, a dance called the gallop, and some interesting country dance figures, the way the Americans have modified the cotillion, and the waltz perhaps . . ."

"Ah," Mr. Rice pounced immediately on the issue. "The waltz, is it? One can hardly think the waltz quite proper."

"But that is the *point*, Papa. It is simply a new style of dancing—there is no hint of the improper about it. I confess, I have danced many a waltz, and I assure you, it is most proper, and although the gentleman's arm does lightly encircle one, it is simply for guidance in the steps. Furthermore, the gentlemen are most properly required to wear gloves . . ."

Polly's father held up his hand. "Hush, girl, don't rattle." He sat for a moment in thought. "Do you truly, upon careful consideration, believe that these dances are suitable for young girls such as Nettie and Francie? For if you teach Nettie, you can be assured that Francie will insist on learning too."

"Yes, Papa. I believe there is nothing improper in the new forms of dancing. I have found that what is improper is often what is defined as improper—even a matter of circumstance—rather than that the action is immoral. And among men of honor and women of virtue, actions that among the dishonorable and unvirtuous might lead to immorality remain innocent. In our own small circle here, and among the families we visit, I cannot foresee any impropriety."

166

"Well argued, my girl," said Mr. Rice. "Come along. I shall talk to your mother, and if she has no objections, I will give my approval."

Nettie waited—on tenterhooks—for the outcome of the parental conference, but Mrs. Rice was merely puzzled that the dance should be considered questionable. Aunt Cat created a moment of tension by taking up the cause of waltzing. Aunt Cat's judgment was held in low esteem, but on the other hand, her actions, while occasionally foolish, were never improper, and so that small moment of danger passed. The council of elders handed down a favorable decision.

The lessons began that very night, with Aunt Cat at the pianoforte, and Polly and Clarissa as instructors. Nettie and Francie learned the basic steps and the rhythm, the "feel" as Clarissa put it, but whenever Polly tried to take the male role, she found herself falling over her own feet and those of her pupils.

"It's just simply backwards," she exclaimed in despair. "I just can't dance backwards."

Clarissa proved little better in the role of a gentleman, and so the sisters and their cousin were discovered by Mr. Rice whirling and twirling about the room, Nettie behind Clarissa and Francie behind Polly, as the learners attempted to imitate their teachers.

"Well, well," said Mr. Rice, "the waltz is a stranger dance than I had thought."

Chapter Nine

The announcement of the engagement of Miss Polly Rice and Mr. Frederick Moresby had appeared in both the local, provincial paper and in the London papers the day before Lady Moresby's dinner party. Consequently Polly and Frederick, in the drawing room before dinner was announced, found themselves the center of their neighbors' interest and well-wishes. Mrs. Ruggles gave Polly one of her enveloping motherly hugs. Squire Ruggles made her an elaborate leg and offered his wishes for her future happiness; then, his eyes twinkling, he said, "I like exceedingly the 'preliminary drawing' you sent over of my Caesar. And my missus likes it too. She's fixing to ask you to paint her favorite tabby—great big yellow fellow he is, too."

Mrs. Ruggles responded with something very closely resembling a girlish giggle. "Oh, la, Mr. Ruggles! You know I've never even thought of such a thing. Don't you believe him, Miss Polly. He will have his little jokes."

The squire winked at Polly, as he tickled his wife under the chin. "Isn't she a cute one, though?" he asked of the world in general.

The rector's old aunt found this byplay in no way diverting. "Really, Squire Ruggles, you have no sense of propriety."

The squire was not only undismayed by the reprimand, but looked ready to chuck the old aunt under the chin as well, when Lady Moresby interrupted by calling his attention to the fact that dinner had been announced.

Conversation was always sprightly at Lady Moresby's dinner table. Mrs. Rice had discovered in her latest botanical journal a new idea—a room called a conservatory, largely of glass, to open off a drawing room or parlor, and separated from the main room only by a pair of glass doors. It gave her an idea for remodeling her little parlor, which was tucked into the southeast corner of the house, and never much used since it lacked well-placed windows as well as space. A conservatory would turn it to some good use. "If only," she concluded, "the price of glass were not so high."

This comment sent some of the gentlemen off on a discussion of the glass tax, and the glass tax to Ricardo's treatise on political economy (which Polly was only beginning to puzzle through), and then to questions of export and import, the price of cotton, and the threat of cheap grain from Ireland and America.

"I'm telling you, sirs," said Squire Ruggles, "that once the United States get going, they'll flood the world with grain. Ain't that right, sir?" he demanded in a loud voice of Alex, who was seated at the other end of the table. Alex had been busy charming Dr. Littleton's elderly aunt, and had not the faintest notion of what the squire was demanding he agree to. Fortunately the

170

squire had no need for an answer, since he was full tilt on the subject of the Corn Laws, which imposed duties on imported grain, and the question was purely rhetorical. "Have a nephew over there," the squire continued. "P'raps you remember him, ma'am. Henry, m'brother's boy" (this latter shouted down to the elderly aunt). "Boy writes from out in what he calls the Ohio Country — says land is cheap, and cheaper farther west, and lots of it — good land, once it's opened and developed. That means cheap grain, sirs. And I say that without tariff protection, we'll all face ruin. The price of wheat was so low last year that it hardly paid off the cost of growing it. I don't mind telling anybody that I was hard put to it last year and that I expect to be hard put to it this year."

Dr. Littleton, the rector, whose sympathies were more with the poor than with the landlords, although he was not prepared in this company to say so, suggested timidly that higher prices for grain and thus for bread would be hard on those who had no land.

This was an unfortunate observation, for the squire had his opinions on that score as well. "Aye, it will be hard on the working people. But who's to benefit from cheap bread? I'll tell you. The manufacturers at the expense of the landlords and farmers, that's who. Helps them keep their wages low. And just explain to me, Littleton, how it is that only the manufacturers deserve protection? Plenty of import duties on foreign manufactures. Don't see why landlords are any different. How is it that we tried to keep the colonies from developing their own manufactures? And lost them to boot for it — ain't that right, sir?" The question was again addressed to Alex, but the general import of the statement was addressed to Dr. Littleton. The rector's opin-

171

ions were firmly fixed, but since they were unsupported by theory or informed by attention to public debates, he could only murmur noncommitally and wish he had never ventured to speak. The squire was getting alarmingly red in the face.

"What blasts me," the squire said emphatically, giving the table a good crack with his fist and causing the dishes in his vicinity to rattle, "are the cloth manufacturers. Get their raw cotton from America without paying any duty, but they've managed to put a duty on imported cloth. Now that don't seem right."

Mr. Rice observed that several leading economists were of the opinion that prices should be allowed to find their own level, resulting in both manufactured and agricultural products being produced where conditions were most favorable, a clear benefit in lower prices to the public and a national benefit in vigorous trade; although earlier theorists, who were not to be discounted entirely, had suggested that self-sufficiency in basic necessities was essential to national security, which did suggest some protection for agriculture and certain basic industries.

This observation fortunately coincided with the removal of the dessert wine, which meant that Lady Moresby, with a speaking look at her husband, could remove the ladies to the drawing room. Polly had listened with some attention as Squire Ruggles's ire dominated all other conversation at the long table. Her diplomatic training had given her the knack of attending with interest even the most boring conversation, and furthermore, she had spent a part of the morning attempting to establish exactly how Mr. Ricardo's definition of rent compared to those of Mr. Say and Mr.

Adam Smith. Mrs. Rice was naturally interested in the price of grain, but the other ladies of the party were becoming restless. Escape to the drawing room was a relief, but as it proved, a questionable one.

Aunt Cat had been holding her tongue on the subject of conservatories until the ladies retired, but she had her own ideas on newfangled notions, and those ideas usually had to do with their dangers. Conservatories were no exception. She had never seen one, to be sure, but she had read Humphrey Repton and she subscribed to publications, and she was certain that the dangers far outweighed any pleasures from indoor gardens.

"Really, Catherine," said Mrs. Rice, "I can't think what dangers my plants pose for me. I certainly do not intend to nibble poisonous leaves or roots."

"Aside from the smells of earth in pots, think of the dampness of the atmosphere, which surely cannot be good for the health. I have also read that there may be dangers from want of oxygen, the plants requiring so much—and when you consider the smallness of your little parlor, I should think the scheme doubly dangerous."

"Wouldn't the fragrance of the leaves and flowers overcome any odors?" asked Lady Moresby. "I myself find that I rather like the scent of damp earth."

"I believe I've read that plants expel oxygen rather than consume it," Polly suggested.

"Well, whatever," Aunt Cat countered. "it can't be healthy."

The younger girls were soon as tired of conservatories and orangeries, of geraniums and exotic plants from America, as they had been of economics (al-

173

though Francie did wonder if it was true that plants could breathe), and it was with severe impatience that they awaited the gentlemen. Their arrival was indeed sweet relief, and Sir Harry's call for whist players the means to even greater relief—a sure insurance against more economics. Nettie immediately begged Aunt Cat to favor the piano over the card table—"you play with such spirit, Aunt Cat—and we must practice the waltz with real gentlemen in anticipation of Frederick's ball." Aunt Cat, who had little love for cards, and much for the company of youth, agreed.

As the drawing room floor was cleared, Frederick, quizzing Polly, for he knew very well her preferences, asked, "And do you prefer the dance floor or whist?"

Polly, whose toes were already tapping as Aunt Cat ventured into the first tune, answered in kind. "You know I'll choose the dance floor. Your mother understands very well the talents and preferences of her guests, even if you do not, sir."

Francie, although not yet out, would turn sixteen shortly, and was permitted to dance at private parties among intimate friends. Therefore, with Squire Ruggles's daughter (the legitimate one), the ladies of the dancing party made five, while even with the squire's older son, there were only four gentlemen to partner them, and one of those gentlemen was Bolling, who like Polly, had recognized Lady Moresby's plan, but had not the confidence to solicit a female hand—even that of a squire's daughter. Nettie's eye, meanwhile, was falling with more and more disapproval on him. An inactive male would never do; more than three men were wanted on the floor if the evening was to be successful.

"My lord," she said, approaching him with a lively smile, "is it that you do not dance, or is it that the choice of partners does not please you?"

"No such thing," he replied, surprised. "Haven't d-danced in an age. D-don't do it any-m-m-more, y'know."

"But you do know how, do you not?"

"Yes, yes, d-danced quite a b-bit at one time, y'know."

"Then I must assume," said Nettie, with her best flirtatious glance, "that the company is displeasing or that you are now troubled with gout?"

"Oh, no. N-n-no, n-not that at at at all." Lord Bolling was nearly undone. "J-just, y'know, don't d-d-d-dance much anymore."

"That may be acceptable at great balls, my lord, but don't you think that in a small company such as this, when there are only four gentlemen to five ladies, that you might make the sacrifice?"

This was such a pointed invitation that poor Lord Bolling saw no escape and, bowing, demanded Nettie's hand for the next dance.

Much to Nettie's surprise, he was an accomplished dancer. In fact, thought Nettie, he was far superior to Alex Chapham, of whose superior accomplishments Nettie had heard from Polly. He was even superior to Frederick. "Now, my lord," she said, as he led her from the floor, "you have exposed yourself as the most excellent dancer imaginable, and there is my little sister, sitting without a partner for two whole dances, and I do think it is terrible to be young and never asked to dance. Don't you think you could do me the favor of dancing just once with my sister Francie?"

Lord Bolling was entirely incapable of resisting such a determined young lady, and before he knew it, he had been led to dance the entire evening away. He had been so severely wounded by his former lady, his self-esteem so lowered, that he could not imagine that Nettie could have any other motive in urging him onto the floor than to fill out the want of partners. He obligingly danced all the remaining dances, and he even enjoyed himself, when he could forget to remember what a failure he was at love.

As the dancers rested following a waltz, in deference to Clarissa's recent illness, Alex suddenly turned to Polly. "I say, Poll, why don't we teach them the way we dance in America? It's so much livelier—maybe because we have to step more lively to keep warm in our harsher winters," he added tactfully.

The younger dancers clapped their hands in delight; Frederick and Bolling, although less enthusiastic, raised no objections, at which Alex and Polly went into consultation, and after some discussion decided that since the dancing party had an extra lady, and four couples were needed to form a square, that Polly should act as the prompter. "I've already discovered," said Polly, when Alex objected, "that I am no good at playing the gentleman."

"Very well," Alex agreed, and assuming charge, turned to Aunt Cat. "Aunt Cat, do you know any good jig tunes or reels? Either will do—or we can even dance to clapping hands." He glanced at Polly before addressing the others. "At the frolics in western Virginia we danced to fiddle music, and in Washington, when we

176

roll up the rugs at small private parties, there is usually a spinnet or pianoforte, but there've been times when we had nothing but our hands to set the time."

"How very interesting," Clarissa remarked.

"We use a four-couple square, just as we do in cotillions and quadrilles," continued Alex, ignoring Clarissa, "but couples work around the square, something like a maypole dance, and the figures are not performed in set sequence."

"I say," remarked Bolling, "how are we to keep from knocking each other down if we don't know the order of the changes? D-doesn't sound possible to dance without knowing the changes."

"The prompter calls out the changes. The fun is in following the directions as well as in performing the figures. And this way a dance can go on as long as the fiddler and the dancers can perform. We usually don't do such marathons—but sometimes—especially at the country frolics, I've seen squares—and running dances too, performed like contests, with people dropping out and substitutes leaping in to fill their places . . ." Catching Clarissa's raised eyebrows, Alex laughed. "But that's neither here nor there. As I was saying, the prompter calls the changes. And when the prompter is really good, he—or sometimes she—inserts all kinds of amusing remarks between the calls for the changes."

"I doubt I can do that," Polly said, "but I can call the changes, and I'll clap my hands in between."

"Let's see," Alex said, "you all know allemande left and right, four hands round, promenade, sashay—that is, *chassee*, the grande moline . . ." Alex checked off the various figures, while Polly helped Aunt Cat select two or three appropriate tunes. "Now, Polly," Alex said, "help me demonstrate the figures that our friends don't know. Do you remember this one? It's like the balance but much more vigorous . . ."

The group became very merry indeed as the dancing got under way. Some confused their left and right hands, went backward when told to go forward, and stood in bewilderment when their partners were discovered across the square rather than by their side. Frederick was feeling a bit stiff—it was years since he had participated in such giggling, breathless gaiety—although Bolling, who could claim as many years as Frederick, had begun to enjoy himself immensely.

Clarissa, noting Frederick's reserve, found occasion to comment on the provincialism of the Americans when the changes of the dance found him by her side. Lord Bolling, panting from exertion, his hair in disarray and his shirt points wilted, steadied his blue eyes on Clarissa from his position on her right, and said, "Damned good fun, I say," and in response to a new call, whirled off.

Frederick himself had no time to reply as the two flanking couples returned to their places and Polly commanded that all the gentlemen swing the lady to their left, by which means they were returned to their own partners, but which resulted in a contretemps between Frederick and the squire's son, the latter being one of those who could only distinguish right from left by remembering which hand he used for writing, and that therefore the other was the left. In the unexpected changes of this American way of dancing, it was proving a disadvantage. Polly called a momentary halt to the dance to tie a handkerchief to his left thumb, remarking that she had had similar difficulties, and had

178

solved the problem by similar means when frolicking in America. Frederick to his surprise found himself laughing heartily.

Clarissa soon declared herself fatigued, but Alex, the irrepressible, insisted that it was just too bad for Polly not to have the pleasure of dancing at least one dance and, after ascertaining that Clarissa felt too inexperienced to call the figure changes, announced that he himself would call them.

"But Alex," objected Polly, "how can you possibly dance and call at the same time?"

"Like a sound horse, I have excellent wind. Come, take your place by Bolling. That's the girl. Ready, Aunt Cat? All right, friends," he announced as they took up the rhythm, clapping in time to the jig tune that tinkled from the pianoforte, "all join hands and circle right . . ."

Clarissa, furious at Alex, was suffering an unusual fate. A pretty girl, light on her feet, who at thirteen had begun practicing flirtatious glances before her mirror, she was not accustomed to play the wallflower. She attempted a look of interesting fatigue without success; the others were too involved in the complications of following Alex's instructions and much too merry. She was angry because the others had not stopped the dancing, as they had before, to allow her to rest. In fact, she was so greatly recovered that they had forgotten the recent assaults on her constitution, and she looked so robust that she was unable to feign a convincing suggestion of delicate health. She was too well bred to openly sulk, and her refusal to rejoin the square in Polly's place when a new dance was begun was gracious, but as she sought to find the proper expression and demeanor for a young miss on the sidelines, she contemplated revenge.

The squire, in the sitting room where the card tables were placed, had caught the cheerful rhythm of the jig tunes, which had hampered his game and drawn a cross word from Dr. Littleton's elderly aunt, a serious and skillful whist player. "Do pay attention," she reprimanded him after a rather severe setback. "Surely you were aware when you led the diamond that Lady Moresby was completely out of that suit and that therefore my nephew must be holding the knave, otherwise I should have led it, you know, when the ace fell."

"Yes, ma'am," replied the squire dutifully, although he did not follow the critique past his own ill-chosen lead. "Careless of me, but those jig tunes in the drawing room unsettled my mind—put all my attention on my feet, y'might say. Didn't know young people danced jigs these days."

Lady Morseby, in charge of scoring, soothed the old aunt by remarking that no great harm was done—squire and aunt had won the game despite his lapse. "And I do believe that supper will be laid out in the dining room by now. I've a particularly choice morsel to show you, ma'am, that Polly tells me is very popular in Brazil. She gave me the receipt and I've been experimenting to adapt it to our English resources . . ."

The squire joined in mollifying the elderly aunt with some teasing references to the lady's presumed gay youth, including much jigging at country parties, which earned him a sharp rap on the wrist from the lady's fan. The squire, unrepentant, favored the old aunt with one of his winks and retired to the drawing room, where he teased Aunt Cat into playing for him while he danced a jig and the former dancers clapped in time, offering many expressions of encouragement and admiration.

The light supper set out in the dining room brought all the dancing to an end. As the whist players and the dancers mingled, Polly found herself laid seige again by Squire Ruggles. Frederick, who had been seeking out his affianced, gave her a barely perceptible but understanding nod, and returned to the drawing room. She has the squire completely charmed, he thought. Then a smile from across the room beckoned; Frederick answered the invitation, smiling in reply. He sat down by Clarissa, who said sweetly, "Mr. Moresby, I have been waiting and waiting for some sign of recognition from you, but alas, I fear that when we met in London I was too insignificant a miss to be remembered."

Embarrassed, Frederick searched his mind to place Clarissa among his London acquaintances. To make up for his lapse in memory, he said, slipping easily into the conventions of flirtation, "I am a rogue for forgetting such beauty, but I can excuse myself that it was only upon meeting you here that I discovered your wit, a quality in women that appeals more to me than beauty."

"Ah," said Clarissa, "that explains it then . . . although you flatter me to think me more than a conventional girl, and one who is largely self-educated. And that badly, I'm afraid."

"You are too severe upon yourself. But tell me where we met. I am now all curiosity."

"At the Stepfordson's ball, two years ago. You danced with me twice, a quadrille and a country dance.

181

I thought at the time you seemed distant and bored, and very soon after our second dance you escaped to the card rooms. I assure you, I do forgive you; I only remind you of the meeting to tease a little."

"I am afraid that London palled the last few years. And you could have been little more than a child two years ago."

"Barely out of the schoolroom, and in my first season. I was very green, and much too silly for any man with any sophistication to notice." Clarissa smoothed a wrinkle in her skirt. "Polly is so fortunate. We had all given up hope of her ever marrying, and we are so happy she has captivated such a fine man as yourself, sir."

Clarissa paused — scarcely more than the time for the drawing of a breath, but long enough for Frederick to initiate some response. When he did not, she continued, as though musing aloud, her auditor forgotten, "She was always such a harum-scarum, so careless in her dress, you know, and always kicking off her shoes and letting her hair fall out of its pins. We always thought that if the right man would offer for her, it would do wonders, and I must say, it has. She's looking really very pretty tonight." Clarissa gave a conscious start, as though only just realizing that she spoke to Polly's betrothed. She laughed. "How I run on. I've always loved and admired my cousin, you know — I looked up to her so when I was a little girl — and her happiness means so much to me."

Frederick was no longer a green youth himself, and was no little bemused by this prattle. There were also certain notions aroused by the idea of Polly in dishabille, which he hastily and with a glance across the room, set aside for later. "Yes, Polly is looking very well tonight. And fortunately, with her hair cut so short, there are no longer any pins to scatter about the dance floor."

"Yes, although it is quite out of style to wear one's hair so short, it *is* the best arrangements for Polly. I do admire her unconcern for style."

Frederick and Clarissa's tête-à-tête was interrupted by the squire, who wanted to discuss the merits of a certain young bull being offered for sale by a breeder in the next county, and Clarissa soon found herself in the toils of conversation with the rector's elderly aunt.

Both Clarissa and Frederick noted, however, that Alex had taken the squire's place, and that Polly was soon laughing heartily at some sally. As another eddy in the assembly parted some groups and brought others together, Polly and Alex were joined by Lord Bolling, and Clarissa drifted like a leaf in the eddy back to Frederick's side. Noting that his eyes were on his future bride, who had at that moment cast an unmistakably saucy glance at Alex, she said softly, "I really can't approve of the freedom of the house that my aunt and uncle Rice allow Polly's American friend. He seems to bring out the harum-scarum in her—she is so abandoned in his company."

"Polly is still under her parents' protection, and if they see fit to welcome young Chapham, I shall welcome him also," Frederick replied stiffly.

Clarissa was aware that she had received a set-down, and hastily and very prettily apologized. "I spoke too freely, and I must beg your pardon, but I hope, knowing how much affection I bear Polly and the respect I have for my uncle and aunt, that you will accept that I spoke—however unthinkingly—only from those motives, and will excuse my indiscretion."

Frederick's quickly replied that, of course, he understood and forgave. He also had spoken hastily. Could she forgive *him*?

Frederick had begun to watch Polly more closely in these last weeks, and he was seeing a different woman than he had seen before — more of playfulness, a flirtatiousness in the way she spoke to other men, and — a sure sign that he had fallen in love, although he did not yet know it — he immediately began to misinterpret every glance from those pretty eyes that was not directed at him.

Although he knew perfectly well that Clarissa's remarks were not innocent, and suspected that some motive other than affection was at work, they were not without effect. Certain doubts had been implanted in his head at the very moment that he was becoming aware of certain feelings invading his heart. Frederick was finding himself when in Polly's presence prey to powerful impulses to get his hands on her, and with a tendency, when she was not present and his thoughts were running free, to dwell on her face and figure, and on what she said when they were together. Now there was something new to think about — how Polly looked at Alex, what she said, how she acted — and how this compared to her behavior when she was with him. And then there was a bothersome question, unworthy though it might be. What *had* their relationship been in America? Just what had Polly's life been like all those years abroad? If Frederick had been a hero in a romance, he might have ground his teeth, for he was no longer under any delusion (if he had ever been) that he was rescuing a nice little lady from certain spinster-

184

hood.

Frederick's ever-watchful mama had now come to a satisfactory conclusion. As she brushed her hair before the ormolu mirror, Sir Harry sat comfortably nearby, clad only in a dressing gown, sipping a final brandy and admiring his wife at her toilet.

"I think," she said, catching his eye in the mirror, "that Frederick has lost his heart to Polly."

"And what makes you think that?"

"His eyes follow her everywhere. I've always considered that a sure sign of love."

"Or infatuation."

"Well, yes, but in this case is there any reason to distinguish?"

"You are, as always in these matters, correct." Sir Harry tossed off his brandy, and set his glass on the tray by his side. "And the lady?"

"I'm not so sure of Polly—she's so tactful, and so friendly with everyone. No doubt it's her diplomatic training."

Sir Harry rose as Lady Moresby lay down her brush, and ran his hand softly over her shining hair. She reached up to take his hand as it fell on her shoulder, and their eyes again met in the mirror.

"Quite frankly," he said, "I'd say she flirts too much with Chapham."

"Why Harry, I would never have expected you to notice such things."

"I notice a good deal, my dear. For example, you were looking amazingly well tonight. Do you know that you are still beautiful?"

He bent to kiss her neck as he slid his hand inside her dressing gown.

She turned about to be lifted in her husband's arms. "Is it too much to hope that our son can have this too?" she asked.

"Probably," he said.

Chapter Ten

Summer was now reaching its prime, ripening, languishing under guileless blue skies. The whole of Tanwell was scented with musk rose, which lingered late that year. Farmers anxiously watched crops showing the first signs of thirst, hoping that each shower would become a deluge. Mrs. Rice and the gardener watered flowers and vegetables in the family gardens, and joined farmers in watching the skies. Frederick and his father discussed the weather over their port and in their rounds of the fields. It was the August dog days.

For the young, it was a summer made to their desire. Jonathan and William were scarcely ever seen, to the relief of their sisters. And it was a summer made for courting, for pretty dresses and parasols, for afternoon drives and morning strolls, and for archery in the afternoons at Tanwell.

Alex, not long after his arrival in the neighborhood, had reminded Polly of their fondness for archery, which they had enjoyed in America, and urged her to rummage up from storage her own and her family's archery

187

equipment, for he himself remained an enthusiast for the sport, however much it might be waning in popularity. Whenever Bolling and Alex were with them, it became their custom to spend at least some time practicing on the lower lawn at Tanwell. As the novices gained in skill, a fever of competition set in. Bolling was appointed Captain of the Target to settle all disputes and to rule on the number of paces from the target for each archer to shoot, according to skill. He held the position by reason of the fortuitous combination of knowledge of the sport and sober judgment.

Clarissa was sitting under a lacy parasol watching an archery contest when Frederick strolled across the lawn.

"Don't let me interrupt," he called to the archers. "I shall content myself as spectator." Seating himself beside Clarissa, he asked politely, "You are not shooting today, Miss Knight?"

Clarissa had given up being interestingly frail, having discovered that it was inconveniently confining. She replied truthfully, "I was detained with my aunt this afternoon, and was like you unwilling to interrupt. The archers are not individually shooting today, you see. It is a hotly contested match. Mr. Chapham and Polly are teamed against Lord Bolling and Nettie."

"Then you and I shall challenge the winners."

"I must warn you," said Clarissa archly, "that I am a most serious competitor. I play to win, and I relish all contests."

Frederick made a small bow. "I suggest then that we make a close study of our prospective opponents. Do I correctly judge that Polly and Mr. Chapham are at this

188

moment the likely losers?"

"You do. My cousin Polly has not the determination of her sister, and Mr. Chapham is much more interested in flirting. Lord Bolling, on the other hand, is so incapable of flirting — or even of conversation — that he has nothing else to do but concentrate on the contest."

"Hmmm," Frederick murmured as Polly at that moment clapped her hands and cried, "Oh, Alex, *marvelous* shot!"

The archers moved forward. Polly, a skilled archer, shot from the regulation sixty paces for women. They moved forward again, and Nettie took her position at the thirty paces Bolling felt her skill merited. Alex's marvelous shot was not enough to turn the tide of battle, for although Polly performed creditably, Nettie hit first the inner white and then a perfect gold to win the contest. "There, my lord," she said as they left the field. "Am I not a worthy partner?"

"Most worthy, Miss Nettie. I b-believe we have won by eleven points. You will soon be the b-best of us all."

"I challenge!" Alex exclaimed. "Polly and I challenge you to a rematch, and *this* time I will pay more attention to the target and less to my partner's lovely eyes." He leered fatuously at Polly, who replied, "And I, sir, will no longer allow my mind to wander to such subjects as that careless American fashion you apply to the folding of your cravat!"

"Ah, now I am to hear republican simplicity maligned — or is it my nationality? Do you mean to imply that Americans are not as talented on the archery range as Britishers?"

As Polly gave her hand to Frederick in greeting,

189

Clarissa closed her parasol with a snap. "I'm afraid, Mr. Chapham, that you will have to wait awhile longer for the opportunity to prove your American skill against ours, for Mr. Moresby and I now demand the right to challenge the winners. You are relegated to the sidelines, where you may gaze into your fair partner's eyes to your heart's content."

"*You,* Miss Knight, I would never dare to challenge—as either man against woman or American versus Britisher. I am intimidated by your skill on any playing field."

Frederick and Lord Bolling took their places as Clarissa tested the bow that Polly had relinquished. She was aware how well archery revealed the female figure, had practiced diligently, and now displayed excellent form although her aim was still wanting.

Polly and Alex seated themselves to watch. Polly could see that Alex was eyeing Clarissa as she experimentally drew her bow, but she was puzzled by the underlying current of dislike in the exchange between him and her cousin. She wondered if she should give voice to her curiosity. After all, she rationalized, I've known Alex for many years, and we have always been friends, so why shouldn't I? She turned to Alex and in a lowered voice remarked, "I detect an undercurrent between you and Clarissa, Alex—"

"Oh?"

"Yes. An undercurrent of . . . of . . . antagonism, it seems."

"You will excuse me, Polly, but I do not like your cousin much, and I fancy that she does not like me, either. I don't know whether it's because I'm American,

190

or she doesn't like my face or my manner. Or that she thinks I perhaps see too much."

"And what can you mean by that, Alex? What is there that Clarissa would not like you to see?"

"Oh, I don't know." Alex answered evasively. "It's just a feeling. Well . . . it's insignificant. And it was unpardonable of me to say what I did. Don't give it another thought. Anyway, look what approaches. Your mother has sent us succor."

The footman and a maid were proceeding slowly across the lawn bearing lemonade, carefully packed in ice from the precious summer store—now nearly exhausted as the hot, dry days lingered.

Polly poured lemonade for herself and Alex, then slipped the heavy quilted cover over the container, which would insulate it and its contents from the summer heat. "The others are so intent on their game we won't interrupt them now." Turning to the footman, she said, "Please take the lemonade and glasses back to the terrace and set out chairs. We will all take our refreshment there later."

The sun was hot, and Polly was hot from exertion. There was no shade near the bench on which they sat, so she gestured toward the noble sycamore tree at some distance from the archers. "Shall we take ours to the shade of that tree over there?"

"You don't mind sitting on the grass? I don't see any benches."

"Oh, Alex. When did I ever object to sitting on the grass?"

"I thought perhaps you had grown out of your romping ways."

191

"Should I, Alex? Grow out of them, I mean?"

"Never. Why do you ask?"

"I will be twenty-five in November, you know."

"What difference does that make?"

"Perhaps I'm feeling a little depressed as I contemplate a twenty-sixth birthday, and then a twenty-seventh, and so on, year after year," she said thoughtfully.

"Then what you need is cheering up."

Soon Alex had her laughing at a tale of diplomatic cross-purposes, and she forgot her approaching old age and the curious antagonism between Alex and her cousin.

"Do you remember Alexi Stoganov?" he asked.

"The Russian chargé in Berlin?"

"Yes, we met him briefly in Ghent. I heard in London that he died not long ago."

"I'm sorry to hear that. He was always so gallant."

"A useful talent in diplomacy. You did know the gossip about him, did you not? That he got his start in the Imperial Foreign Office by providing services in the Empress Catherine's bed—which, I must say, if she was as repulsive as she's been described to have been in later life, was certainly deserved."

"Alex! How perfectly scandalous! I don't believe it."

"Whether *you* believe it or not, *I* intend to. I've heard that many an Imperial diplomat began his career prone and upside down."

"Alex!" exclaimed Polly, scandalized.

"Can't you imagine that fastidious old gentleman Stoganov as a youth in that Byzantine court plotting his future in diplomacy as he dressed—or undressed rather—for the evening's official engagement?"

"Alex, really, you know that repeating such gossip to an unmarried lady is the height of impropriety, but oh, dear . . ." Polly trailed off into giggles, remembering the so-proper gentleman and his so-proper wife. "He certainly married a high stickler in the end, though, did he not? Perhaps as antidote!"

"Oh-oh. Caution, my girl. Here comes your intended, looking not at all pleased."

Polly looked up to see Frederick crossing the lawn toward them, and indeed looking not at all pleased.

When he reached them, he spoke in perfectly civil tones. "It seems that Miss Knight and I have defeated Miss Nettie and Bolling, although how it came about I'm sure I don't know, and I am sent by my partner to fetch you both for a match."

Frederick extended his hand to assist Polly to rise. "Goodness, Frederick," she said as she brushed grass from her skirt. "Don't you think it much too warm for further exertion today? Let us rest a bit. My mother has sent us lemonade. We can return to the tournament when the sun is lower."

"An excellent idea," said Alex.

Later, brushing her hair in her little chair by the window, Polly remembered the exchange between Alex and Clarissa. She puzzled over it for a time, with no satisfactory conclusion, and then turned to another incident of the afternoon that provided even more food for thought.

As she preceded Frederick and Alex to the terrace, they had by gestures and calls made it known to the

193

others that refreshment awaited them. Clarissa and Nettie walked off the field together, arm in arm. Lord Bolling, who delayed a moment searching for a misshot arrow, followed several paces behind. Nettie, saying something to Clarissa, made a broad gesture, and a folded handkerchief she had tucked in her sleeve fell unnoticed to the grass. Bolling picked it up and, with a hasty glance at the others waiting under the tree, placed it in his pocket. He had been unaware of Polly watching from the terrace.

She expected him to return the handkerchief, but when he did not do so, an idea suggested itself to her. As they all sat together drinking lemonade and talking, she watched Lord Bolling and her sister as closely as she dared. She believed that Bolling looked at Nettie with more tenderness and admiration than friendship would explain, and that Nettie, far from repulsing him, was openly encouraging him.

As she reviewed the previous days, she thought she could remember certain other signs that Lord Bolling was developing a *tendre* for her sister. He was very quick, she recalled, to attend to Nettie: to offer his arm, to place a cushion for her, to retrieve a book left carelessly by the stream. She could not think that Lord Bolling, who was Alex's friend, and who had impressed them all with his soberness and his gentlemanly manner, could be trying to make a conquest of Nettie, or even engaging in a casual flirtation. She believed he was more likely unaware how marked his attentions were. But Nettie . . . Polly was almost convinced that she, at least, knew what she was doing. Really, it would be too bad of Nettie to make sport of the feelings of a

194

man so recently wounded. But on the other hand, it would be a most ineligible match should Nettie be entertaining any serious hopes of Bolling. He was divorced to begin with, and she was too young for him in any event. She had insufficient experience of men to decide so soon on a partner in life. What did she know of love, except for the usual passing fancies for one of the neighborhood boys? As for him, he might well shy away from an attachment so soon after an unprosperous marriage, or even consider Nettie's birth too lowly. Polly resolved to observe the two of them very closely in the future, and if her suspicions were justified, it would be necessary to speak to Nettie.

She drifted off into other memories of the long afternoon. After their lemonade on the terrace, she'd accompanied Frederick to the stables with the intention of visiting the kittens after she'd waved him off, but he chose instead to accompany her. "I must learn to like cats, as you, my dear, must learn to like dogs." They sat in the hay and watched the kittens. She held them in turns on her lap, and Frederick stroked them tentatively with one long finger. They had stayed for nearly an hour, talking of this and that and playing with the kittens, until at last, with reluctance, he said he must go.

She preceded him down the ladder from the loft and stood watching as he, too, descended. The cows were not yet up for the afternoon milking; all was hushed and dim. He looked over his shoulder, saw her standing below, and hastily completed his descent. She'd not been aware what he'd seen in her eyes, although on thinking about it now, she suspected that he'd read something of the muddle: that they were alone, that he was handsome and lean and agile, that he'd smiled and stroked her cheek when she'd asked if there were any puppies at Moregreen for her to visit. Had she moved into his arms, or he into hers? She couldn't remember. It had been so pleasant, those few moments of their embrace. They had simply stood in each other's arms, his cheek against her hair. She lifted her face for his kisses; then they'd heard a step outside, and parted.

Well, she thought, as she lay in her lonely bed. This is love-longing. It was a description she had always remembered from a collection of fifteenth century letters in her father's library: the correspondence between a prioress and her superior. Girls who were given to the church by their families, wrote the prioress, but who had no vocation themselves, were too often "seized by the love-longing." They wandered off. Some never returned. Others came back, "their bellies big," and on their knees outside the gates, they begged to be readmitted.

So Polly wandered off to sleep, her mind and senses filled with Frederick and the love-longing.

Someone else had discovered the growing attachment between Nettie and Bolling long before Polly. Bolling had a title, an older and ranking title compared to the mere Baron attached to the Odious Gentleman Clarissa was urged to wed. The Odious Gentleman's title was of recent acquisition, whereas Bolling's went back three, or perhaps four centuries. (Aunt Cat could not be certain without a peerage, and naturally her

196

brother Giles Rice, who detested the aristocracy, did not have one.) Clarissa had expected her aunt to show some interest in Bolling as a possible suitor in place of the Odious Gentleman, but the scandal attached to his house reduced his worth in her eyes, an estimate that was reinforced when he appeared in person and it was discovered that he had no conversation, that he stuttered when he did speak, and that he had no address at all. Aunt and niece were in accord on the subject of this male personage, if not the Odious Gentleman: he was not worth the effort to attach. Aunt Cat further considered the Odious Gentleman not only much more lively and polished than Bolling, but probably richer, while Clarissa had soon detected Nettie's interest in Bolling, and would not for the world have interfered. Nettie was the one friend in the whole world to whom she was loyal. And if that was not sufficient reason by itself for her lack of interest in Lord Bolling, there was yet another point. He had shown absolutely no interest in her from the very beginning, having eyes only for Nettie.

As Polly was drifting off into her dreams, Clarissa and Nettie were gossiping companionably on Nettie's bed. The two girls had gone together to the archery range to search for the lost handkerchief and, when they did not discover it there, retraced their steps to the terrace and into the house. Clarissa, much more familiar with the arts of romance than Nettie, immediately guessed that it had been found and appropriated by an admirer, who could be none other than Bolling. With an arch look, she suggested the possibility, but Nettie was not to be teased into an open admission of interest.

Clarissa renewed her efforts during their bedtime

gossip but with no more success. For the first time in her life, Nettie found that she did not want to confide in her cousin. She did not know why; she only knew that whatever was going on between herself and Lord Bolling was not for girlish gossip. She had a feeling that whatever it was, it was a delicate thing that belonged only to the two of them, and that she could not discuss it even with her best of friends. So she parried Clarissa's questions and her teasing by bringing up the subject of the Odious Gentleman, a certain distraction.

Chapter Eleven

Not many days after, Alex and Lord Bolling brought news from the village. Market day was to be enlivened by a traveling troupe offering a marionette show, a high wire performer, and a lady juggler — an event that absolutely required the attendance of all. A party was arranged, and a message sent to Moregreen for Frederick.

After some discussion of the advantages of wheels over shanks mare, the party determined, since the day was cool, on walking in order to better enjoy the beauty of the countryside, which was cleansed of dust by a recent rain. Polly arranged for the stabling of Alex's and Bollings's horses until their return to Tanwell. There was a general flurry of gathering parasols and bonnets, and soon all but Francie, who was spending the day with a friend in the neighborhood, set out on foot for the village, a matter of a little over a mile.

The road to the village from Tanwell was hardly more than a country lane and carried only local traffic, which meant that all six of the party could walk abreast if they chose, and with little expectation of meeting any vehicle other than a farm cart or two. However, it is seldom that six people long find it convenient to walk abreast, and so they proceeded toward the village in parties of threes, twos, and fours, according to who fell behind examining an interesting plant, or hurried ahead to have a longer enjoyment of a view, who quickened pace or lagged behind. If Frederick thought that Polly perhaps walked rather too frequently with Alex, he could not have been certain that it was by design, for he found himself as frequently by Clarissa. Only Nettie and Lord Bolling might have been noticed—had Frederick been interested—to be more often walking together. Polly noticed, however, and although she was unaware of it, so did Alex, who had long since concluded that his friend was taken with Polly's little sister. Alex had not yet concluded that Clancy's admiration would lead to anything of a more serious nature, but was gratified for his friend. Miss Nettie was not shy about soliciting Clancy's good opinion, but she was at the same time maidenly and modest. It was just what Clancy needed—a demonstration by a sweet young person like Nettie that just because one woman had found him wanting, another did not. Would do him a world of good, thought Alex.

They arrived at the village common just as the tight wire walker took his place to begin his third daring walk across space since the day began. The common was not crowded; although the village of Merton's Green had some pretension to importance as a trading center for the area, it was outranked by a larger town ten miles distant. Market day was lively enough, but the stalls were closing by the time the Tanwell party arrived. Farmers' wives, with their eggs, cheeses, chickens, and vegetables, and the vendors with their miscellany, were packing their wares. Their customers were drifting away. Laborers and farmers and their families had work to attend to in these long, busy days of summer. Nonetheless, many paused to take in the final show of the morning. There were also boys and girls from the village, some of their elders who could leave their shops, many housewives, several maids, and a number of the shiftless, all of whom together made a sufficient crowd for the performers to gain a few more pennies.

The Tanwell party joined the audience in front of the high wire performer, and with the other spectators held their breath during each daring feat and sighed with pleasure with each recover. They cheered in appreciation as the lady juggler tossed various objects in varying numbers into the air while balancing various other objects on her nose or forehead. They laughed at the marionette show, an adaptation of the old favorite, *Punch and Judy*. During the performances, Alex and Bolling restrained the others from succumbing to the calls of the pieman and the orange seller with the promise of a cold collation and many "Chiney oranges" awaiting the party at Crossfield Cottage.

The housekeeper—Mrs. Lewis, the postmistress's nephew's wife—showed the ladies upstairs to a retiring room where they could refresh themselves. There was scented water in the pitchers, towels in plenty, and discreetly visible in a small adjoining room, a lidded wooden commode which concealed a chamber pot. A young girl—the postmistress's nephew's wife's daughter — was just laying out small bars of soap on the basin stands. The housekeeper introduced her and said, "Alice will give you any assistance you may need," at which Alice bobbed a curtsy. "She will show you below when you have refreshed yourselves," her mother added, and the girl curtsyed once more. Alice proved to be adept at performing the office of lady's maid, and when Polly complimented her, she smiled broadly, curtsyed again, and said proudly, "Me mum — my mother — trained me, ma'am. She served in a very great house before marrying my father, ma'am."

"Are you looking for a position, Alice?"

"Not yet, ma'am. Me mum thinks I'm not old enough."

Polly smiled at her kindly. "I'm sure you will have no trouble finding a position. Your mother has taught you well."

"Thank you, Miss Rice. May I show you downstairs now, please?"

The gentlemen were assembled in the small parlor, ready to repair forthwith to the dining table. The housekeeper had, as Alex promised, prepared a fine collation, and a large bowl of golden oranges decorated the center of the table. The meal was served in courses, continental-style, for which the housekeeper and Alice, in the kitchen, were thanking their lucky stars. Mrs. Lewis had been given very little notice of the luncheon party, and had been required not only to send for her daughter, but to press into service her husband and the "young lout" who weeded the garden. "Thank goodness for Mr. Chapham's high-flown ways," she remarked several times to her helpers. "Such a crazy way to eat, I said to him when he explained it all to me. So what if the Frenchies do serve their meals one dish at a time? What is that to a good Englishman? But then Mr. Chapham pointed out that he was a good American, and he had me there." So Mrs. Lewis ran on. While in the dining parlor the guests remarked on the novelty.

After a discussion of the morning's entertainment, and country fairs and traveling shows in general, Alex expressed curiosity about the principal sights of interest in the county, particularly a picturesque spot in the neighborhood that he had heard often mentioned.

"The spot is lovely," Polly responded, "but if I remember it accurately, I'm not certain that it would hold much of interest for you, Alex. We wouldn't visit America to see magnificent cathedrals or ancient churches—indeed, could not—it's yet too new a country. On the other hand, Americans can hardly be impressed with our natural wonders when theirs are so much more magnificent. I'd recommend rather that you visit the curious monuments at Stonehenge, or ancient castles and Roman ruins."

"Although I've read that the climate is more violent in America than in England," Frederick remarked, "I had not thought of the North American continent as one of the great natural wonders. The Falls of the Niagara excepted, of course."

"It is just that everything is on a grand scale in America. The thunder and lightning in summer storms, the extremes of heat and cold . . ."

Alex looked up from peeling an orange. "Polly arrived in America just in time to experience some of the violence. Eighteen sixteen was the year without a summer—they actually had ten inches of snow in June in New England that year. New England's an area where

203

the snows are always heavy. For instance, on many of the farms the barns are attached to the houses so the farmers can care for the stock without having to cut through drifts that attain heights of ten, fifteen, sometimes twenty feet. But even in New England, ten inches of snow in June is unusual."

"How frightfully uncomfortable," remarked Clarissa.

"I should like to see such d-drifts," said Lord Bolling.

"So should I," echoed Nettie. "I can't imagine so much snow!"

"I believe a volcanic eruption is the suspected cause of your 'year without a summer'?" Frederick asked. "We had a very cold winter in England associated with the eruption."

"So I've read," Alex answered. "The winter in Washington was also unusually cold. Do you remember the sleigh rides, Polly?"

"Indeed I do. But it is not just the violent climate that is so magnificent . . ."

Clarissa, who found nothing of interest in a conversation in which she had no role other than audience, said, "I do not understand how even 'violent' climate can be considered interesting. I for one find the constant talk of weather one of the most persistent bores of life in the country."

Lord Bolling turned to Clarissa and said reprovingly, "P-p-pardon, Miss Knight, b-but you must remember, you know, that the w-welfare of the country rests on g-good w-weather for crops." Lord Bolling always felt uncomfortable with argument, which worsened his stammer, but as a landholder he felt it necessary to instruct the young lady from London.

"That is certainly true," concurred Frederick, "and

204

I'm afraid, Miss Knight, that you will have to bear with our country fascination with weather. But what I find puzzling is that such violent and surely uncomfortable weather can be described as magnificent."

"I suppose it does seem odd," Polly said thoughtfully, "but it is appropriate to the magnificent scale of the continent itself. Nearly all the rivers here, even those that rise in the mountains, are narrow in comparison, and the falls of no great height. In the lowlands they run placidly to the sea. But in America the lowland rivers are so broad, so immense, the floodwaters from snowmelt or storm so turbulent and uncontrolled; and it is impossible to imagine until it is experienced the grandeur of the Falls of the Niagara, and even more impossible to imagine the roar of the vast quantities of water spilling into the gorge below. One must actually shout to be heard above the roar."

"And the spray, rising from below the falls . . ." added Alex.

"The rainbows arching through the spray," said Polly in antiphony.

"The ground shaking under one's feet."

"Oh," cried Nettie. "How I should love to see it!"

Polly, gratified to be able to speak of an experience that had affected her deeply, said, "I should like to have you see it, Nettie. For you all to see it. Even the colors in America are violent. Here in England, the light is softer. But in America, the sun is brilliant and strong, with an intensity that I have experienced nowhere else. So extraordinary. There is haze over the Blue Ridge Mountains—they derive their name from it—but as one views them from afar, one sees them as under an intense light—so difficult to explain the effect. Or to paint. And in the fall, the leaves turn bright red or brilliant yellow in so many and varied hues, interspersed with greens and browns. The prospects are magnificent—they almost beg the painter to record them—yet I could never capture them. The prospects seemed to shrink under my brush, and the brilliant fall colors to turn to mere colorful daubs."

Alex bowed gallantly to Polly. "I thank you, Miss Rice, for your appreciation of my country." He then turned to Nettie. "I hope that someday you may visit America, Miss Nettie. My mother and father, who as you know live in Washington, would be delighted. We Americans are perhaps overly fond of showing off our continent, just as we are sometimes overly prone to boast about our republican liberties."

In the kitchen, young Alice, who with the aid of the loutish young man had been clearing the table of the final course during this exchange, said to her mother, "Cracky, ma'am, you should hear them talking about America. A waterfall so big that it near shakes the earth and rumbles like thunder—and snow in June . . ."

"What kind of language is that, miss? We do not use words like 'cracky.' And you would do better to attend to your chores. Here, help me get this coffee ready to serve."

In the dining room, the conversation had turned from country entertainments in America to the more sophisticated society of Washington and New York.

"You must remember that the majority of us are transplanted Britishers, after all, and although we hope to build a new race on new soil, we cannot help but carry with us the customs and manners of Europe and England. We have a season in Washington, just as you do in London and the provincial towns here. Girls come out when they reach the proper age, young men gamble and race horses, we dance and go to the theater, attend drawing rooms . . ."

"I think, however," Polly interrupted, "that you would find a broader spectrum of political and religious opinion at a drawing room in Washington. Consider, Alex, at the drawing rooms at Duddington House. The proprietors," she continued, addressing the table, "are the Carrolls, a wealthy landholding family. One of their ancestors signed the colonies' Declaration of Independence, and the family is still prominent in public affairs. And they are Catholic. The brother of Mr. Carroll is a Jesuit priest, and often appears at the drawing rooms and dinners. He founded a college in Georgetown, which is a town near Washington, that is open to all faiths. John Quincy Adams, the present Secretary of State, is a Puritan. Dolley Madison is a Quaker — although there are those who say she is a fallen Quaker, for she does not wear gray, and she dances . . ."

Alex had noted Clarissa's increasing boredom, in contrast to Nettie, who was hanging on every word, and decided it was time to turn the conversation into channels closer to home. "Very true, Polly. Someday, Moresby, I hope you can visit us in America, and as I assured Miss Nettie, even though I should be languishing in some consulate at the ends of the earth, my family would be most happy to receive you — any of you" — he gestured expansively — " and to help you see and understand America." As Alex began to fear that he would be required to run on frightfully before he could get the conversation into those other channels, Alice appeared with the coffee.

207

"Ah, the coffee has come. May I suggest that we take it in the pretty little garden attached to the cottage?"

In the bustle and confusion of leaving the luncheon table and finding seats in the garden and pouring coffee, the subject of America was forgotten.

Frederick, too, had observed Clarissa's lack of interest turning to boredom, and finally to a sullenness which she was not able to hide. He could not but sympathize. However interesting the subject to others, and therefore however willing they were to listen, for a young woman who had no great curiosity it could not but be tiresome. He exerted himself to find and introduce topics that would interest her, and allow her to take part with something other than murmurs of awe and feigned appreciation.

The conversation thus turned to the latest gossip from London reported in recent newspapers, then to a literary review in the *Edinburgh Review,* and finally to the "Peterloo massacre" in Manchester. Polly became quite exercised on the latter subject, joined (surprisingly) by Bolling, who although hardly sympathetic with the demonstrators, could "not quite approve" attacking unarmed people. Then someone remembered a scandal of some proportions involving the mayor's wife in a nearby town, who had been accused by a store clerk of stealing ribbon and other trifles, culminating in the theft of a valuable shawl — a theft that could not be overlooked. A subject was discovered with which everyone could be happy. At last Frederick drew attention to the lateness of the hour, and the party prepared for their departure.

As they walked homeward, well satisfied with the day's entertainment, Nettie stopped and gestured across the fields. "Let's not go home the way we came. We can cut across the field to the path through the woods and cross the stream on the bridge near Tanwell."

"The afternoon sun is quite warm," Polly observed, "and except for crossing the field, the way Nettie suggests is much more pleasant at this time of day."

Lord Bolling surprised them all again by taking a hand in the decision. "Seems much more sensible to take the cooler p-path, if Miss Rice and Miss Nettie will lead the way."

"Follow me, then," Nettie said. "There's a gate into the field just a little farther on."

"When you speak of crossing a field I am assuming that there are no bulls loose in it," Alex remarked. "I have a considerable interest in scientific agriculture, but only from a theoretical point of view in the matter of bulls."

Clarissa, with a hand to her bosom, gasped. "Oh, I should probably just die of fright if I encountered a bull! As many years as my aunt and I have been visiting Tanwell I have never become quite easy with the larger animals that abound in the country. I shall have to stay as close to Mr. Moresby as possible, I believe, if we are to take to the wilds."

"Oh, pooh, Clarissa," Nettie exclaimed. "My mother would not think of letting her farmer keep a mean bull. And if he did, he would be sure to keep it closely penned. Anyway, everybody crosses this field. The squire's workers go to the village this way and have been doing so for years, and so do people from Moregreen and Tanwell, for it's shorter."

Alex, perceiving that he had made an error in mentioning bulls, stepped to Clarissa's side. "With Nettie and Clancy—for he is a country fellow at heart, you know—we should be perfectly safe even without Frederick, and Polly is also familiar with the larger domestic animals. So"—he swept off his hat and bowed—"lead on, Nettie."

They crossed the field without incident other than meeting two laborers returning to the village from Moregreen, who pulled their forelocks in greeting as Frederick stopped for a moment to confer with them. Polly, who with the others was waiting at a little distance, observed the expression on Alex's face at this undemocratic form of salute, which rested on the centuries of distinction between those who owned landed property and those who did not. She felt a sudden sense of shame.

When Frederick returned to them, he addressed Polly. "They say one of your mother's cows is down, Polly. She's just in the little hollow over there. I think I'd better have a look at her. These men will then walk up to the farm house to leave word if she needs attending." He turned to the others. "So if the rest of you would see Polly home . . ."

"No, no," Polly protested. "I'll come with you. If she needs attention, I can carry word back to my mother, although, of course, our farmer will want to attend to her at once. If the men are mistaken and nothing is wrong, then I have merely walked a little farther than the others today, which I assure you will not harm me."

"We can all go," Clarissa said. "The poor cow."

Frederick opposed this plan. "If she is in pain, she may not react well to so many people. I have seen the gentlest animals attack when under stress. If Polly does not mind such an interlude to her walk, I will be happy

210

to have company, but the others of you must go on."

The cow was at the bottom of the hollow when Frederick and Polly and the laborers came upon her. She lay with her legs folded under and her head twisted back against her shoulder.

"We tried to get her up, Mr. Freddy," said the older of the two laborers, with another stab at his forelock, "but she don't seem like she can. Look like the milk fever to me."

The younger laborer, omitting any further gestures of respect, said, "Her calf be over there, sir. Him be just a little mite."

Frederick went down into the little hollow to examine the cow, while Polly mused that the calf looked as rickety as its mother. The inspection was brief. Frederick was soon beside her again.

"I'm afraid Old Joe is right, Polly. Her eyes are sunken, and she feels cold to the touch. She appears to have dropped her calf only recently. It is much too young to be one of the spring or early summer crop."

"It must be the cow my mother calls Spot. I heard her asking our farmer if a cow named Spot had calved yet."

Frederick turned to the two laborers. "If you would be so kind to inform Mrs. Rice's farmer, we will all thank you very much."

"We'll go right along, Mr. Freddy," said the elder, with another pull at his forelock. "Good day to you, ma'am. My regards to your mother."

As Polly and Frederick made their way toward the woods, Polly said, "Mr. Freddy?"

"Yes, Old Joe has known me since the cradle. His compromise with my maturity is to call me Mr. Freddy

211

rather than Master Freddy."

"Were you really called Freddy in your youth?"

"Occasionally, until I was old enough to put up a good row about it."

"You were right to do so. You aren't really a Freddy sort of person."

"And what is a 'Freddy sort of person'?"

"Oh, someone less substantial. Less intelligent, less dignified, less honorable, less commanding of respect."

"Am I all those things, Polly? And nothing else?"

He stopped her as they entered the cool woods. He put two hands on her shoulders and looked questioningly into her eyes. "Nothing else, Polly?"

She looked away. What answer did he want? She stole a peep at him from under her lashes. "I should think such a formidable list of compliments would be enough for any man for one day, sir."

Frederick tried to keep the disappointment from his voice as he released her. "Very well, my dear. I'll let you off for now."

Polly frowned. Somehow she had made a mistake. Was it the light answer? Did he want her to be more serious? Why hadn't she said that he was the kind of person she liked to be with? That he was a restful person? That he was gentle and kind? That he made her feel protected? She sighed involuntarily, and they walked on in silence.

Frederick was also asking himself questions. What had he wanted her to say? Why hadn't he insisted? Why hadn't he kissed her? He glanced down at her, and thought she looked fatigued.

"You are looking a little fatigued. Shall we rest a bit?"

"The stream widens and becomes shallower farther

212

on, I remember, and there's a great large boulder that's just right for resting on."

"There are several places where the stream flows around and over rocks."

"But we had one favorite place—Peter and Gussie and I. It was such a lovely childhood, Frederick. My mother never scolded us for coming in mud-stained from our rambles, or Gussie and I for hitching up our skirts to climb trees—not even when we tore them on limbs and fences. Of course, she had so many other children still in the nursery to worry about, and we had to wear old clothes on our excursions, and were required to mend them ourselves. Peter's always said he would make a fine sailor, for he knows how to mend his own clothes. Sometimes I think Jonathan and William suffer from being the last born—although we older ones, as we sat sewing up rips and tears, often thought we suffered for being the first born." She was silent a moment, considering. "My mother is not so easy in her ways as she was then."

"We all change as we grow older. But how I envy you your brothers and sisters! It's lonely growing up an only child."

"And I look sometimes on the calm and peace at Moregreen, and remember that Peter could be an awful tease, that Nettie was always bothering Gussie and me, that there was always a baby with the croup. And how I hated mending and wished I had more hours just to be alone."

"You and I must try then for a compromise, must we not?"

Two squirrels ran chattering along a limb above them, and they stopped to discover the source of their

213

dismay. "Whatever the problem is, it must be a matter between squirrels," Frederick decided.

"They were playing tag, perhaps," volunteered Polly. "Before the big chestnut outside the window of our mother's dressing room fell, we often amused ourselves watching their games."

They soon came to a place where the stream widened. "This is the place I remember," Polly said. "Can't we go across here and rest on the other side in that little grassy glade?"

"The stones are too far apart, I'm afraid, for a lady to cross," Frederick said, walking to the bank to study them. "The opposite bank is very steep here. In any event, it's only a short distance now to the stepping-stones near the Tanwell bridge."

"Peter and Gussie and I often crossed here. From this spot on it's prettier on the other side. And," she added, "this was much the best place for wading. We could take off our shoes and dabble our feet in the water. Would a Frederick sort of person approve?"

"The bank is steep, and probably slippery. The water was up after the rain." But Frederick saw her disappointment. "If you don't care if your dress gets muddy, a Frederick sort of person would approve. The water here is shallow due to the breadth of the stream at this point, no doubt because of the gradual erosion of the bank on this side."

"Engaged people could even go wading, could they not?" Polly asked with a touch of mischief, and an undercurrent of challenge.

"Why could they not?" answered Frederick, taking the challenge.

He had no reason to be ashamed of his legs, which

were well muscled, hairy, and shapely — nor of his feet, which were well formed and free of corns, bunions, or other disfigurement. He was not self-conscious strolling about in his birthday suit in circumstances in which nudity was appropriate, but whatever the guardians of female delicacy and general propriety might rule on engaged people wading in streams, he felt remarkably silly with his naked feet and lower legs protruding from his trousers.

They clambered barefoot down to the broad, flat rock that sat solidly in the water near the bank — a rock that the mightiest torrents could never move, Polly commented. She, at least, seemed comfortable with bare feet, and gave no hint of guessing how awkward he felt. Before seating themselves to dangle their feet in the water, Polly tossed her shoes, and Frederick his boots, onto the opposite bank. Polly sent her bonnet sailing also, but it was caught by the breeze and dropped in the stream. Frederick reached a long arm out for it and returned it dripping to her.

"Well," she said philosophically. "I never liked it anyway." She prepared to give it another toss, at which Frederick took it from her. He waded across the stream to deposit it safely on the bank.

"Is this a revelation of a hidden propensity to waste that will send us both to the poor house?" asked Frederick, knowing perfectly well it was not.

"No, only my mother's philosophy: never cry over spilt milk."

"Or tossed bonnets?"

Polly looked at him in surprise, but his expression was so bland that she was uncertain whether it was a jest, or only a remark made before he thought. She

215

made no answer, but sat down and dangled her feet in the water, observing that it was wonderfully cool. Frederick sat down beside her and for a time they enjoyed the woodland silence. Polly thought about a painting, and Frederick thought about Polly.

Polly's thoughts wandered to the cow, and then to the laborers' habit of forelock pulling. She could not refrain from suggesting to Frederick that one aspect of reform, among the many that were being demanded by reformers, might be the ending of this particular custom. It was a small thing but so *symbolic*.

"Your time in the Americas has certainly given you some advanced ideas," Frederick said. "You have taken up the radical philosophers, including Mary Wollstonecraft, and you've become quite a little republican. You are of the opinion that England is representative of tyranny?"

"No, not at all. And I am not about to cry the superiority of the Americas. Both Brazil and the United States are still burdened with slavery. The Americans are not at all eager to join England in enforcing international agreements against the slave trade, agreements that they themselves have signed, and Brazil is presently the prime market for slaves. Cuba is a good market also, but of course, since it is smaller, more slaves are sold in Brazil. But we must remember that our own government has not managed to outlaw slavery yet in the West Indies because the planters' representatives and the merchants who depend on the sugar trade cry that they would be ruined."

"You are well versed on the subject of slavery. I hadn't realized."

"It's a particular concern of mine. It must be abhorred by all thinking people. I am in correspondence with people in America—in the United States—and here in England who hope to end the slave trade entirely and to eventually end slavery wherever it exists."

"Why haven't you told me this before?"

She turned to Frederick and, with a gesture of appeal, said, "Do you mind, Frederick?"

He took her hand and kissed it. "I honor you for it." She was still gazing at him with what he thought was a question in her eyes, so he released her hand and, leaning toward her, kissed her lightly. Her response was unexpected: a startled, "Oh!" Then she began to laugh. "Oh! Forgive me. I'm sorry. I think a fish took a nibble at me. It tickled."

Once their laughter ended, an uncomfortable silence fell between them, as both secretly cursed the fish. Frederick was conscious of an overpowering hankering, Polly of a great desire to be properly kissed. But how to get started again? There seemed nothing to do but take up their conversation once more.

"There is much to be done to improve the lot of the people in England, I admit," Frederick stated, "and I wonder now that I spent so many years in so many frivolous pursuits. I seem to have kept all my serious thoughts confined to my library, and all my active attention to serious matters confined to the breeding and feeding of my cows."

"Well," she answered, "I long ago decided that if you read Shelley for his political convictions—convictions that have caused him to be labeled an infidel, a jacobin, a leveler, and goodness knows what else, you cannot consider me such a radical."

"You mistake reading to discover the opinions of

others with reading to confirm one's own opinions. I confess that I read *Queen Mab* to discover why it created such a stir, not because I agreed with the political point of view. And I confess also that I mentioned it to Miss Knight merely to tease the girls. They were so obviously reveling in the romance, that I thought to challenge their understanding of the social and political implications of the work."

"Oh," said Polly. It was a very flat "Oh."

"I believe that for the last few years I've been stifled by the life I was leading. Sometimes when I used to read accounts of Captain Cook's voyages, or Vancouver's, I'd wish I'd gone to sea, or become a serious scientist so I could have accompanied the explorers of new worlds. It's a little childish, I suppose. But if I had had a brother, I might have left my inheritance to him and gone off to America — I think North America, since I have no facility with languages." A memory of his former mistress came into his mind unbidden. Would he, in different circumstances, have followed her to America, married her, and started a new, freer life? He thrust the thought aside, put his hand over Polly's, and smiled into her eyes. "We're very serious for two people with their shoes off and their feet dangling in the water."

The touch of his hand was galvanizing. "Well," she said, as briskly as she could, "I expect we should go. Now it's up the other side, and that looks more formidable than I remember. Isn't that odd? Usually places remembered from one's childhood seem smaller when seen again in adulthood."

"Perhaps a piece of the bank has slipped away due to flooding. Or maybe you remember another part of the stream. How many years since you've seen the spot?"

"Oh, goodness—it must be all of ten years."

"Streams do change, you know—rocks are displaced in high water, banks cave in . . ."

"I was so sure I remembered the glade on the other side that I didn't really look closely at the rocks. This rock, for example, seems flatter than I remember, and there were hollows on the upstream side that I don't feel in this one. . . . Well, we have burned our bridges—or tossed our shoes. Shall we try to reach the other side?"

Frederick helped her rise and, after making sure he had good footing on the rock, explored the bank. "Here," he said, when he had positioned himself securely, "give me your hand."

He was standing with one foot braced on a rock at the stream's edge, and the other firmly planted higher on the bank. He turned and extended his hand. Polly took it, carefully eyed the bank for foot and handhold, and jumped. As she snatched her hand from Frederick's to catch at a protruding root, he was thrown off balance. The rock shifted under his foot (or his foot shifted on the rock) and he went down. They both slid to the bottom, Frederick breaking Polly's slide by awkwardly throwing his arms around her. They began to laugh as they came to a halt at the stream's edge.

"Oh, dear, I'm all mud," Polly gasped.

"You certainly are," agreed Frederick, endeavoring to pick dry leaves and stray twigs from her hair.

"Do you remember how much fun it was to get dirty when you were a child? Or was it different—growing up alone?" she asked, perfectly still under his touch, her eyes on his, and the laughter on her lips.

"I had friends," he answered, reaching across her for

a handful of mud, his eyes still on hers.

He saw the moment she realized his intent. With a push at him she sprang up and began to clamber up the bank, careless now of her skirts.

Frederick, equally unmindful, was after her, and she was barely over the top of the bank when he, too, was over. He caught her around the waist and whirled her about in his arms. In seconds all the play went out of the day; by the second kiss it was very serious indeed, and by the third they were clasped in each other's arms and beginning to feel the blood rushing here and there to various seats of passion. All reserve was lost in their kindling desire.

The sound of approaching voices somehow penetrated their self-absorption, and they parted. Polly, her face flushed, picked up her shoes and sat down on the ground, and with great concentration began to put them on. Frederick, with more presence of mind, sat down on a log and put on his socks before attempting his boots. He was just putting his foot into the second (while Polly was stuffing her stockings into her pockets), when Alex and Lord Bolling reached the spot on the path that lay directly across the stream.

"Oh, there you are," Alex called. "We wondered what had happened to you."

"Were you looking for us?" asked Polly, with an edge of annoyance in her voice.

"No such thing. Clarissa lost her reticule — she thinks she left it just at the edge of the woods where she stopped to examine a clump of mushrooms. So Clancy and I, like knights of old, set out to retrieve it."

If the two men noticed that Polly and Frederick were

a little heated, and in much disarray, they gave no sign. "Well, we'd best be getting on, or we'll be caught by nightfall. We still have to get back to Tanwell for our horses," Alex continued when neither Frederick nor Polly found anything to say. "If you'll excuse us."

"What was wrong with the c-cow?" Lord Bolling could not help asking.

"Milk fever," Frederick answered.

Frederick and Polly found little to say to each other on the walk to Tanwell. They both had much to ponder, although the sudden incandescence of their response to each other had not quite made its way into full consciousness. Polly was thinking principally along lines having to do with her mother's caution against passion. Frederick certainly hadn't rejected her; but would he, on consideration, be shocked? A few more minutes and she would have been ready to toss her bonnet for sure. Frederick meanwhile was considering how completely he had misjudged his fiancée; as he had already begun to suspect, she was not at all the tame little spinster he had supposed her. He was temporarily dazzled by his prospects, and he kissed her hand before they parted on the Tanwell steps.

Chapter Twelve

"Whilikers!" breathed Jonathan.

Mr. Rice closed the cover of Captain Bligh's account of the mutiny of his ship and his subsequent nearly four-thousand-mile voyage. Although he had read it when first published, he had thought it sufficiently interesting to read aloud to his family, and that it might be beneficial for Jonathan and William, who unlike their brother Peter when their age, showed no serious tendencies.

"Isn't that the most amazing tale?" Polly asked.

"What happened to the mutineers?" Nettie wondered.

"Killed each other, most likely," answered Mr. Rice. "They were found a few years back by an American ship—or rather, one mutineer and several women were found."

A lively discussion followed, in which all joined, but when the last word was said, a silence fell on the group. Jonathan and William were excused, Francie excused herself, Mr. Rice picked up his newspaper, and the ladies gave their full attention once more to their different occupations. Little Pug lay at Aunt Cat's feet, wary eye on a cat. After a time, Mrs. Rice broke the silence. "When you send the book back to young Tommy Ruggles, Polly, you must tell him that we all enjoyed it, and thank him for all of us. I fear we kept it a disgracefully long time."

"I'm sure Tommy doesn't mind how long we keep the book. And I certainly will thank him. He's a nice lad."

After another silence, Aunt Cat, thinking to introduce the subject of Clarissa's marriage yet another time, but by a roundabout route in order to avoid her brother's censure, with a great sigh asked Mr. Rice if he remembered her Bertie, her "dear husband, so gallant and handsome," a younger brother who had gone to help put down the rebellion in America and had fallen in a distant battle called Cowpens—"such a funny name for a battle."

"Perhaps a strange name for a battle," responded Mr. Rice, "but it is also a famous battle—a double envelopment, a feat that has been accomplished only a few times since Hannibal encircled the Romans at Canae."

Five amazed pairs of eyes turned on Mr. Rice.

"Beg pardon, sir?"

Four pairs of eyes shifted to Nettie with unspoken condemnation.

"A double envelopment, my dear. Banastre Tarleton in command of cavalry and foot soldiers was pursuing the Americans, when their commanding general—a chap named Morgan, I believe—decided to stand and fight at a meadow called Hannah's Cowpens. Some of our own generals like to lay to luck all the battles the Americans won, but there was some brilliant soldiering

224

by the Johnny Rebs, and this was one of those times."

"I'm sure that was the case, Mr. Rice," interposed Mrs. Rice. "Now . . ."

"Yes, and in this case all the more amazing because the Americans were retreating; they were fighting a *defensive* battle, you see. Now, in a double envelopment, both flanks of an enemy are enveloped while the center is held . . ."

Aunt Cat suddenly came to life. "Really, Giles, I think it most unfeeling of you to dwell so long on the battle in which my poor dear Bertie lost his life! It may be terribly interesting to you — the advances and retreats and double whatevers and flanks and centers, but to me war is something quite different — quite different indeed." She scooped up Little Pug and cuddled him in her lap for comfort.

Mr. Rice, immediately sorry he had forgotten his sister's sensibilities, coughed and said, "There, there now, Cat. You're quite right, of course. Terribly thoughtless of me."

Aunt Cat was never one to give over an attack easily. "Just think," she said, a faint tremor creeping into her voice, "how you would feel had Peter been killed at Waterloo. I can tell you — it would be quite a different thing indeed, all this interest in things military."

"Now, Cat, I've admitted you are right and apologized, and I will keep my mouth tight closed for the rest of the evening. What more can I do?"

"Come, Catherine," Mrs. Rice added, with her usual brisk address. "Your Bertie is long gone; your brother has apologized, and we are free to pursue whatever topic you prefer." It was a mistaken invitation, as she soon realized.

Another sigh was fetched up from the deeps of Aunt Cat's ample bosom. "My Bertie was all that a young girl could ask for. But I'm sure that if I had not met Bertie—who was so suitable in every way, so completely acceptable to my family—that I would have been completely willing to marry a man chosen by my father. It is only an accident that we happen to fall in love with the proper person for marrying."

Mrs. Rice, who had married for the perfectly sound reason that Mr. Rice was a perfectly proper person to marry, and whom she had always regarded with affection if not with love, saw no reason to contradict her sister-in-law. She offered a noncommital murmur.

Mr. Rice pretended he had not heard. His opinion of their rake of a father was not high, and that he had had any qualification for choosing spouses for his children was too ludicrous to discuss.

Clarissa, however, was not willing to allow her aunt's remark stand unchallenged. "How can you be so unfair, Aunt Cat?" She impatiently jabbed her needle in and out of the embroidery she was working. "You married for love; you're always saying so, yet you don't think it matters whether I even like that odious old man."

Mr. Rice, irritated out of his resolve of silence, looked as stern as he knew how to do. "I will not have any more squabbling on this subject in my presence."

Nettie, emerging from one of her seeming abstractions, exclaimed, "I would *never* marry for anything but love! I think Clarissa is absolutely right. Why . . . why . . . marrying a man without love would be like living with . . . with . . . your brother for the rest of your life." Nettie then bethought herself and amended, "I don't mean I don't love my brothers, but it's sort of a respect-love — well, not respect in the case of Jonathan and William — but it's very dull, whereas love, I mean real love, is exciting and consuming and, well . . ." Nettie's voice trailed off and she dropped her eyes before the amazed gaze of her parents, her aunt, and her older sister. "I know I'm not saying it very well, but you all know what I mean — Aunt Cat was just saying of my Uncle Bertie . . . well, you know what I mean," she ended lamely.

Her four elders were all thinking along exactly similar lines: that it was time that Nettie learned a few facts of life. Living with a husband was not quite like living with a brother, whether there was love or not. But Clarissa put down her embroidery and, going to Nettie's chair, hugged her, and whispered, "You are my very dearest friend."

Polly replaced the brush and comb on her little dresser, blew out her candle, and assumed her favored attitude of repose and thought in her chair by the window. She gazed thoughtfully across the parks toward Moregreen. She really must have a talk with Nettie. But what could she say? How would she explain the relationship called love — which she wasn't sure she understood — and the act that sprang not only from lust, or from love, but from the prosaic suitabilities of begetting heirs and leading an upright life? She suspected that Nettie was feeling the same love-longings with which she had so long been plagued, and that had made her so susceptible to the kisses and caresses of Dom Felipe, and that young officer, and . . . oh, well. And that amazing episode by the stream! She simply

227

must talk to Nettie.

She found an opportunity the following evening, as they sat alone in their mother's dressing room working at one of the tasks associated with one of their mother's everlasting charities.

"Nettie," she began, "I can't help noticing that Lord Bolling's affections are becoming fixed on you, despite his obvious attempt to disguise the fact, and it is also impossible to avoid the observation that you are encouraging him."

Nettie started to interrupt, but Polly overbore her. "No, Nettie—I'm sorry to sound censorious, but pray let me finish. And when I have, then you may speak in your defense. I know that it is the custom for girls to wed when they are barely out of childhood, and to much older men—perhaps that is the way nature has intended. But I can't help wondering if you really wish to attach yourself to a man who is fifteen years your elder, and furthermore, without first having some experience in the world. I cannot believe that you seek fortune or a title, so I must presume that you are enamored with the idea of love and of the freedom that marriage permits. I *must* caution you, my dear, that it would be a great mistake to let romance—the idea of romance—cloud your good sense . . ."

"I will not be still any longer!" Nettie cried. "How can you say such things to me? I assure you that I fell in love almost the instant I saw Lord Bolling."

"Oh Nettie, how can one be in love from merely seeing someone?"

"I'll thank you, Polly, not to interrupt me until *I* have had *my* say. Maybe I wasn't in love with him from the first minute, but I certainly found him very attractive and interesting, and the more I know him, the better I like him. I'm not sophisticated like you. A retiring life with Lord Bolling, which wouldn't be much different from the life we lead here, is exactly what I want. Furthermore, what has your sophistication gained for you? You have had your romances, I suppose, but for some reason I cannot understand, have never wanted marriage with any of the men who might have loved you, and now you are marrying, what have you got? A man you don't say you love, but *respect*—a marriage of convenience just like Mama and Papa's . . ."

"But theirs has been a good marriage . . ."

"Don't interrupt me! I'm excited when Lord Bolling walks into the room, I like to look at him, I like to be with him, I love to have him touch me; my—my—my heart even beats faster when he touches me."

Polly, recognizing the signs of various emotions said to be associated with love, was silenced.

"And you—" Nettie continued. "Frederick may be more handsome than anybody, and more sophisticated"—Polly was wearying of the word—"but you haven't anything like Lord Bolling and I have. Just a dull, uninteresting, marriage of convenience! And," Nettie added, lost to all feeling but her anger, "I'll wager it won't be more than a year before Frederick takes up a mistress, so there."

Having crowned her oration with this devastating conclusion, Nettie's anger subsided, and with it the consciousness that her sister was looking very much stricken, and then—with the utmost horror—that a tear was sliding down Polly's cheek and dripping from her chin onto the half-sorted bundle of rags in her lap. Another tear followed, although Polly made no move and no sound.

"Oh, Polly, forgive me!" Nettie dropped to her knees and threw her arms around her sister. "I'm so sorry, my love. I'm so sorry. I was angry. Frederick would never do that."

Polly freed herself gently from Nettie's clasp and searched for her handkerchief to dry her eyes. "There, there, Nettie. Of course you didn't mean it. I'm crying for shame. Just because Lord Bolling would not be to my taste as a husband is no reason he shouldn't be to yours. Goodness, if it weren't so, how would we ever pair off? We must do so, you know, like the animals on Noah's ark." A watery giggle escaped her. "The squire and his wife are the elephants."

Nettie giggled also. She sat back on her heels, and studied Polly's face as she dried her eyes. Nettie's incautious words had been prompted by a conversation with Clarissa the night after the party at Moregreen, a conversation that had worried her ever since. Should she tell Polly?

"What is it, Nettie? Is there something else you want to say? You have my permission to castigate me to your heart's content. I deserve it all for being so pompous."

"It's just something that Clarissa said," Nettie answered, still fainthearted.

"And that was?"

"Well, Clarissa said . . . oh Polly, this is awful! I didn't want to listen, but then I did want to, and then I didn't want to tell you, and I'm still not really sure I should, but I've wanted to tell you for a week now, because . . . well, because . . ."

"Goodness, my head's in a muddle. What *are* you trying to say?"

"Well." Nettie took a deep breath. "Clarissa says she met Frederick in London last year. Her illness quite put her out for this year's season, but she expects that had she been well enough to go about . . . well, this is awful . . . but she intimated that she might be the one engaged to him."

Polly was looking at Nettie in disbelief. "But Frederick gave not the least sign that he'd ever met Clarissa."

"Well, that's true, but Clarissa says that he told her one time when they went riding together that he did remember her, but preferred that you not know it."

"That doesn't sound like Frederick at all, Nettie." Polly was truly puzzled. If she had been asked to describe Frederick's character in one word, she would have said that "honorable" was his most outstanding characteristic. That he was truthful, and blessed (or cursed) with a strong sense of rectitude she had never doubted, and it was in fact these characteristics, which she now believed she had immediately sensed, that had drawn her to him, and was the basis for the respect in which she held him. Yes—respect—whether Nettie thought so or not, surely essential to a marriage. . . . And surely, the passion between them . . . that, with the affection she was certain he felt for her . . .

"Go on," she told Nettie. "I may as well hear it all."

Nettie continued reluctantly. "She also said that after seeing the two of you together, she had come to the opinion that your match with Frederick was only a marriage of convenience and for your sake she hoped that it would end. She said that there was obviously no *love* between you, and that you deserved more. And she

231

also said, oh, Polly, I'm sorry to tell you this; she said that Frederick was known for his beautiful mistresses, and that it would take much more than respect to . . ." Nettie faltered. Clarissa had been very much to the point, and Nettie wondered if her mode of expression might not be just a little vulgar.

"Yes?" Polly prompted. "It would require more than respect to . . . what?"

"To, well, to keep him in your bed. *There,* I've said it. That's all."

The sisters were both silent for a moment. Then Polly said, "I can't understand why Clarissa would talk that way to you. It is really beyond the bounds of all propriety, no matter what the truth may be."

Nettie realized suddenly that she was still sitting on the floor at Polly's feet. She rose and brushed her skirt before sitting down on a nearby chair. "I think it's because she is so unhappy, Polly. Really, she has always been one of my very best friends, and we've always shared everything with each other. Maybe she doesn't quite realize how I've come to love you. You were away so many years."

"Yes," said Polly, rising to pace the room. "I can't think that she could have forgotten that you are my sister unless she was just dreadfully unhappy. Desperation at her situation is surely the answer, surely the reason that she would behave so improperly."

"Do you think so, Polly?" Nettie's face brightened. She and Clarissa had been friends for so very long.

"Yes, I think that must be it. We will pretend that I know nothing about this, and we will behave to Clarissa just as we always have. She needs our understanding — perhaps we can even suggest to Aunt Cat that it would be better not to push for the marriage. But Nettie . . ." She looked fixedly at her sister, and Nettie thought she saw something of her mother's authority peeping from Polly's sober face.

"Yes, Polly?"

"I think it would be best if you told Clarissa, should she attempt to discuss with you again the affairs of Frederick and myself . . . I think you should tell her that you cannot discuss your sister's affairs, even with her."

"But I *didn't* discuss your affairs, Polly! I just listened." Nettie felt like a guilty little girl.

"I know, my love, and you felt mixed up in your loyalties. The way to avoid such problems is to refuse to be drawn into another such discussion, even in the role of unwilling listener."

"But I thought you should *know*," Nettie burst out. "Anybody can see how much Frederick likes you. But I think Clarissa wants Frederick. Haven't you noticed how she flirts with him? And I must say, Polly, the way you laugh and joke with Mr. Chapham is not entirely proper either!"

Polly, who had ceased pacing to stand by the window, and who had been momentarily distracted, as she often was, by some artistic possibility in the scene she was viewing, was wrenched rudely from her distraction. Now here was *another* complication!

She turned to stare at Nettie. "Has Clarissa been saying that my behavior with Alex is improper?"

"No, she's said nothing. I've just been noticing that you seem so friendly with him that if I were Frederick I'd be jealous. I'd certainly be jealous if Clancy behaved that way."

233

"Clancy?"

"Yes, I think of Lord Bolling as Clancy. And he has asked me to call him Clancy when we are alone, although we never are. But I was talking about you and Alex, and I shan't be scolded for speaking of Lord Bolling as Clancy. What about the way you behave with Mr. Chapham?"

"He's an old friend. We knew each other when we were both so young. I was just nineteen when I went to Ghent with Uncle. Alex was as young and green as I was. And in America, my duties as my uncle's hostess sometimes seemed more onerous than I could bear. Alex and his family were so kind to me — and to Uncle. We had such fun at their farm in Pennsylvania, and in the summer at their place in the mountains of Western Virginia among the settlers there. That's where Alex and I learned some of the dance patterns we were teaching you . . . and Alex pays attention to all kinds of people — he thinks nothing of talking to the commonest laborer as though that person were his equal in station and rank — it's the spirit of democracy in America. Alex is just so free and easy with everyone — it's his way — and such an old friend, I hadn't realized . . ."

"Well," said Nettie, having regained a little of her confidence, "I think Mr. Chapham's wonderful, and I agree that he's one of the easiest persons to be around, but *I* don't flirt my eyes at him, and giggle with him under the trees and in corners."

Suddenly Polly laughed. "Have I been flirting my eyes at Alex? Really?"

"Yes, you have, and you know it. And you should stop it right now. You could begin by being more, um . . ." Nettie searched for the word and found it.

234

"More circumspect! So there!"

"Well—" Polly laughed again. "I'll flirt my eyes at Frederick, although what he would say to such simpering I can't imagine." The idea of flirting with Frederick struck Polly as so incongruous that she actually giggled again.

Nettie, happy to see Polly recovering her spirits, laughed too, and the sisters went down to their dinner in the happiest of moods.

Polly reflected lengthily on Nettie's description of her feeling for Lord Bolling, which Nettie, at least, seemed to recognize as that illusive emotion called love: (1) excited when he walks into room, (2) likes to look at him, (3) likes to be with him, (4) loves to have him touch her. At the latter enumeration she proceeded to (5) heart beats faster. Am I? she asked herself. Am I in love?

It had just slipped right into her mind like the imperceptible approach of dawn. There was no bolt out of the blue. She felt absolutely no different than she had the moment before. How was this feeling different from what she had felt for Felipe? There was a sixth point in the enumeration, when it came to choosing a husband. Could she live with the man the rest of her life? Perhaps, technically, this was not a point necessary for love, but it certainly was necessary for marriage!

Well, she must flirt more with Frederick, less with Alex; find more time alone with Frederick . . .

If only Frederick had a little of Alex's dash! He was so *serious!* Only reading *Queen Mab* to discover Shelley's point of view!

235

They were always being interrupted. This very evening — their eyes met constantly across the dinner table, they'd escaped to the dusk of the garden, and then Jonathan and William were scampering around chasing fireflies. She must find a way.

The archery tournament went on, but owing to the accident of pairing Polly and Alex, and Clarissa with Frederick, Polly had less chance than she hoped to flirt. It seemed also that there was never a minute to be alone with Frederick, and for the first time she began to regret the presence of Alex and Lord Bolling, of Clarissa and Aunt Cat, of her sisters and mother. There were simply too many people underfoot at Tanwell. Even her father, even her young brothers, managed to get in the way. Mr. Rice found Frederick a sound conversationalist with sound views on economics, and went out of his way to be hospitable; Jonathan and William were hero-worshipping Frederick along with Alex. They even admired Lord Bolling, for these men engaged in outdoor pursuits as well as indoor (in fact, Jonathan and William had never seen any of them read a book, which is all their father ever did), and had been flattered to be included in an overnight fishing expedition where they actually went out in boats and fished from the middle of a river!

She couldn't even lure Frederick to her side by painting his portrait. The one begun shortly after their engagement, although it remained unfinished, no longer required that the sitter be present. Her painting could nonetheless provide her the opportunity to be alone and Frederick the opportunity to find her alone. She had in any event been longing for her brush.

Polly announced her intentions to her friends as they sat on the terrace drinking tea: that she had been shockingly neglectful of her painting, and would be unable to receive any visitors before one o'clock. She had been eager to paint outdoor scenes—in the orchard, the garden, the fields—before the leaves turned, and while some of the trees were yet laden with fruit and the early fall flowers were in full bloom. So each morning Polly took her paint box and her easel and folding stool to the garden, and each morning she worked alone. Frederick did not take the hint. She lost herself in her work, and did not consciously listen for his footstep, but from time to time an uneasy thought intruded into her concentration. Why didn't Frederick take his opportunity to be alone with her?

As a matter of fact, Frederick often thought of Polly. But each time the impulse came to him to look for her under the trees or among the flowers, he hesitated. Polly's painting was important to her; he should respect her wishes. And in any event, he had been neglecting important work around the estate.

Pursuing their mutual misunderstanding, Frederick and Polly longed to be together, but remained apart.

Chapter Thirteen

The first hints of autumn were in the air—a subtle scent of ripening grain, a cast to the days of a sun retreating to its winter solstice. Alex and Lord Bolling were leaving within the week, and the ball that Frederick had promised to Nettie in the summer would be the final gala of their visit.

The night of the ball found Moregreen lit brilliantly by a great quantity of candles. Every window in the house was aglow, even those in the broad passages that connected the two wings with the main house. Lanterns lit the refreshment pavilion erected on the first grassy terrace in front of the house, and in the formal garden at the back the many lanterns, hung on posts, on trees, and lining the garden wall, left only occasional shadows.

The long drawing room and the dining room, on either side of the great central hall, had been opened by means of sliding doors to form an enormous reception or ball room across the entire front of the house. A stairway rose from the center of the hall to a wide landing, from which two flights on either side ascended to the second floor. The great hall below and the hallways above, which by day were flooded with light from the large arched windows above the landing, were now more softly lighted by the great chandelier. The glass-paned doors, on either side of the central stair, were opened wide to allow passage into the lantern-lit gardens.

Lady Moresby had not found it necessary to invite families from five counties—one county had provided more than enough guests. All the neighbors of any pretension had been invited, and the drawing room, dining room, and great hall were filled with the high and the middle levels of county society, while others of their number sampled punch in the pavilion or strolled in the gardens. In such a crowd neither the Paunceforts nor the Darrows would be able to fix upon Alex and his terrible nationality (in any event, Alex had quite won neighborhood hearts), and the large number of Herbert girls was nicely balanced by the large number of Pendleton-Blockworth boys.

Polly danced the first dance with Frederick, and promised him as many more as he should like. She rapped Alex on the arm with her fan when he proposed they stroll in the garden, and told him sternly that two dances were his limit, and that they would not be teaching any American dances this night.

Frederick, on his part, had deliberately avoided contracting many dances, for in fact he cared to dance with no one but Polly, and also—as he told her, he felt it his duty as host to be available to partner any unlucky girls for whom partners were wanting. Polly suggested he give one of those dances to Clarissa, which she virtuously felt was a demonstration of faith and trust. It was bad luck that one of the two dances promised to Alex was the very one for which Frederick had dutifully engaged Clarissa, and worse luck that it was a waltz, but it was sheer blindness that she failed to note the change in Frederick's demeanor or the stony hauteur that masked his displeasure.

The seemingly small incident had loosed in Frederick a flood of pent-up jealousy. Clarissa, noting his expression, saw the opportunity for which she had been waiting so long, and of which she'd nearly despaired. In the middle of the dance she suddenly swayed toward him, and as Frederick involuntarily tightened his arm about her waist to support her, she drew back and murmured, her head drooping slightly in order to look up at him pathetically from under long lashes, "Do forgive me, Frederick, but I am feeling faint. Perhaps if I could step outside for a moment . . ."

"Of course. Here, take my arm." Clarissa draped herself on his arm and with faltering step allowed herself to be led through the doors that opened onto the garden from the great hall.

"Let me help you to that bench over there," Frederick said solicitously, gesturing toward a well-lighted spot near the doors.

"Let us walk instead. I fear if I do not exercise a bit after leaving the warm room, I shall take a chill."

"Wouldn't it be better that you rest? The exertion of walking . . ."

"Oh, no. I shall be perfectly all right. Walking slowly, with your arm to support me, will restore me. It's just that the waltz requires so much exertion, and one does become dizzy, you know."

241

They slowly paced the length of the garden, and on the third turn, at the end near the latticed arbors on each side of the gate leading to the kitchen gardens, Clarissa suggested that they sit down.

"Are you feeling better?" Frederick asked, still solicitous, but uncomfortably aware that there were no others in the garden.

"Yes, I am no longer so faint, but . . . oh, Frederick . . ." Suddenly Clarissa's voice broke. Was that a tear in the corner of her lovely eye, glistening in the light of the lantern that hung overhead? Whatever it was, Clarissa dashed it away as though in disgust at herself. "Forgive me, I'm a foolish child." She bowed her head and clasped her hands in her lap, wringing them in the most delicately anguished manner.

Frederick had a dizzying moment of déjà vu. Had he not witnessed this scene before?

"I'm afraid I shall cry," she whispered. "Could we not step beyond the gate? I don't want to cry at our last engagement together—the last time I shall be happy." All Clarissa needed to bring a real tear to her eye was to think of the Odious Gentleman who was waiting in London to claim her hand. The real tear fell, and splashed on that delicate appendage, followed quickly by another.

"Oh, please," she breathed on a sob. "Please let's step beyond the gate for a moment—just until I recover myself."

Frederick had no wish to disappear into the dark kitchen gardens with this dangerous young female, but he could hardly deny her in her distress. He gave her his hand, and then his arm, and opening the gate, escorted her through it. Clarissa, without pausing to

242

ascertain whether any other couples had sought the sheltering darkness beyond the garden gate, threw herself upon his chest and burst into a storm of tears. She was crying in earnest now.

There were no benches on which Frederick could seat her and then stand by supplying handkerchiefs, so he had little choice but to hold her in his arms. He was not so dishonest with himself that he denied an unbidden desire to kiss and fondle, even as he sought for a way to extricate himself from the embrace. After all, except for that one trip to London following his engagement, he had been abstinent.

At last he said, taking his arms from around the sobbing creature and putting his hands on her shoulders in order to hold her at a distance while still giving an appearance of concern, "Here now, you have cried enough. I'm sure that if you make it firmly known to your aunt that you do not want to marry the gentleman, she will come around. You can't be forced, you know, to marry against your wishes."

Clarissa's answer was to fling herself back into his arms, and lifting her tearstained face to his, demand in a throbbing voice, "Oh, Frederick, why could it not have been you?"

Her arms went around his neck, twining insidiously, as her willowy form swayed against him. His head went light, and he kissed her.

"Oh, Frederick," she breathed, "I have loved you from the very first moment."

Reality hit Frederick like a cold slap, and a chill went racing up his spine. He pushed Clarissa from him, and then, ever the gentleman, put his hand under her chin, and looked into her shocked eyes. "Forgive me for my ungentlemanly reaction. I should be whipped for kissing you. It meant nothing. I am in love with Polly."

There. He had said it. To himself, to Clarissa, to the world in general. "I love Polly," he repeated.

"You kissed me because you love *me,* I know it." Clarissa actually stamped her foot.

"No, I do not. And you do not love me. You just don't want to marry that other man and are trying to find a way out. But this isn't the way, my dear." Frederick was quickly working out a role as Old Uncle Frederick. "We should never suit. To begin with, I don't like romantic poetry, you see." Noting that Clarissa was preparing to cry again, he quickly dropped any thought of bantering his way out. "We shouldn't suit because, whatever you may have talked yourself into thinking, you don't love me. And I love Polly. You wouldn't want a man who loves another woman."

"You kissed me," Clarissa said accusingly. "I shall tell Polly that you led me out here and kissed me."

"And I shall tell Polly the truth," Frederick said grimly. "The truth is that I kissed you because I haven't kissed Polly enough. And that's something I plan to remedy. Now, let's go back inside."

"I can't go back inside. I look *awful.* My eyes will be all red, and I've torn my skirt, I know, on some horrible bush out here."

Although Frederick could see no tear in her skirt, Clarissa insisted that every woman would notice it as soon as they were in the well-lighted rooms. So with something close to desperation, he put his mind to work on a solution. The retiring room for the ladies was above the drawing room, reached by means of the great staircase. However, they could gain access to it also by entering the passage that connected the kitchen wing with the main house and which gave access to a stairway cleverly concealed in the fireplace wall between dining room and breakfast parlor, and from which the servants could pass unseen from their quarters in the attics above to the kitchen below. When he suggested it, however, Clarissa would not hear of it: with its large serving pantry and commodious cupboards, there would surely be servants working in the passageway, or if in the unlikely event it was deserted, then someone might be in the retiring room and see her with her eyes all red.

Well then, he would bring Polly or his mother to her. She just *absolutely* wouldn't be able to bear that. He then suggested that he take her to the kitchen, and ask the housekeeper if Clarissa could use her sitting room above the kitchen to mend her torn skirt. No, that wouldn't do — it was certain that there would be servants there, including some from Tanwell, and they would gossip. At last Frederick hit upon the idea of fetching a mirror and his mother's sewing box from her dressing room, meanwhile secreting Clarissa in the library at the end of the opposite wing, where she could repair the ravages sufficiently to present herself to public view again.

Several servants were in the kitchen passageway, as Clarissa had insisted they would be, preparing the supper that would be spread beneath the pavilion on the front lawn. Frederick marched by them trying to look as though he were not bent on a nefarious errand. He ran up the servants' stair and, after a quick survey of the hallway, moved swiftly into the open and to his parent's chamber door. It was closed, but fortunately

245

not locked, Lady Moresby (after carefully putting certain items under lock and key) trusting her guests to respect closed doors. Frederick opened the door boldly. Should anyone be within he would simply close the door again with an apology and think of something else, although what else he couldn't think. The room was fortunately empty, and he quickly located the sewing box and a hand mirror in the adjoining dressing room. Another furtive survey of the hallway, a moment's wait until two laughing young ladies disappeared into the retiring room, and he was back down the servants' stair, and reunited with Clarissa, who still stood in the shadows awaiting him. She had been making good use of her time by carefully and surreptitiously ripping loose a ruffle.

Frederick led Clarissa through the bookshelf-lined west wing passageway to the library. He instructed her to stand in the shadows while he checked the room, a lucky precaution, for he intruded on two gentlemen drinking from a bottle holding something much stronger than punch and discussing the latest horseraces at Newmarket. He apologized for the intrusion and led Clarissa instead to a small study which occupied the space that in the opposite wing accommodated the pantry. His luck was holding. The room was empty, and a servant had evidently just replaced the single candle on the small desk between two floor-to-ceiling shelves of estate record books. He drew the curtains, even though he didn't think that anyone would stray so far from the pavilion as to be looking in this window.

"Now, can you manage?" he asked, feeling ungentlemanly, but anxious to escape.

Clarissa prepared to cry again. "Where are you go-

246

ing?"

"Back to the ballroom, of course. There is by now undoubtedly at least one lady who is feeling neglected and probably very angry, and there will soon be two. We've been gone from the ballroom close on half an hour, you know."

"Please don't go." Clarissa favored him with her prettiest pout.

"I cannot stay with you here."

"But what if someone came upon me?"

"They would say 'excuse me,' and promptly withdraw."

"Please, Mr. Moresby, will you guard the door? I *promise* I will be quick. I promise. Please?"

So Frederick found himself again delayed while Clarissa, with an eye on the clock, dallied long enough that she hoped Frederick would miss another dance. I'll fix Polly, she thought grimly. If the engagement is broken, who knew what might happen? And no matter what did, Polly wouldn't have him.

Frederick, fuming outside the door, at last could bear it no longer. He simply had to knock on the door.

"What is it?" came the muffled answer.

"Do you need anything? Are you nearly finished?"

"Just a few minutes more."

She kept her promise, and left the library before another five minutes passed. Frederick was amazed. She looked radiant. There was not a trace of a tear, no reddened nose or eye. He stared.

Clarissa actually thought she might be blushing. "What is it?" she smiled tremulously.

"Nothing. Or, that is, I was promised ravages, but you have emerged ravishing instead." Oh, God, he ad-

247

monished himself, shut your mouth. He clamped his teeth together firmly and vowed to say no more.

Clarissa took his arm as they proceeded down the passageway to make what Frederick hoped would be an inconspicuous entry, and delivered, in a gentle voice, her coup de grace. "Although I am disappointed that I have not engaged your affections, Mr. Moresby, I wish you well. Truly I do. So I will warn you." She stopped him at the door. "I would try a little harder to find out about the relationship between Polly and Mr. Alex Chapham if I were you. You know, of course, that Polly spent most of her time in Brazil with French artists, and I believe that she had a lover there. You may think she's a respectable country girl, but if you question her closely, you will find that she is something quite different."

Frederick merely made a stiff and nearly imperceptible bow. To make such an indelicate accusation against a cousin, the daughter of an aunt and uncle who had shown her nothing but kindness, was so ill bred, so improper, that he was stunned. His training as a gentleman had not yet deserted him, however. He opened the door, Clarissa still on his arm.

But his luck had at last flown. Not only had one partner discovered his absence when he failed to claim the dance promised him, but she was standing near the door with Polly, to whom the dance then in progress had been engaged. Polly had long before noted his absence, and Clarissa's as well, and she was trying to control her annoyance as the lady beside her went on about how she would scold Mr. Moresby when he returned to the ballroom. At that moment the door in front of her opened, and there stood Frederick, with an

248

absolutely radiant Clarissa looking up into his face — actually making calf eyes at him. The lady standing beside her saw them at the same time. "Why there is that naughty Mr. Moresby!" she exclaimed playfully, and then, suddenly aware of Clarissa and recollecting to whom she spoke, she subsided into something very like strangulation. In fact, for a moment she did feel that her breath had been cut off. "Excuse me," she gasped, and departed hastily in the direction of the retiring room to recover herself.

Polly turned away, but Frederick was beside her before she could move, having literally removed Clarissa from his arm, and left her standing, to be claimed by whoever wanted her. His gentlemanly training, as well as his luck, had finally failed him.

"Pardon me, Polly. Miss Knight felt faint."

Polly smiled, but her eyes glittered dangerously.

"It is our dance, I believe," he said.

Polly continued to smile and stepped into his arms. They swung easily into the waltz. Frederick realized that she was ramrod rigid, her muscles so tense that she trembled. She seemed to look into his face, but her eyes were focused somewhere in the vicinity of his nose. He felt his nostrils flare self-consciously and silently cursed. She stumbled and, from sheer necessity, relaxed slightly. They finished the dance without further mishap.

"We are engaged for supper," he reminded her.

"Yes."

Short of making a scene, there was no way that he could follow any one of his several impulses. He could certainly not, at a ball, and in his parents' house, accuse Polly of having had a lover, which seemed the

249

uppermost impulse. Earlier in the evening, he could perhaps have lured her outside for some dallying in the shrubbery, but the present glitter in her eye suggested that a trip to the shrubbery would be more likely to end in disaster and a scene that would embarrass them both, and possibly the guests as well. Whatever he wanted to do—and it was plenty—he was wise enough to know that he should calm himself before straightening out his affairs with Polly, and give her time to calm herself as well.

They moved through the rest of the evening automatically. Frederick maintained an iron control, responding courteously to everyone who spoke to him, dancing dutifully with distressed girls without partners, smoking a Havana cigar in the garden with an old neighborhood chum. Polly was so angry that she was not angry, and was reminded of how, when she was a child with Peter and Gussie, they had pressed hard on their canker sores to make them hurt so much they stopped hurting.

Alex, always alert, did what he could. What a trooper, he thought, as he swung Polly down a country dance. Frederick was twenty different kinds of fool to let that little cheat Clarissa get him outside. Probably tried to seduce him. But just then he looked up and saw such a look of fury on Frederick's face as he watched the two of them, that Alex suddenly had a premonition. Oh, Lord, worse than he'd thought. He sought Frederick out later to test the water, but discovered that he was to get no satisfaction in that quarter. The water was solid ice. Frederick was perfectly polite and pleasant, and reminded Alex that he expected him to call before departing for London. He was so formidably correct that Alex, for once, was afraid to dare.

Nettie had also noticed the absence of Frederick and Clarissa, and managed to find an opportunity to hiss at Clarissa, "You will never be my friend again," under cover of an apparently friendly cousinly exchange. Clarissa merely smiled at her.

The terrible evening finally ended, with the principals still trooping so valiantly that few of the guests were aware that anything untoward had happened. The scandalized lady who with Polly had witnessed Clarissa and Frederick's entry, observing Polly and Frederick dancing together in seeming amity, decided on the spot to seal her lips forever. Sir and Lady Moresby, engaged in their role as hosts, and Mr. Rice in the card room, remained blissfully unaware. Aunt Cat, sitting with the chaperones along the wall, was too much engaged in gossip, and too unobserving in any event, to note the comings and goings of the young people. Lord Bolling, who had eyes only for Nettie, could not help being aware that Nettie was angry with Clarissa, but was in the dark about the cause. Only Mrs. Rice, more perceptive than her matter-of-fact efficiency led others to expect, had made any note of the undercurrents of anger. She had seen Clarissa depart the ballroom with Frederick as she descended the stair from the retiring room, and drew accurate conclusions about the various hostilities she observed in progress during supper.

At last, near three o'clock, the ball was finally over, and by three-thirty the Tanwell family was jolting uncomfortably toward home. The Rice carriage had come along the lane used for communication between the two houses, since it was shorter than by the public road. Tonight this back road was chosen also to avoid the

251

certain traffic jam on the main road as carriages departed. The entire family—the three elders, the three young women, and Francie—uncomfortably crowded, jounced along in silence. Polly was cool to Clarissa, and Nettie, who was simply beside herself, had determined never, ever, to speak to her again. Mr. Rice and Aunt Cat supposed that the girls were too tired to chatter, although Mrs. Rice suspected otherwise. Francie, as though to prove the conclusions of the former two, fell almost instantly asleep, her head on her mother's shoulder.

Chapter Fourteen

Frederick was at Tanwell barely after breakfast asking to see Miss Rice. He knew he was unpardonably early, but he had only with difficulty contained himself from arriving earlier. He knew that the Tanwell household would lie late abed after retiring so near the dawn (with the possible exception of Mrs. Rice), but he also knew Polly to be an early riser. Surely Polly and her mother will be up by eleven o'clock, he told himself, as he dismounted and handed his horse to a groom.

The footman, Robert, showed him into the drawing room, with somewhat less than his usual bright-eyed cheer, having been sent to Moregreen the night before to assist with the serving. Mrs. Rice received him and, after some initial courtesies, left him to cool his heels for a considerable time before Polly, looking militant, arrived.

"Well," she said, fire in her eye and ice in her voice. "You wished to see me?"

Frederick was firmly controlling his temper. He was the one who *appeared* at fault, and he was not going to let his anger prevent him from getting Polly by herself so he could accuse her of having lovers. Although Clarissa had mentioned only one, he had now multi-

253

plied the one to several, and had even given fleeting thought to calling Alex out. The sensible streak in Frederick had immediately vetoed this notion—in fact, he had even chuckled at his own foolishness. Surely Polly would not have been so freely friendly with Alex had he ever been her lover, or were they lovers now. And when would they find the time, anyway, in the whirl of parties and games and sports that had been keeping them all at a gallop since Alex arrived. A sincere apology and a straightforward explanation therefore seemed the best strategy for the opening round.

"I came to explain to you about last night. I don't know what Clarissa has told you, but I can guess that if there was any truth in her story at all, it was much distorted."

"Yes?" said Polly, and sat down, her hands clasped primly in her lap and a politely inquiring look on her face. Frederick had a strong urge to shake her.

"I can't talk to you here." He made an effort to speak calmly. "Polly, listen. This is foolish. I can explain. We are not children to ruin our lives by hasty judgments. Come riding with me. Let's find a quiet spot where we can be alone to talk and where no one will disturb us."

"Considering how some people have been throwing themselves at you, we may have to ride a considerable distance."

"Polly, please."

"Oh, all right," Polly said ungraciously. Then, a little ashamed of herself, she said, in a more civil tone, "I must change. If you will excuse me?"

"Of course." Frederick sat down again and idly picked up a book, to which he gave not a minute's attention. His mind seemed stuck on one theme, which

254

went round and round and round—Polly's lovers, Polly's lovers, Polly's lovers. Her told himself firmly that Clarissa had shown herself to be devious and scheming, that she had mentioned a lover as a means to strike at him for rejecting her advances, that she had long been undermining Polly's character; and then he found himself right back at the same point: had Polly had a lover? Lovers? He could not seem to get himself beyond that point to consider whether it mattered, or what he would do if she had.

Polly's horse, saddled and held by a patient young groom, stood beside Frederick's as they descended the steps in front of the house. They mounted, and silently turned their horses toward Moregreen and the ride that skirted the stream and entered the woods beyond. However, Frederick halted before they had gone more than a few yards and said, "Let's ride out to the meadow above Moregreen. We are not likely to meet anyone there, and there is that old stone wall at the upper end where we can sit and talk."

Polly nodded, and they turned their horses from the path to cross the park and enter the fields behind the Moregreen stables. They let their horses set the pace, and did not speak to each other until they reached their destination.

If Frederick had had room for any thought other than alleged lovers, he might have considered more carefully the possible turmoil in Polly's mind, but because he was not thinking clearly, he made the mistake of supposing that all that was needed for her to forgive him was an explanation of his lengthy absence from the ball in the company of Clarissa, and that he would then be free to play the innocent and righteous accuser. Such attention as he gave to his course of action was devoted to organizing his apology into the most acceptable phrasing.

They dismounted, Polly sliding from the saddle before Frederick could offer to help her. Leaving the horses contentedly grazing nearby, they sat down on the low wall—a section of an ancient stone fence that remained in place only as a token to bygone generations.

"May I explain to you, Polly, about what happened last night?" Frederick asked with a humble air.

"I thought that was the reason we were here."

With this lukewarm encouragement, Frederick recounted the entire episode, not omitting the kiss, and emphasizing strongly the reason for it. His phrasing, although he repeated exactly what he had said to Clarissa about that kiss, was unfortunate, suggesting to Polly's unreceptive mind more a general masculine need for kisses than any specific desire for her kisses. And with characteristic caution, he had omitted any reference to love. While the question of Polly's lovers remained unanswered, how could he go so far as to tell Polly that he loved her? He did not expect that she would melt into his arms after his explanation, but he expected some softening. Instead, and to his considerable surprise, her expression remained as aloof as when she entered the Tanwell drawing room.

"One can hardly blame Clarissa for assuming that you would welcome her advances, considering what passed between you in London, and the fact that you have been encouraging her for the last month to think you were developing a *tendre* for her," Polly stated coldly.

"What? What did you say? What have I been doing?"

"I said that you have been *encouraging* Clarissa, and that—"

"I heard what you said, damn it. And that is certainly an odd way of looking at things. Encouraged Clarissa, did I? That damned little hussy has been using every trick in the book on me. I'd like to know how you think I could have escaped her when you were spending all your time with that damned American."

"Oh! So it's my fault that you were out in the garden for an hour pawing and kissing Clarissa?"

Frederick was so mad he could no longer sit still. He leaped up and strode off a few paces to recover himself, returned, and opened his big guns. "All right, I've told you what happened in the garden and why, and you can believe me or not as you choose. Now, let's have a little explanation from you, my girl. Tell me what you and Chapham have been doing behind my back."

"Behind your back! Well! I should have expected some such nonsensical accusation. But for your information, we've done nothing behind your back! Alex is an old friend. His family was very kind to me in America, and he deserves—and merits—hospitality from mine."

"*Hospitality?* That is amusing. How many other men have you been hospitable to?"

A sudden stillness settled on them—it seemed to Polly as though even the birds, the insects, the wind over the meadow became still. She felt the blood leave her face and her heart constrict. She stood up slowly, and facing Frederick, she said stiffly, "What are you accusing me of, Frederick?"

"I'd like to know a little bit more about your past, I

think." Frederick's voice had become deadly. His eyes were narrowed and his mouth was a hard line. He looked—and felt—quietly murderous. "You are no inexperienced spinster; that was made very clear to me not long ago by your own lips. And if you will pardon my bluntness, by your body against mine."

Polly gasped. It was as her mother said. Men did not expect their wives to show passion. And worse, it was apparently grounds for suspicion if they did. She lost her head completely—no rational arguments from free thinkers, from Mary Wollstonecraft, from American republicans, from French novels, or French artists came to mind. She was as lost to reason as Frederick. "*You* accuse *me*, you monster! How dare you? How dare you? You with your mistresses and whores."

"Mistresses and whores?" Frederick found himself stamping his feet like that silly Clarissa, and set himself in motion for another turn, while Polly yelled at his back, "Yes, mistresses and whores! How many, Frederick? Do you still have one waiting for you in London? And when did you and Clarissa meet in London? You haven't answered that question. Just why were you hiding *that* from me? How—"

This raving was cut off by Frederick grabbing her by the shoulders. He barely restrained himself from shaking her. "I never met Clarissa in London. And I've had only three mistresses, by God, and a whore from a decent house now and then. Now you tell me, madam, just how many men you have been mistress to."

At this speech her rage was so great that she thought something might burst in her head and she would fall over in an apoplexy. But with her rage a cold anger enveloped her. "Take your hands off me."

258

There was such contempt in her voice that Frederick's hands fell to his sides.

She walked to her horse. "Please help me mount, Frederick."

"No, by God. We're going to finish this discussion if I have to drag you back here and sit on you."

"Very well." Polly walked back and sat down on the wall. "I have been mistress to no man, and never shall be." With that she closed her lips firmly. Her eyes did not waver before his demanding stare.

"Just what does that mean? I'll be damned if I understand you."

"Well, I understand you. Your ideas are not advanced at all. I was completely mistaken about you. Mary Wollstonecraft was right. Marriage, as practiced in England, is a form of slavery. And I've seen enough of slavery in America and Brazil to know its horrors."

"And just what does that mean? My ideas may not be as advanced as yours, but by God, I càn speak to the point."

"Very well. To the point. Slavery means all rights belong to the master, none to the slave — that the slave is owned body and, if the master chooses, body and soul. Fortunately, I have a choice; I can become a slave or I can remain free. I thank you, Frederick, for helping me choose. I choose freedom."

Polly arose, straightened her skirts, and went to her horse. She led it to the wall. 'You needn't help me mount, thank you." She reined her horse around and looked down at Frederick. "Our engagement is broken," she said.

Frederick was now as angrily calm as Polly. "A wise decision," he snapped, and turned away to his own horse. Polly was off at a recklessly hard gallop before Frederick was mounted. He did not follow her, nor turn his own horse toward Moregreen, but headed for a lane that bordered a long field and then joined a country roadway where he, too, could ride hard and fast and dissipate some of his anger.

Polly handed her heated horse to a groom, and said, "Please rub her down well. I've given her a hard ride, I'm afraid."

She entered by the kitchen door, intending to search out her mother to tell her — quite calmly — that she had broken her engagement to Frederick, but was met instead by the cook, who the minute she saw Polly, cried, "Oh, Miss Polly, the most terrible thing! Miss Clarissa has run away!"

"Run away!" Polly's first thought was an irrational sense of relief. She would not have to face the child, pretending nothing was amiss, or — should she feel another way about it, when she began to feel again — give her a scolding she would never forget, a scolding such as Aunt Cat should have administered long ago, she thought nastily. Then reason prevailed, and she repeated, "Run away? Where is my mother? I must find Mama immediately."

By following her ears she soon found the more distracted of the household. Aunt Cat, emitting loud wails, had collapsed on a sofa in the drawing room, where Francie was chaffing her hands. Little Pug, cowering beneath the sofa, whined in unison with his mistress. A bottle of smelling salts lay on the floor, some of its contents scattered on the rug and imparting a pungent odor to the room.

Nettie, on her knees attempting to gather the spilled salts together, turned a stricken face to Polly. "You know about Clarissa? Oh, Polly, it's my fault. I scolded her last night and called her a—a—a—cheap flirt."

"Well, so she is," Polly replied bracingly, "but I doubt that your calling her one is the reason she ran away." Now that she was no longer facing Frederick with her blood up, his explanation seemed likely true—in fact, Polly was convinced that it was true. But, of course, that wasn't what mattered. . . .

Aunt Cat wailed from the sofa, "I can't think why Nettie would call Clarissa such a thing. And Polly agreeing! Such a terrible thing to say of my sweet girl. If anything has happened to her, I will just die. Oh, dear, I don't think I can support it!" Aunt Cat prepared to swoon once more, but Mrs. Rice, who had entered during this speech, said sharply, "Do sit up, Catherine, and stop being foolish. Whatever Nettie may have had to say to Clarissa and for whatever reason, it is your fault, and to some extent Giles's and mine that she has run away. If you will sit up, you will feel much stronger. Polly, ring for tea—or no, coffee and a spot of brandy will be better. And put Pug out. His whining is distracting. Now, Catherine, I'll read Clarissa's note to you again."

Mr. Rice came in as Francie and Nettie were helping Aunt Cat to sit up. And behind him was Lord Bolling.

"Clancy!" exclaimed Nettie, forgetting formal address. She had actually forgotten, in the excitement of Clarissa's departure, that it had been agreed between them the previous evening that he would call in the morning—this morning—to request her hand of her

261

father!

"What is this, Mr. Rice?" Mrs. Rice asked in some consternation.

"You will forgive me," said Lord Bolling, "for intruding at such a moment, but I encountered Mr. Rice in the hall, and d-d-d-d- . . ."

Mr. Rice took over. "The thing, is, my dear, that this young man has come to claim Nettie's hand, but having heard of the uproar from a groom — really, it's shocking how fast news travels among the servants — in any event, as I was saying, having heard of Clarissa's sudden mysterious departure, he immediately claimed the right to assist us in this emergency in light of his, um, love for Nettie, due to which he feels that our problems are very much his problems."

"Oh, sir," wailed Nettie, mortified at this public announcement of her affairs, and all mixed up with the affairs of that unconscionable flirt besides.

"There, there, child. I have given my permission."

As Nettie went to Lord Bolling, he strode to her, and took her hand. Polly felt her heart constrict again, and thought that really, it was a hard day for her heart, indeed. She could scarcely bear to look at the besotted pair.

Nor could Aunt Cat. "I do think," she declared "that when my child may be in danger, alone on the road, prey to highway robbers and to pushing men, and to goodness knows what fate, that we might be thinking of something besides engagements."

Mrs. Rice, at this reminder of the really serious matter that confronted them, said, "Forgive us, Catherine. We are, of course, happy for Nettie, and in our surprise have forgotten momentarily. I and, I am sure, Mr. Rice will be grateful for Lord Bolling's help, and with your permission I will read Clarissa's note, and you can perhaps help us guess where we might begin our search."

"Happy, ma'am, to be of service," Bolling said.

Mrs. Rice thought privately that Bolling was not likely to be much more help than Mr. Rice, but she smiled at him kindly and opened the note.

"Dear Nettie," the note began. "I address this note to you as one of my dearest and oldest friends, despite your anger with me. I am going away to seek shelter with a friend who I know will welcome me. Despite all my protests, Aunt Cat and my guardians insist that I must marry an odious man, and if I do not, they threaten me by telling me I shall receive no dowry when I do wed. I will, of course, have control of my own fortune in another seven years. In the meantime I prefer to live in poverty, to marry a poor man, if, undowered, I must, than to marry a man I neither love nor respect, and who indeed is totally repulsive to me. As my circle of friends is known to Aunt Cat, I suppose that I will soon be found in my sanctuary, but I would have you warn her that if I am brought back and further urged to marry That Man, I shall only run away again, and that I shall run to a place where I cannot be found. I will not marry That Man. Forgive me, Nettie, for stealing your pocket money, and ask Aunt Cat to forgive that I stole from her reticule. I have never stolen so much as a sweet before in my life, and so you may know how desperate I am. At all events, I shall repay you and Aunt Cat as soon as I am able. Please forgive, your distracted Clarissa."

A silence, except for Aunt Cat's snuffling, followed the reading of this testament.

"She seems very d-determined," said Lord Bolling. "Now, if I may suggest a course of action?"

"Do, please," said Mr. Rice.

"P-perhaps Miss Knight's aunt can tell us with whom among her friends she might be most likely to shelter. And if you, sir, or Mrs. Rice, or someone in the household knows the time of the stage d-d-departures from various points nearby, and if you are w-willing to take Mr. Chapham and Mr. Moresby into your confidence, we can the three of us pursue the d-different d-d-d- . . ."

"Directions," Nettie said gently.

"Thank you, my dear," Lord Bolling said fondly (giving Nettie's parents and sisters an instant vision of the future), "and since we will be on horseback we can have c-confidence in one of us overtaking her. She cannot have had more than a few hours' start."

"Yes," Mrs. Rice said. "We didn't return from the ball until nearly four . . . an hour for preparations while she waited for all to be asleep . . . it is now twelve. That's nearly seven hours, but we must assume that she walked to the stage, since there are no horses missing from the stables. So that would make only six hours' head start."

"It's my opinion," offered Mr. Rice, "that this escapade is more for show than seriously meant. I expect we will easily overtake her. My guess is that she took stage in the village for the town of Ifford, where she will

264

have a choice of stages to the north and west this morning, and this afternoon to the south and east. Rather than waste time waiting for Frederick, I suggest that I accompany Lord Bolling to the village, and with Mr. Chapham we shall surely have a sufficient search party."

"*You*, Mr. Rice?" exclaimed Mrs. Rice.

"And why not, my dear? You have perhaps forgotten that I was once a hell-for-leather young fellow, and although I am no longer young, I still sit a horse well enough and have a certain endurance. Rest assured, however, that if the chase seems long, I shall leave it to the younger pursuers."

Polly offered a silent thank-you to her father for eliminating Frederick from this chase; it would have been simply too humiliating to involve him in an intimate family affair when they were no longer engaged and the family had no claim on his time or interest. And on top of everything in an affair involving Clarissa. It would have been the outside of enough!

Francie was left to attend Aunt Cat — of all of them she had the most soothing touch and, being innocent of all knowledge of Clarissa's intrigues, was better suited to the task than either Polly or Nettie.

With the men preparing to retrieve the truant, and Aunt Cat momentarily soothed, the time had come for Polly to tell her mother of the broken engagement. However, first she must tell Nettie how pleased she was that Lord Bolling had declared himself.

As they shut the door quietly behind Francie and Aunt Cat, Polly turned to Nettie and hugged her. "Oh, Nettie, I'm so happy for you. What a shame that such a wonderful event should be temporarily overshadowed by this emergency."

Mrs. Rice gave her daughter a kiss and a small smile. "I'm not sure I approve your marrying a man so much older, my dear, although it is so often done. I've sometimes thought, considering that we are so much longer lived, that it should be the other way around—that women should marry boys, rather than men marry girls." Both Polly and Nettie stared at their mother, and she laughed and said, "But come, I am happy for you, Nettie, and since I have raised you to be a sensible girl, I trust that you have made a sensible choice."

"Thank you, Mama," Nettie said as she hugged her mother.

The time had come for Polly to make her own announcement. It would do no good to wait for a more propitious time—indeed, what time more propitious than now, when a new engagement balanced a broken one?

"Mama, I wish to speak to you a minute. And you too, Nettie, if you will?"

"Why yes, child," answered her mother. "What is it?"

"Could we sit down, please? And someplace where servants aren't likely to intrude."

Her mother gave no hint of surprise, but Nettie cast her a look that Polly could not interpret. "Let's go in the library," her mother suggested.

When they were seated, Polly informed them both, with at least an outward show of calm, that she and Frederick had agreed that it would be better to break their engagement.

Nettie reacted with vehement negation. "No, Polly! You can't! You shouldn't! Oh, what have you done?"

Mrs. Rice was less dramatic than Nettie, but no more willing to accept the announcement. Because she had been aware of the undercurrents during the previous evening, and having eyes in her head, she suspected that Clarissa had been much at fault. Go easily, she cautioned herself, and consider carefully before making a reply. "Are you sure, Polly, that you have been entirely sensible?" she asked at last.

"I assure you, Mama, it is much the best thing. It was a mistake. Both Frederick and I have had misgivings from the very first. After so many years of independence, I don't believe marriage would suit me; I shall be much happier unwed." Polly saw a disposition to argue rising in her mother's eyes, and added, "And, forgive me, ma'am, I'll appreciate it very much if you will not fuss at me."

"I do not intend to fuss at you, Polly. However, permit me to say this. I think you have made a hasty decision that both you and Frederick will regret, and I trust that one of you, when your anger has cooled, will have sense enough to know it. That is all I will say. Now." She pushed her hair purposefully under her cap. "It's time I attend to the day's duties. The cows still give milk, the hens continue to lay eggs — although very few after the August heat; there are several bushels of early apples to be prepared for drying, and we all will still be hungry by dinnertime, despite broken engagements, offers of marriage, and runaway girls." With this, their mother left them, and Polly was alone with Nettie, who showed no inclination to refrain from fussing.

"Oh, Polly!" she cried, before Polly could also get to the door and escape. "How *could* you?"

"It was very easy. And I assure you, Frederick made no argument. I am telling you again, Nettie, that it is for the best, and it is what Frederick and I both want.

267

Now I'll thank you to say no more."

Nettie was vacillating between regret that she had suggested that Clarissa was trying to become Polly's rival, and annoyance that Polly hadn't used the information sensibly. "Oh, it's all my fault! If I hadn't told you what Clarissa said, this would never have happened. How could you *be* so foolish, Polly—I told you to warn you. Why didn't you *listen* to me?" Then another painful memory returned, and her hands flew to her cheeks. She covered her face in shame. "And I'm responsible for Clarissa running away. I was so mad at her I just told her she was a cheap flirt, and it was pretty low of her to make trouble for you when she was a guest in our house. I've just made a muddle of everything!"

Polly was thoroughly exasperated, but she controlled her annoyance with Nettie, wisely recognizing that she was not quite herself at the moment. "No, Nettie, you have not been responsible. It's Clarissa and Frederick and I who are responsible, not you. You told Clarissa nothing that wasn't true. She has behaved very badly, but in her favor we must recognize that she was probably desperate and grasping at any solution to escape a marriage she did not want. When she returns, we will treat her as our cousin and friend, with no accusations."

"I'll find it very hard to do."

"And so shall I. But we must. Now, I think you should go and relieve Francie, who may be reaching the end of her patience with Aunt Cat. I'll change, and then I'll come down to relieve you. All right?"

"All right." Nettie sighed. "What a dreadful task we have before us! I do hope that Clarissa has not managed to get far away. And that she's not done something

268

foolish. I couldn't bear it if she were in danger."

"I doubt that she is," Polly reassured her. "Now run along, and I'll join you shortly."

A messenger arrived just after their dinner, bearing a sealed note from Mr. Rice to his wife. Mrs. Rice opened it and read:

"My dear wife,

You may convey the facts I am about to communicate to you, but not the sense, which latter is one of high irritation. Clarissa was seen at the inn in the village awaiting the stage, and known to all who saw her as 'the Rice's young niece.' Several of the good villagers took it upon themselves to tell her that she should not be traveling unescorted and, in fact, had finally made up their minds to send a delegation to Tanwell to inform us of her escapade just before the young men and I made our appearance. She was equally identifiable— her person and her countenance, although not her connections with us—at the posting inn at Ifford. She made no attempt at disguise, and I would say had rather called attention to herself than maintained the modesty of manner and reserve that one might expect of one who hoped to remain undetected. But enough. I write in haste to tell you that I have determined to accompany young Chapham and our future son-in-law Bolling in their pursuit of our wayward niece. Considering that she is a silly chit indeed, I think it wise that I be of the party when the quarry is taken. Do not expect us before tomorrow; we shall not undertake a return journey without rest. I am, Madam, your Devoted Husband."

As if to prove the old adage that it never rains but it pours, Polly received a visit that same afternoon that caused her much agitation. She was sitting with Aunt Cat, who had fallen into a fitful sleep, when a maidservant cautiously peeped into the room. On Polly's beckoning her to enter, she whispered that a woman was in the kitchen asking for Miss Rice. The maid, who had been born and raised in the town, was uncertain who the woman was, but by the conscious look on the face of young Mary Riggs, that little miss knew very well.

Polly found Martha Riggs waiting for her by the door, her baby in her arms. Polly greeted her courteously, and Mrs. Riggs, after dropping a clumsy curtsy, said, "Can I speak to you, miss? Private like?"

"Of course, shall we step outside? It's cool and pleasant in the garden."

"If you'd just walk along with me to the gate by the orchard, miss. I wouldn't want your mother to see us."

As they walked together down the path, Mrs. Riggs inquired politely for the health of Mrs. Rice and others of the family, after which Polly questioned Mrs. Riggs on the health of her children, and particularly the baby.

"Baby's doing tolerably well, miss. The milk your mother sends made all the difference in the world. And the other children, aside from some coughing—the weather's so changeable in September—are in health."

"Who attends the other two little ones when you are out, Mrs. Riggs?"

"Oh, my Patsy. For all she's only seven, she's right watchful. And," she added proudly, "Gilly, even though he's not yet seven, is near as good. I have good children, as your ma says. I'm truly blessed in that way."

Polly reflected on her brothers, Jonathan and William, ten and eight, who had no responsibilities, and on the differences that a station in life could make to childhood.

When they reached the gate to the orchard, Mrs. Riggs shifted the baby to her other arm, and then back again, and finally, unable to find other occupation, began nervously.

"I don't rightly know if I should tell this to you, miss, unmarried like you are. But your ma won't pay any attention to me, and I couldn't go to your pa, him being a man and all. And I heard you was to be married soon, so you will be learning what's expected of a married woman. I suppose it's the same among the gentry as with us."

From this introduction and from her previous acquaintance with Martha Riggs, Polly easily guessed to what the visit pertained. "I assure you, Mrs. Riggs, that you need have no reserve. You may speak freely with me. My mother has told me that she has explained to you the use of a small sponge."

"Oh, miss, I'm so glad I'm not wrong in speaking to you on such a subject." Despite her relief, a deep flush darkened her face. She looked off across the field to avoid Polly's eyes. "The thing is, miss, this babe is near three months now, and since my milk's dried up, I'm even more likely to get in the family way than usual. A suckling babe never kept me from catching afore, so now I ain't suckling . . ."

271

"Is your husband forcing his attentions on you so soon, Mrs. Riggs?"

"Oh, la, miss, that's some way of saying it!" Mrs. Riggs laughed bitterly. "I'm hardly out of childbed afore that man is 'forcing his attentions.' I shouldn't say it, but it was a terrible day for me when I gave in to him. I was just a girl, miss, and crazy to know a man. I didn't know any better. And when my old dad found out I was carrying, I thought he'd kill me. But he was a strong man, miss, a mighty man. I guess the only man Mr. Riggs was ever afeared of. My dad made Riggs marry me. That was a terrible day too. I'd rather 'a bore the child alone and raised a bastard than the life I lead now. But ain't it funny, now — out of that evil man has come my darling good children."

Polly was so overwhelmed by this tale that she did not know what to say, so she offered to hold the baby instead. But Mrs. Riggs, once launched, needed no encouragement. Nor did she need sympathy now she was recovering her strength and her baby gaining in vigor. Life was hard, but suffering was the lot of most of the world. She no longer prayed that Mr. Riggs would desert her, as her neighbor's man had, and she was now entering a stage in life when she could have hope of her children as a defense against an abusive husband. More than one son had turned on his father to defend his mother, and her Robbie was getting to be a big boy. "You see, miss, I just told Mr. Riggs that I'm going to use that thing Mrs. Rice told me about, whether he likes it or not. I told him I ain't going to bear another child to have it die — like this one would have, if it hadn't been for Mrs. Rice. And I ain't going to lose my health, or maybe die, and leave my young ones to his

272

mercy. I told him he could look where he pleased and welcome, but if he comes in my bed, I'm going to have the say-so."

"Was he very angry?"

"Oh, my. Knocked me down, he did. 'Think I want all these brats?' he kept yelling. I couldn't help but laugh, miss. If it's my fault, then he shouldn't care if I use that thing. But I didn't laugh long. He's got no sense, miss. Now he's threatening terrible things against Mrs. Rice. Says she's made me defiant, and the thing is sinful. He's talking among the other men, and I'm downright afraid for her, miss."

"Oh, surely, Mrs. Riggs, angry as he may be, he would not physically attack my mother."

"Oh, I don't think he'd do anything open, but something sly, some harm to her, or to you, or to her livestock. But he's a terrible man in anger, and we can't trust that he mightn't actually injure her if his anger overcame him. It's the way she talks to him, and that angers him awful."

"Thank you for your warning, Mrs. Riggs." Polly handed the sleeping baby to its mother. "I'll speak to my father tomorrow. I'm sure he will think of something."

"Thank you, miss. I could never forgive myself should I cause your ma harm. She is a good, kind lady, and many's the ones who say so, but this business, miss, it don't set right with some people, even some of the women."

"Don't worry anymore, Mrs. Riggs. I'll warn my mother and speak to my father."

"Won't do any good to warn *her*. I've done that."

"Very likely you are right. Well, as I said, don't worry. My father will think of something."

273

Polly returned to the house in a state of frustration. She could not speak to her father until the following day; she could not vent her anger toward Clarissa; a thousand things had occurred to her since morning that she should have said to Frederick. She wanted to cry, but could not indulge that desire until she could attain the privacy of her bedroom at the end of the day. Aunt Cat tried her patience unmercifully. Nettie persisted in discussing her folly. She had lost Frederick, just as Nettie, and her mother, had warned — flirting too much with one man, too wanton with another. It didn't help that Frederick in his anger, as in his passion, had given her a hint that there was something, perhaps not dash exactly, but something waiting to flare beneath his consistently calm and controlled exterior and his careful and judicious opinions. Her spirits fell to such lows that she thought she could not endure. But endure she must; so she scolded herself roundly, and then went in to her mother to inquire how she could be useful. She said nothing, however, of Mrs. Riggs's warning.

By three o'clock that afternoon, Moregreen was in nearly as much turmoil as Tanwell. Frederick rode up to the stables shortly past one o'clock, but his horse was so lathered, and his expression so forbidding, that the groom who received the horse was too frightened to impart the exceedingly interesting gossip that had arrived from Tanwell. Frederick strode into the house and, as luck would have it, encountered his mother just emerging from the dining room, where she had been occupied in returning to their places various small articles that had been removed to safety during the ball.

274

One look at his face was sufficient to tell her that something was wrong, and she said, with some fright, "What is it, Frederick?" imagining Sir Harry found in a ditch with at the very least a broken leg, and soon to be borne into her presence on a litter.

"Polly and I have just broken our engagement, and I want to hear not one word about it. Is that clear?"

Her first reaction was relief that her husband was still in one piece, followed instantly by motherly disapproval of her son. *"Broken your engagement?* What foolishness have you been up to?" Lady Moresby had not the least notion of taking orders from a son, even one who had attained thirty-two years.

"I am going upstairs to pack for London and will be leaving immediately. If you will excuse me, ma'am."

"Frederick, you come back here this minute!" his mother said in a voice she had not used since he was sixteen.

Frederick turned on her. "I'll thank you to mind your own affairs. I won't be questioned by you, or by anyone else. This is my business, and I won't have meddling. No matter how much you might have connived to get me to marry that woman, it has done you no good, and it will do you no good to scheme to get me to apologize. I wouldn't marry Polly Rice if she were the last woman on earth!" By the time this cliché had fallen from his lips, Frederick was shouting. His mother had gone white; her lips were parted and her eyes were wide with horror, while both hands clutched a Dresden mandarin to her bosom. They stared at each other for a moment, and then Lady Moresby burst into tears.

"Tears will gain you nothing," Frederick stated coldly, and disappeared up the stairs.

275

Lady Moresby, still clutching the Dresden mandarin, wobbled into the drawing room and sank down upon the elegant Chinese Chippendale sofa. Frederick had not spoken to her so cruelly since he was eight years old. She dried her eyes—it had been merely the shock, she realized—that had made her cry. Frederick had been very angry, either at Polly or himself, and the very violence of his announcement was a glimmer of hope.

Lady Moresby was a kind employer, and always interested in her servants' welfare, their families and affairs, but she never gossiped with them about the interesting doings of her neighbors as seen by their various relatives employed in other houses about the neighborhood. She was equally careful that as little gossip as possible leave Moregreen via the servants by confining disagreements and upsets to private apartments. She realized that every servant in the house must have heard Frederick's announcement of his broken engagement and the horrid, low-bred way he had yelled at her; what she did not know was that every servant in the house also knew that Mr. Frederick the night before had spent the better part of a half hour in the garden with Miss Knight, that she had wept on his bosom, that he had probably kissed her, that Miss Rice was hopping mad, that Miss Knight had run away sometime in the middle of the night, and that Mr. Rice and the two young gentlemen from Crossfield Cottage had gone off to bring her back. Nor did Lady Moresby know that two and two had been added up very quickly to make five, or in this case, possibly five and five multiplied to make twenty-five. Whatever the sum, it was certainly mounting up to an interesting day all around in the servants' quarters.

Frederick was out of the house in half an hour, without a word to his mother, who had wisely retired to the small sitting room where she was pretending to read a book. She had already discovered that it would be impossible to control her impatience while waiting for Sir Harry to come in from somewhere on the estate. As she stared at the book, occasionally turning a page for effect, she tried to remember exactly what he had said he intended to do that day. She had been reading a letter when he put down his newspaper and said, "Well, Eleanor, I'll be . . ." Then he had said, ". . . and I should be back in time for dinner." From long habit she had heard what was essential she hear (he would be back in time for dinner), and that was all she had heard. What was the middle part of that sentence? She tried again. "Well, Eleanor, I'll be — — — — — — this morning, see — — about a cow that Frederick — —, and I should be back in time for dinner." Very well, Harry was going to see a man about a cow — apparently at Frederick's request; he should be home in time for dinner, so he was neither going a long distance nor a short distance. Now, someone about a cow, and at intermediate distance, and for Frederick. She repeated the sentence again, and this time managed two more words: "driving over." So he would be driving, not riding, and he would be driving over, not up or down, and that must mean he would be on his way to the Herberts — now she was on his trail all right — for the Herberts were the most enthusiastic dairy farmers in the county, except for Frederick. Lady Moresby pulled the bell rope, and soon had sent a footman scurrying to the stables with instructions to saddle her horse. She sum-

277

moned her maid, ran upstairs to change to riding gear, and was downstairs and out the door in the record time of twenty minutes. Even if she missed Harry, she was at least doing something, and if she didn't meet him on the road within half an hour, she would turn around and be home in time for dinner herself.

But as she cantered sedately around the bend that skirted the Masden copyhold, she sighted Sir Harry just topping the rise ahead.

He waved and halloed as she came nearer, and as she reined in beside him, he drew his horse to a stop.

"Well, this is a surprise," he said. "Nothing amiss, I hope."

"Well, I rather fear there *is* something amiss." She quickly reassured him that no lives were in danger (although from the state of Frederick's temper when he was last seen, she feared there were perhaps some limbs in danger), and related her news.

"Well, I'm damned," said Sir Harry.

Lady Moresby dismounted with the assistance of her husband, who tied her horse to the back of the gig and helped his lady up into the vehicle.

As they drove toward home, Lady Moresby gave her husband such details as she could—which were few enough, to be sure. "You know, Frederick hasn't shouted at me like that since he was eight years old," she concluded. "Remember when he wanted to bring his first hunting hound into the house, and I—" Her voice broke.

"Now, now, no tears, old girl. My guess is that the shouting at you was shouting he wanted to, uh, shout at Polly."

Lady Moresby sighed. "I knew that, of course. But

278

oh, Harry, I shall be sorry if they do not make it up. I have become so fond of Polly."

"Well, not much we can do about it, is there? Tell you what. We'll have a nip of that French wine Frederick brought from London. And we won't bother to wait until the sun's over the yardarm either."

Frederick meanwhile was setting a steady pace toward London. He planned to spend the night at the White Ox, some twenty-five miles distant. Although he was still in a stew, his anger was subsiding, and his thoughts running in less repetitive channels. With each new review of his fight with Polly, it seemed more foolish and irrational. Although she could have accepted his explanations and apologies . . . and there he went again, on the same old go-round. Several more miles, and it was more foolish yet. He did love Polly, and he would be very much mistaken in his judgment if she hadn't at least begun to love him. Or if she didn't, he could make her love him. Was he going to blight his life over a misunderstanding?

As for Polly and Chapham, all he could now see in their banter was the easiness of old friends. It had been so open, so devoid of suggestion, of anything hidden, that Polly's assertions could only be true. Contrasted with Clarissa's insinuations, her suggesting glances and studied attitudes, it now seemed all innocence. He had let jealousy interfere with judgment.

Recollection of Clarissa led to a byway: Polly had accused him of knowing Clarissa in London, of "something passing between them." Now, where in blue blazes did she get that idea? Had Clarissa been telling Polly lies—insinuating that they had met previously? Well, in fact Clarissa did claim they had, he remembered . . . that night when Polly and Chapham taught them that American romping cotillion. Which he had only half believed, since he had absolutely no memory of any previous meeting. Clarissa said he'd danced with her at a ball. Perhaps he had—Lord, how could he remember every green chit he'd danced with since he first went to town? But certainly nothing had happened between them. Clarissa had obviously fabricated some tale, or at least hinted at something to Polly. Should he put any credence, then, in Clarissa's hints of shadowy lovers in Brazil? Brazil, of all places!

But now the evil thought had once again popped up. Polly had said she had been mistress to no man and never would be. Did that mean she denied lovers? "Oh, to hell," Frederick muttered aloud. Did it matter? Perhaps he should read this Wollstonecraft woman. Was marriage slavery? If he considered his father and mother, or Polly's parents, it didn't seem so. In those two well-regulated households there was an easy companionship, a sharing of responsibilities, respect between the parties.

But take the Holstead-Evans case. Martha Holstead-Evans had been married off to that rake the Earl of Cornwellan when she was a mere fourteen or fifteen. After the marriage there were two, or was it three, babies, almost literally on each other's heels. Enough in any event to ensure the succession. Then he deserted her, left her at one of his country estates with the children, and set up housekeeping with his mistress. Gossip had it that his wife had finally taken a lover, for although her husband had deserted her (in actual fact, even if technically he still provided her support), and although he lived openly with another woman, she could not divorce him. One infidelity on her part, however, was sufficient for him to divorce her on the grounds of criminal conversation. She'd been in her early twenties when she made her desperate bid for freedom, if he remembered correctly. What had happened to the countess anyway? It was his first year at the university, a long time ago, and he'd not have remembered even that much of the ancient scandal, except that a friend's older brother knew one of the lady's brothers.

Remembering Martha Holstead-Evans put Frederick on a different plane of thought entirely. He had not been a thoughtless or dissipated young man, but he'd been wrapped in cotton wool for years. That time when his friend Hastings was trying to interest him in causes and talked him into visiting that foundling hospital . . . hadn't the countess been one of the directors? Or a relative of hers? Hastings had sent him off on that visit accompanied by a young lady philanthropist whom he remembered as one of the most beautiful women he'd ever met. His heart had not really gone out to those infants, some of them collected from gutters and rubbish heaps and back alleys, where destitute or gin-ridden newly parturant mothers abandoned them. His attention had been all for the woman he accompanied. He'd been much more interested in trying to flirt with her, to animate her beautiful face with laughter . . . to distract her from her dedication. . . .

That brought him back to Polly, who although certainly not such a classic beauty, was blessed with a sweetly charming face and a sparkle that arrested the attention. Dash it all, he had probably been in love with her from the very first, even while they were both pussyfooting around pretending to be so rational in the arranging of their lives.

She had been pretending too, he realized in a burst of insight. There had been passion there that she'd concealed until that moment by the stream. And he'd been such a stick since Chapham had appeared out of the wilderness, behaving so correctly while all the time sulking with jealousy—and envy too, when he got right down to it. He'd envied Chapham for Polly's smiles, but had been too stiff to encourage them for himself.

By this time, Frederick had brought his horse to a walk, and was not making any great progress at all, at least toward his destination. It would be nightfall before he arrived if he didn't get jogging. He urged his horse to a faster pace. He had almost—but not quite—worked himself into the notion of turning around and going home.

He was well known at the inn, for he often broke his journeys there, and because he always tipped well, he was liked and served with cheerful readiness. By the time he was fed and had settled down by the small fire to drink a good French brandy that the innkeeper kept for him and a few other favorites, Frederick was not only ready to go home, but ready to forgive most of Polly's sins and all of his own.

Chapter Fifteen

While Frederick sat by his fire, Clarissa was facing her uncle in the private sitting room of another inn a good many miles away.

Mr. Rice might think Clarissa a silly chit, but then, Mr. Rice was accustomed to silly chits, having four daughters, and he had discovered that even silly chits are often susceptible to kind and reasonable words. Of course, in the case of his daughters the governing influence was his good wife, not his silly sister Cat, but it would do no harm to begin with Clarissa as though she had some sense, and if such should not be the case, he could change his tactics easily enough.

There had been no doubt that Clarissa was the young woman who ostlers and yard boys, innkeepers and guests had seen entering the northbound stage. Once the next stops on the line were discovered, and schedules checked for any possible connections where she might transfer to another coach, they could set off with reasonable assurance that they would soon overtake her. They inquired carefully at each stop and the one transfer point they passed before they saw the stagecoach in the distance, but the answer was always the same. "Aye, a pretty girl, yellow hair, yes, yes, a light blue pelisse, matching bonnet. Unattended, yes. Yes, she got back on the stage with the other passengers."

Mr. Rice now settled back with his brandy — a slightly more robust brandy than the one favored by Frederick — and looked at Clarissa, who sat calmly on the settle across from him staring into the fire.

"Well, Clarissa. I've sent Chapham and Bolling off to the taproom in order for you to tell me your story. Now I want no lies or excuses, no missish simpering, and no poetic Byronic romancing." Observing the quick and slightly startled look that she darted at him before letting those thick lashes veil her eyes again, he smiled. "Oh, I know you've been leading Nettie astray with all this modern poetry."

"Polly told you!" Clarissa said, a nasty edge to her voice.

"No, Polly didn't tell me. But the fact that you think she did makes me wonder two things. One, why do you young people suppose that your elders are blind? And two, why do you think that Polly, who is an honorable woman, and who has shown you much kindness, should be a tattle?"

"I hardly know how to answer your first question, sir. But I meant no insult to Polly. It was just that she caught Nettie and me reading Keats once, and we knew that you had forbidden Keats . . ."

"Yes, so I had. Probably foolishly, or at least so I thought when Polly convinced me that the waltz was a respectable dance."

This was too obscure for Clarissa, and she was too

284

tired to care. She sighed, and returned her gaze to the fire.

Mr. Rice smiled again. "Now Clarissa, as I said. I want you to tell me exactly why you undertook this escapade. I cannot believe that you really wanted to escape detection, so I must assume that you either felt you must draw attention away from some other event or that you wished to emphasize your position in regard to the man you have been ordered to marry, or perhaps both."

"I won't marry him."

A singularly persistent little mind, thought Mr. Rice. "Perhaps the fault is partly mine, Clarissa, in the matter of your marriage. You probably are not aware that I am your guardian with the trustees of your fortune, and that I have something to say in your future."

Clarissa's head came up in surprise.

"Yes, I was right. you didn't know. Well, I never bothered to tell you, nor to exercise my rights of guardianship. Your Aunt Cat has seemed capable, you have seemed happy, and—I know my sister well—she does not take kindly to advice. Or, shall we say, she takes advice only when it pleases her. And I will confess that I have been lazy. My own family is large, my interests scholarly . . ."

Clarissa's eyes had now taken on something like a dawning hope.

"Well," Mr. Rice continued. "I am now acting as your guardian; I am not unsympathetic, and I am prepared to listen. Let's hear your story."

Clarissa was not a bad young woman—only, as Nettie had observed, a young woman who had garnered from society some false ideas of right and wrong, and who had been brought up in an atmosphere that was not con-

285

ducive to a flexible and rational search for solutions. She had seen one course open to her: to attach or entrap another eligible man. But then she had been brought to the country, and of the three eligible men, one — Alex — didn't like her, Lord Bolling never gave her a glance, and only Frederick seemed susceptible, especially since Polly . . .

"Yes?" Mr. Rice murmured encouragement as Clarissa hesitated. "Polly is not perfect, my dear. Please speak freely."

"Well, it seemed clear that it was a marriage of convenience, and Polly was always flirting with Mr. Chapham."

"Yes, you may find some comfort in that; although another's misbehavior does not excuse one's own. However, I will assume you now have the true facts of the case?"

"How do you know?"

"Because if Frederick had been susceptible to your charms, you would not have needed to run away."

Clarissa began to cry. "He said he loved Polly," she said in a muffled voice.

"Why yes, that's been obvious for some time. You see, Clarissa, you were blinded by your own wishes. I don't know what has happened that Frederick felt he had to tell you that he loves Polly, but you must have been foolish enough to suggest that he loved you."

Clarissa sniffled and applied her handkerchief to her nose.

"I imagine you've learned your lesson, and we need say no more about that."

"Should I apologize to Polly?" The tears were now brimming over, and she applied her handkerchief to her eyes.

"I'm not sure we can decide that now, since we don't know how Polly feels, or what harm you have done."

"Nettie called me a cheap flirt."

"Well, well, we needn't go into that now." Mr. Rice was getting bored with girlish confessions. Clarissa's handkerchief was sodden, and the alternating applications to eyes and nose repelled him. He searched out his own spotless handkerchief and handed it to her. "Come now, let's have the rest of the story. Let's hear about the odious marriage."

After a good blow and a general wipe-up, Clarissa said, "The man is forty-five years old; he's a widower with two children. He is supposed to be handsome, but he's *old*."

"Is that so bad? Girls often marry men who are much older. I have heard it said that a girl of twenty who marries a man of forty can look forward to a merry widowhood."

"How revolting."

"Well, yes, I suppose it is in this sentimental age."

"Anyway, Aunt Cat and the trustees want me to marry him because he's terribly rich, he has a title, and they think I won't be able to make any other match as good." Clarissa paused, her lower lip caught between her teeth. "As long as I am confessing, I suppose I should say that Frederick was more attractive than Alex because he has more money — a lot more money. But I had a lot of time to think today, and I've decided that even if I am never offered for by a man who is rich, that if it comes to a choice, I prefer someone I can like and respect to someone with a lot of money."

"Is it possible that you have grown up a little?"

287

Clarissa saw that he was regarding her with a hint of the old fondness, and cast herself at his feet to lay her head on his knee.

A pretty gesture, he thought cynically, but nonetheless he patted her head. "Get up, child. The floor is cold — they're speaking of an early frost tonight, and we mustn't have you getting sick again."

When Clarissa was seated, Mr. Rice said, "Let's consider some other lessons learned. I suspect that if you had taken a different approach with your Aunt Catherine, rather than tears and protests and sulks, that you might have won your case. She is not a strong-minded woman, you know; I'd rather call her pig-headed. Firm resolve is the best weapon against pig-headedness, not tears and sulks, which only aggravate. Although Cat was ready to agree to anything you might demand when I left, I suspect that she will, once you are safely returned, forget those resolves. But I think, if I lend my voice to yours, and if you remain pleasantly firm and sensible, that we shall succeed in bringing her round. And I will further have a word or two with your trustees. They have control of your money; they do not have control over you."

Clarissa was on the brink of tears again, so he rose and stretched and decided he needed another brandy. He suggested that it had been a long and tiring day for her and perhaps she should retire. Tomorrow, after all, they must make an early start.

So Clarissa was sent off to bed, and he then joined Alex and Bolling in the taproom, where they all sat late by the fire enjoying a sensible conversation concerning economics, politics, and international affairs.

* * *

288

At Tanwell and Moregreen, agitation remained at high pitch. Aunt Cat wept, and repeated often, "Oh, if only I had listened to her! I would never have forced her to marry him if I had known she felt so strongly."

Nettie's agitation, although unexpressed, was nearly as great as Aunt Cat's, for she could not help feeling that it was all her fault. Polly, who had remained stonily calm throughout the day, gave way to grief in the privacy of her chamber. Mrs. Rice had some concern for the effect of strain on her husband, and an even greater concern for Polly, who she sensed was affected by her broken engagement more than she admitted.

Lady Moresby, who was apprised of the crisis at Tanwell by her husband when he came in from the stables, had immediately sent a note to Mrs. Rice offering any assistance, should it be necessary, commiserating on the broken engagement, and informing her that Frederick was on his way to London in a great pet. In the evening Sir and Lady Moresby sat by the fire in the small sitting room, only slightly calmer than the inhabitants of Tanwell.

Mrs. Rice greeted Clarissa calmly when they returned the next day. After Aunt Cat had fallen on Clarissa's neck with lamentations (but no promises, her brother noticed), Mrs. Rice said firmly, "You will excuse us, I'm sure, Catherine, but I would like to speak privately with Giles and Clarissa."

"Well, I'm sure I wouldn't push in where I'm not wanted," Aunt Cat huffed.

"Nothing of the sort, Catherine. I simply have some

information to impart to them that you will admit is rather awkward. It is my intention to make the final days of your stay as pleasant as possible by an airing of our difficulties. You are already *au courant* and I see no reason to bore you with repetition."

Aunt Cat sniffed, and shed a tear.

"Now, Catherine," Mrs. Rice said, "Clarissa and Giles are tired from their journey and anxious for a cup of tea. You know you have many little chores to do if you are to leave when planned, so run along and do them and I will send Clarissa to you as soon as I can."

Mrs. Rice ushered her husband and niece into the library and closed the door. After tea was poured, she said, "I thought, Clarissa, and you, Giles, that it would be better to hear our news immediately, and from me. Polly and Frederick have broken their engagement. Polly insists that it had nothing to do with you, Clarissa, except to precipitate a discussion between them that made it clear they would not suit." Mrs. Rice caught a gleam in Clarissa's eye, which she had a strong urge to extinguish. "If you are thinking, Clarissa, that this gives you an opportunity with Frederick, you are wrong. You are too immature for a man such as he, and it is my own belief that the engagement will be reinstated when they have both had time to consider. I also suggest that you consider carefully your role in 'precipitating' the discussion of which Polly speaks. Now. A happier piece of news." She turned to Mr. Rice. "I don't suppose you have told Clarissa of our new engagement?"

"No, I left that to the ladies."

"Then" — Mrs. Rice turned back to Clarissa — "you will be happy to know that Nettie is affianced to Lord Bolling."

"Nettie *what? Engaged?* But she was to have her come-out this season! Aunt Cat and I had it all planned!"

Mr. Rice was beginning to regret that he had promised to save Clarissa from the widower.

Mrs. Rice continued evenly, "I'm sure that Nettie will have an opportunity to enjoy London after she is married, and of course we will all be in London for Polly's exhibition."

When Clarissa had been excused, Mr. Rice burst out, with unusual force, "That chit ought to be laid over my knee! She has as much sense as a chicken. She thinks of no one but herself and her flirtations and pretty clothes. It would serve her right if I handed her over to the widower she so despises."

"Oh, she's not a bad girl, just thoughtless." Mrs. Rice indicated the tea tray. "Let me pour you another cup of tea, Giles, and you can tell me what you have decided to do about the disgraceful arrangement Catherine and the trustees have made. Can't you step in as her guardian? I don't think we can ignore that this whole lamentable business with Frederick was perhaps the result of Catherine's attempt to force her into a distasteful marriage."

"I'm more interested at the moment in this bad news about Polly and Frederick."

Mrs. Rice handed her husband back his teacup. "I don't suppose you noticed at the ball that Frederick was absent for some time with Clarissa?"

"Surely Polly won't allow herself to be swayed by jealousy, especially when Frederick presented himself here so promptly yesterday morning to set things to rights—or such I presume to have been his errand."

"Yes, I myself am surprised that Polly would take

291

such a step over such an incident, which—knowing Clarissa—was probably contrived. Polly is a level-headed young woman, despite her artistic tendencies." She paused to fetch a sewing basket from a nearby table. After selecting a pair of underdrawers in which William had in some mysterious fashion torn a gaping right-angled rip, she looked up to find her husband watching her with amusement.

"Are we not wealthy enough, Amelia, to donate our torn underdrawers to charity—especially a pair as worn as those?"

Mrs. Rice responded with one of her faint, sardonic smiles. "I am puzzled, Mr. Rice, that you so readily acquiesced to an alliance with the Danvers and their titled house."

Mr. Rice showed no surprise at the change of subject. "Well, so you might be, had not Bolling shown himself over the summer to be a sensible man."

"And had your daughter not so obviously shown her inclinations." She snipped off a length of thread. "He does have really remarkable blue eyes."

"Yes, I had been preparing myself for the event. It has been obviously imminent almost since Bolling first appeared. I admit that I would have preferred a son-in-law somewhat more republican—Chapham, for instance—but Bolling will suit well enough." He waited for a response to that bit of nonsense, but when it was not forthcoming, said more seriously, "But have I—we—been mistaken about Polly and Frederick?"

And so Mr. and Mrs. Rice drank tea together and discussed their family problems for a companionable half hour. They did not discuss, however, although they were both conscious of it, that had they not neglected a duty to Clarissa, this unfortunate incident might never have occurred.

Frederick awoke with the same tiresome question rattling around in his brain. His first thought as he came fully awake was "Has Polly had a lover?" At the same time he was conscious of an early-morning languid longing. He wanted Polly there to make love to, and then they would breakfast together, leisurely, and then make love again. Unless Polly was shy by daylight. He got out of bed and prepared to shave and dress in order to banish erotic thoughts. Contrarily, he wanted to hear her laugh, to watch her at her sketching — even, crazier yet, to see her eyes flash as she discussed some farfetched notion. "Oh Lord," he said aloud. "I'm in a bad way."

There was no question though, in this early morning light, of returning to Moregreen. He was clearly not yet ready. That he loved Polly he could not deny, but could he accept for a wife a woman who had had lovers — a lover? In fairness, although Polly had not denied lovers, neither had she confessed to having had lovers. Could he marry her not knowing — for he was convinced she would never tell him. It would be like her to insist that he accept her past, in the blind, so to speak. She would stand on her radical notions about female equality in matters of this nature.

Well, his thoughts continued as he entered the high road for the last leg of his journey, it's what we're trained to. Polly has been living in a different world. What do I know of diplomats and artists? And after all, here in England wealth and aristocratic titles were licenses for women (once married) to take lovers. The practice was

293

even more common among the French, with whom, he surmised from Polly's casual chatter of her life in the Americas, she had spent much time. And the Americans, although they were said to be quite as stuffy as the English despite their radical politics, were—according to both Chapham and Polly—willing to permit young men and women to associate freely with each other—to go about unsupervised together without anything thought of it. Would that not breed an easy give-and-take between them?

He would go on to London, take temporary lodgings, and seek out artists. He must learn something of Polly's life, while separating himself from the scenes of their courtship and estrangement.

He turned over possibilities for an introduction, and at last hit upon a means. His old friends Hastings had become something of a patron of the arts as well as a philanthropist. Perhaps Hastings could introduce him into the appropriate circles. And Polly would be in London soon for the exhibition of her work. Frederick, contented with his plan, found he could lay aside the burning question and observe the Welsh women and the Irish, who with a smattering of English, were harvesting the early fall crops on the truck farms that supplied the London markets with fresh vegetables. It was not in Frederick's nature to worry about a problem once he had determined on a course of action.

The uncomfortable task facing Polly of informing her father of Riggs's threats against her mother was quickly accomplished. She had never seen him in such high dudgeon. He grew red in the face, leaped to his feet, and with an evident effort to bring himself under control, paced the room. His right hand clenched in a fist, he struck it repeatedly into the palm of the other. "The upstart! The presumption!" he exclaimed. "The gall of the man."

Polly sat quietly, waiting for the storm to subside, but when her father at last had himself under control, he simply said, "I will attend to it. You may rest easy."

"What will you do?"

Her father turned on her a stern eye and a forbidding face such as she had not seen since forgotten days of youthful folly. "I will attend to it. That is sufficient. You are excused now to accomplish whatever duties your mother requires or tasks you yourself have in train."

She opened her mouth to protest, thought better of it, and said simply, "Thank you, sir."

When she was gone, Mr. Rice set himself to serious consideration of his course, but after lengthy deliberation, no more effective action occured to him than to present Riggs with a warning that should any untoward accident occur to any of his family, his dependents, or his property, that Riggs would be held responsible, and that if he heard any more reports of threats or his mutterings among the laborers and cotters, he would have the sheriff on him. He considered briefly the possibility that Riggs might not hold clear title to his little plot, but could not bring himself to take action that would cause more suffering for the man's family than to the man himself. He did not want to confront Riggs in his own house; he did not consider it wise to belittle the man in front of his wife—which would likely get her a beating, and possibly fill him with so much resentment that the warnings would not have sufficient effect.

295

Mr. Rice therefore altered the pattern of his daily exercise in order to walk or ride within sight of the grog shop where Riggs spent a significant portion of his time reinforcing his bad temper. His aim was to intercept Riggs before arrival at this dispensary of cheap spirits and inferior ale when he would be sober and more susceptible to advice. Within four days he accomplished his purpose, overtaking Riggs on the narrow byway that led to the groggery.

Mr. Rice mixed his threats and warnings with some man-to-man comments on the advantages of keeping one's place in the conjugal bed without adding to one's responsibilities in consequence of it. To suggest any kind of consideration for Mrs. Riggs would obviously be useless, and Mr. Rice was not the kind of moralist who let principle hamper effective tactic. The end he sought was the protection of his own wife (and inevitably the women to whom she preached), not the impossible task of changing Riggs's moral posture. And if it opened to public speculation what went on in his own bed — well, he expected that his wife's activities had already accomplished that.

Riggs was practical, as well as cynical and suspicious, and had little faith in the evenhandedness of justice when a poor man faced a rich man, but neither was he one to grovel in front of the gentry. Warnings and threats of the sheriff might have made him defiant and stubborn, had Mr. Rice not offered an argument to buttress his forced conversion that would leave his bluster and swagger intact. The number of children for which he was responsible was already of a sufficient number to prove his past and present virility, and if he could blame his wife for the cessation of pregnancies, he would never need to expose his continued virility to question. He could wink and grin and remark on having more coins in his pocket for drink and fellowship, even if he got on the old woman every night.

Mr. Rice, whose intention it had been to implant some of these notions in Riggs's not entirely adequate brain, felt a temporary self-repulsion. He made certain that he found time and occasion to reassure Mrs. Riggs, and to hint that whatever new tack her husband took, she should not contradict him, unless he once again began to threaten Mrs. Rice and her work. He was so observant of her modesty, and thanked her in such a gentlemanly way, that his star ascended to a position not far below that of his wife. For his own part, he tried to forget as quickly as possible his encounter with Riggs and to remember that Martha was a worthy woman with well-behaved children who had deserved his help. His own wife, he trusted, would now be free to pursue her eccentric course. It certainly would do no harm as long as she confined her efforts to respectably married women.

Chapter Sixteen

Summer was at an end. The leaves were beginning to turn, although Polly noticed, even in her distress, how muted were the colors compared to those in America. When the late September rains and fogs permitted, she spent many hours sketching and painting along the stream, in the woods, in the orchard, even in the fields where the laborers were at the harvest. When shut within, she worked on the long overdue portrait of the squire's ox, Caesar. It was a means of avoiding her family, and a poultice for an injured heart. She did not believe that the poultice could effect a cure; her art had become rather an analgesic, a deadener of pain. The unfinished portrait of Frederick, begun after their engagement, she turned to the wall, along with other false starts.

To her relief, Clarissa and Aunt Cat departed soon after the ball. On the final day of their visit, Clarissa sought out Polly in her orchard retreat and attempted to apologize. She even brought herself to explain that at the Moregreen ball she had felt faint during a dance, had asked Frederick to take her to the garden, and that she had wept because she was so overcome by the thought of her impending distasteful marriage. "Frederick was very kind to me, Polly, as he would have been to any lady in

299

equal distress, but that was all. I swear to it, cousin."

"There is no need to swear to the truthfulness of your story. I believe you, Clarissa." Polly took up her brush and turned her eye to her sketch book.

"Don't dismiss me like that, Polly. You haven't given me a chance to say I'm sorry if I caused any difficulty for you, and I *am* sorry. I truly, truly am."

Polly controlled an impulse to sigh and roll her eyes heavenward. Instead she again lay down her brush and held out her hands. Clarissa clasped them in her own and repeated again, "I am sorry, you know."

"I know you are, dear." Polly drew her down and kissed her. "Now run along and finish your packing. We artists are a selfish lot, and if you keep me from my painting any longer, I shall lose the light effect I am trying to catch with this quick watercolor sketch. So run along. I assure you, you are forgiven whatever sins you care to name."

"Only one thing more, Polly. If you could tell Nettie that. We have always been such good friends and I should hate to lose her. I feel that she's harboring a coldness toward me because she thinks it's my fault you have broken with Frederick."

"Of course, my love. Now *do* run on."

"Promise?"

"I promise."

Polly turned resolutely to her sketch, and Clarissa — finally — gathered up her skirts and, stepping carefully to avoid the few rotting apples, left at last.

Clarissa was not completely satisfied with the interview, or with herself. She had not confessed her insinuation to Frederick that Polly had been involved in scandalous affairs. But, she thought in self-justification, she had said she was sorry — for everything — and her

300

Aunt Rice had told her that Polly did not blame her for the broken engagement. And if Frederick had told *her* that he loved Polly, surely he had told Polly. And so Clarissa forgave herself.

Alex was the next to leave. His last few days at Cross-field Cottage had been so taken up with arrangements for departure and for farewell calls that he had had very little time for his friends at Tanwell. Nonetheless, he observed that Polly was dispirited, despite her determined cheerfulness, and so he exerted every effort to call as often as he could and to try to elicit smiles and laughter with his banter. But when the time came to present himself to say farewell, he had a more serious question to ask. As they strolled across the park toward a favorite spot by the stream, he said to her, with a touch of wistfulness, "We deal so well together, you and I, why don't we love each other?"

"Because," Polly answered, looking up at him with affection, "you are unprepared to be faithful to any woman. You should have been an Englishman—or better yet, a Frenchman—who could marry for convenience and keep a mistress or two on the side."

Alex laughed and squeezed her arm. "You are wrong, but I'll not argue. It does puzzle me, though."

They seated themselves on a rustic bench by the stream and for a while sat silently together, listening to the water slipping along its course and to the birds winding up their morning chatter.

At last Alex broke the silence. "Has Frederick misunderstood our relationship? I would not have it be a cause for your broken engagement."

"Perhaps he did, but willfully. He had no cause to think we were other than friends."

"No, Polly. You're wrong. It was my fault. My damnable easy ways. I've landed us in the bucket for sure."

"I think it's in the basket, not bucket."

"Whichever, it's damned uncomfortable. I should have recognized that you were no longer the homesick girl I first met in Ghent, with too many responsibilities heaped on her head, needing to be cajoled out of her loneliness. Nor were you any longer the playful companion of my youth . . ."

"Our youth, Alex."

"Yes, of our youth. You, at least, have grown up. You're a recognized artist, and you're . . ." Alex hesitated, then took her hand and lifted it to his lips. "You've become a lady."

"Oh, pish-posh," Polly said, withdrawing her hand but smiling at him. "Nettie said I flirted with you too much, and I guess I did. But it's always been so—including Ghent, my innocent—and I suspect always will be, even if we meet as doddering ancients. But Frederick had no time for explanations, or to allow me to admit I had acted with impropriety. He accused me rather of scandalous behavior in general."

"The cad!" On a moment's reflection, he added, "But it's hard to believe such a sensible fellow would leap to such a conclusion from our mild flirtation, if such you choose to call it."

"No, he had reason. I've never been quite as proper as ladies are supposed to be—I seem to be cut from a funny piece of cloth. And Frederick had a right to assume that if I flirted so casually with you that I might with others, and that perhaps there were incidents less innocent than casual flirtations in my past."

"More likely our Miss Clarissa put the maggot in his brain. I never could quite like that chit."

"I've thought of that. But that isn't really important. The important thing is that he believed whatever she insinuated, or at least suspected it, and that it made a difference to him." Polly considered for a moment the propriety of her next statement, then made the decision to speak frankly. "I shouldn't say such things to you, but perhaps the very reason that we don't love each other, except as friends, is why we have always been able to discuss subjects that are ordinarily considered indelicate between men and women who are not husband and wife. The thing is, Alex, it just makes me mad. I know *he's* not virginal."

"Well, yes, love, but women are different."

"Oh, Alex. Not you too? Haven't you read accounts of the South Seas? Those women don't seem to be confined and constrained as we are here. Are they so different from us? Or we so different from them?"

Alex was not sure that the reported standards of the South Seas were appropriate for civilized nations. "Those people are savages, Polly. They aren't civilized; they aren't Christians."

"Well, perhaps I shall become a pagan." Polly rose purposefully. "Come, let's stroll and talk. Tell me your plans. How long do you think you'll be stationed in Germany? When will you leave London? Will you be there long enough to see my exhibition?"

"I leave immediately for Germany. I will certainly write, and I'll try my best to wheedle a quick trip to London from my stern superiors, although whether I'll be able to make the opening is doubtful. Now, to return to

303

the subject we were discussing . . ."

"Absolutely not!" Polly reached out to pull him to his feet and, with this gesture, returned them to their normal footing.

They said their formal adieus before they left the shelter of the woods.

"May I kiss you good-bye?" Alex asked.

"Of course."

His kiss was not brotherly, and he held her for a moment. Looking down at her, he said fondly, "We could be more than friends and flirts, couldn't we, Paula my love?"

"Possibly. In the South Seas."

He let her go with a brotherly shake. "What a saucy lady you are!"

As they walked toward the house, Polly said, "Nettie tells me that Lord Bolling will stay on at Crossfield Cottage for a time."

"Yes, the old boy can't believe his luck in capturing such a young and pretty treasure. He bores me for hours worrying that he's too old for her, that he swept her off her feet, that he should have waited until she saw more of the world. I tell him that his Miss Nettie was probably ready to marry and settle down when she was twelve. How did a sister of yours ever turn out so sober? Why, I think she's older at eighteen than you are at—what did you tell me? Twenty-four? She is certainly older than you were at nineteen."

"You must remember the difference in our circumstances. Although I was well trained in household management, there was Gussie to take real responsibility while I pursued my studies. I spent so much time with drawing masters and with my instructor in watercolor, and then I was thrust into a new and wonderful world.

304

Nettie has led a routine and quiet life here in the country, and since Gussie married, has borne all the responsibilities of an eldest daughter, and at a very young age."

"No, Polly. Responsibility never sobered you. She's a different girl altogether. She'll be a good wife to Bolling. They will live contentedly in the country, occasionally coming up to London for one of your exhibitions or to visit museums and historical monuments. They are orderly people — very orderly — but I believe deeply in love."

Chapter Seventeen

As soon as Frederick was settled in his temporary quarters, he called on his friend Hastings.

"Heard you were in town, old man," said Hastings, heartily shaking Frederick's hand. "Wondered when you'd get around to call."

"I thought I might run into you at the club. I went there a few times to dine, but according to old Grimes you very seldom cross the threshold there anymore. I needed to hire a valet—I lost Peters a while back, you remember. And I had other business to attend in order to get settled for a few months in London. So it hasn't been neglect of you, old friend, as I hope you understand."

"Of course. I supposed you had business to attend to. Knew you'd get around as soon as you could."

"I presume that married life has had a progressively settling effect, if you're so seldom at the club."

"Yes, I'll admit it has. My philanthropic work takes more and more of my time and interest. I've been working with Martha Holstead-Evans. You recall no doubt that I arranged a visit for you to a foundling hospital in which she had an interest. In any event, we've been trying to find a director for a new foundling home we've

307

established in the country. And when I'm not engaged in similar activities, I find it more to my liking to gaze at my paintings, or enjoy the company of my little Julie and the babes about our feet."

Frederick expressed a desire to pay his respects to Mrs. Hastings and to view the babes.

"I'll send word to Julie to join us for tea in an hour, and bring the children for a brief interview. We do not impose them for long on others who have no reason to dote on them as we do. You can stay to tea, can you not? And the entire evening, perhaps. We haven't seen you for so long."

When they were comfortably settled with glasses of wine in hand, and after the preliminary pleasantries and inquiries into the health and whereabouts of relatives and friends, Frederick said, "Odd you should mention Martha Holstead-Evans. I was just thinking about her."

"Indeed?"

"Yes, I'm not quite sure what recalled it to mind, but I was remembering a visit to a foundling hospital with her."

"You aren't by chance finally developing an interest in good works, are you? You don't have to be a Methodist or a Quaker, you know. Lots of good Anglicans in philanthropy and causes."

"No, no causes yet. I must confess, Hastings, that I have need of your advice, but on another subject. I hope you won't think me lacking in my desire to renew our friendship because of it."

"No, why should I? Good Lord, man. I've never seen you so foolishly apologetic. Has something been going on I'm not aware of?"

"Afraid my foundations have been shaken a bit this

past summer. Probably what I needed, but it doesn't make it more pleasant. The thing is, that I have what will strike you as an odd request. I want to meet some artists."

"Yes, it does strike me as an odd request. May I ask the reason, or would you rather that I not?"

"You needn't ask permission to question me, for I came prepared to tell you my reasons. All in confidence, of course."

"Of course."

Frederick took a restless turn around the room. He came to rest by the fireplace. One arm on the mantel, he began, "I have become engaged — or rather, I was. You might say that we have separated for a time — I, at least, needed time, I realize now, to think it over more carefully. She's an artist, you see."

"An artist," Hastings murmured. "Not quite what I expected of you."

"Yes, I'm a pretty sober fellow, as you know. I'm not sure I can accept the free and easy company of artists, but I wouldn't think it right to deny my wife social and professional intercourse with her colleagues." Frederick did not feel it necessary to elaborate further on his reasons. "She has been opening my eyes, you see."

"So you want to find out if you can support the society of artists. Understandable. You should know that I'm not a great patron — like Lord Blackstone, for example. I take risks with unknown artists and so am better known in the circles of the lesser known." Hastings set his glass on the table at his side. "By the way, who is the artist? May I ask?"

"Of course. Her name is Polly, Polly Rice. Some fellow here in London is preparing an exhibition of her work."

Hastings reached for the decanter to pour more wine. "Do sit down, old man. Polly Rice, hmmm? It's Jedro who's setting up the exhibition. Good man. He's a dealer who's trying to promote exhibitions of artists' work. Most painters can't afford to establish their own galleries or even attach an annex to their studios where they can exhibit their work. Don't know whether he'll succeed or not, but it's a step forward." Hastings sipped thoughtfully. "Believe I've heard there's some controversy about Miss Rice's work. Something about a naked Indian, I believe."

"A naked Indian?" asked Frederick, puzzled. "I've seen several of her portraits of Indians and they're always clothed in robes or some sort of apparel."

"Well, I'm just passing on the gossip. I've been looking forward to the exhibition. Thought if she's as good as I've heard, I'd pick up one or two of her works. But you said you'd like to meet some artists. One of our bluestockings entertains artists on Thursdays. Would you like to accompany me? I must warn you, there may be a few literary people and perhaps others like myself. We philanthropists are always looking for patrons for our causes wherever we can find them."

For the remainder of the hour the two men discussed the latest political events, the welfare of Frederick's dairy cows, and Hastings's philanthropic projects. Mrs. Hastings then came in with the children, two well-behaved youngers of six and four, who after renewing acquaintance with their "Uncle Frederick," were taken away by their nurse, leaving the adults to drink their tea in peace.

310

When Frederick returned late to his lodging after a satisfactory evening with his old friend, he found that his newly hired valet-butler-man of all uses had left him a tray of biscuits and a bottle of port beside the chair in front of the fireplace. The fire was banked, but required only a log and some stirring to set it ablaze. He made himself comfortable, reflecting on the wisdom of his choice of a temporary hire, and that he might well take on the young man permanently. He needed a valet, and it was too much to ask his father's aging attendant to assist him. Even as little assistance as he needed personally, his clothes still required care — and it was too inconvenient to hire someone every time he came to London. He poured himself some of the port, ate a biscuit, and then picked up the note that also lay on the tray. He broke the seal, opened it, and glanced at the signature. "Well, what is this?" he muttered. The note was from Alex Chapham.

He read with mixed feelings. After preliminary expressions of regret that Frederick had not been in when he called on returning from the country, Alex went on to explain that he had hoped for a week in London before departing for his post in Berlin, but that the American minister, Mr. Rush, insisted he leave posthaste for reasons too dull and boring to catalog. That being the case, he had hastened to call once more to take his leave and thank Frederick for the hospitality he had enjoyed at Moregreen. He had been disappointed to miss him again, but since he was scheduled to leave early on the morrow, there was nothing for it but to take his leave by pen. Alex then turned to a subject "of a more personal nature," and hoped he would not offend if he spoke frankly.

Frederick was seized with a sinking sensation. Was Alex going to tell him that he had asked for Polly's hand and been accepted? He scanned hurriedly through the remainder of the letter, which satisfied him that his worst fears were not fulfilled. He tossed off what remained of his port, and poured another. Then he set himself to read the final paragraphs more carefully.

"I began to suspect," Alex wrote, "on the night of the ball at Moregreen, that you might have misconstrued the relationship between Polly and myself. As I hope she has told you, she and I are old friends, beginning with Ghent, where I was a young and very lowly aide to one of the American peace commissioners. Our friendship ripened in Washington, but, at least on the past of Miss Rice, it has never been anything more. The friendship was enhanced by our frequent meetings in Washington, where her uncle and my mother and father formed an equally agreeable friendship. We were often together, and because of it, and that we were both so nearly of an age (I am barely two years her senior), we became like brother and sister."

[Alex had had some qualms as he wrote the last lines; there had been too many kisses, and he believed that he and Polly could have become lovers eventually, even if not husband and wife. He decided, as his pen hovered over the paper, that he would leave it to Polly to correct his statement if she chose. If not, no harm done.]

"Polly would not like it that I have written to you thus. She feels, I believe, that she was unreasonable in her anger, from what little she would say, but seems not convinced that you might have reached the same conclusion about your role in the dispute. Again pardon me, but it has been said that it takes two to quarrel, and although I hasten to add that she said nothing of a quarrel, I assume that there must have been some heated discussion. I, too, saw the languishing Miss Knight lead you from the dance floor, and I still quiver from the black looks that you shot my way as I danced with Polly.

"I add only this: It is my hope that the two of you will meet in an atmosphere of calm, and resolve those misunderstandings that have parted you. As I grew to know you, I came to realize how right you are for Polly. I say that with envy, for did I not believe that you would lend her the anchor she needs in the exciting world that will soon open to her, I would attempt by every means I command to change her opinion of me—to see the 'brother' as 'husband.' "

[Alex had smiled as he firmly wrote "husband" instead of "lover." Maybe Polly was right; he was bad husband material.]

"I need not tell you that Polly is a woman of great integrity. I don't suppose I could sway her if I tried, for I am convinced that her heart belongs to you and always will. That she saved herself so long, and did not succumb to the conventions that continually press girls to marry before their twenties, is demonstration of the depth of her attachment to you."

[Alex had consulted several dictionaries to discover that exactly right word, "integrity." He was determined to set Frederick's mind at rest on the score of Polly's purity, and he considered those words "saved herself" and the inept wording of the last sentence masterly strokes.]

"I hope that I have not lost your regard, and that you will not allow a mistaken jealousy to prevent our meeting in the future when I am again in England. Let me humbly say that I have not emerged unscathed from this pleasant summer. I hope it has taught me to contain my American brashness, and assume a more proper manner even toward such old friends as Polly. With sincere regards, I remain, Alexander Stone Chapham."

Frederick regarded the fire for a time, drank some more port, and then read the note again. What the thunder was the fellow trying to say? Another glass of port, which neatly finished the bottle, and it all began to fall in place. The damned American was telling him he hadn't crossed the finish line with Polly and suspected that no one else had either. Then he felt a strong revulsion at the coarseness of his thought. He wouldn't have anybody, not even himself, thinking that way about Polly.

He wadded up the note to throw in the fire, then decided against it. He heaved himself out of his chair — it was too damned low for a man with his long legs — and looked around for a place to stow the thing. His eye

314

came to rest on the desk in the corner. He lurched against a table as he made his way across the room. Too much furniture in the place anyway. And, he admitted with a spontaneous chuckle, he'd had his share of intoxicants since the afternoon. He stuffed the note in a drawer.

He was disguised all right. Tomorrow his new valet would have to rustle up the hock and soda, for he was going to have the devil of a headache. He threw himself across the bed without removing his clothes. His last thought was that Chapham was a good enough fellow, after all.

The rooms were already filled when Frederick, accompanied by Hastings, arrived at the bluestocking lady's Thursday evening salon, featuring artists. Their hostess was exceedingly pretty, tall and slender, clad in a gown of the latest fashion, with a pair of spectacles perched atop her very pert nose. Frederick learned within the first minutes of their acquaintance that she had been nearsighted from birth. She had been punished by her first governess for trying "to make out her letters with her nose," but a second governess had convinced her parents that it would be sensible to get her some eyeglasses. "I tell everyone I meet this story," she confided to Frederick, "because I want people to learn that reading and study do not necessarily cause nearsightedness." She then introduced Frederick to another woman, who although plain, plump, and spotted, was remarkably clear-eyed, and who was soon monopolized by two gentlemen eager to discuss Hazlitt's latest essay, leaving Frederick free to look around for an artist.

All the women were conventionally dressed and coiffed except a lady in one corner of the room clad in billowing bloomers of the sort supposedly favored in Eastern harems. Several of the men wore open collars, with scarves knotted around their necks rather than the conventional high shirt points and neckcloth, and a few seemed to be bent on bringing dishevelment to a high art. One young man was stretched on the carpet at the feet of a lady well past her heyday. In another corner of the room, as Frederick strolled about, two painters (or such he supposed them to be) were in deep discussion of Goethe's color theories, and he found two others in a spirited argument about the best shop in which to buy artists' supplies.

A man who introduced himself as a doctor interested in medical illustration, and another who cheerfully confessed he was an opium eater, had soon attracted a small group by their animated discussion of the massacre in Manchester, where a large number of people demanding annual parliaments and manhood suffrage had been ridden down by militia. There had even been women among the demonstrators, which made the crime more heinous, although the doctor contended that they damn well shouldn't have been there in the first place. Other people joined the group, and soon Frederick was hearing of a number of needed reforms that he had never known were needed. "Although one rather thinks," drawled a flawlessly dressed gentleman, twirling his quizzing glass, "that it would be as effective to put one's suggestions for reform in a bottle, and like Percy Shelley, cast them into the sea, as to make demands of the present government."

"Demonstrate that the Whigs will be any better."

"Oh, hardly, old man. The lot of them could disappear in the sea with the bottles and we'd be none the worse for it."

Frederick left the group to sample other opinions, and found the plain lady with the magnificent eyes still arguing, now with one of the open-shirted and scarved fellows, who was denouncing Hazlitt for his traditionalism in art. "Nothing wrong with Rembrandt, of course, but Hazlitt—like old Reynolds and his crowd—thinks there're inviolable laws of composition. Don't hold with that at all."

Hazlitt's clear-eyed devotee said, "He may be a traditional painter himself, but surely you've read his essay on Turner. What was it he said? That Turner doesn't paint scenes of nature, but the elements through which they're seen—that his landscapes are paintings of earth, air, and water. Something of the sort."

A hitherto silent member of the group essayed an opinion. "Must have been reading Goethe. He says there ain't any form—at least what we see with the old optics. Says light, shade, and color make up form."

The conversation was off on a discussion of light in painting, and of color theories (West's use of the spectrum as opposed to Turner's use of the primaries and secondaries), which left Frederick at sea.

He found a painter named Quartermain extolling Napoleon for looting continental art treasures and bringing them to Paris, where he had put them on display for all to enjoy. "Whatever you have to say about Bonaparte—personal aggrandizer though he might have been—he had a belief in the people. In Paris, art is no longer the possession of the priviledged few . . ."

"But really, Quartermain, what possible good could a

common laborer get from viewing a Rubens? Should be pearls before swine I'd say. Has to be a line drawn somewhere!"

"It wasn't the *French* people who defeated Bonaparte," a woman named Olivia Greve remarked. "*We* defeated him, not they, and with the aid of some of the most absolutist governments in Europe. Tyrant or not, his bond with the people was mystical."

"Oh, I say, Olivia, that's rather too thick."

"My dear, you aren't thinking," an elderly lady cautioned. "It may seem in retrospect that the revolution was an exciting overthrow of ancient shackles, but may I present the perspective of one who witnessed the tumbrels rolling toward the guillotines, devouring king and commoner alike?"

"Excuse me, ma'am, but I was speaking of Napoleon Bonaparte, not the revolution." The discussion was well on the way to a replay of the French Revolution and the Napoleonic Wars, with art forgotten.

Frederick drifted on, and with him drifted Quartermain, who had begun the argument with his mention of Napoleon as a benefactor of art for the people. "Still can't mention Bonaparte's name without getting into some silly discussion on the revolution and the war. A dead bore. Well"—he peered at Frederick through his spectacles—"you a painter too?"

Frederick confessed he was not, but that he was acquainted with one. Quartermain had not heard of Polly, of her exhibition, or of the naked Indian, but when Frederick mentioned her book of engravings of American plants, although Quartermain was not familiar with it, it did remind him of his trip to America. "Couldn't do the continental tour, you know, with Boney loose. So I went to America, and found it a damned exciting country."

They discussed America until joined by one of the Hazlitt group. "Now they're arguin' about old Reynolds and his rules of proportion," the newcomer reported.

"Well," said Quartermain, "I can't say I agree with the Paris art crowd who're saying that Greek and Roman statues are eyesores, but I've always thought it hard on our ladies that they had to be held up to Diana."

"I say, that reminds me of a frightfully droll story Ragge was tellin' me. About Spenser. Have you heard it?"

"One hears so many stories about Spenser."

"Well, stop me if you've heard this one. But if you haven't, it's too good to miss. Seems Spenser got a commission to paint this beauty — regular angel — daughter of some duke or other. He takes one look and begins to wonder how he can get his hands on this morsel." In an explanatory aside to Frederick, he said, "Spenser's big weakness. Word gets around. Pretty soon — no commissions."

"Get on with your story, Renshaw," Quartermain said.

"Well, first off, Spenser decides that she must be painted as a Greek goddess — flowin' draperies, bare feet and all. Then he starts lecturin' her about art, and how Sir Joshua said that a lady's hand should be the length of her face, and all the rest of that nonsense — all the time tellin' her she has the proportions of Diana, but not exactly the whole truth, since he wasn't usin' the sacred proportions of the divine Diana, but whatever the girl's happened to be. When he got down to comparison between her big toe and her nose, he's kneelin' on the ground holdin' the sacred part in his hand — the girl's gettin' more and more skittish—and he just can't help himself. He's got to kiss that toe."

"Revolting!" declared Quartermain, laughing nonetheless.

"Well, yes. Prefer noses myself. So—she jerks her foot back and kicks him. Hits him right in the eye. Was black for two weeks. Lost the commission besides. Then he made the mistake of confessin' all to Twameley, who thought it was too good a story to keep to himself. Spenser gets mad, has some words with Twamely, they square off at each other, and Twameley lands him a facer and blacks the other eye."

Amid the general laughter, Quartermain was reminded of another story about the unlucky Spenser and his amours, but as others joined the group, Frederick found an opportunity to move away.

In the course of the evening he heard discussions of Fuselli and the morbidity of his work, the weird art and poetry of Blake, and much about the relationship between poetry and art. He learned that it was necessary to do portraits, and messotints of family seats, in order to live, but that painters had a vision to serve as well. There was talk of the new painting in France, of the freedom which should be the artists' right, and whether it was better to study in France or Italy. And should a painting portray "something," or only what "is"? Frederick didn't understand the difference.

He was attracted by an animated discussion in a corner among two men and a woman. He joined their circle, which almost immediately brought them to a self-conscious halt. When he apologized for intruding, the woman laughed and said, "It's just that you caught us discussing something other than art, literature, or

320

reform. We were discussing the advantages of phaetons over curricles, who is the best carriage maker in the kingdom, and the merits of Mr. Ragge's new stallion." Frederick petitioned admission to the circle in order to clear his head, confessing that he was acquainted with an artist — his neighbor in the country, in fact — and had come tonight with his friend Hastings, who as they knew was a collector; that although he was very interested in all the aforementioned subjects (especially art, owing to the aforementioned acquaintance), he also happened to be interested in horses, and in his own opinion, the best carriages . . .

Later, after exhausting the topic of transport, and the related subjects of the new road-surfacing techniques and the predictions of self-propelled steam road vehicles, the lady turned to Frederick and asked, "What is the name of your neighbor, sir? Perhaps we know him."

"My neighbor's a woman, ma'am, not a man. Her name is Polly Rice."

"Polly Rice . . ." she repeated speculatively. "I don't believe I know her."

"Know her name," interjected Ragge. "Did a book of engravings. *Native Flowers of the Americas*. Good, clear drawings, all the parts there, but hardly art."

"Polly Rice," said the third member of the party, the same Twameley who landed Spenser the facer. "Been cogitating. Ain't she the one Jedro's showing next month?"

"Believe you're right," agreed Ragge.

Twameley, still cogitating, added, "Bit of a scandal there, I've heard. Something about a naked Indian."

The woman looked at the men with amusement. "A good clear drawing with all the parts there?"

321

"Oh, that's good, Sally. Very good, indeed! All the parts there! Ha, ha."

"Better hope, Sally, that she don't do miniatures," said Twameley.

"Well," said Sally, looking wicked, "if the Indian is like some gentlemen, no doubt a miniature would be sufficient."

The two men burst into guffaws and Sally, with a flirt of her fan and a toss of her head, walked off. Frederick, although he shared the men's amusement, was mildly scandalized. He was even more so when Ragge said confidingly, "Oh, that Sally's a dasher. Married old man Millington—one of those Nabob fellows with pots full of money—when the old boy was in his dotage and she was about sixteen. Died within a twelvemonth. He did, not Sally. Then she married a Frenchie while she was over in Paris studyin' art durin' the peace in 1802. But then he went and got himself killed fightin' for the Corsican, so Sally was in something of a spot."

"Kept her skin, though. She got herself out of there, right and proper."

Ragge, nudging his friend, said, "Twameley ain't one to boast, but Sally was his mistress for a while—although pretty sure it wasn't his parts she was discussin'."

"Well, should think not," Twameley said. "Sally didn't go off for that reason, I can tell you."

"Sally's got her convictions. Twameley's right there."

"Couple of other fellows she lived with after me—don't remember their names. But she says now she'd never put her neck in the yoke again. Much more interesting this way, and she ain't mistress to nobody, she says—no matter whose bed she's sharing at the time—says she's mistress of herself alone." Twameley obviously admired his former mistress; his gaze rested on her fondly as she stood by the refreshment table in conversation with the woman in bloomers. "Thing is, Sally got some ideas over there in Paris. Some of the women in the revolution were terrors—although Sally says they were betrayed in the end—couldn't meet to rabble-rouse, or something like that. Queer business. She'll tell you all about it if you ask her. Some woman over there, whose husband joined the Restoration government now Boney's gone, who can't paint anymore, or can't show her paintings, or something like that. You should ask her. Give you an earful, Sally will."

"And how about that Frog philosopher?" Ragge prompted.

"Oh, him. She talks a lot about some fellow named Fourier. Fellow says sex is a fundamental passion, and a chap—or a female even—ought to try out everything, near as I can make out. Now I don't hold with all of his ideas on what's proper to try out . . ."

Frederick had heard of the philosopher only in relation to his notions about abolishing cities and bringing up children in some kind of communities called phalanstries, and that only because he met a man whose parents had taken him to America to give the idea a try—an unsuccessful try as it turned out, neither the wilderness nor the noble savages being as friendly as the utopians had hoped.

"You're read Fourier?" Frederick asked Twameley, hiding his amusement at such heavy matters for a man who seemed so unlikely to be interested in Utopian starts.

"Tried, you know. Thought it might help with Sally. Frightful lot of jibber-jabber. A few good ideas. Stands

323

to reason. Couldn't write as much as he did without a few getting in."

"Damned good painter, Sally," said Ragge, summing up. "But you can't tie her down." He looked around the room. "Now take Clara Wheelock over there, Aubrey Wheelock's wife. She's been illustratin' poetical works, and now she's tryin' to do fashion illustration. Got herself a studio where she works every day, but every night she goes home to Aubrey and their two young ones, and they sit around their fire and drink tea just like their neighbors, who're all lawyers and merchants — petty bourgeois, you know. Wheelock — that's him over there talkin' to our hostess — he's a cartographer for the Admiralty; did damned important work for the government durin' the war."

Frederick was by now feeling overwhelmed and, as soon as he could gracefully get away from Twameley and Ragge, went in search of Hastings. "I've about had as big a dose as is good for me for a beginning," he said to his friend.

They walked along the now nearly deserted streets toward their club, where they expected to take a nightcap.

"Well," Hastings asked, "what did you think?"

Frederick pondered for a moment before answering. "You know, I said to Polly one time that I never really gave much serious thought to anything but breeding and feeding my dairy herd, despite all the reading I've done over the years. I was telling her that I managed to get my hands on a copy of *Queen Mab,* and read it just to find out what Shelley said that was so shocking."

"Complete nonconformist, Shelley. And practices what he preaches. Didn't bother to divorce his first wife

324

before eloping with old Godwin's daughter by that woman — what's her name? Wollstonecraft. But I've never read *Queen Mab*. Preachy, I've heard."

"Yes, he goes on about the tyrannies of religions and governments, about the rich and powerful living on the backs of the poor and powerless. It didn't seem to have any application to my life. My family's always been good to those dependent on us. Damn it, Hastings, I've been getting a feeling lately that I don't entirely like — that I've been blind to half the human race!" Frederick then recounted his meeting with the formidable Sally and her admirers.

"Yes, Sally has a reputation. But she can back it up with so much chapter and verse from some philosopher or other, throwing in Amazons and feminists in France, that pretty soon you get the idea that she's right."

"Well," Frederick replied, "it remains to be seen how Sally and the others I met tonight stand up to the scandal if Polly really has painted a naked Indian."

"How about you, old friend?"

"Whatever I may decide about marriage, I will stand witness to Polly's integrity and to her rectitude and delicacy of mind."

"She may need more than that from her friends, and — no offense — from those who love her."

"Of course." Frederick instantly realized that he'd sounded stiff and priggish. "Oh, hell, Hastings. I've got to have some time. I'm too cautious, I know, but . . . well, what more can I say? I have to have some time."

"No one knows your cautious ways better than I, Frederick, and you've needed some stirring up lately. But I also know your liberality of mind. Perhaps you should call yourself thoughtful rather than cautious.

Judgment without prejudice. I've always said it was unfortunate you didn't go into law and from there to the bench."

They turned in at their club, handed their cloaks to the porter, and made their way to two vacant chairs near the fire. Brandies in hand, they settled back comfortably.

Hastings, holding his brandy up in order to admire the rich color brought out by the glow of the fire, said, "Told you this was a radical set. Too bad you didn't have a chance to meet Clara and Aubrey Wheelock. Conventional as you'd want in their private lives." He then remarked thoughtfully, and with regret, that there had been few philanthropists at the gathering, but then, there seldom were many on artists' night. Had Frederick realized, by the way, that that fellow Twamely was one of his most reliable contributors to causes, whereas his friend Ragge spent all his money on horses and his collection of fine prints?

Chapter Eighteen

September passed away, and with it the rains and fogs that had contributed to the depression of Polly's spirits. The first days of October were bright and cloudless. As the weather changed, her natural eagerness revived. Her London exhibition was foremost in her thoughts, and the anticipation of long visits with Peter and Gussie. She had seen them much too briefly on her return from Brazil. That Frederick also was in London she could not ignore as a further reason for her improved spirits, although she still saw no way out of their impasse. She had been wrong to flirt so openly with Alex, and she would admit that she was wrong, but she refused to excuse her past life or justify it to Frederick.

She made an uneventful trip to London, accompanied only by a maid, a week before the rest of the family in order to assist with the arrangement of her exhibition. The trip itself lifted her spirits. The weather was cool and comfortable, the countryside basking in crisp October, and as the miles rolled away under the wheels of the carriage, her thoughts turned to a renewal of her wardrobe. She must have a new dress for her appearance at the gallery. She would also order a ball dress in the latest style — fuller at the bottom and in some filmy material over satin, a cashmere shawl, a new hat. She would order a coat made, fur trimmed and with full sleeves and a muff, in

327

which to face the English winters, so severe after the gentle climate of Brazil. Gussie had written of a shop that sold artificial flowers made with such skill that they could be mistaken for real blossoms, but in colors that announced that they were creations, not imitations; flowers to match the ball dress, to wear in her hair, and perhaps to trim the dress.

Sir Harry and Lady Moresby left the same week, to take one of their "little jaunts" before settling themselves at the Clarendon Hotel for their brief stay in London. They intended on their jaunt to visit two or three famous gardens, in pursuit of Sir Harry's plan to establish a more extensive garden at Moregreen, and to include also Hawkestone Park, which had a reputation for its beauty, and for the sublime situation of the Red Castle. Lady Moresby did not share Sir Harry's enthusiasm for ruined castles, but she was anxious to see the re-creation of a New Zealand Maori hut, another feature of the place, for she shared with Frederick an interest in the explorations of Cook and his successors, particularly in the South Seas.

After a brief visit to London, Lord Bolling returned to Crossfield Cottage to accompany Nettie, her parents, and her sister on their journey to the city. The two boys, Masters Jonathan and William, were left behind, to the satisfaction of all. The family intended to stay but three nights with Gussie, and then Mr. and Mrs. Rice, with Francie and Nettie, would go as guests to Lord Bolling's townhouse in Berkeley Square, Lord Bolling meanwhile lodging with a cousin. Only Polly would stay on with Gussie. It was true, as Gussie insisted, that she could accommodate them very well, with only the most minimum discomfort, but Mrs. Rice insisted that in her second pregnancy Gussie needed rest, particularly as her delivery date was so near.

They arrived late in the afternoon. Gussie was at the door to meet them, and by her side her husband. Julian Furneaux was a former soldier, and he bore himself as though on parade. Although he had family connections among the aristocracy, he had no aristocratic pretensions. Like the family into which he had married, he was content to take a place in the wealthy middle class. A genius at intricate finance, he was a friend of Nathan Rothschild, having come to the latter's notice for his role in the final deliveries of gold to the Duke of Wellington during the Peninsular Campaign. He thought himself well mated in Gussie, for like her brother Peter, she had an immediate grasp of financial matters — and financial matters were his only interests, except for his growing family and a seemingly uncharacteristic devotion to the sport of boxing. He stood quietly, a little apart now, observing the family reunion.

Gussie was in her seventh month, and so was not going about in public, which meant that she was doubly delighted to have company. It did get boring shut up in the house all the time, confined to her modest garden for exercise, and she wished often that she could be in the country where she could take long walks, despite her bulk. She was delicate, she knew, because she had been told so, and her doctor had recommended that she rest at least three hours a day, but she felt if she could exercise a bit in the fresh air that it would do her no harm. She had never been ill in the country. She was certain that boredom made her feel sluggish, and expected her family to remedy that problem.

Mrs. Rice, after a quick kiss on her daughter's cheek,

329

stepped aside to allow the others to greet her. This second infant was coming very soon after the first. It was true that the births would be no closer than her own first two — Peter and Polly — but after this pregnancy she really should rest for a time. Nonetheless, she was looking very well, and Mrs. Rice's motherly worries abated.

When the greetings were over and they had refreshed themselves, they met in the back parlor, where Gussie and her husband awaited them beside a laden tea tray. Polly came hurrying in, her cheeks and the tip of her nose reddened by the cold and her eyes sparkling. At the moment, at least, Mrs. Rice observed to her husband with an exchange of glances, Polly looked in good spirits.

Lady Moresby sent a note to Frederick at his temporary lodging as soon as they were settled at their London Hotel to ask if he was free to come round soon, and before they made their plans for the week of their stay in London. He replied promptly and, at four o'clock that afternoon, presented himself at their apartments.

"Are you free to join us for dinner, Frederick?" asked Lady Moresby. "I have always thought the dining room here excellent."

Frederick agreed to dine with them and asked about their other plans.

"I've some shopping, and your father some business, but nothing that could not bear waiting. Polly's exhibition, of course. Do you expect to attend?"

"I presume you will want to go the first day, but I thought it would be more tactful if I went around a day or so later."

Lady Moresby regarded him thoughtfully, but re-

330

frained from the question she wanted to ask. What could be of such consequence that it could keep apart two people so obviously well suited? However, she remarked only that they would be calling at Gussie's. "Have you called, Frederick?" she asked.

"No. I've not thought it necessary. I don't know Polly's sister well, nor her husband at all."

"Now that the family's here, you must, no matter what is between you and Polly. I really think, Frederick, that you should accompany your father and me when we call."

"You are right, of course, ma'am," Frederick replied.

The visit was made the following afternoon, but to the disappointment of them all (including Frederick, although his disappointment was mixed with relief), Polly was not in.

Polly was standing by Mr. Jedro, the two of them gazing at a full-length portrait of an Indian, entitled "Black Wing." The Indian's cloak was thrown casually over one shoulder and arm, but so gracefully that it fell around him like a king's royal robe. His entire strong, lithe body was revealed, painted and gleaming with oil. Only a breechclout hid his nakedness.

Polly was frowning. "I never intended, as I have twice written you, sir, that this painting should be exhibited or sold. That I was even in the studio with the man would have been scandalous — let alone that I painted him from life. Furthermore, once word spreads, it will discourage people from coming to the exhibition — especially those on whom we must depend for sales — which you and my brother Peter have both emphasized as the purpose of this display."

331

Mr. Jedro was a large, bulky man, with a halo of wispy black hair surrounding a bald pate, and a large Roman nose dominating an otherwise undistinguished face. He was soberly dressed, for he had discovered that he could say and do the most outrageous things if he hid himself behind a formally proper exterior. At the moment he was contemplating one of his outrages: to show a full-length painting of a near-naked man, painted from life by a female artist. And a near-naked savage at that. The whole thing was downright revolutionary and would surely stimulate sales. His immediate task, however, was to gain her permission to show it. He adjusted his voice to its most reasonable tone to answer her objection. "You do not understand the value of sensation, my dear. Consider the mobs at Murray's when the new canto of *Don Juan* appeared."

"That may be, but Lord Byron has been driven from England.

Mr. Jedro nimbly changed course. "For his scandalous behavior not his work. And in any event, this Indian has not been inconsiderate of his modesty. If you will excuse the vulgarity, he has, after all, chosen to chastely cover his private parts. You see, I speak frankly with you, as one lover of truth to another. Come, Miss Rice."

"You know perfectly well, Mr. Jedro, that no one will believe that this portrait was painted from a plaster model. My uncle would no doubt have confined me to my room for a month had he known what I was doing. We thought it a lark—the two young men who sneaked me into the studio. And the painter whose studio it was— I won't even tell you his name . . ." Remembering, Polly suddenly laughed. "He was so angry with us at first, but when he saw that I, at least, was serious, he let me stay.

332

And then"—she as suddenly sobered—"in Brazil . . ."

"Very interesting, I'm sure," replied Jedro, who was not at all interested. It was not method, but result, that mattered to him. "However you accomplished it, the painting is superb."

"Nonetheless, it must not be shown. I do thank you for your appreciation, but I would not be so unthinking as to cause my family embarrassment. And my sister is soon to marry a respectable man who has already suffered great embarrassment at the hands of a profligate wife. I myself . . ."

She stopped. Why should she consider Frederick? Trying to be honest with herself, she conceded that she valued Frederick's opinion more than ever since admitting her own impropriety of conduct. She could not help hoping for a reconciliation, nor ignore her fear that a scandal would destroy any possibility of a renewal of their engagement.

Jedro broke in on her thoughts with another change of direction. "I undertook the supervision of your botanical engravings because I thought them worthy, and for the same reason I agreed to sell your work when your brother approached me. But I admit to another reason." Mr. Jedro prodded himself into an oratorical frame of mind. "Women, like men of the lower orders, are not expected to have the capacity to achieve greatness—or even a superior understanding. I believe John Keats to be a poet who will one day outrank Byron; yet, because he is of humble birth, it is assumed by the critics that he cannot be as great."

Mr. Jedro, although he never forgot the primacy of monetary gain, did believe sincerely that human progress was served in art, as in science, by exploration, experimentation, and a search for truth. The scientists studied physics to determine laws of nature. Artists, he believed, should search for new ways to see and new ways to put what they saw on paper and canvas. And who knew what wonders were locked up in women of all classes and in men of the common herd? This Miss Rice, now — a perfectly respectable female, nothing out of the ordinary way about her. Yet in some of her work he saw passionate feeling. And that Indian! Didn't she realize that she had painted Rousseau's noble savage? Of course her technique was not so well developed as in some of her later work — but it was one of those rare cases of flaws enhancing rather than detracting from a work. And how had she achieved such facility with the human figure?

Lost in thought, Mr. Jedro had not heard Polly's comments on Keats and, assuming they paralleled his own, merely murmured in response, "Yes, yes. How true." Ignoring the puzzled look Polly gave him, he turned to her and with solemn face pronounced, "Your work shows the same daring experimentation generally that our young poets attempt in their work. And with color — the daring that Turner is accustoming us to, but there is a delicacy of touch to your brush that —"

"Oh, do stop, please," Polly begged. "You begin to sound like a critic. It is enough for me that you like my work and are willing to undertake the sales. But are not my other paintings sufficient to demonstrate woman's capacity — inferior as mine may be to a Turner or a West . . ."

Mr. Jedro quickly returned to the straightforward honesty he preferred, but that he had found most artists did not. "It is not inferior, my child, if we consider your work in comparison with work of those men when they were your age. I've never deceived you by suggesting that your work is yet great. It is good; it is promising; the two new oils you have brought me show that you are achieving ever greater skill in the medium, and a few of the water-colors—this painting of Niagara Falls, for example—are superior. As for the Indian portrait that we were discussing, it could not be better. It is one of the best works in the exhibition."

The door opened unnoticed as Polly replied, "You are persuasive, but what has the portrait of the Indian to do with women?"

A discreet cough drew their attention to Lord Bolling. Nettie, not given to discreet coughs, asked, "Yes, what does a portrait of an Indian have to do with women.

"Nothing at all," said Polly.

"Everything," said Mr. Jedro. "I am trying to convince Miss Rice to allow me to exhibit this magnificent painting, but she argues that because the chief—"

"He was not a chief," Polly interrupted.

"—is, uh, not in proper London attire, and the fact that the artist is female, there will be a scandal."

"You *know* there will be a scandal!" Polly exclaimed. "We were discussing whether or not to create one, Mr. Jedro."

Mr. Jedro continued to address Bolling and Nettie. "Miss Rice was just asking, as you entered, what the portrait had to do with women. I was preparing to answer that question. . . . Shhh, shhh, Miss Rice. . . . But before I go into that, let me say that it is one of the three best works in the entire collection, and I want it shown. However, the reasons I want to show it are not only because of that fact (although that is my primary reason), but also to demonstrate what a woman can do. I furthermore believe

335

that art should have no limits; that the artist has a right to paint any subject, and in any way he, or she, sees fit, and to exhibit it publicly."

During this statement of philosophic principle, in which Mr. Jedro had omitted only the profit motive, Nettie had been gazing mesmerized at the painting. She had, like all children resident at Tanwell through the centuries, closely observed the naked Adam in the carvings that decorated the dining room at Tanwell. She had studied pen and ink illustrations in books. But she had never seen, in gorgeous color, such a bold, proud, and straightforward display of masculine muscle and sinew. Coming to life with a start in the pause that followed Mr. Jedro's speech, she emphatically exclaimed, "Well, I agree! Of course Polly must show her best work."

"Nettie, do think! When women can't study unclothed human bodies in life classes, even *female* bodies and in *draperies*, what will be said of a woman who has painted an unclothed man?"

"Who cares about gossip? I am not afraid!"

"But censure? Social ostracism?"

Mr. Jedro, recognizing an ally in Nettie, intervened. "Miss Rice. You exaggerate!"

Lord Bolling, more thoughtful, and with some experience of gossip and scandal, was more cautious. "Your sister has a right to wish to avoid scandal, my dear. It is not easy to be the subject of g-g-gossip."

Polly, in order to cut short a discussion which must be painful to Nettie's future husband, held out her hand to Mr. Jedro. "I'll think about it and let you know tomorrow. Your oratory has stiffened my backbone, but I'm not sure it is sufficiently stiffened, and I must still consider my family. Please do not expect my agreement."

336

In the carriage, as they returned to Gussie's, Nettie took up the attack. "You say that you must consider your family, Polly. Well, if that is so, then you must consult your family. I insist that we do so before you make you decision."

"A family conference?"

"Yes, a family conference. I hadn't thought of calling a meeting, but it would be just the thing!"

Lord Bolling observed that Nettie had made an important point. "You can hardly make a d-decision based on family c-considerations without consulting their opinions."

"Surely it would be thought a strange way to go about making decisions — calling everyone together to consult them on such a subject? Wouldn't it be better to ask each one privately?"

"It might, if the exhibition were two weeks from now rather than two days."

Polly did not answer immediately. Then she said, "Perhaps you're right, Nettie. But first I must speak with our father. If he has no objection to exhibition of the painting, then we can speak to the others."

"What a famous idea!" Nettie exclaimed, with a touch of sarcasm. "You know how Papa is. He will never agree."

"He agreed to let me teach you to waltz."

Lord Bolling again intervened. "I think, my dear, that if Mr. Rice objected in a general d-discussion, then the rest of the family would also disagree. Perhaps it might be b-b-b . . ."

"Best?"

". . . to obtain his opinion p-privately, as your sister suggests."

Polly went immediately on their return in search of her

337

father. She found him in the small library, which Gussie set aside for his exclusive use whenever he came to London.

"Excuse me, sir, may I interrupt? I have a problem I wish to lay before you."

Mr. Rice invited her to join him by the fire, and, looking at her kindly, rubbed his hands together and said, "I should never say so to Gussie, but I will be glad to retreat tomorrow to my future son-in-law's residence, which I hope may be better heated. Well, now, you tell me you have a problem?"

"It's not a terrible problem, Papa. It's only a question of propriety, and I need your advice."

Polly quickly told the story, describing the portrait, how it came to be painted, and Mr. Jedro's arguments. Mr. Rice listened without interruption, leaning forward with his hands to the fire. When she finished, he settled back in his chair and took a good look at his first daughter, his odd child. She looked so much like her sister Gussie, yet it was Nettie who was most like Gussie—both with quick intelligence, and that appearance of abstraction when they listened to a conversation. Polly was an odd mixture: her mother's practicality, a disorder about her and an impetuosity that had no precedent in either family. But her talent was his own pleasure in visual detail made manifest. The passive emotional resonance of his response to a great painting was vibrant and active in his daughter. Although he had submerged this emotion in the more intellectual pleasures of scholarship, he had recognized his young daughter's obvious talent, and was encouraged by her response to the visual world to believe that she might share the same mysterious affinity that was his. He had spared no expense for her drawing mas-

338

ters, securing at last a man who refused to engage in the teaching of drawing as a genteel ladies' accomplishment. When the master was satisfied with his pupil, he recommended to Mr. Rice a young watercolorist to instruct her in a medium in which English painters excelled, and who was equally as exigent. Once released from the discipline of teachers, she had imposed discipline upon herself. She was, he fully realized for the first time, an artist. As his daughter, she deserved his counsel, but as an artist, she deserved his respect. First, however, he wanted to see the painting.

Mr. Jedro was visibly nervous as he unlocked the door and ushered Mr. Rice and Polly into the room. The fading afternoon light was bad for viewing. Should he light a lamp?

"No need for that," Mr. Rice assured him. "I have come only to look at a painting in order to give my daughter advice. I am not here as an art lover."

Mr. Jedro had the wits to hold his tongue.

The examination was soon over. Mr. Rice thanked him, took Polly's arm, and escorted her from the gallery to the bows of Mr. Jedro, who with great difficulty was still holding his tongue. As they emerged into the street, Polly's father drew her arm through his and patted her hand. "I cannot give you advice on whether you should allow the portrait to be shown or not, for you alone will bear the attacks on your delicacy. But I can give you assurance of my support should you do so."

"Thank you, Papa."

Mr. Rice handed Polly into the waiting carriage. He raised the window to shut out the rain that had begun to fall while they were in the gallery, took off his hat and brushed it, called unnecessary directions to the coachman, settled his hat on his head, fingered his cravat, and at last spoke. "The body is exceptionally well executed, Polly. Am I wrong in my belief that a knowledge of anatomy is a necessary preliminary to painting the human figure?"

"Well, you see, Papa, one did occasionally see Indians very scantily clad, and in Brazil, it is a tropical country, sir, and the slaves . . ."

"Yes, I see."

This was one of Polly's guilty secrets—her interest in unclad bodies—but, she thought defiantly, it was only after she had begun to study her own body and how its lines changed with movement—as best she could in uneasy secrecy and with inadequate mirrors—and after she had seen men with arms and chests bared that her drawings and paintings of clothed bodies came alive. She had needed to know what lay under the clothing. Well, she might as well confess all.

"I finished the painting you just saw in Brazil. I had anatomy lessons there from one of the French artists. He thought it wrong that women could not study the human figure. But when it was discovered that he brought live models into his classes, he was threatened with deportation. My uncle was very angry with me, but fortunately it was thought that I, and the two other women who dared enter his studio, were innocent girls saved from a degenerate mind."

Polly began to cry, surprising herself as well as her father. Mr. Rice was for once at a loss. He had been more moved by the painting than he cared to admit—deeply moved by the dignity and grief he saw in the man's face—and with his emotions roused, Mr. Rice was not certain he could respond with his characteristic thoughtfulness.

While he sorted hastily through his confusion for an adequate word to comfort his daughter, Polly regained her control. Drying her eyes, she added, with only the slightest tremor in her voice, "Even in France, where women receive more encouragement than we do here, you know, it is not thought proper for them to study from live models. Oh, Papa, I do fear that I will embarrass you all!"

"It was not thought a woman's province to do historical or allegorical paintings, Polly, but Angelica Kauffmann did so, and was one of the founders of the Royal Academy."

"Yes, and no woman has been allowed to become a member since!"

The bitterness in Polly's voice surprised him even more than her tears.

"Well, well, you can exhibit with the Academy, nonetheless."

"Yes, if my paintings are approved by the Hanging Committee."

"Well, well," he murmured again, unable to think of anything else to say.

Polly could have said that he didn't understand, for indeed, he did not. He had never experienced that particular suffering that so many men and women, through the centuries, have endured—the creative spirit, seeking recognition and release. Polly herself did not understand it. She only knew that Mr. Jedro was forcing her to make a decision, although perhaps from motives she could not respect, to continue to struggle to paint the way she wanted to paint. She *would* show the Indian, and she would let Mr. Jedro sell it to whomever wanted it! Then she remembered her previous concern for her family's opinion, even for Frederick's, and that, as her diplomatist

341

uncle had taught her, in any conflict, compromise is essential unless one is willing to risk war. She was foolish to concern herself with Frederick's opinion — that was over and done with — but her family was another matter.

That very evening, at Nettie's insistence, a note was sent round to Peter, and to Aunt Cat and Clarissa, asking that they join them for discussion of a family matter.

Lord Bolling was the first to speak: that as one who had suffered from wagging tongues, he could testify to the pain that gossip could cause the target. His observation of society, however, led him to believe that scandal seldom attached to the relatives and friends of the victim, and that it rather tended to gain them sympathy. He, for one, was prepared to withstand any criticism or calumny that might come his way owing to an association with Polly through his dear Nettie, but he did not pretend that scandal could be avoided.

Clarissa, whose mood had changed from impatience on receipt of the summons to horror as she learned the reason, exclaimed, "Polly, how *could* you? I will not have another season ruined! I will not!"

Aunt Cat's bosom heaved in agreement. "It wouldn't be so terrible if he wasn't a *real* man." At a quizzical look from her brother, she bridled. "Well, I mean, after all, there she was . . ."

"And there he was," Peter finished.

Exactly. And don't you laugh, Giles," she added, catching Mr. Rice attempting to hide a smile. "I don't know much about art, I admit, but I do know that it is just improper for an unmarried lady to look at a man without his clothes. There! I can speak right out if I have to."

342

Peter remarked that since the family fortunes were secure and showing every sign of increasing, there was no likelihood of financial suffering from a scandal, and he agreed with Mr. Jedro that the scandal (if, in fact, there should be one, of which he was not at all convinced) would enhance the sale of Polly's work. After all, no one could be certain she had painted from life. He furthermore believed the scandal would be confined to a small circle, and soon forgotten.

Polly replied that he knew nothing about it. "Aunt Cat has surely made clear what the general reaction will be."

Gussie swallowed her fears of social ostracism and agreed with Lord Bolling that it was Polly who would have to withstand the brunt of criticism, and that the decision was therefore hers. If the family stood by her, it would take some of the sting from the scandal. Her husband, who saw no harm to his own position in the society he valued, supported his wife.

Clarissa, near tears, cried, "You needn't care, because you're married, Gussie! But I am not, and now I never shall be. Oh! I will have to marry the baron after all, and he's so *old!*"

Turning to Clarissa, Gussie said, "But you are so clever, Clarissa dear, that I'm sure you will be able to find a way to take advantage of such scandal as there may be."

"Yes," Mr. Rice remarked, his amusement at Gussie's barb carefully hidden behind a sober countenance only his wife could interpret. "A little scandal associated with a young lady, just a pinch of daring, is titillating to young swains, if my own experience is any guide."

"What does 'titillating' mean?" Clarissa asked suspiciously.

"Why, a little exciting, intriguing."

343

"Oh," said Clarissa, at once beginning to be reconciled to a notorious relative.

"Just so!" exclaimed Aunt Cat. "Why, Giles, remember when Lord Axton's sister ran off with the butler, how interesting the other girls became? I don't believe one of them had had a suitor before that frightful event, but in the end every one of them was married, and very well, too."

"Are you suggesting, Cat, that a family with too many unmarried girls should sacrifice one of them to the butler?"

"Oh no, of course not, Giles. You know perfectly well what I mean. I agree with Lord Bolling. There are just any number of examples, you know. No one cuts Sir Timothy Shelley because his son leads a scandalous life. Indeed, one pities him!"

"Yes, pity is so much more pleasant than ostracism."

Francie, who had taken no part in the discussion, asked, "What is ostracism, Papa?"

Mrs. Rice had opposed Francie's inclusion in the conference, believing her too young to understand the implications or the consequences. She now spoke, in a sharp tone, "I will explain to you later the meaning of the word, Francie."

Mr. Rice, across the family circle, glanced at his wife questioningly, but she looked away without response.

Clarissa, almost worked around to a different point of view by visions of titillated suitors, decided to exercise her French. "I am beginning to agree with Uncle. It is just too bourgeois to be so concerned for propriety."

Mr. Rice, considering again that he should have turned that young miss over his knee long ago, said repressively, "It is not 'bourgeois' to be concerned for propriety, Clarissa. The argument Mr. Jedro has made—it is, in fact, two arguments—is that Polly's painting of the Indian is one of her best paintings, and second that no artist should be barred by convention from painting any subject. I am not sure I agree that any subject is permissible; a civilized society must recognize some restraints. However, our decision is whether we are willing to undergo the criticism that may attach to us through Polly—such criticism as is often the lot of those who attempt to change the standards by which society is regulated. Polly saw beauty in that young Indian, and she could only have achieved the success that she has by painting from life. As she once told me, among women of virtue, and men of honor, actions that among others might be thought questionable remain innocent. I have given her my own approval."

Whether to avoid a lengthier lecture from Mr. Rice, or from conviction, there were murmurs of acquiescence, however reluctant. Gussie's brilliant young banker offered to pour wine; Aunt Cat protested that she and Clarissa were shockingly late for the rout at Mrs. Barrington's; and Peter was also engaged. So a reduced family circle was left to drink wine together.

Polly accepted a toast by her brother-in-law— "To painting and the painter"—but she excused herself shortly and went to her room, pleading fatigue from the preparations for her exhibit, although in truth she had had little hand in them. It had been a long and difficult day. And on top of it all, she had missed Frederick when he called with his parents. If only she had had just a moment to speak to him!

When Mr. and Mrs. Rice gained the privacy of their

bedchamber, Mrs. Rice could at last unburden herself. "Really, Giles," she scolded, "you should be ashamed of yourself for giving Clarissa the idea that it is smart to be involved in scandal."

"Yes, I admit readily that I gave in to my baser qualities. I could not resist."

"You have an unfortunate habit of making fun of people. Of poking at their weaknesses and encouraging their foolishness."

"Why, Amelia, am I so very bad then?"

Mrs. Rice did not like quarrels, and besides, Mr. Rice was so tolerant of her failings that she never felt quite right in pointing out his. It was unfair! And moreover, he had the habit of admitting so readily to his errors. It was really quite provoking, especially when she was angry or upset, as she was now. She turned away without speaking.

Mr. Rice looked thoughtfully at her rigid back as she sat at the dressing table loosening the braids that she had recently taken to wearing. Her hair was graying, and he speculated for a moment on the passing of time, trying to recall the lines of a poem that teased his memory.

"Well, it *was* wrong of you, Giles," she remarked in the silence.

"Yes, my dear. It was. But you have already chided me for that, and I have admitted my error. Is there something else amiss?"

She turned to him, and he was surprised to discover tears. Everybody seemed turned to watering pots today! His wife was not a woman who cried often; he could have counted the times on the fingers of his two hands, had he had a moment to reflect. The tears told him instantly that there was more to this than displeasure at his really unpardonable behavior with Cat and Clarissa, even though

346

he knew full well that he had won their acceptance more quickly and easily by the course he had taken than by any high-minded arguments.

"Why, my dear, what is it?" He leaned toward her and took her hand. "Come, Amelia. These tears have nothing to do with Cat, or with Clarissa."

She drew away her hand and searched for a handkerchief. He took his own from his pocket and handed it to her.

When she had recovered herself, she said in her normal, controlled voice, "Well, I am angry with you, Giles, for such underhanded tactics, but I do know quite as well as you that it was the quickest way to win Clarissa's and Catherine's acceptance. It is your acceptance to which I object."

He was surprised. "You mean that you do not approve the public showing of the Indian's portrait?"

"No, Giles, I do not. It will create a scandal; you know it will. And it will make it even more unlikely that Frederick and Polly can make up their differences."

"Do you think Frederick is the only man who will ever want to marry Polly?"

Mrs. Rice rose to open a window. "Doesn't it seem close in here? Perhaps fresh air will clear my head." She stood by the window a moment looking out. At last she said, "I want Polly married, and settled; having children and leading a respectable life. I don't want scandal in the family. Nettie is marrying a divorced man. And Francie is reaching the age when such things make a difference to a girl."

Her husband did not answer immediately. At last he said, "Why, Amelia, I'm surprised at you. You are the last person from whom I would have expected to hear such

347

sentiments."

She looked at him in surprise. "I don't understand you, Giles. My family were ordinary respectable people and I have always been an ordinary and respectable woman."

"Have you, Amelia?"

"It is unusual, of course, for a woman to oversee the agricultural affairs of an estate, but it's perfectly respectable."

"I'm not referring to that. Think a minute, my dear, and be honest."

"I suppose then you mean that my father took up Methodism and became a preacher. Of course that was unusual for our class, but there was nothing disreputable about it."

"No."

"Then I don't know what you mean."

"I think you do."

Mrs. Rice turned back to the window. After a moment she said, "I suppose you are referring to my efforts to help a few poor women." Her voice was flat.

Mr. Rice went to stand at the window by his wife. "Come sit by me, Amelia." He led her to the bed, and pulled her down beside him. "Do you remember that our farmer came to me to report mutterings against those efforts? Do you know that I have had to speak to Riggs and threaten him with severe reprisal should he harm you? That Polly has spoken to me of her concern, because of threats reported to her?"

"It's only that fool Riggs," Mrs. Rice said, her mouth set in a stubborn line.

"No, it's not just Riggs, as I'm sure you know. Do you realize, Amelia, what you are doing?"

She replied angrily, "Yes, I know what I am doing! I

am helping desperate women!"

"But it is not respectable work," Mr. Rice replied gently. "It is indelicate for a woman to discuss such subjects. And furthermore, you are encouraging debauchery—telling respectable married women they can behave like prostitutes."

Mrs. Rice gasped. "How can you say such a thing, Giles? The women I help are loyal to their husbands; they have children; their motives are pure."

"No, my dear. You are undermining the morals of respectable women."

Mrs. Rice stared at him aghast. "You don't believe that."

"No, of course, I don't. But that's because I know you, and I know the women to whom you have given help. They are deserving, morally upright women. Nonetheless, you are defying the conventions, and discussing openly what is not discussed in polite society. Furthermore, many reformers would oppose your efforts. They have spoken against Malthus's recommendation of late marriage because they believe the purpose to be to limit the numbers of the poor in order to relieve us of the trouble of improving their lot."

"I have never cared for the opinion of polite society. And as for your last argument, I care nothing for reformers!"

Mr. Rice took her chin in his hand and turned her face to look into her angry eyes. "Did you say you have no care for polite society?"

Suddenly her anger was gone, and in its place he saw her familiar fleeting, sardonic smile. "You trapped me. I should have been more cautious."

"Yes. And you should know that Polly stated, when she

reported threats against you, that she cared not at all about polite society's opinion, only that you not come to any harm."

Her face softened. "So I'm not respectable? Well then, I suppose I must accept that my daughter is not."

"Yes, I think you must." He shivered. "Do you think we could have the window closed now?"

"Of course. I'm sorry. I didn't notice how cold it had become, I was so angry with you. And this house is always so cold anyway!"

He watched her from the edge of the bed as she crossed to the window. "Do you mind that we must share a room and a bed for another night, Amelia?"

"Of course not. Particularly since I've turned our bedroom into an icehouse."

"Do you remember that inn not far from Bath?"

He was rewarded with an enigmatic glance. "Yes, that was a very cold inn, and a very cold night, Mr. Rice, but a very warm bed."

It was the closest they had ever come, in their long years together, of open acknowledgement of pleasure in each other.

Before they went to sleep, Mrs. Rice murmured, "You know, don't you, Giles, that for my daughters' sakes, I would stop talking to the women."

"Yes, my dear, I know it. Now go to sleep."

Chapter Nineteen

According to Mr. Jedro's way of thinking, the exhibition of Polly's work had been a success. He sold most of the oil pantings and all of the watercolors, including, for an exceptionally good price, the portrait of the Indian. Mr. Jedro was further gratified by the number of essays and critiques, despite the novelty of such an exhibition, and considered the money he had spent publicizing it as money well spent.

The portrait of the Indian had created, if not a sensation, at least some sensational speculation. Had it been, in fact, painted from life? Mr. Jedro would not say, merely looking mysterious. However, he advised Polly to respond to all questions by stating that she wanted to be judged by her work, not by the circumstances in which it was painted. She elected to follow his advice.

Although the critics were far from an accord on whether the model was animate or not, *The Sun* made what Mr. Jedro considered the authoritative pronouncement. "It is too much to believe that Miss Rice could have found in America either a classical statue or a suitable plaster model from which to paint the form of the Indian, Black Wing. It is equally too much to believe that after faithfully painting a lifeless body, she added a head from life. The vigor and unity of the work forbid it." Nonetheless, the critic suggested that Miss Rice, for her own welfare, would be better advised to confine herself thereafter to landscapes and leave the human body, at least unclothed bodies, to the less delicate sex.

Another critic ignored the controversy entirely, judging Polly an unformed artist, still experimenting to find her medium. He suggested she concentrate on watercolor, in which she seemed both most daring and to command "the surer brush." The essay continued in similar judicious vein, described her Indian paintings as "a highlight," noted her youth, criticized the "excessive color," and looked forward to another female name joined with that of Angelica Kauffmann on the list of England's illustrious artists.

One critic commented that it was possible Miss Rice had committed an indiscretion, but that it did not detract from the quality of the work. (This caused Mr. Jedro a hearty laugh. "In fact, *improves* the quality," he told his wife.) *The British Press* held that a woman painting a nearly nude man — no matter whether from life or a plaster cast — was indicative of the debauched standards of the age. But the majority concentrated solely on the scandal, without mention of Polly's work at all. One such expatiated long on the many outlets females enjoyed for their talents that would not offend decency: they could do miniatures, paint pleasant landscapes, decorate workboxes, and press flowers under glass. Genteel ladies could also paint flowers, and he reminded his readers that Miss Rice had done a very attractive book of engravings.

For her part, Polly weathered the storm well, cocooned within her family and a growing acquaintance among sympathetic artists. Mr. Benjamin West, on whom she called shortly after the exhibition, was no longer in good health and perhaps for that reason was overly critical of

352

her work. But he had a fondness for young artists, and for Polly because she so openly and enthusiastically appreciated his native America. His criticism was tempered with that fondness. Her connection with Lord Bolling, whose family was old, established, and of some influence, also was an advantage to her in weathering the storm. And a moneyed family, as Peter had insisted, had a certain immunity, particularly a family such as theirs—a family that was no bourgeois mushroom upstart.

Frosts in November hinted of future snowfalls. In Gussie's small garden the berries were bright red among the shiny green of the holly. Hundreds of sparrows hid among the leaves, and when Gussie or Polly took their exercise in the garden, the birds rose in clouds, filling the air with a whirring of wings. The poor old mad king lay dying; the regency of his son was coming to an end. Not far distant, a baby named Victoria, granddaughter of the king and niece of the regent, lay gurgling in her cradle.

The "little season," for which Mr. Jedro had timed Polly's exhibition, had brought a number of people back to town, and social engagements and public entertainments had increased. Frederick was in a period of hiatus in which he seemed unable to make a decision or any positive move. It was as if it were enough that Polly was in the same city. So he waited, uncertain what he waited for, and in the meantime he renewed former acquaintances and returned to some of his former amusements. He was seen often at his club, at social gatherings, and at the theatre, but he was never observed in the company of any member of the opposite sex.

After the excitement of Polly's exhibition abated, after their parents and family returned to Tanwell, Polly and

Gussie had time to recover their old sisterly intimacy. It was not long before Gussie knew the whole story of Frederick and the quarrel, although she was not certain why Polly could not have said to Frederick quite simply that she had always been virtuous, even if she had been perhaps a little fast.

"Goodness," Gussie said. "My Julian wasn't the first man I'd ever kissed."

"I know. It was just that Frederick suspected me of behavior that, were I a man, would have been reason for admiration."

"Surely you can't think that a woman should be admired for a series of lovers?" Gussie picked up the little cap she was embroidering for her new baby. "Are you sure you're being quite fair to Mr. Moresby?" she asked, as she bent her head over her work. "Frankly, Polly, I think Clarissa should be called to account for her meddling. I've known her longer than you have, and while she can be marvelous company, she's also selfish and self-centered."

"I can't be certain that Clarissa insinuated I'd behaved improperly."

"Then how otherwise would he have come to suspect you?"

"Nettie said I flirted too much with Alex—Mr. Chapham. And I did. Frederick could easily think that it was a sign of wantonness."

"That's too silly to believe. Didn't you ever flirt with Mr. Moresby?"

"No. One doesn't flirt with men like Frederick."

"Why not?"

"He's too stuffy."

"Stuffy? Do you mean serious?"

"I suppose so," Polly said defensively. She wasn't sure what she meant, except that she irrationally felt that Frederick should have forced her to deny Clarissa's insinuations and, in whatever event, not allowed her to break their engagement and then ride off. Why hadn't he recognized words spoken in anger?

"Well," Gussie said, "You're pretty stuffy yourself. I've thought it was because of worry about your exhibition, or because you were feeling badly about Mr. Moresby, but maybe you changed more than I thought while you were being a diplomatist."

Polly looked at Gussie in surprise. "I don't think I've changed."

"I think you have."

Polly was shocked into silence. Had she been the stuffy one? She'd always trod a carefully proper path with Frederick. That day by the stream, when Frederick, teasing, lighthearted, reached for a handful of mud, and then they were in each other's arms . . . A blush rose with the memory, and then other memories besieged her, of conversations, quiet walks, laughter as they met in the allemande, tender moments, Frederick as he examined that poor cow. She shuddered with the desolation of her loss, while Gussie quietly plied her needle, her expression composed.

"Mama seemed to think I was too hoydenish, and after all, I was twenty-four when I came home, and it was time for me to acquire more dignity. And with Francie and Nettie looking up to me, she said — and she was correct — I needed to present a better example."

Gussie uttered an exclamation of disbelief. "Oh, really, how could Mama suggest such a thing! If Nettie and Francie need example, it's how to be a little more light-

355

hearted—a little less proper and well-behaved! Sometimes I think you, and perhaps William, maybe Papa occasionally, are the only ones in the family with any lightness of spirit to leaven our seriousness. Why, it's only because of growing up with you that Peter and I aren't depressingly proper and sober-minded."

"Perhaps Mama was less proper herself when we were young. She seemed more concerned for propriety when I returned from America than before I left." Polly was suddenly struck with a memory of Mr. Riggs. "Bless me!" she exclaimed. "I'd forgotten about Riggs and his wife."

Polly's description of their mother's activities among the poor was received with amazed exclamations from Gussie and a good deal of interest. "And to think! She never said a word to me! She might have told me!" Gussie ran on in like vein for some time, truly angry with her mother for not equipping her *own* married daughter with such useful information, until the striking of the clock reminded them that it was time to change for dinner. As Gussie put away her embroidery, she reverted to their earlier conversation. "But you know, Polly, you must think of something, whether you call Clarissa to account or not. That is, if you truly love Frederick. You do, don't you?"

Polly sighed. "Yes, although it took me forever to realize it. In fact, Nettie had to tell me. That is, she told me how she felt about Bolling, and when I thought about it, that seemed to be the way I felt about Frederick. But oh, Gussie, I did wish he had a little more dash!"

"Let's hear no more of that, now," Gussie admonished as she turned to greet her husband, who had just come into the room.

* * *

356

Gussie was nearing her due date, and Polly thought to stay with her through her lying-in and for a time after the baby was born, and then she would decide her future. To her surprise, Gussie denied her.

"I won't have you setting yourself up as a maiden auntie," Gussie scolded. "I won't have you called on by all and sundry to help out whenever birth or death or disaster strike. That's what you were doing for Uncle Peyton, no matter how exciting it was to live in America. Now you're helping Mama and Papa. Soon you'll be helping Nettie get settled. No, Polly, I won't have it. You can come to visit me, but just to visit — not to help out — and you will have to expect me to introduce you to hoardes of eligible men, and you can't stay long enough to keep you away from your painting."

Polly asked with some irony if it would be all right if she stayed on for a short while at least. She'd like to do some visiting, some further refurbishing of her wardrobe, and had been offered a commission for a portrait of a gentleman who had such an interesting face that she was eager to do it. "And I've met a woman named Clara Wheelock who does illustrations for a fashion house. She's married and has children, and works in a studio not far from her home in Marylebone that she's asked me to share. I thought perhaps I could arrange for a hackney to call for me every day and bring me home at night. Do you think you could put up with me for another few weeks?"

Gussie went to her sister and gave her a hug. "Oh, Polly. I love having you here. Your idea sounds marvelous. Just think — a studio!" She hugged Polly again. "We'll send our carriage for you, of course. But," she added, "you can't help with the new baby, because I'll have a woman to do that. You are a painter. And anyway, you

357

should be married. And I am determined that you shall be. As soon as this tiresome pregnancy is over, I will give a brilliant round of parties. I'll have you married to some rich London banker, and then I shall have you in London all the time instead of so far away in the country."

"If I stay in London, I'll more likely find myself wed to an impecunious painter, or to some eccentric art collector."

"How exciting!" Gussie clapped her hands. "Have you met someone? Tell me."

"It's true, I've met more men in these three weeks than I'd meet in a lifetime in the country, but I can't so readily forget Frederick, even if he doesn't have any dash . . ."

"Oh, well, love, as I've tried to tell you, dash isn't everything. And I must say that one wants steadiness in a husband. Dash is for lovers."

"Why Gussie, how naughty you are!"

So the two women chatted and chaffed each other as though they still were girls. Nonetheless, Gussie, who knew Polly so well, saw sadness and loneliness in the droop of her mouth. One evening, when she thought Polly was looking particularly sad, she decided to take matters in hand, and later, in the privacy of their own chambers, she spoke to her husband.

"Do you think, Julian, that you could arrange a small theater party?"

"But my dear," Julian replied, as he removed his cravat and folded it fastidiously, "you know you cannot go out."

"Yes, I know. But Polly is so sad, and she needs cheering up. There's to be a presentation of *A Midsummer Night's Dream* and I'm sure she would enjoy it. If you could ask some young man, with perhaps the Gardiners — say you've received tickets from someone, or that the young

358

man needs an introduction to the town, or that the Gardiners insist you meet a young acquaintance — or that their young acquaintance wants to meet Polly. Anything."

"You're making up a novel, Gussie. I can't produce from thin air people who have young men who need introducing, or who have tickets to entertainments that they want to bestow on me."

"Oh, Julian! You know very well that — at least with the Gardiners — it would be a conspiracy. The young man will be innocent, of course." Gussie frowned in thought. "Or you could entertain business associates, and need a hostess."

Julian Furneaux did not enjoy intrigue, but he had been a very good conspirator in the life-and-death business during the recent war of getting funds to the Duke of Wellington in Spain, and he was not incapable of carrying out one of Gussie's suggested intrigues. Within the week he was sitting in a theater box with Polly, the Gardiners, and a young Frenchman ordered by his father to London to study the workings of the London Exchange.

Frederick, with two young men, was watching the same performance. One of the young men was the brother of an old school acquaintance who now resided year-round in the country. With a friend the young man called on Frederick soon after their arrival in London. Both were in the naval service, and prepared to enjoy to the full their weeks of freedom from duty. Frederick invited them to join him at the theater that very evening.

As the first act came to an end, he suggested that they stretch their legs. They were preparing to exit in order to pace the passageway, when he caught sight of Polly. She looked extraordinarily beautiful. Her short hair curled forward on her cheeks, and two flowers over each ear, held in place by a bright band strung through her curls, formed a frame for her face. The light shawl about her shoulders did not hide the depth of her décolletage. As she rose to greet an elderly lady, her shawl slipped from one shoulder, revealing her figure, her breasts high above the slim waist and the graceful flare of the skirt. As though she felt his gaze, she turned her head and looked directly at him. He bowed; she smiled warmly and inclined her head, then turned to speak to the elegant gentleman who was busily adjusting the shawl around her shoulders.

"I say," his friend's young brother asked, "wasn't that Miss Paula Rice you bowed to?"

"Yes," Frederick answered, hiding his surprise. "You are acquainted with her?"

"Oh, yes. Knew her in Brazil. Rio was a regular port of call. On the South Atlantic station, you know. What's she doing in London? Is that her husband with her? We always wondered, didn't we, Knyvyt, why she didn't marry that Filipe fellow who was so gone on her. Common knowledge that he offered for her."

"Well," said his companion, "Miss Rice always was a sensible one, even if she was all the time hanging around with that French chit and those artists. The Dom had money, but the way they keep their women locked up over there—well, too confining for Miss Paula by far." He glanced across at Polly again, who was studying him and his friend quite openly, with a slightly puzzled expression. "But I say, Woodruff. Why are we wasting our time standing around here? Let's go say hello."

They started off, and then, remembering their manners, halted. Woodruff asked politely, "Care to accompany us, sir?"

"No, thank you. I won't intrude on your reunion with Miss Rice. But please convey my regards."

"Right," said Woodruff, anxious to be off.

"We'll rejoin you immediately, sir, as soon as we pay our respects."

Frederick sank back in his seat, and then promptly got out of it again. He couldn't sit there looking at Polly's reunion with those two sprigs, but then again, he couldn't sit there pointedly not watching. So he made his way into the passageway, where he paced until the curtain for the second act was called.

He couldn't stop himself from glancing repeatedly in Polly's direction, and sat through the rest of the play staring at the stage with his mind on Polly. He seemed unable to control his head from turning her way, or his eyes from seeking her face. Once he caught her looking at him, but she tilted her chin in a disdainful gesture and looked away. Frederick had some satisfaction in thinking she was angry. If that warm smile had been an invitation to forgive and forget, as he hoped, then that disdainful tilt of the head was anger that he had not responded. Could it be that she wanted reconciliation too? He had made unforgivable accusations for which he was heartily sorry, but which continued to loom — great obstacles in the path of their reconciliation.

He felt it necessary to invite his two young companions to supper and for a brandy at his club after the theater, and then found it necessary to listen to Polly's praises sung. There was no hint in their conversation of anything more than lighthearted flirtation, although there was speculation about "that Filipe fellow" and why Polly hadn't married him. They were calling on her the next day; she seemed settled in town for a time, which was

361

news Frederick considered worth his time to hear, although otherwise he was thoroughly exasperated with them and with himself. So Polly had been loved, had apparently received a proposal of marriage, and had refused it. Where the thought of lovers had maddened him, the idea of a correct proposal was pleasingly respectable. Until there appeared in his imagination a formidable Spaniard — or Portuguese rather — but they surely looked alike — with smoldering eyes, no doubt, and a taste for passion. Frederick was called back to the present when the young Woodruff said, "I say, sir, this must be a crashing bore for you, listening to our reminiscences about Brazil."

Frederick assured them it was not, ordered another round of brandy, and encouraged the young lieutenants to talk about their naval service and their ships. He asked some questions about reform in the treatment of the men on His Majesty's ships, but found the young officers uninterested in questions of impressment, or of punishments and pay for the lower deck. So he listened to their stories, and after a decent interval excused himself in order to return to his lodgings, where he could brood in peace.

Frederick was finding himself caught, and without will to resist, in a round of balls and routs and parties. Although he had never been a member of the high life to which Clarissa and her aunt clung, their different circles were not exclusive. When they intersected, he was always polite, but distant. Clarissa, released from the clutches of the Odious Gentleman, had all of London to fish in, and Frederick often glimpsed her batting her lashes at a circle of admiring young fellows. He would have thought her no

362

longer on the catch for him, except for the artful allure in the curve of her smile whenever she managed to catch his eye. He took great pains to come no closer than the distance of a room.

He saw her again at a polite musical evening he attended as a favor to a friend. The music bored him, the conversation bored him, and the refreshments bored him. He seemed to be stalled in a mire of social activity and indecision, wanting Polly but unable to make up his mind how to initiate a reconciliation. In the week since the theater he had spent every evening sitting by his fire drinking port and brooding, until he was beginning to feel himself a dissolute. But that was exactly where he wanted to go at that moment—to his fire and his port.

He was just making his way toward his hostess when Clarissa intercepted him. Treating him to a flutter of lashes, she said, "Mr. Moresby, I determined to intercept you when I saw you yawning during the performance of that terrible Italian soprano. I just had to find a kindred soul with whom to commiserate. Why anyone cares to listen to such noise! Are you as weary as I of such demands on one's time and patience?"

"How do you do, Miss Knight." Frederick bowed politely.

Clarissa sparkled up at him as she executed a curtsy in return. "But how formal you are!" she chided him.

With what he knew would be unpardonable rudeness he opened his mouth to reply that their relationship had never gone beyond the formal, at least in his case, when from somewhere behind him he heard Polly's name. He turned involuntarily. Two women stood near them, with a gentleman in knee breeches. One of the women wore an elaborate turban over her coal-black hair; her compan-

363

ion, a slightly younger woman, had contented herself with an ostrich plume.

"Whatever you say, sir, she must be a wanton," the haughty woman in the turban said.

"I was not arguing that point, Lady Annette, only that Jedro has never said the Indian was painted from life."

Clarissa caught at Frederick's arm, whispering urgently, "They're talking about Polly, oh, I know it!"

The younger woman, suddenly recognizing Clarissa, attempted to halt the discussion by stepping forward to speak to her. "Clarissa, dear, how are you? I haven't seen you for weeks! Have you been in the country?"

"Well, who is your friend, Jane?" the haughty lady asked, eyeing Frederick with interest.

Unable to avoid making the introduction, Jane presented Clarissa to her companions, and Clarissa in turn necessarily presented Frederick. She had managed to transform her desperate grip on his arm to that of a confiding young girl on the protecting arm of an attentive male. "Mr. Moresby and I have known each other ever since this summer. We met in the country." With a coy glance at Frederick, she added, "It was such a lovely summer."

"Please don't let us interrupt your discussion," Frederick said, ignoring Clarissa's statement and a light but insinuating pressure from her hand resting on his arm. "I couldn't help overhearing that you were discussing Miss Rice's paintings, and whether the Indian's portrait was painted from life. I can assure you that to my certain knowledge, it was."

The woman sniffed. "It is unimportant whether or not she painted from life. The painting is of a real person; it is not an illustration of a classical story; it is not allegorical,

364

nor is the subject legendary. It is a portrait. To paint a full-length portrait of an unclothed man suggests a prurience of mind; a truly genteel lady would have been interested only in the head. A face, particularly the eyes and the set of the mouth, speaks of the inner character of the subject — but a body — what has it to tell of interest, except to those whose interests are low-bred?"

Jane, with an embarrassed sidelong glance at Clarissa, asked tentatively, "Might not beauty of form be sufficient reason for an artist?"

The gentleman in knee breeches raised his quizzing glass to study Jane more closely, and the haughty woman in the turban raised her nose.

"Miss Rice," pronounced the latter, "has demonstrated herself to be a shocking wanton with immoral propensities and no delicacy."

Something snapped in Frederick's brain. It was as though a river of ice was breaking up in a spring thaw with an excess of crashing and rending. Removing Clarissa's hand from his arm, and taking Jane's, he said, "Madam," looking earnestly into her startled face, "I salute your defense of Miss Rice. She did see beauty of form, and that is all that needs saying, except that she is a painter of talent and a lady of high moral character. I hope to marry her, if she will have me." He turned to Clarissa, and bowed. "I leave you, Miss Knight, to defend your cousin from further attacks on her character. I am sure, knowing the high regard in which you have always held her, that you will do it well." He smiled blandly as her large brown eyes, no longer flirtatious or sparkling, but dagger bright, looked angrily into his own. He waited for a reply, but he had succeeded in tying her tongue, which gave him enormous and no doubt unworthy satisfaction. He inclined his head to the woman in the turban and to the gentleman by her side, who was now studying Frederick through his quizzing glass. With a last, satisfied glance at Clarissa, Frederick turned on his heel and walked out of the house. He thought it unlikely his hostess would miss him.

His impulse was to run immediately to Polly and beg forgiveness on bended knee, or to snatch her from the bosom of her family and carry her off without waiting for forgiveness. Such a plan of action did not, however, strike him as practical at midnight on a cold wintry evening, and in any event a lady of high moral character would demand, or certainly deserve, a proper marriage license, at the very least. In front of his fire, with his port and biscuits, his course of action became clear. Of course he was going to marry Polly. A special license, and then, no matter what Polly might say about it, he would have her.

He was in a veritable fever: the special license, rooms reserved at Clarendon's, his new man alerted to prepare for just about anything—a trip to the continent, or to one of the watering places. What matter that it was dead winter? A carriage to rent—he could hardly carry Polly off in a hackney coach, or slung across his saddle, although the latter idea did have a certain flair.

"Miss Rice, please," Frederick said to the stiff-looking butler, presenting his card.

"I am sorry, sir, but Miss Rice is not in."

"Mrs. Furneaux, then."

"I'm sorry, Mrs. Furneaux is not receiving."

"Damn it, man, out of the way! I will either see Miss Rice or Mrs. Furneaux or I will break your head."

"Sir! I have my orders."

Frederick had not forgotten the lessons from his youthful days on the town, when it had seemed the ultimate in sophistication to be seen at Gentleman Jackson's Boxing Saloon. He landed a smart blow on the butler's jaw, just at the moment that a footman stepped out of a room to the right of the entryway. The footman's surprise was so great, and his sense of hierarchy so firmly fixed, that his first thought was to help the butler to rise, although the impulse was quickly followed by the recognition of his duty to protect the house. Frederick had never achieved sufficient ability to spar with Jackson himself, but he had been quick, and in the footman's instant of hesitation, Frederick struck the second blow. He ran up the stairs without waiting to determine the result. The footman was quickly on his feet, being younger and more agile than the butler, and was setting up a hew and cry even as he pursued Frederick up the stairs. A maid popped out of a room in front of Frederick, duster in hand, and on sight of him screamed and sank to the floor. He turned to give the pursuing footman a stopper when a voice above, brimming with all the outraged authority of a lady of the house, demanded, "*What* is going on down there?"

Frederick and the footman, as well as the butler, who was now foggily making his way up the stairs, looked up at Gussie. Before Frederick could open his mouth, the footman — recalling his duties — lunged at him. Frederick caught the movement from the corner of his eye, whirled, and struck again, this time with his full strength. The footman stretched his length upon the floor beside the maid, who was just getting up.

Gussie was hanging over the banister above looking down at them. "It's all right, Hawkins, I know Mr. Moresby. He was a neighbor in the county. Perhaps you

367

should see to Gregory, who I believe Mr. Moresby has rendered unconscious, after you show my guest to the library. I will join you shortly, Mr. Moresby." With that, she turned and disappeared.

The butler would clearly have liked to throw Mr. Moresby out of the house, but he kept his countenance valiantly blank as he opened the library door and asked if Frederick would care for any refreshment. Frederick declined. "I will just need a few moments with Mrs. Furneaux. Thank you, Hawkins."

The butler, with what in a less perfectly trained man would have been a snarl, said, "Very good, sir," and closed the door more forcibly than necessary.

Frederick had not long to wait before the door opened and Gussie entered.

"Where is she, Mrs. Furneaux?" Frederick asked, forgetting even the most perfunctory courtesies.

Gussie sat down awkwardly in a fragile Sheraton chair, and said, "Please sit down, Mr. Moresby."

"I came for Polly, Mrs. Furneaux. Where is she? Is she here and refusing to see me?"

"No, she is not here. Were you accompanying her somewhere?"

"No, by God. I'm *taking* her somewhere."

"Please stop pacing and sit down, Mr. Moresby. How can we speak rationally with each other when you won't even stand still?"

Frederick at last sat down, but he clearly was poised to spring up at any moment and resume his pacing.

"Now," Gussie said. "Tell me where you are taking her and why."

"First of all to be married, and after that . . . I don't know. Wherever she wants to go."

"Really Mr. Moresby, you take me by surprise. Has Polly anything to say to this?"

"Nothing whatever."

Gussie giggled.

Frederick's spirits soared. "Can you tell me that Polly doesn't still love me, Mrs. Furneaux? I'm sure she's told you about our engagement and about our foolish quarrel. She's told me so much about you, and when you both were youngsters, and how close you have been as sisters, that she must have confided in you."

She smiled at him, causing Frederick's heart to give a great painful thump. She looked so much like Polly, and that smile was so dear, it was more than he could bear. He leaned toward her and took her hand. "Please Mrs. Furneaux — Gussie — please tell me where she is."

"She shares a studio with a woman named Clara Wheelock who does fashion illustration." Gussie paused, eyeing him speculatively; then she said, "Yes, Mr. Moresby — Frederick — you *are* doing the right thing, I am sure of it. Yes, you must carry her off. It is just the thing!" Gussie, forgetting her accoucheur's instructions against sudden movements, bounced from her chair, and made awkward haste across the room to a small Sheraton desk, from which she took a paper and a pen. Not bothering to seat herself, she quickly wrote out the direction. Frederick was instantly at her side, and only with effort restrained himself from snatching the paper from her hand. He did seize her hand to rain two kisses on it, and then, unable to control his excitement and gratitude, he kissed her cheek. Then he was gone.

Sometime later, Gussie, on hearing her husband come in, left her couch and started down the stairs, remembering to hold the banister and move with all deliberation.

He saw her from below. "Gussie, what is it?" He ran quickly up the steps and caught her in his arms. "What is it?"

"Oh, my darling," cried Gussie. "Mr. Moresby does have some dash after all!"

Julian Furneaux, who had thought to hear that he would soon be a father again, was understandably puzzled.

Frederick ran up the first flight of stairs two at a time to come face to face with a well-dressed gentleman who had been regarding his hasty ascent with curiosity. After a second of surprise on Frederick's part, and study on the other's, the gentleman said, "I say, haven't we met before?"

Frederick, on a closer look, recognized one of the guests from the bluestocking lady's salon. "Yes, I believe we have. At Miss Tibkin's."

"Of course. Remember the conversation well. We spoke of horses. But for the life of me, afraid I didn't catch the name."

"Moresby, Frederick Moresby."

"At your service, sir. Archibald Twameley."

The two men started up the second flight together. Twameley, with a sidelong glance at Frederick, said, "Don't let me slow you down, old man. You seemed in a bit of a rush, I thought."

"Too much of a rush for five flights of stairs."

"You're going to take tea with Clara too?"

"No, Polly Rice. She shares a studio with Mrs. Wheelock."

"Forgot you and Polly were neighbors in the country. Quite a stir she gave the prissies, what?"

"Indeed she did," Frederick agreed.

They fell silent as they continued on up the stairs. When they arrived at the top, Twameley said, "Always open house at this hour." He opened the door and walked in, with Frederick close behind him.

The room was large and light and cheerily furnished. Three men were looking through some drawings stacked on a desk, and a man and woman stood talking quietly by a window. Polly, with Clara, sat with another group: a woman in elegant walking attire, and a gentleman wearing a dressing gown over full evening dress, whom Frederick immediately recognized as Twameley's friend Ragge.

Standing nearby, the dashing Sally was holding forth on a review of Byron's *Don Juan*. ". . . recognized the quality of the poem, but said it was 'poetry such as no brother could read to his sister, and no husband to his wife!' If that isn't a clear statement of the foolish protections by which we are confined . . ."

Polly, occupied with pouring the tea, assumed that Sally was expecting a reply, and said, "It presumes, of course, that we must be protected from the lustier side of life, that we—" She looked up to hand the cup to Sally, and instead saw Frederick approaching. "Frederick," she whispered.

Sally, who had broken off her speech to greet Twameley and the familiar-looking gentleman who accompanied him, stared from one to the other. She later claimed that she heard a thunderclap as Polly's eyes met Frederick's. Before her own bemused eye, and Twameley's quizzing glass, Frederick went straight to Polly and said, "I've come to carry you off, Polly."

"Frederick," she said again.

371

"I say," said Twameley.

Frederick, unaware that he looked foolishly love-smitten, was however aware that he had not shaped up his plans adequately. He had no idea how to go on, and had not taken into account that he might find Polly in the company of a large number of other people.

Polly, coming suddenly to her senses, said, "What do you mean, carry me off? Carry me off where?" Her emotions were turbulent. "If you think, Frederick —"

Frederick strode around the table and pulled her to her feet. He touched her lips softly with his fingers. "Hush, now, my dear. I have something to say." He turned to the others, "If you all would step outside for a few moments, please. I have something to say to Polly, but I think I can do it more effectively if we are alone."

Sally was the first of the hypnotized viewers to come to life. "Twameley, for goodness' sake! You are forever organizing committees. Get these people out of here."

"Yes, yes. Of course. Here, everybody, let's step out on the landing."

Ragge put down the teacup he held in his hand; Clara Wheelock shooed her elegant fashion model before her; the three gentlemen at the table and the couple by the window followed her; and Twameley offered Sally his arm. He turned as he closed the door behind them all, and favored Frederick and Polly with a grin. "Take your time, my pets," he said.

"Now, what is the meaning of this?" Polly said as sternly as she could, although her voice sounded breathy and her heart was beating desperately.

"Why, love, I have told you. I have come to carry you off."

Polly was near tears. She sat down suddenly, and

picked up her teacup. After a determined sip, she put it down again. With her head bent, she said unsteadily, "I don't understand, Frederick, how you can just burst in upon me like this, and expect me to fall in your arms. You have been in London ever since—ever since . . ."

"Ever since our foolish fight, my darling."

"And you haven't called—except once, and you didn't come to my exhibition . . ."

"But I did. I went twice, and I even bought a painting. The Falls of the Niagara." He dropped to one knee beside her. "Polly sweet, I love you." Then, as he caught her expression of rising rebellion, he said, "I warn you, I will carry you off by force." He took her hands very firmly in his own.

Unable to resist, she raised an eyebrow and asked, "As your lightskirt?"

"I was only recently defending your honor to the most strapped-up lady I have ever met. Now wouldn't it look odd if I carried you off to live in sin?" He relinquished one of her hands in order to pat his pocket. "I have very thoughtfully and foresightedly provided myself with a special license."

"I shall continue to paint naked men."

"Only when I am there as chaperon."

"I shall continue to hobnob with artists and their patrons." She smiled impishly and made an encircling gesture with her arm. "People just like you saw here."

"Delightful."

"I'll need to change my dress first."

"I hope that means yes, because my knees are getting very tired."

"How thoughtless of me. Do get up." Frederick rose, a little stiffly. "It's a good thing I decided to marry before

373

many more years pass. I won't be capable of that position much longer." He pulled Polly to her feet again. "Polly, my love."

Her face was buried in his shoulder, and he was kissing her hair when the door burst open, and Twameley and Sally danced in, followed by Ragge, Clara, and the others.

"You have been peeking," Frederick said accusingly over the top of Polly's head.

"Here, old man. Let her go. Let me shake your hand. Congratulations. Polly, a kiss." Twameley parted the lovers and, after his kiss, delivered Polly into the hands of the ladies, who showered her with more hugs and kisses.

"Did we hear somethin' about a special license, Moresby?" asked Ragge. "I say, I know a clergyman not more than a mile off. Be happy to do the trick for you. Needs the business, don't you know."

"But I must change my dress," Polly cried. "I can't be married in this old dress."

"You look beautiful, my love," Frederick said, kissing her hand.

"Frederick, do stop." Much to her annoyance, Polly thought she might be blushing. She helplessly bestowed a doting gaze on him, and then, herself forgetting they were in company, impulsively clasped his hand in her own. He drew her again into his arms.

"Stop this shameless display," Sally said, again parting the lovers. "We've a wedding to prepare for."

"Who cares about clothes?" Clara asked. She held Polly at arm's length a moment. "Let me just pin your lace a bit straighter."

The model in the elegant walking attire looked injured. "That's a funny thing for a person to say who's making her money off Madame Celeste." She adjusted her skirt, and looked around to gauge the effect on the company.

"Oh, come off it, Sissy." Ragge pinched her cheek. "Let's you and me get married, too. My friend charges less for doubles."

Sissy sniffed. "A rake like you? I wouldn't marry you if you were the last man around."

Twameley, overcome by the idea of his friend Ragge as a rake, went off into howls of laughter.

Ragge looked at him severely. He shed his dressing gown and straightened his waistcoat. "Here, now, Twameley. We have a job to do. Our friends are gettin' married today. Have to have somebody to stand up with 'em—you can do that. I've got the clergyman in mind, and our young friend here can get us some hackneys." He turned to one of the company, a very young man who looked to be on his first venture as a man about town. "Run out, there's a good lad, and find us two hacks—no, better make it three. I say, Moresby, how did you get here?"

"I have a carriage."

"Two then. Shake the old legs, lad."

"Let's all go," Sally said excitedly.

"Quite right," Twameley agreed. "Clara, stop fussing. Polly looks fine."

Before Frederick and Polly could protest, they were in the street, where with much shouting by their companions two hackneys were secured to carry the wedding party. Frederick's elegant rental equipage set off, Ragge on the box with the coachman to give directions, followed by two ancient vehicles pulled by the veriest nags.

They were almost immediately halted by shouts from

375

behind them, and Sally descended to purchase some frozen-looking flowers from a frozen-looking old lady. After a consultation, the company was led on a lengthy detour to the shop of an artificial florist. There the entire party, except Frederick and Polly, who were rightly presumed to be whispering lovers' vows to each other inside the carriage (at last clarifying all the little misunderstandings that preceded the discovery that they loved), and Ragge on the box (to keep an eye out that the prospective bride and groom did not escape them) descended on the shop to purchase artificial flowers to the extent of their combined purses.

The clergyman was just the kind Ragge would know, according to Twameley ("Just hope he's the real thing," he whispered to Sally), but he performed the ceremony without mishap. Frederick and Polly were then carried off to a nearby coffeehouse, where they were treated to an impromptu wedding dinner and toasted many times—all on the cuff—and then bundled back into their carriage, slightly groggy. The two decrepit vehicles followed them to the doors of their destination, the Clarendon, which Frederick had unwisely revealed, his tongue loosened by wine and the confusion and hullabaloo. Polly was kissed again by one and all, and Frederick's hand was again wrung; Sally and Clara and the two other ladies of the wedding party tossed artificial flowers in their path as they entered the hotel. It was a thoroughly disreputable wedding.

"I'm surprised," said Frederick, as he closed their door and shot the bolt, "that they didn't come up to undress you and put you to bed."

"Why, Frederick!"

"*I* don't think, you see, that you need to be protected

from the lustier side of life." He suddenly caught her in his arms. "You do love me, don't you, Polly?"

"Oh, Frederick, I do, I do, but we haven't had time to think. Do you *really* forgive me? I did behave disgracefully, I know."

"How could I not forgive you, when you have so much more to forgive?"

She put her arms around his neck.

After an interval, she said, "I must tell Gussie where I am."

"Gussie knows I've carried you off, but if it will please you, we'll send a messenger."

"Gussie knows?"

"Yes, dear. How do you think I found you?" Frederick had unfastened Polly's pelisse and removed his cloak. He was now setting to work on such fastenings as he could discover in Polly's dress. "In this emergency I must act as your maid," he said, discovering a button. A few more buttons, and he asked, "By the way, love, what was Ragge doing with that dressing gown over that eye-catching evening ensemble?"

"He was our model."

"Ummmm?" responded Frederick, somewhat distracted by what he was uncovering.

"Clara was doing a fashion illustration of a gentleman's dressing gown, and I was doing his portrait, which he wanted in evening dress."

"My word," said Frederick, as Polly's dress slipped from her shoulders.

Polly and Frederick sat on a rug in front of the fire, wrapped in blankets and quilts from their bed. A half bottle of champagne and two glasses sat on a small table near them.

Frederick, who thought the romantic poets' flights too fanciful, found running through his mind as he stared at the flames lines from Shelley—not on politics—but to one of his rumored amours. "My heart is quivering like a flame . . . I am dissolved in these consuming ecstasies . . ." His thoughts wandered lazily to remembered physical repletion and the way his new wife had so willingly come into his arms. He felt a smug satisfaction that he had accomplished a deflowering with such finesse that his darling had not known the depth of patience and control it had required to keep his hot blood from the boil. I have no life . . . but in thee . . . he thought contentedly, echoing Shelley.

Polly, for her part, wandered through a jumble of different thoughts. How had she come to be blessed with such a man? To be loved and to love, for that moment at least, she thought must be a pinnacle of life's experience, akin to those rare moments when she achieved the expression with paint on canvas of a vision in her mind.

Surely Frederick was unlike the men her mother had described, for he had so deliberately roused her to passion. And then, when suddenly, with something very like a groan, he rolled away from her and she lay, surprised and confused, he turned to her again, still breathless, and whispered, "That was for me, my darling, but soon . . ." had he really quoted a poet? ". . . 'we will taste the life of love again.' " She'd trembled in his arms, vibrating to his caresses, until he entered her again, and this time . . . "how sweet, sweet, sweet . . ." How much she still must learn of this man who—would she ever have thought it—could woo her with lines from *Endymion*. She knew now what it was like to lie in a man's arms, tonite, tomorrow,

378

and fate willing, all the nights of her life. Her body was remembering "the very tune of love" and she was pleasantly conscious that she was naked as the newborn babe in its receiving blanket.

She shifted her position to lean her head for a moment on Frederick's shoulder. "Tomorrow, my dearest, I really must get some other clothes."

"Of course, my sweet. Tomorrow." Frederick drew her into his arms and, with some adjustments, managed to get them both wrapped in one quilt. "Where shall we honeymoon, my pet?" he asked, kissing her hair and fondling her breast.

"Didn't you once say perhaps America?"

"I think I prefer to journey through France on a donkey, subsisting on fruit and wine, like Mary and Percy Shelley."

"Oh, Frederick, you don't, really."

"Then where would you my love?"

"I was thinking of Berlin, and bread and beer—"

We will not, dear reader, intrude longer on the rompings and murmurings of the lovers, but draw a curtain on the scenes of passion that followed this remark.

Chapter XX: Epilogue

Did they live happily ever after? Of course not. There were times of happiness, but there were also times of sorrow. There were times when they were estranged and times when their lives ran on oiled wheels. There were moments of passion, and moments of anger. But they lived a long life together, and they died still loving each other.

Lady Moresby and Mrs. Rice were well satisfied with their mutual grandchildren, for Frederick and Polly had five children, two boys and three girls. Nettie and Lord Bolling, as Alex predicted, lived contentedly in the country, coming up to London occasionally to visit their relatives, to attend Royal Academy exhibitions when Polly's paintings were hung, and to view national monuments. Nettie and Gussie both joined Polly in her fight against slavery, and they had the satisfaction of seeing their labor rewarded in 1833, when the practice was abolished in all British dependencies. Gussie's husband, Julian Furneaux, as he had always expected, became a director of the Bank of England.

Alex was on friendly terms with them all, visiting them whenever his diplomatic assignments in various European capitals allowed him a short time in England. He was eventually appointed to the Court of St. James, where he represented his country for six happy years. During his tenure as ambassador, he was introduced to a young American girl, brought to England by her father to capture an earl or a duke, but for whom nothing would do but she must have Alex. Although they had no children, their September-May marriage was happy for the few short years they were together. Sailing alone on a visit to her family in America, her ship was lost at sea. Alex never remarried.

Clarissa, as she deserved, married a handsome and wealthy man. Both brought up to flatter and please, it was not until they married that they discovered they did not like each other very much. They pursued independent interests—he with his mistresses and his club; she with a succession of flirts. She did not, however, take a lover, as she threatened to do that day in the summer house with Nettie when she was nineteen. She bore children as she ought, three of whom died in infancy, which caused her some grief. She was kind to her foolish Aunt Cat until the old lady died at the age of ninety-two and in mid-life turned to religion.

Clarissa's new piety puzzled her relatives, but Nettie at last discovered the inspiration. Although Nettie and Clarissa were never close again, they visited each other occasionally, and once, as it happened, Nettie arrived during the hunt season. Among the gentry gathered for the chase was a handsome, silver-haired clergyman dressed for riding and unaccompanied by a wife. Clarissa became well known, if not well liked, for benev olent works under the guidance of the silver-haired pastor.

Polly continued to paint, although she sometimes wept in frustration when it seemed that her household, marital, maternal, family, and community duties kept her too long from her easel. On the whole, however, she considered herself fortunate. And so, on the whole, did Frederick. Although he had many interests, and became well known for his work for political reform, his greatest satisfaction, aside from his family, remained the breeding and care of his dairy herd. He only occasionally regretted that he had not become a scientist and sailed with some explorer.

By the end of the century Polly was ranked among the minor painters of England, and of her best works it was said that probably a man had helped her with them. Seventy years later an era of feminism retrieved her from obscurity and elevated her to a rightly deserved place in the development of nineteenth century painting.

Did Polly ever paint another nearly naked man from life? Yes, she painted Frederick several times, and completely in the buff, but those paintings were destroyed by one of her grandchildren, in 1897, the same year that Queen Victoria celebrated her diamond jubilee. Pictures of his grandpa naked were bad enough, but that his grandma painted them was worse.

And the portrait of the Indian, Black Wing? It is still in private hands; the stir that it caused long since forgotten.

383

ZEBRA'S GOT THE ROMANCE
TO SET YOUR HEART AFIRE!

RAGING DESIRE (2242, $3.75)
by Colleen Faulkner
A wealthy gentleman and officer in General Washington's army
Devon Marsh wasn't meant for the likes of Cassie O'Flynn, an
immigrant bond servant. But from the moment their lips first
met, Cassie knew she could love no other . . . even if it meant
marching into the flames of war to make him hers!

TEXAS TWILIGHT (2241, $3.75)
by Vivian Vaughan
When handsome Trace Garrett stepped onto the porch of the
Santa Clara ranch, he wove a rapturous spell around Clara Ehler's
heart. Though Clara planned to sell the spread and move back
East, Trace was determined to keep her on the wild Western fron-
tier where she belonged — to share with him the glory and the
splendor of the passion-filled TEXAS TWILIGHT.

RENEGADE HEART (2244, $3.75)
by Marjorie Price
Strong-willed Hannah Hatch resented her imprisonment by Captain Jake Farnsworth, even after the daring Yankee had rescued
her from bloodthirsty marauders. And though Jake's rock-hard
physique made Hannah tremble with desire, the spirited beauty
was nevertheless resolved to exploit her femininity to the fullest
and gain her independence from the virile bluecoat.

LOVING CHALLENGE (2243, $3.75)
by Carol King
When the notorious Captain Dominic Warbrooke burst into
Laurette Harker's eighteenth birthday ball, the accomplished
beauty challenged the arrogant scoundrel to a duel. But when the
captain named her innocence as his stakes, Laurette was terrified
she'd not only lose the fight, but her heart as well!

*Available wherever paperbacks are sold, or order direct from the
Publisher. Send cover price plus 50¢ per copy for mailing and
handling to Zebra Books, Dept. 2381, 475 Park Avenue South,
New York, N.Y. 10016. Residents of New York, New Jersey and
Pennsylvania must include sales tax. DO NOT SEND CASH.*